A Man Who Heals

Stefani Wilder

Tipped Z: Book 3

Stefani Wilder is a pen name for Robin Stephen

text copyright © 2017 by Robin Theodora Stephen Deutschendorf

stefaniwilder.com
robinstephen.com

Cover photography by Ashley Rose Williams (Phillips), Rocking Lazy A Photography ©2018. All rights reserved.

PRINT ISBN: 978-1-946238-07-8
E-BOOK ISBN: 978-1-946238-06-1

Brown Wing Press
Iowa City, IA
brownwingpress.com

First Brown Wing Press Edition

BOOKS BY STEFANI WILDER

A Man Who Rides
A Man Who Starts
A Man Who Heals

Vaquera's Haven
Vaquera's Bronc

For my husband: tireless first reader and secret genius behind so many Tipped Z details

Chapter 1

The path through the forest was narrow, dark, and creepy. I hesitated before the first trees, turning to look at the empty field behind me. The sun was a bright ball in the flat blue sky. The grasses danced and swayed, insects flitting here and there on the breeze.

I turned back to the forest, checked the time, and muttered to myself. There were any number of reasons going into this forest alone was a bad idea. I'd spent weeks preparing. I was as ready as I could make myself. Still, I knew the odds were against me.

I took one last look at the verdant field behind me. It was still empty. Whatever happened as soon as the trees swallowed me from view, Buttercup and I were on our own.

We went on. I had my sword equipped. The blade caught the last light of the sun and threw it back briefly. Then the trees shouldered up around us, their trunks heavy and dark, their branches high and reaching.

The trees were dead. Every one of them. As I steered Buttercup along the path, the stark branches reached like skeletal fingers towards the bleached sky. I scanned them for any sign of life, my heart beginning to beat a little harder in my chest.

"Come on, you evil queen." I spoke to the trees in general, knowing my quarry couldn't hear me. "Send out your minions."

To my left, a tree came into view. It was dead like the others but stood out from its fellows for the way it gleamed oddly in the shadows. For a moment, I thought it had been stripped of its bark. I nudged Buttercup closer, and then I could see.

The tree was draped in the pale, shifting strands of a massive spider web.

Behind me, I heard a terrible thud: the solid impact of a large, dense body hitting the ground. Wheeling Buttercup, I didn't hesitate. My sword was already swinging as I turned. I barely had time to take in the grasping mandibles, the coarse hairs on the raised, slashing legs, before I struck.

My blow landed, but seemed not to make much impression on the massive, carapaced creature before me. The spider, easily half the size of my horse, simply struck back.

There was a flash of red, and I swung again, this time using my special attack. Buttercup heaved forward as I snatched a second blade out of its scabbard and rammed the spider with both weapons, the impact of my horse's charge backing the blows.

The spider buckled, its legs curling up as it rolled onto its back and died, releasing a spray of dancing gold coins I moved forward to collect.

I paused to assess the damage. The red flash at the edges of the screen had meant I'd taken a critical hit. These spiders always used a super-powered strike to initiate combat, but follow-up blows weren't so bad. Which meant it had been stupid of me to panic and go for my Double Slash Charge attack. It had a long cooldown period, which meant I would not be able to employ it again for quite a while. I'd meant to save it for the queen.

In my desk chair in my dim apartment, I shifted and sighed, taking a sip of DragonFire. The red carbonated beverage fizzled pleasantly on my tongue. I glanced at the clock again. 2:15am. I shouldn't be drinking an energy drink at this time of night, and I shouldn't be embarking on this quest right now either. I should return to the field, which was a save point, pour the rest of my highly caffeinated beverage down the drain, and go to bed. I wanted to be at work by 8:00 am.

"Right," I said, staring at the dead spider. It had begun to fade, the gross details of its hairy legs growing translucent in the forest's shadowy light. As I watched, the corpse blinked out of existence.

It was time to move on. Beating this forest and the boss within was my last quest before I could clear this section of *Heroes of the Totem Spirit* and gain access to three new portals. My avatar, PonyPrincess090, was leveled up higher than should have been possible given my current access. I was even on the Elite Squad, a list of players whose XP gains and various other stats were crunched by an algorithm and placed at the top of the constantly changing leaderboard. Elite Squad status was almost unheard of for someone with my access level. And yet, whenever I came into these creepy woods, I got my ass handed to me.

The problem wasn't me. It was the forest itself. According to the lore of the game, it had been deliberately designed so it couldn't be cleared by a single player alone. The spiders could only initiate their supercharged attack if no player had them within their field of vision. Coming in with a group with multiple players to keep an eye on the trees made clearing this zone child's play.

I found this maddening. I did not want to come in with a group. That was the whole point of games. I played games *instead* of having friends, not to make new ones. The last thing I wanted a game to do was to force me into relationships with other players.

And so, for quite a while, I had been intent on giving the game designers the finger by defeating this zone alone. I had spent the last several weeks doing nothing but preparing to face the dread queen and her minions. The problem was, I'd already failed. A couple more surprise hits like the one I'd just taken, and I'd be dead. At this rate, I'd never even reach the queen, much less defeat her.

Taking another sip of DragonFire, I sat up a little straighter. My apartment IRL was dark and warm, smelling of reheated pizza and DragonFire's faint bubblegum tang. As my desk chair creaked again, I spoke to Buttercup as if my computer-generated horse/totem/partner could hear me. "Okay, this was a bad idea. We're going back."

I turned around, orienting for a view of the path I'd followed into the woods. I'd expected the forest to look the same as it had before—

trees with bare branches and dark trunks, still and empty and throwing shadows across the gray ground.

This is not what I saw. The trees were still there, sure. But now they were seething with spiders like the one I had just killed.

I sat a moment, frozen with shock. My stomach curdling, I watched as even more spiders crawled around trunks to fix their beady, creepy eye-clusters on me. "Shit," I said. "Shit, shit. Shiiit."

There was nothing for it. I ran.

Running in a video game is, fortunately, nothing like running in real life. If it had been up to my actual skinny-fat legs to save my bacon, I never would have made it past the first tree. But actual physical exertion was not required of me, and I had Buttercup, who I'd invested almost as much collected XP in as my own avatar. She was a force to be reckoned with. Also, she had a mithril chainmail horse coat that imbued her with enhanced defense, not to mention enchanted shoes that gave her kicks stun power.

We barreled through the forest, spiders leaping down at us from every side. I swiped at the ones I could reach. Others bounced off Buttercup's mailed haunches. But quite a few hit their mark. More red flashes lit my screen. I used one healing potion on me, another on Buttercup. Those were rare and hard to find, and it hurt me to part with them. I had one more, but I couldn't use another for 30 seconds, which was an eternity in game time.

By the time we plunged back past the last trees, I was down to 1/6 of my life. Buttercup was in better shape, but not by much.

We galloped out onto the plain. We were now free of the quest zone and into a save zone, but one of the rules of *Heroes of the Totem Spirit* is you have to destroy any minions that follow you out of a quest zone before you can save or leave the area. I steered Buttercup to a hillside and turned to see what we would have to face.

Five of the terrible spiders had followed me out of the woods. They were not as fast as Buttercup. I'd put a little distance on them, but they scurried with heedless ferocity through the swaying grasses, mandibles clashing. With desperation, I looked at my Double Slash Charge indicator. It still had two minutes and twelve seconds of cooldown. The great thing about that attack was it affected multiple foes. You could pull it out in a melee situation and floor every monster within reach. But it wouldn't help me now. I'd used it up on that first dratted spider.

As I watched the five horrendous creatures scuttle towards me, I felt the dull sense of resignation that comes with inevitable defeat. I spoke to Buttercup again. "We're doomed, old girl." Had she been a real horse, I would have reached down and patted her sweat-soaked neck, possibly taken a little snip of her mane to remember her by. But she wasn't real. There was nothing to do but eject us both from this nightmare before the killing blows fell. I reached for my keyboard, intending to force quit out of the game.

In *Heroes of the Totem Spirit*, HotTS for short, signing out in the middle of a quest has the same impact as dying. Which is to say you lose all your unsaved gold, mana, and XP. But the game also has another particular feature. It's one of the new generation of MMORPGs that puts a special emphasis on making the stakes of gaming higher, thus forcing more realistic play styles on the players. They accomplished this via the totem animals.

Every time I died, I lost Buttercup.

It was my least favorite aspect of the game, but also part of what made it so compelling. At the beginning of the game, every player chooses a totem animal companion. As the game progresses, players can invest experience and resources to make that companion into a fighter or a healer or a source of extra speed or endurance. Without an enhanced totem animal, certain quests aren't possible to win, but putting XP and resources into your companion is always a risk. While in other RPGs, you can die and respawn endlessly with little consequence, in HotTS, death is a massive setback.

I hated losing Buttercup. I could always make her again, I knew, but it would be months before I had her back to this level, and her mithril coat was so rare a find it was basically irreplaceable.

Full of bitter regret, I watched the spiders come. Call me a coward, but when facing a battle I know I cannot win I prefer to crash the game rather than watch Buttercup die.

I had my fingers set lightly on the control, alt, and delete keys when a blur of movement sprang onto my screen from the left. A figure appeared: a hulking warrior in black and red plate mail, hurling himself at one of the charging spiders with two curved, glistening blades drawn. Behind him a massive wolf—black pelt a hulking shadow in the idyllic grass of the field—bounded forward to engage a second spider. Above the warrior's head floated the name Hawkeyez777.

With a surge of hope, I snatched my hands away from the fatal buttons. I scrambled to set myself up to meet the charge of the remaining three monsters.

It was all over in an instant. Hawkeyez777 and his wolf avatar tore through their foes. I dispatched one spider while Buttercup stunned another with a kick. I took a hit from the third in the process, but it wasn't the supercharged first strike that would have killed me. It was just a normal blow, and I survived long enough for my savior and his companion to come to my aid.

Soon, all five spiders were curling up and releasing their spray of coins. I was down to the tiniest sliver of life, but it didn't matter. I felt a ridiculous rush of relief as the words, 'Progress Saved,' flashed across my screen.

I would not lose Buttercup. Not today, anyway.

As the defeated spiders faded to nothing, Hawkeyez777 turned. The field was peaceful again, lit with soft sunlight, dust motes dancing, the grass swaying. The great wolf turned also and moved to stand at the warrior's side. I made sure my mic was enabled and said into my headset, "Thanks, man. I got in a little over my head there."

The warrior's face did not change, of course. Video games have gotten pretty darn sophisticated, but none that I know of can link an avatar to its controlling human's facial expressions. When Hawkeyez777 spoke, the warrior's mouth moved in a clumsy approximation of speech. Though he'd enabled the option that passed it through a filter so it sounded both oddly deep and also somewhat robotic, I had grown used to it over the course of our interactions in the MMO environment. "Watch yourself, pony girl. I might not be here next time."

Then he turned and ran off over the hillside, his hulking wolf bounding at his side.

I like to think I'm the kind of nerd who doesn't look like a nerd on the outside, but this belief is probably delusional. The truth is, I invest a lot more time and effort into the appearance and wellness of my HotTS avatar than my own human body. Which means, at the very least, I am the kind of nerd who looks a little unhealthy.

I admitted this to myself as I splashed cold water on my face the morning after my ill-fated assault on the spider forest. In the mirror under the harsh glow of the cheap fluorescent lights in my bathroom, all I could see were the rings under my eyes, my pale skin, and my hair that was neither long nor short but was, in any case, devoid of signs it had been paid attention to beyond getting washed and brushed in this century. Certainly, there are other habits that can make a person skinny-fat, pale, and sleep deprived. Drugs, for instance. But we nerds get this way because we exist almost entirely in other worlds—the worlds of books and games—in order to escape reality.

"Idiot," I said as I stared into my bleary eyes. "You shouldn't have stayed up so late. You shouldn't have tried to take on the spider forest alone. And you need to stop drinking DragonFire after 5:00 pm. Got it?"

The me in the mirror looked remorseful, but I knew better than to think she would change. With a little grimace, I turned away. I didn't look good, but it didn't seem worth the effort to try to do anything about it. As I dragged myself into my jeans and black t-shirt, raked a brush through my hair, and grabbed a DragonFuel bar from the box that sat open on my desk next to my gaming rig, I tried to remember the last time I *hadn't* felt like warmed over roadkill on my way to work.

I failed.

I left the sleeping area of my studio apartment, grabbed a case of DragonFire from the fridge, rescued my keys and shoulder bag from the counter in the kitchenette where I'd left them the afternoon before, and stepped out into the Tucson morning.

It was 7:40 am. Time to head to work.

Outside, the late August sunlight fell glaringly into the dim recessed entryway that led into my studio. The heat was already a building weight in the air. I locked my door, catching a whiff of gasoline and creosote on the already-very-warm air. Turning, I made my way along the dry sidewalk that led past the blank stucco faces of the other apartments until I reached the parking ramada. I walked past that to the uncovered spaces, approaching my faded purple(ish) Ford Explorer.

I addressed my vehicle in an ironic tone. "Good morning, Bessie." Sidling in between my parking space and the next, I unlocked the door and slid inside, knocking a few empty DragonFire cans off the passenger seat to make room for the fresh case. I tossed my bag on top before turning the key in the ignition. The engine stuttered to life. I tore open the energy bar and chewed it down as I piloted out of the parking lot to join the dense flow of commuters making their way to dreary office jobs.

It was only Tuesday, and I already felt done in enough that a month of weekends would do me good. Swallowing the dry bar, I groped into the passenger seat for a can of DragonFire.

Fifteen minutes later, I had arrived at my destination. The parking lot of Humanilism Enterprises was still relatively empty as I steered my Ford past the security checkpoint and into an empty parking space. I was one of the minority of people who preferred to arrive so early. As I secured my vehicle and walked into the reception area of the repurposed warehouse Humanilism had turned into an open floor plan office, the building had a cool, quiet feel.

My case of DragonFire under my arm and my bag over my shoulder, I gave the girl sitting at the odd metal podium within the large front doors a slight nod. I held up the ID badge I wore around my neck. She waved me on by. I didn't recognize this girl. It seemed to me they changed on a thrice daily basis, the same one never returning to her post after I had seen her once. They all had the same bored, blank-eyed look about them. I wondered what this girl could possibly do to stop someone from entering the building uninvited. Maybe she had a red button behind the podium that, when pressed, would cause a massive cage to rise up from the smooth concrete floor and thereby trap the miscreants.

Although why anyone would want to force their way into the offices of Humanilism Enterprises, I had no idea. As I pushed my way through the second set of doors and looked out over the expanse of long tables, the red brick wall with the company logo applied in thick white paint looming over the tiny people below, I felt another sliver of my soul roll over and die out of sheer inability to face another day in this place.

The problem wasn't an aesthetic one. Humanilism had won awards when they opened this office. The large windows glittered in the early sun. The brick wall added an air of rustic charm. The long tables were smooth, made out of recycled wood, sanded down and lacquered to a dull sheen. Most of the workspaces were empty, with a few stations occupied by those still on from the night and other early starters like myself.

I stood a moment, surveying the available options. No one who worked here had their own, assigned space. Every day was a crapshoot, each employee claiming a work area upon arrival. It was one of the reasons I preferred to come in early.

There was a good place open today: a slot on the end of one of the long tables close to a small fridge at one of the beverage stations. I stashed my case of DragonFire accordingly and went to a storage locker, where I traded my shoulder bag for my company-issued laptop.

Five minutes later, I was settled in place, booted up and logged in, waiting for my first assignment of the day. It could be one of two things. Tech support for the do-it-yourself website builder BlockWeaver, or manually reviewing do-it-yourself ads for a local Tucson newspaper's website.

Technically, I worked for Humanilism, but Humanilism rented me out to other companies that needed humans for the myriad of thankless tasks that allowed the internet to run. My job title was, in fact, just that. Human. I was a Human assigned tasks that were still beyond the capabilities of bots.

I never knew which hat I'd be wearing until I logged in, and sometimes I got switched back and forth several times a day. I never knew which I hoped for as I waited for the system to register my presence and assess where the greatest need for me was. They both came with their own particular flavor of psychic pain.

As I waited for my assignment, I settled myself, popping open another can of DragonFire and glancing around the bright space. Tony sat slumped at a workstation further down the row. He saw me and raised a pale hand in a wan greeting.

The spinner on my screen disappeared, a message in the chirpy, thin, letters of Humani Sans Light taking its place. "Good morning, Jordan! Your first assignment today is: Ad Review."

I clicked 'Proceed.' As my queue loaded, I thought fleetingly of Buttercup and the enchanted world of *Heroes of the Totem Spirit*, of Hawkeyez777 and his flashing swords, his kickass wolf companion, and the field with its swaying grass and dancing dust motes. Why couldn't real life be more like a video game?

The first ad popped up. I focused, bringing all my attention to bear. The ads were text-only classifieds, and they'd already been cleared by the automated checker. My job was to review them for the less obvious grammatical errors the algorithm couldn't catch, and also flag ads that seemed seedy, illegal, inappropriate, or otherwise off.

It wasn't difficult work, but it was surprising how clever the trolls could be. If I let something slip by, thus allowing an ad that was obscene or shady onto the newspaper's website, I would lose a lot of Merit points.

The first few ads were no-brainers. One was for a house cleaning service, another for an AC repair company. But the third one stopped me short. Not because there was anything wrong with it, but because it was out of the ordinary.

RANCH HORSE RIDING LESSONS
Come to the historic Tipped Z Ranch for a unique opportunity to learn the traditional ways of the vaquero from a 5th generation rancher.
tippedz.com/lessons

I stared at the ad, my performance timer quietly racking up seconds in the corner. I could spend however long I needed at any given task, but there were several bonuses for working fast. For one thing, my work schedule was not based on hours, but a measure called "Interactions."

Each task I completed earned me Interactions. Once I completed my quota for any given day, I was free to go home. Or I could stay late and get a head start on tomorrow's Interactions. Or go home early and fall behind. When I worked didn't matter, as long as I kept up on a week to week basis. Sometimes I would get a text letting me know about a surge in demand in one of my skill areas. I could earn extra Interactions and Merit for coming in on short notice to meet the need.

Working fast, working extra, or working well also gained me Merit. Merit was the official currency of everything within the Humanilism ecosystem. It could buy you everything from a day in one of the secluded workspace nooks along the edges of the open office, to extra vacation time, to literal physical goods in the Humanilism store.

So I had every reason to be efficient. Still, something about the ad arrested me. I felt myself quietly entering a moment of personal crisis.

I thought again of Buttercup. I had spent a ridiculous amount of time leveling that horse up, earning her armor and special attacks, riding her around the HotTS environment. I thought of what Hawkeyez777 called me. *Pony girl.*

I spent hours of every day in that virtual world. And yet, I hadn't ridden a real horse in years. I hadn't even seen one in the flesh for nearly as long—not since that terrible day at that terrible auction when I saw the real Buttercup for the last time.

My timer box gained an amber tint, warning me my Merit-Earning window was narrowing. I couldn't access the internet while I was logged into the work system, but there was a notepad app I could pull up. I did so, copied and pasted tippedz.com into a blank note, and clicked 'Approve Ad.'

In an uncharacteristic show of follow-through, I called the Tipped Z that very afternoon. I called because their website didn't have an automated scheduling system. Or even a contact form. It had only an email address and a phone number. Fearing my moment of determination would run its course before I heard anything back if I sent an email, I scraped together all my meager courage stores, tapped the number listed on the website into my phone, and placed the call.

I hate phones. I hate them even more than I hate interacting with people in real life. Which is to say I lose the ability both to parse human language and formulate intelligible responses when speaking via the telephone.

My brother's diagnosis of this problem is "weirdo loser," but the various shrinks he had coerced me into seeing over the years have a different way of putting it. The most recent one told me I am "highly introverted." He'd explained further in earnest tones while leaning forward in his leather chair. "It requires a large expenditure of energy on your part to socialize with other people. You thrive on being alone, on intellectual pursuits, and in calm, quiet environments."

There was no doubt I spent a lot of time alone, but I'm not sure even the most generous onlooker would describe what I did when left to my own devices as "thrive." Still, his words had allowed me to begin to set aside the nagging suspicion I'd carried my whole life: that I was deeply and irrevocably defective.

Having a label for my hatred of the telephone did not make calling strangers any easier, though. As I listened to the phone ring and ring after dialing the Tipped Z, I nearly panicked and hung up. Just when I was pulling the phone away from my ear, the ringing cut off and a cheery, female voice said, "Tipped Z. This is Nora."

My palms felt damp and my mouth felt dry. I shifted the phone from one ear to the other and licked my lips. I said nothing.

The woman spoke again, less certain now. "Hello? Tipped Z. This is Nora."

I'd been sitting in my desk chair, having pulled up the ranch's website immediately upon returning to my dim little apartment after work. It was 4:30, and I was feeling jittery, most likely because I had consumed roughly my body weight in DragonFire but hadn't eaten anything since the energy bar. I began to pace around my cluttered sleeping area and managed to blurt out, "Yes. Hi. I saw your ad."

There was a pause. I froze in front of my window. The blinds were drawn, but they were old and crooked and let light through in irregular slivers. I tried to straighten one sagging section with my free hand, but it drooped back out of line as soon as I let go.

Nora spoke again, sounding even less certain. "My ad?"

My heart was pounding now. I felt I'd rather be facing a giant spider than having this conversation. I fumbled on, groping for words that would make her understand. "On the website. I mean, the classifieds. The self-serve ad. For riding lessons. Ranching." I paused, aware of how incomprehensible I must sound. I sucked in a breath, closed my eyes and focused. "You offer riding lessons. Correct?"

There was a sound in the background, a murmuring of other voices and the crackling of someone covering an old-school style phone receiver with a hand. Then the voice came back, louder now and full of laughter. "Oh, the ad!" She sounded suddenly energetic. "Yes," she said, as more voices sounded in the background. "Aaron is offering lessons. How about Sunday at 7:00 am?"

I blinked, the sudden shift in the conversation taking me by surprise. How about Sunday at 7:00 am? I was usually asleep at that time. I doubted I had any plans.

Still, I let another moment drag by in silence. I was aware I was once again behaving like a person who is not competent when it comes to interacting with other people. I sensed Nora beginning to wonder if the line had dropped.

I had so many questions. Who was Aaron, for instance? A 5th generation rancher, evidently, but what did that even mean? Was he a grizzled old cowboy? A young bronc-riding upstart? How much did lessons cost? Was I supposed to arrive at 7:00 or have my horse ready at 7:00? Did I bring cash? A check? A credit card? What would I be learning, precisely? I could already ride quite well, after all.

None of these questions made it to my lips. Certain this amused woman was about to give up on me and end the call, I blurted the only sentence my muddled mind could form. "That sounds great."

"Wonderful!" The voice sounded truly enthused, as if my decision to call and schedule a lesson had made her day. "What's your name now? So I can put you on the schedule?"

This should have been an easy question. Most people, after all, know exactly what their name is without having to think about it.

Unfortunately, my case is a little less cut and dry. I despise the name my mother gave me and choose to go by a different one. While I am aware that many, many people do not go by their given name, I always feel a strange compulsion to explain to people that while my name is Faith, I go by Jordan.

Whenever I attempt to explain this in my brother's presence, he interrupts me, overriding my introduction and saying on my behalf, "This is Jordan," then muttering in an aside to me a moment later, "No one wants to hear your life story when they've just met you."

He was in the same boat, so he should know. Still, perhaps it was the residue of the public school system and being called by the wrong name the first day of class by every teacher for years and years, but it felt dishonest to introduce myself as Jordan without first explaining about the Faith thing.

So once again, there was that strange pause, the scrambling of my ridiculous mind, the sensation I was about to miss my chance. There was another rustle in the background, followed by a thud of some kind. Hearing this seemed to jerk me out of my suspended state. "Jordan," I blurted. "My name is Jordan."

"Jordan!" Nora sounded thrilled. "I've got you down. We'll see you Sunday."

I'd been afraid the Tipped Z would be hard to find. The directions provided by Google looked a little strange, with this goofy jog thing branching off a one-way street. Prepared to get lost, I left early only to find myself going through a four-way stop to proceed along a one-way loop that flipped me around until I was nearly back at the stop sign, at which point I found myself faced with a large, new-looking sign that said, quite plainly, "Tipped Z," followed by an arrow pointing right.

Approaching the sign, I looked right. And it was just as the map had shown. A narrow, rutted driveway partially hidden by a hedge of flowering magenta flowers passed between two normal lots and then curved back around to bend gradually as it carried on, leading me off into an expanse of empty land.

I drove for a few minutes, watching the dust billow up in my rearview mirror. I reached a gate, which was open, with another sign mounted overhead. At last, I found myself driving up to a low barn structure with a massive, ancient truck parked out front.

Beyond the barn stood a house with a wide porch. Parked to one side of the house were a more modern looking truck, a featureless sedan, and a motorcycle.

I opted for parking at the barn, steering Bessie in beside the monstrous vehicle already there. As I parked, I saw the truck's passenger side door was open. Somewhat incongruously, mounted to the bench seat within sat two car seats.

Stopping, I killed my engine and looked at Bessie's dashboard clock. It was 6:45. An indecently early time to be awake even, much less somewhere other than in bed. My conviction I would get lost had caused me to allow more time for the drive than necessary, and now I was way early.

I stepped out of the car anyway, the warmth of the early sun rushing in as soon as I opened my door. Before I'd taken so much as a step, suddenly there were four dogs standing next to the truck, staring at me with sharp, bright eyes. They were odd-looking dogs, all wiry hair and muscle, ranging in color from light with spots all over to solid gray to mottled brown.

I'd never been comfortable around dogs. They were descended from wolves, after all. These four seemed to expect something from me, so in the least offensive tone I could muster, I said, "Hi doggies. Good doggies."

They didn't move. I was considering climbing back into Bessie when I heard a woman's voice sound from inside the barn. I quivered but didn't move. Hadn't I read somewhere that you can trigger a predator's attack instinct by running away?

I waited, and the voice seemed to draw closer. Soon, I could make out another voice sounding along with it, this one also female, but lower and quieter. I waited.

At last, the speakers appeared. They stepped out a small door in the side of the barn and walked towards the massive truck.

They were not what I had been expecting, although after I saw them I was no longer sure what sort of people I had thought I'd meet out here. One of the women was tall and tan, with a long blonde braid hanging out the bottom of her flat-topped hat. She was lean and toned except for the small bulge of a pregnant belly contained within a slim-fitting tank top.

The other woman was shorter and not as lean, with kind eyes and a baby clinging to one hip plus a toddler holding onto the index finger of her free hand.

It was the second woman who saw me first. She noticed my predicament with the dogs. "Oh," she said, her tone startled. "Fuzzface, Chet, Lop, Peach, that's enough." The dogs instantly stopped staring, their group breaking apart. She added, to me, "You must be Jordan. I'm sorry. I hope they didn't scare you. They're harmless unless you're an unruly cow."

The dogs had scared me, of course, but it seemed pointless to say so. Besides, I was too busy stifling my desire to explain that while I did prefer she call me Jordan, my real name was Faith. The words cued up like the roll on a player piano and scrolled along inside the silence of my head. Though I refused to pronounce them, they occupied too much of my attention. I managed the tiniest of nods.

"I'll be right with you," the woman said. Then, she added, "I'm sorry. This is Nora, and I'm Erin. I'm the one who will be giving you lessons."

I felt stunned by her words. Erin. Not Aaron. I had pictured a grizzled codger or a young musclebound upstart, not this kind-faced mom who looked less than a decade older than me.

As the dogs wandered off to do whatever dogs do on ranches, Erin turned to inspect the truck, speaking to Nora. "I don't know." She seemed to be gazing at the two kiddie seats with an expression of deep mistrust. "Are you sure they're safe? Why don't you just take my car?"

Nora, who was in the process of climbing up behind the steering wheel of the ancient vehicle, waved a dismissive hand. "After we went to all that trouble to put the new belts in? Come on, Erin. I'm going two miles on a private dirt road. I think the kids will survive."

Erin approached the truck's cab and heaved the baby up into the seat in the middle. As she did so, I noticed the toddler looking at me. When I looked back, I found myself arrested by the sight of him.

The kid couldn't be more than two years old, but he stood there in full cowboy regalia. He wore tiny boots, a tiny flat-brimmed hat, tiny jeans, a tiny button-down shirt, and the most serious expression I had ever seen on the face of a child. As he waited for his turn to load, he fixed me with his wide, blue eyes.

I felt more exposed in front of that kid than I had with the dogs. "Hi," I said, emboldened by the thought that he might be too young to even understand human speech.

The kid reached up and tipped his hat.

Chapter 2

"Okay," Erin said, squinting against the bright glare of morning sunlight reflecting off the arena sand, "Why don't you go ahead and mount, then."

We were in an arena now. The sun hung above the distant mountains, and the heat was building by the minute. I looked from the coarse, horse-hair rope in my hand to the placid gray gelding standing next to me, then back to Erin. My new riding instructor ran her hand down the neck of the gleaming bay mare who stood beside her, a slight, encouraging smile on her face.

Right, I thought to myself. *Mount.*

I turned a little, running my mind back over everything that had happened since the rumbling, rust-splotched truck had trundled away with the two kids and one of the dogs inside. Erin, looking vaguely worried, had led me into the barn, through a large, dim room full of hay, then out a large open door so we came upon two tacked horses standing at a hitching post in the steep morning sun. Erin had turned to me with an air of mild embarrassment. "I'm so sorry, Jordan, but it sounds like Nora didn't get many details over the phone. What would you say your riding level is right now?"

At the sound of my preferred name, the "my name is actually Faith" loop cued up again, beginning to play beneath my thoughts. It did this, constantly. It was what my brother did not understand. While he could introduce himself as Gregory and be done with it, I had to deal with this urge to explain every time I heard my name spoken by anyone who didn't know *the truth*. It was a glitch in my programming, a redundant loop of specious reasoning. It was foolish. The explanation was both a waste of time and irrelevant to everyone but me. I knew that. Still, it would not quit. My relentless internal monologue tripped me up all the time in moments like this one.

Erin was waiting for an answer. I, in my distracted state, said, "Oh. Experienced. Very experienced."

"Great!" The word was chipper, but something in Erin's tone lacked conviction. Her eyes had flicked over my black t-shirt and plain jeans but then settled on my well-worn leather boots with their high heel and smooth sole. The sight of them had seemed to confirm my otherwise questionable story. She added, "I won't bore you with the basics, then."

The horse had been saddled and bridled already, so there was nothing for it but to take the rope she offered me and follow her into the arena, leading the gray gelding.

Now I stood there, dumbfounded. It wasn't that I didn't know how to mount a horse. The stirrup was there—wider than I was used to and constructed out of wood with some sort of reflective metal on the outside and a leather lining—but perfectly recognizable. It was the rope that was the problem. The horse wasn't wearing a bit. It had this sort of woven rawhide loop around its nose. The reins were tied onto that, draped around the horse's neck and looped on the saddle horn. I'd never seen a set-up quite like it before, but it was all comprehensible enough.

The problem was this whole extra piece of rope, the end of which I was holding and had used to lead the horse into the arena. Was I supposed to ride with three reins?

I looked at Erin, hoping for a clue, but her horse was wearing headgear of a totally different nature than mine. The bay mare most definitely had a bit in her mouth, with a set of reins attached and looped around the saddle horn. Under the headstall attached to the bit, she also wore a little wrap-around thing like my gelding did, but much thinner. Tied to that was what seemed to be a second set of reins—tiny skinny ones—woven of horsehair and with a loose end like mine, which Erin was holding in her hand.

I looked at her horse, looked away, and looked back to be certain. But, yes. I hadn't been wrong. The horse was literally wearing two separate pieces of headgear, both with their own set of reins.

I began to fear I'd made a huge mistake.

Erin stood quietly as I tried to parse all this, watching me with a patient air. I looked at the gray horse behind me. He was large and solid and possibly falling asleep. I swallowed, reflecting on the fact that my video game version of Buttercup never provided these kinds of challenges. To mount her, I pushed a button. And voila, I found myself on her back.

Another moment passed in suspended silence. All around us, the landscape was huge and bright and empty. The barn structure lay behind Erin. As I watched, a pale horse appeared in a pipe corral off the side of the barn, wearing a fly sheet and ambling out from under a ramada to move to a water trough. In every other direction, empty land stretched on and on. I could see the tidy lines of dividing fences, mesquite and creosote along the ridgetops. How much land did they have out here? Enough to get lost in, I thought.

There was a movement behind Erin. She turned slightly, looking over her shoulder as a man on a quad pulled up to the arena gate, dismounted, and came in. As this new arrival approached Erin, half jogging to cross the large, sandy space. I saw something in her posture go a little bit stiff.

Erin turned as the man stepped up to face her. I, desperate to think about anything but my predicament, looked at him too.

I was used to meeting people in an artificial environment. Every person I encountered in *Heroes of the Totem Spirit* wore a skin. These skins were not real, but every player invested considerable time and resources in the appearance of his avatar, from the facial features and body composition down to the armor, weaponry, and other sundry accessories. I think it's safe to say pretty much everyone I knew in that fantasy world put on the most impressive front possible.

But even in that fantastic environment, this guy would have made me look twice.

It wasn't that there was anything showy about his appearance. He was taller than Erin, but not tall. He was lean, but not thin. His hair was dark brown, his eyes a bright brown, and he walked with a certain strange care—as if concentrating on every step.

He was also breathtakingly, stunningly, attractive.

"Hi Grant," Erin said.

Grant wasn't wearing a hat. He wore jeans, boots, and a gray t-shirt. And yet there was something so cowboy about him, the sight of the quad he'd left by the gate struck me as strange. It seemed like he should have been riding a black stallion or something.

He glanced from Erin to me, and back again. There was something a little cold and glittery in his eyes. "Nora said the colts in the south lot need hay, but the gate's open and the lot is empty."

Erin glanced at me, rubbed her forehead, and stood a moment in silence as if perplexed by this piece of information. She fidgeted with her rope, frowned, and fidgeted some more. Then, moving more as if she was acting out of reflex than any real, conscious decision, she took the horsehair rope she was holding, pulled it through her belt, turned, and swung onto her horse.

"I'm sorry," she said, picking up her two sets of reins as she set the rope that had been her lead down on the other side of the horn. "I have no idea what she was talking about. She's back at the Rocking J now, with the kids. Why don't you give her a call?"

I may not always be super quick on the uptake when it comes to conversation, but I am, and always have been, a keen observer. Acting quickly for fear I'd forget what I'd just seen Erin do if I delayed, I imitated her, shoving the trailing rope through my belt, setting my foot in the stirrup, and swinging up onto the gray gelding's back.

The man was looking at Erin with a stymied expression, but as I swung up onto my horse his eyes flicked over to mine. And caught.

They were brown eyes, but on the light side, almost with an amber tint to them. There was something sharp in the way he looked at me, something behind that gaze that was both pitiable and a little foreboding.

Erin, seeing us looking at one another, seemed to realize it was customary for humans in the same place to become acquainted. She blurted out a flustered introduction. "Oh, sorry. Jordan, this is Grant.

Grant, this is Jordan. Jordan is my ...um... my new student. Riding student."

On cue, the Faith reel sprang to life in my head again. *I do like to be called Jordan. Thank you for calling me Jordan. But just FYI my real name is Faith. Not real in the sense that that's what you should call me, but real in the sense that that's the name I was given when I was born. But please, please, call me Jordan.*

Fortunately, none of these words made their way to my lips. And Grant, it turned out, was not as polite as the two-year-old with whom I'd interacted earlier. In his defense, he had no hat to tip. In any case, he did not acknowledge me in any way other than to maintain that eye contact a moment longer. Then he turned and strode back off in the direction of the gate.

Erin, looking hot and pinched, watched Grant for a moment before shifting her gaze back to me. She seemed relieved to note I was on the horse's back. With an effort, she focused, the lines of worry smoothing out of her face.

"Let's get started, then." Her tone had a forced, bright quality to it. "Loosen your reins a little. Around here we hold any excess in a coil, like this, but if you're more comfortable that way at first, that's fine. Today I just want to see how you ride. Will you ask Duke to walk out, please?"

I walked from the guest parking spaces past a glowing pool, making my way onto a smooth walkway that led up to the bright façade of my brother's condo. Like my apartment, it had a recessed entryway. Except while my entry amounted to little more than a short, dank hall, his had an overhanging arched portico, a large potted palm, a doormat, and a glowing stained glass panel in the heavy, polished wood of the door itself.

I paused to orient myself, shifting the mini-case of DragonFire under my arm. It was the first Tuesday of September. Gregory and I spent Tuesday evenings together, always. It was a tradition we began back when I started college. Gregory had convinced me to move into the dorms on the grounds I'd have a more complete college experience that way. He'd moved as well, abandoning the latest in the string of cheap apartments we'd occupied since running away from our mother and taking a room in a house full of struggling artists.

I'd been 18. He'd been 20. We'd found it disorienting to not be living together for the first time in our lives. We'd started the Tuesday dinner tradition, and never stopped.

I enjoyed Tuesdays with Gregory. And yet, I always had to steel myself a little before walking into his world. It hadn't always been this way. Gregory had lived in plenty of iffy places, often with rather iffy house-mates.

Not anymore.

I slipped my key into the lock, worked the deadbolt, and set my hand on the heavy, antiqued knob. As the door cracked open, music spilled out—something jazzy—along with a trickle of dry, cool air. I stepped onto the luminous rust-red tile floor of the entryway.

I stood one more moment just inside the door, blinking. Gregory had always been one for light. When we were kids, he was forever at war with our mother over how many lights it made sense to have on at any given time. He never turned lights off when he left a room, never wanted to exist in even semi-darkness. I, on the other hand, avoided the light like a grub.

We were opposite creatures in so many ways, Gregory and me. It was only our shared trauma that made us friends.

I pushed the door closed behind me, the heavy latch clicking, and shot the deadbolt home. "Jordan?" Gregory's voice sounded from up the hall. "Sister dear, is that you?"

He knew it was me, so I said nothing. I walked to the bamboo mat positioned below the pegs for coats and stepped out of my black Vans. By the time I had straightened, Gregory was there, standing beneath the blazing chandelier that hung within the arc of the curved staircase that led to the second floor. He held a glass of white wine and looked poised and well groomed, as usual. He was barefoot, wearing a collarless button-down shirt open at the throat and pale linen slacks. He was breezily and effortlessly handsome, my brother. Another way in which we were opposites.

He came forward to meet me, relieving me of the mini-case as he eyed it with his trademark distaste. "I'm certain every time you drink one of these, it takes a few minutes off your life," he said, turning and leading me back into the kitchen.

"Oh, and that doesn't?" I thrust my chin at the glass of wine as he rounded the corner and set the glass on the granite counter-top so it made the cool clink of glass on polished stone. Gregory disappeared behind the refrigerator door, then came back to me, his expression lofty.

"A glass of wine relaxes me at the end of a long day." He lifted his glass and took a sip. "Really, Jordan, this is a very nice Riesling. Can't I tempt you?"

This was a ritual between us—one I found irritating. I shouldered past him and retrieved a can of DragonFire from the fridge. I popped the top, took a sip, and met my brother's disapproving gaze. He sounded on the verge of despair as he said, "Can't I at least get you a glass?"

I set my can on the counter, dumping my bag onto one of the stools tucked beneath the island. It promptly slid off and fell to the floor. I saw Gregory twitch. His condo was, as usual, immaculate. It was as if he expected a crew from the local paper to show up at any moment to photograph him in his native environment.

Which, for all I knew, happened to him on a regular basis.

I plopped my body on the stool next to the fallen bag, trying to ignore the screaming of every muscle in my legs as Gregory forced his gaze up off the floor and began to take in other aspects of my appearance. I sipped my energy drink and, in an attempt to forestall the inevitable question, went on the offensive. "So, how was your week?"

Gregory was frowning—the expression manifesting in mild dimples at the sides of his mouth and a single crease between his well-formed eyebrows. When *I* frowned I looked like Yoda sucking on a sour patch candy. That's the lottery of genetics for you.

"My week was fine." The words were perfunctory, distracted. "I delivered that show up to Phoenix Art Museum, and the opening went well." He paused.

He was an artist, my brother. And a very successful one. It still surprised both of us, I think, how vastly his circumstances had changed since we'd lived together. He'd transformed from a high school dropout into an internet sensation, literally overnight.

It had happened my junior year at the U of A. At the time, he was working two serving jobs to help with my tuition. Still, even then he managed to paint enough to have a small presence around Tucson. That weekend, he had a show opening at a small gallery downtown. During the reception, a local Instagram celebrity wandered in, posted a snap of one of Gregory's paintings along with a rave comment, and wandered out again.

The post went viral. Overnight, Gregory's previously modest little Instagram account exploded with tens of thousands of new followers. His show sold out, along with every piece of work he had for sale on Etsy at the time. That had been surprise enough. But then he'd gotten a message from an art agent in New York. It was an offer to represent him, get him into galleries all over the country, set prices, negotiate shows, basically do all the difficult legwork of being an artist, all in exchange for a cut of the profits.

Gregory had accepted the offer thinking it a good laugh. At the time, he'd said to me, "I only feel bad she'll be working for free. A cut of the profits is only a wage if there are actual profits to cut." He expected the surge in interest to pass, his small notoriety to fade.

But it didn't. He called me often in those days to freak out about the places his agent wanted him to show and the price tags she wanted to attach to his work. But he did what she said, and the work always sold.

Eventually he learned to trust her, at which point he threw himself into painting. He quit serving but worked longer and harder hours than ever to produce enough work to meet the demand.

It had paid off, though. Four years later, the momentum had slowed but not died. Gregory's work was in demand. He'd shown all over the country. He was a minor social media celebrity and also a rich person. Still, while he'd insisted on paying off my student loan debt and purchased his condo outright, he otherwise lived frugally, saving against the day his luck ran out.

Now, his eyes were narrow and interested as he scrutinized my face. "Seriously, Jordan. Is that a sunburn? Have you been..." he paused for dramatic effect, "...*outside?*"

I'd known he would notice. Still, it was irritating. I tried to slouch on my stool but that was difficult to manage without a chair back of some kind.

Gregory moved around the counter, tilting his head at me like a fascinated dog. "It *is* a sunburn. That is legitimately skin with some color to it." He stepped back, assuming an exaggerated air of suspicion. "Who are you?" His tone was dark. "What have you done with my sister?"

Gregory was forever hounding me to get more exercise, eat better, and generally, "Take care of yourself a little." At regular intervals he let slip exasperated remarks along the lines of, "You could be absolutely gorgeous, Jor, if you'd try just the *teeniest* bit." To which I always affected shocked hurt at the implication that I wasn't gorgeous as I was.

It was another of our annoying rituals. I knew I'd gotten the short end of the stick as far as family looks went, and found his persistence at trying to convince me otherwise mystifying. No amount of effort could enhance what wasn't there to begin with, so why bother trying?

I sipped my DragonFire, more disgruntled than ever. "Oh stuff it. I had a horse riding lesson, that's all. I didn't think to wear any sunscreen."

I looked up in time to see Gregory change. He had a persona. I suppose everyone did. But Gregory's was so polished and exaggerated, and also so seamless, I often forgot all about the terrified but fierce boy I'd grown up with. We'd been a team all through childhood, and by team I meant he protected me even though he'd been sorely in need of protection himself.

For a moment, his polished, successful artist's skin fell away, and I saw the brother I remembered from the nights we'd spent barricaded in the bathroom, listening to our mother rage on the other side of the locked door. "Jordan," he sounded astonished. "That's great."

I frowned down at my can. The DragonFire was a little warm, its flavor cloying and sticky on my tongue. "Yeah," I said, the words so foreign they seemed to snag on some invisible obstacle on the way out of my mouth. "It was fun, actually."

"Fun!" Gregory repeated the word with so much enthusiasm, I winced. He walked around the counter, picking up his glass and my can. "Come on, let's sit somewhere more comfortable. Dinner is in the crockpot so we can eat whenever."

We retired to the living room, where an abstract oil painting in gold and blue dominated one wall and tasteful, spare furniture sat positioned around the airy space. I pried my beverage out of Gregory's hand and threw myself into an armchair that looked more like a sculpture than a place to sit, cocking my leg over one arm and glaring as Gregory settled neatly onto the thing he called a settee and I called a couch. He'd resumed some of his breezy air, but his expression remained focused. "Where did you ride, then? Was it, like, a group thing? With friends?"

I barked a laugh at that, almost snorting DragonFire. Friends? Sometimes his optimism was astonishing.

I shook my head. I had a mild headache and my legs really were so sore. It was depressing, how sore they were. I'd ridden Duke for an hour as the solid, patient horse had obediently walked, trotted, and cantered around the arena and Erin had watched me with an intensity I'd found unnerving. There had been a time I could ride a horse for half a day and not feel it when I woke up in the morning.

Not now. My legs had felt rubbery by the time I'd dismounted. When I'd woken up on Monday, I'd felt as if someone had stabbed them all over with small, barbed needles. They'd been even worse this morning. The muscles all up and down my thighs screamed every time I so much as wiggled a toe.

"Don't be ridiculous," I said to my brother. "I saw an ad, is all, and decided to take lessons."

My brother looked dubious. "Do you need lessons?" Gregory himself had never ridden a horse in his life. "I mean, didn't you used to *give* lessons?"

I felt a cramp coming on in one sore thigh. I shifted around in my chair. "Yeah. I mean, sure. But those were kids at a summer camp. This is different. Ranch riding. It's a real working ranch with cattle and everything. They ride in this certain way. It's super specific."

It was super specific. I had learned this after Erin had watched me ride Duke. As we'd made our way back to the barn under the baking sun, she'd explained about the thing my horse was wearing (a hackamore) and the thing her horse was wearing (a two-rein) and then given me a detailed account of the way they trained their horses, the goal of their style of riding, and the things she would have me do differently if I stayed on as her student. "You have a good seat and I can see you're very comfortable on a horse," she'd told me kindly, "but you use your hands a lot. Our goal is to operate the horse off the seat and legs."

I had wondered how riding with two sets of reins fit in with not using your hands very much, but hadn't asked. If I was being truthful, I wasn't that interested in the whole ranching tradition thing. But Duke had been lively and relaxed at the same time, despite the fact Erin told me he was over twenty years old. I had felt something uncoil inside me as I had ridden him around that arena, something tight and tangled and uncomfortable I hadn't even realized was there.

"The first lesson is free," Erin had told me as we untacked the horses, carrying our gear into the barn and placing it in a massive tack room with walls hung with saddles and bridles, all gleaming and scrupulously clean and organized. "After that, it's $60 for each lesson, which will last approximately an hour."

We returned to the horses. I began rubbing Duke's pale coat with a rubber curry, high on that unique scent of a dusty horse covered in a sheen of sweat. While I wasn't exactly rolling in dough, my rent was low, my expenses minimal, and my job paid a pretty decent wage. I could afford $60 a week, probably without even feeling it.

Now, looking across the gleaming tile floor at Gregory, I felt that loosening in my chest again just thinking about that vast landscape, the blue, blue sky. "I'm going again on Sunday."

My brother smiled and raised his glass, leaning forward. "Cheers to that."

Despite myself, I smiled too. I stretched out my arm, touching my dull, soft can to the rim of his luminous glass.

⚙

I stared at the spinning progress indicator on the screen of my laptop, trying not to notice the sandy feeling of fatigue in my eyes. I groped for my can of DragonFire, took a sip, and blinked hard.

The progress indicator disappeared, replaced by the words, "Good morning, Jordan! Your first assignment today is: Weaving Consultant."

I sighed, slouching down in my chair as a wave of exhaustion broke over me. It was Thursday morning, and I was so tired I'd almost slept through my alarm. I was tired because my night with Gregory had, as it always did, put me behind on my HotTS XP accumulation. I'd had to stay up extra late last night to stay on the Elite Squad. Like most games of its kind, HotTS has all sorts of ways of rewarding its most active players, handing out special artifacts and various other boosts for people who logged in every day and played obsessively, like I did. When some of these were within reach, it was a waste not to put out a little extra effort to earn them.

Now, as I shifted in my chair, I felt the residual soreness in my legs. My mood darkened further. The bright, airy space around me felt oppressive, the constant mild chatter of my colleagues' keyboards invasive and ceaseless. Also, my nose was peeling.

My queue loaded, and my first Interaction of the day appeared on my screen. When I was at work for BlockWeaver, I did not review static text. I talked to real live people, trying to help them fix their real live problems. At the beginning of each Interaction, I first received a summary of the issue that supplied me with the user's name and a description of their problem. One of these opened now, and I narrowed my eyes in annoyance.

Name: your mom
Question: boobs?

I tapped the 'Flag' button. "Loser," I muttered as the chat window was whisked away to be reviewed by one of my superiors before being dismissed. As soon as that window closed, another appeared.

Name: Nancy
Question: i need the words to be green but there black

I took another sip of DragonFire, steeled myself, and hit the 'Accept' button. A chat box appeared, my canned greeting already in place. I pulled up Nancy's website in a different window and added an extra question. "I'm happy to help with this. Which words are you referring to?"

I hit send. As I waited for Nancy to reply, my bleary mind drifted back to the previous evening: all those hours spent in *Heroes of the Totem Spirit* studiously avoiding the spider forest. There were plenty of easier quests in the portals I had access to. There were tunnels you could go down, some of them offering endless foes, no escape, and no penalty when you died. You could try to match your high score from the last time you went in. There were also quest zones you could endlessly repeat, gathering resources and XP every time.

Beyond all that, there were the other players. MMORPG stands for Massively Multiplayer Online Roll-Playing Game, which meant everywhere you went in HotTS, there were other people around. You could speak to them, trade with them, duel with them, and participate in quests with them. The latter, in fact, was particularly encouraged.

The chat box changed, Nancy's answer appearing below my question. "the black ones."

I closed my eyes for a moment, trying to summon patience. All the words on her website were black.

I was about to type in my same question again, tweaked slightly so as not to appear condescending, when Nancy wrote again. "top the words on top."

I checked Nancy's theme settings. She'd chosen a color scheme in which all headlines were black. I explained this to her, suggesting she could choose a different color scheme and providing her instructions on how to do so. She, in turn, pointed out she wanted a green heading, and none of the available color schemes offered that option.

Although I was supposed to help the BlockWeaver users I interacted with fill in the website templates they paid $7.99 a month to use, it wasn't possible for me to make substantive changes to the appearance of these sites. This was because all BlockWeaver's themes had been "designed by professionals" and were "locked to preserve their aesthetic integrity."

In short, Nancy wanted green headlines, but green headlines were not something I could give her. At least, not without doing things I was not technically encouraged to do.

I took another sip of DragonFire, surprised to note the can was almost empty already. "Sheesh," I muttered to no one in particular. "I need to cut back." Then I returned to the chat box, trying to explain that THIS theme did not have a green headline option, but other themes BlockWeaver offered most certainly did. Nancy should have a look at the other themes and pick one that included a theme that had green headlines.

Her answer came back quickly, her annoyance apparent. "prefer this theme but want green headlines."

In the corner of my screen, my Interaction box turned amber. I was almost to the end of my Merit-Earning window.

I thought longingly of Buttercup, my dim, quiet studio apartment, the simple brutality of fighting a giant spider. I also thought of Hawkeyez777. I'd seen him around a few times since he'd come to my rescue that day, but we hadn't spoken. I kept hoping to run into him organically. I wanted to ask him something.

As I mentioned, MMORPGs encourage interaction between users. Individual players can create group quests, either inviting other specific users to participate with them or opening the quests to anyone. I joined up in open quests sometimes, as doing so got you more XP. But what you earned the biggest points from was organizing such quests.

I'd never done that. Even within the fake world of HotTS I was so massively introverted I hadn't made any friends.

It was why I couldn't beat the spider forest. I now believed the lore that said it was impossible to clear without at least two players. After my near-disastrous last attempt, I had decided there was nothing for it. I needed help. I was determined to ask Hawkeyez777 to take on the quest with me, but so far hadn't gotten up the guts to do so.

I stared at Nancy's message, feeling a dull headache erupt behind my right eye. Recklessly, I flipped to the window that contained her website and navigated to the nearly hidden custom CSS panel we weren't really supposed to use. I typed in, "H1, H2, H3, H4, H5, H6 {color: green !important;}"

I flipped back to the chat window. "Please refresh your screen. Headings are now green."

There was a long pause. I stared in consternation as my Interaction timer crept closer and closer to the tipping point where I would cease to gain Merit. "Tonight," I told myself. "You will ask him tonight."

At last, Nancy's reply appeared, and it made me want to bash my head on my keyboard in despair. "oh ok," she said. "thats the wrong green."

It turned out I didn't see Hawkeyez777 that night despite logging into *Heroes of the Totem Spirit* the moment I got home from work and staying up until almost 2:00 am. This was an excessive amount of playing, even for me. But I had a problem. Basically, it took more XP to progress your avatar and your companion with each successive level gained. Thanks to how long I'd been stymied by the spider forest, the only realms I had access to were geared for lower level players. This meant most of the foes I faced were no match for me, which meant I got little credit for killing them, which meant I had to take on tons and tons of pointless battles in order to rack up enough points to stay on the Elite Squad.

It was taking me all the time I didn't spend at work just to accomplish what should have been possible in three or four hours a day. And beyond the sheer time needed for progress, my situation was mind-numbingly boring. Facing the same easy foes over and over again, galloping Buttercup around the familiar environment to undertake the same repetitive quests—it was all starting to wear down my spirit.

Late that night, after I'd gained my required XP for the day, I took to loitering near the entry portal: the place new players appear when they logged in. Hawkeyez777 was distinctive with his red and black armor, his hulking wolf, and his twin blades. I was hoping to catch him on his way into the world. To entertain myself, I browsed the goods on offer from various merchants set up around the portal, got challenged to one or two duels, and wasted a good deal of time.

It was all to no avail. Hawkeyez777 did not show.

Giving up at last, I logged out of the game and shut down my computer. As the screen turned off, the whirring of the fans died and darkness fell in my apartment. I sat for a time in the stuffy silence. I hadn't turned on any lights. There was only the orange sleep indicator on my monitor and the crooked slivers of streetlights bleeding through the blinds.

"Tomorrow, I guess." I mumbled the words into the darkness, rubbing my eyes and tossing my empty can of DragonFire into the large cardboard box I kept beside my desk for this purpose. It made a dull clink as it fell, shifting other empties with its weight. I swiveled in my chair, looking at my rumpled bed. I was tired. Very tired. And yet something kept me from turning in.

I stood, stretched, and wandered into my tiny kitchen. The fridge light was bright and lurid when I opened the door. I gazed with disappointment at the empty shelves. There was a pizza box with a slice or two left inside, my case of DragonFire, a carton of milk, and a selection of condiments on the door I had no recollection of either acquiring or ever using. I closed the door again and wandered over to throw myself into my sagging armchair, dislodging several pairs of jeans that had been draped over the arm in the process. I gazed at them in mild confusion, unable to remember if I'd put them there because they were clean or dirty.

I rubbed my forehead, the skin of which was still tender with sunburn. Closing my eyes, I thought of the Tipped Z: that expansive sky, Duke's solid bulk, Erin's attentive gaze. Inevitably, the thoughts led me to other memories of riding.

The real Buttercup rose up behind my eyes. She had been a horse I'd considered mine—a horse I'd been promised. We'd spent hours upon hours together. Growing up the way I had, I should have known better than to trust in a promise. But the ranch camp I'd gone to every summer from the age of six had been transformative for me. It was the first place I ever felt safe. It was the first place I ever felt comfortable. It was the place where I turned from Faith into Jordan. Foolishly, I had assumed it would exist forever, and that the people who were in charge would honor their word.

I'd been wrong on both counts. Of course.

One of my legs began to fall asleep. I sat up, turning again to look at my bed yet still strangely reluctant to surrender to my need to sleep. Could I devote myself to horses again? Real ones? It felt like a betrayal. Riding once was one thing. But if I kept taking lessons I would be in that kind of world again. I would get to know other horses, another barn, another way of doing things.

I seemed to hear my brother's voice in my head. *You get stuck, Jordan. That's your problem. You dwell in the dark places and let the past dictate the present. You've got to live for now.*

I couldn't count the number of times he'd said this to me. I could even concede he was right. Refusing to ride horses because you had once loved a horse you had lost was ridiculous. It was insane. It was ludicrous on every level. But so was spending all your free time devoted to a world that didn't exist.

I was a master of the absurd, evidently.

I sat up, my forehead still stinging. I should have picked up some aloe on the way home from work. For that matter, I should have shopped for some food too, and cooked a meal for once instead of living on take-out and leftovers and energy bars. I should have sent

Hawkeyez777 a direct message in HotTS, simply asking him if he'd be willing to take on the spider forest with me. He'd doubtless already beaten it himself. I was seeing him around a lot less lately, most likely because he'd gained access to the three portals I could not yet enter.

I closed my eyes. Suddenly, inexplicably, I thought of Grant—the guy at the Tipped Z who'd come up to the arena on a quad and asked about the horses he was supposed to feed but couldn't find. There had been something about him, something sharp and glittery, something that seemed to put Erin on the defensive. What was that about?

My mind was drifting. I started to sag out of my strange pose and fall. I jerked awake, realizing I was ridiculously uncomfortable in the armchair. I squirmed out of it, stepped out of my jeans, and shuffled off to brush my teeth in a muzzy haze of fatigue.

As I came back out of the bathroom a moment later, my phone lit up. It sat where I'd left it, next to my keyboard. The sight of the glowing screen made my heart clench in anticipation of not goodness.

I looked at the clock next to my bed. 2:17.

It was my mother. I knew it without looking. Knew it from the way my stomach turned sour and the taste of bile rose in my throat. In spite of the stuffy atmosphere, I felt suddenly cold. *Don't look at it.* I told myself. *Just go to bed.*

I walked over to the glowing phone and stared down.

There was a notification on my lock screen. "5 application updates available."

I felt the terror sag out of me in a thick wave. I stood for another moment, listening to the distant hum of Tucson traffic, before turning and collapsing onto my bed.

Chapter 3

"Is Duke okay?" The question jerked out of me the moment Erin and I stepped out the back of the Tipped Z's low barn structure and I saw two horses standing tied, just like last Sunday. Except today there was no Duke. A compact, sturdy sorrel stood next to Erin's horse in his place.

Erin looked at me, an expression of mild amusement on her face. "Given your riding level, I thought you might prefer a more youthful mount." Her tone was casual, not like she was handing out a huge compliment or anything. Still, I couldn't help but feel a swell of pride. I'd reached Level 2, it seemed. And quickly. But along with the pride came a strange prick of fear. She hadn't, after all, answered my question.

"He's all right, though? Nothing's wrong with him?"

It was Sunday again. I was back at the Tipped Z. I'd arrived on time today. There had been no pregnant Nora, no tiny yet polite cowboy to tip his hat at me. There was only Erin with the two horses. They stood in the quiet sun, already groomed and saddled.

The truth was, I'd thought about Duke frequently all week. I'd thought about my next ride on him, the things Erin had briefly touched on about the hackamore and the way it was different from a bit predominantly in how you could use the weight of the heel knot and the reins to encourage the horse to find the natural balance point of each movement. In my head, when I'd pictured my second lesson, I'd been picturing Duke.

"Oh, he's fine," Erin said, walking to one of the red horses and replacing its rope halter with the skinny hackamore I'd noticed before. "He's a patient soul. He's a doll with the kids and the brand new beginners, but he's got a little arthritis in the hocks and we don't subject him to more rigorous work anymore."

I felt relief at these words. Real relief. Yes, I had actually gotten that attached to a horse I'd ridden once. Don't judge me. It's the way I am.

Erin settled the hackamore in place and jutted her chin at a thicker version of the same thing hanging off the horn of the other saddle. "You can go ahead and put that on Sally if you'd like."

I felt another little thrill at the casual way in which she suggested this. I'd never put a hackamore on a horse before, but it looked less complicated than the rope halter the animal was tied with. So I proceeded with confidence, stepping up to set a hand on the gleaming copper coat of the mare's neck and saying, "Hello, Sally girl," in my soothing horse-whisperer voice. The mare flicked an ear at me. After I removed the halter, she lowered her head into the rawhide nose loop when I held it up in her direction.

"Sally is one of Nora's bridle horses," Erin said conversationally as I hung the halter on a hook near the hitching post, "but Nora's not riding much right now, so this girl could use the exercise."

I remembered Nora's lean frame and small bump of a belly. I was trying to decide if it was safe to ask when she was due when the sound of a scuffing boot made me turn.

Grant stood behind me, having evidently just walked out of the barn. His sudden proximity was startling. I jumped back a little to bump into Sally's solid shoulder. "Hi," I blurted. The word was quick and false, jerked out of me like a speeder pulled off its trajectory by a tractor beam.

Grant looked from me to Sally and back again. I was possibly making it up, but I felt there was something disapproving in his expression. He stepped forward and pulled a saddle string out from where it had gotten caught beneath the skirts, releasing it so it dangled down past the saddle pad like it was supposed to. "Hi," he said. I remembered the tension between him and Erin from my first lesson, the way their words had seemed to spark against each other, hinting at underlying conflict.

His hands as he touched the horse were slow and soft. They were well-formed also, with wide palms and smooth fingers. I felt a little thrill at how close he had to come to me to accomplish his task. I could smell him as he moved, a blend of gasoline and dust and something a little sharper I couldn't name.

"You remember Jordan, Grant?" Erin said, easing a large, elaborate bit into her mare's mouth and looking at him with an echo of the hardness from last week in her eyes.

"Jordan." Grant repeated my name like it would be on the Friday quiz, extending one of his nice hands in my direction. "Sorry. I was in a bit of a hurry last week." Something about the way he said this suggested there had been a conversation between him and Erin about his entrance into the arena, but I couldn't fathom what might have been said.

I put my hand in his. It was wide and warm and rough, the clasp firm but not hard. It was such a strange thing, I thought, this gesture of greeting we did. A man's grip told you a lot about him. I wondered what it would feel like to shake Hawkeyez777's hand.

I opened my mouth to tell Grant that whatever he was apologizing for was no big deal. Instead, the defective part of my brain hijacked my tongue, taking over before I knew what its intentions were. "My mother named me Faith, actually. It's weird. I know. But I go by Jordan. I have for a long time."

There was a beat of strained silence. Grant held still for a moment—as if he'd just noticed I was a large, angry snake and I might strike him if he moved. My palm began to sweat against his.

Erin, having finished bridling her horse, stepped over to hang up her halter next to mine. She said, "Jordan is a lovely name. We debated between Jordan and Raquel when we were naming our daughter. We went with Raquel, but it was a near thing."

Erin's kind words smoothed over the roughness of my awkward digression. I got the impression Erin was good at this kind of smoothing. Grant smiled faintly, extracting his hand from mine. His eyes flicked to Erin, then back to me. He said, "Well, it was nice to properly meet you, Jordan." Then he turned on his heel and walked away.

I had enjoyed riding Duke. In spite of being so old, I'd found him responsive and willing. And in comparison to the camp horses I'd known—animals who tended to make extra, extra sure their rider really was definitely asking them to move their feet before taking an actual step—he was downright spritely.

Sally, though. Sally was a different story.

Erin told me about bridle horses and what the term meant as we led the horses to the arena. I have to admit I wasn't totally paying attention. My mind was stuck on Grant, my embarrassing gaffe, and Erin's smooth response. The good news, anyway, was Erin and Grant both knew about Faith now. The ridiculous piece of me that still insisted I inform people of her existence could now be quiet in their company.

So I was a little distracted as I swung onto Sally's back, but I did hear Erin say, "So she's going to be very responsive to your seat and legs. Use your balance and leg position to steer. She won't ever need to be pedaled or kicked."

The words got through the static in my brain, but only just. I gave a small nod. Erin, now mounted as well, was saying, "Okay, walk her out and see how she feels to you. Sit up straight in the saddle and open your hips a bit. She should…"

I didn't hear the rest of what Erin said because I sat up and opened my hips. Sally walked out in a smooth, even gait.

All in an instant, thoughts of Grant and Faith and Hawkeyez777 evaporated. I shifted my seat, and Sally shifted with me. I turned to stare, goggle-eyed, at Erin. She gave me a knowing smile and bent down to run a soft hand over her mare's black mane. There was something distant about the way she watched—as if she was seeing me and some fond memory at the same time.

"On a horse like that," she said, "the reins are for collection. Not steering and definitely not stopping. You do all that with your seat."

The hour that was my allotted lesson time seemed to pass in a heartbeat. Sally was alive and soft, precise and energetic. This isn't to say we could accomplish everything Erin put us to without trouble. Erin wanted me to work on a lot of small precise movements, like asking Sally to move one specific foot one step to the left. I wasn't great with these. But I knew the deficiency was in me, not the horse.

By the time I stepped down and we headed back to the hitching post, I was drenched in sweat. It was a hot morning. The sunscreen I'd smeared over my peeling forehead and nose felt thick and oily. My legs had mostly recovered from last week's abuse, but as I led Sally back across the sand, they had the telltale wobble in them. I knew I'd be suffering again by morning.

And yet, as the dust stirred up by Erin and her mount encountered the sunscreen residue on my face and clung there, I found myself smiling—literally smiling—as I thought of that feeling of lightness that went through Sally's entire body when I asked her to pick up the canter.

"Good ride, I guess?"

I blinked, looking up, and was startled to see Grant. I had nearly reached the hitching post. He'd come out of the barn again, carrying a halter in each hand. His tone wasn't necessarily anything other than friendly, yet I caught an underlying current of some kind. Irony? Disdain? I wasn't sure.

Nevertheless, I felt heat come into my cheeks beneath the sunburn. The effects of my magical ride began to recede, the black waters of self-consciousness rising up to take over my internal landscape of uncomplicated joy.

I should have ignored him—given him a cold look or maybe the finger. Instead, I answered with enthusiasm, unable to contain my prattling tongue. "Sally's amazing."

I glanced at Erin. She was watching Grant like a squirrel watches a prowling cat. It was weird, I thought, Erin's apparent dislike for this guy. She seemed like such a mild, friendly person. So far I hadn't seen any evidence to suggest Grant deserved the coldness.

Grant didn't look at Erin, but he did move off, saying nothing more to me. I watched him walk across the dusty yard to a gate, which he opened and went through, closing it behind him. He moved with an easy competence, not in a rush, but his body language still somehow infused with a sense of purpose.

I looked at Erin, who was easing the bit out of her mare's mouth. "What the deal with Grant, then?"

It was a bold question, one I probably wasn't authorized to ask. But my tongue had been loosened by the amazing ride followed by Grant's strange question. It could say anything in this state.

Erin's brow pinched as she turned to hang the bridle up, then replaced her skinny hackamore with the rope halter. I took it upon myself to remove Sally's hackamore as well. As the moments dragged by and Erin said nothing, I began to think she wouldn't answer.

I tied Sally to the hitching post with a quick-release knot, which I saw Erin note with approval. Finally, she let out a soft sigh. "He's my husband's second-cousin. Or something. Maybe there's a 'once removed' or two in there. Basically, he is the son of my husband's father's uncle's son. I think. He came in to help since Nora can't ride for a while and I'm..." she paused, "...pretty busy with the kids."

It wasn't really an answer. It explained Grant's presence at the Tipped Z but didn't shed any light on the evident tension between the two of them.

Or maybe it did.

I might have said something more, pried a little further, but Erin pulled her mare's saddle and headed for the tack room, closing the door on the conversation.

I left the Tipped Z that day in a state of glowing contentment—a feeling that faded gradually as I made my way through the suburbs and back into the crush and press of Tucson traffic. As I squinted at the sun flaring off windshields, stopped at traffic lights, and navigated my Ford into the concrete jungle of the city, the feeling of Sally beneath me washed out to a mere echo. By the time I parked and made my way into the dank entry of my apartment, all I could think about was the sensation of the dust clinging to the sunscreen on top of my burned skin.

I worked my key in the lock and stepped into my apartment. I stood a moment in the dark on the other side of the door, disoriented by the crooked slivers of light that stabbed through the blinds. As I did so, I became aware of the disaster of the place.

My housekeeping skills had never been great in the first place. While first Gregory and then college roommates had kept my messy side in check for years, ever since getting my old place that side of me had, perhaps, gotten out of hand. Every surface was cluttered. A stack of junk mail sagged on the kitchen counter next to the bag of paper towels I had purchased weeks ago. One roll sat next to the bag, partly used, while the rest waited patiently in plastic for their turn. Next to that was my stovetop with its crooked electric coils. This was entirely covered in a map of the greater world of *Heroes of the Totem Spirit*, which I had printed sheet by sheet and scotch-taped together in hopes of finding something fun and interesting to do that wouldn't require first beating the spider forest.

I flipped on the overhead light. It flickered endlessly, throwing out harsh light in florescent spasms. I turned it off again and took a few steps forward.

The living area was no better than the kitchenette. My overstuffed chair was a shapeless lump under piles of clean laundry I had never bothered to put away. My bed was unmade, the sheets wadded into a knot in the center. The door to the bathroom hung ajar because the knob didn't latch, the nightlight showing an expanse of countertop populated in toilet paper much the way my kitchen counter hosted paper towels.

Under the lack of tidiness, there was the cheapness of everything. The linoleum in the kitchen and bathroom bubbled in places. Several of the cabinet doors in the kitchen hung crooked on their hinges. In the bathroom, only cold water came out of the tap for roughly a century until it turned scalding hot. The tub had a permanent, rust-colored streak below the endlessly dripping faucet. The fan rattled when turned on, and there was a strange hole in the floor behind the toilet I tried not to pay too much attention to.

You don't have to live like this. The thought rose up inside me, buoyed to the surface by the fading residue of the good mood riding Sally had given rise to. I thought of Gregory's spotless, light-filled condo, his shining floors, his perfect furniture, his knack of never leaving anything out of place. His way of living was the antithesis of how we'd grown up. Mine was taking my mother's neglect when it came to housekeeping to its logical extreme.

Standing there in the doorway, I decided I was going to clean up. I could imagine my apartment as it would look when I was done. Blinds open, surfaces cleared, floor mopped, everything tidy. It still wouldn't be anywhere near nice, but at least it would be livable.

There was a set of stylish hooks mounted on the wall next to the front door. Gregory had installed these back when I'd moved in. I could remember him standing there with the elegant handheld drill he'd brought over, along with a laser level and drywall screws. He'd hung the hooks in an even row, explaining to me how being tidy was about habits. All you had to do was not put things in places they didn't belong. Ever. You took the extra few seconds to put them where they were supposed to live all the time. In my case, when I came in the door, I should hang my bag on these hooks. This would prevent me from tossing it onto my kitchen counter. According to Gregory, as soon as even one single item was out of place, you were giving yourself tacit permission to create more clutter.

The hooks were empty now except for a plastic lightsaber I'd somehow acquired one Halloween in college. It was set across the top, preventing the hooks from being much use. I removed the lightsaber and hung up my bag, then added my gray canvas jacket—which had been living on the back of my armchair since late spring—to the hook beside the bag. I stood for a moment, armed and feeling quite proud of myself. Then I looked around for a place to put the lightsaber.

This was the problem. Gregory said to put everything where it belonged. But where did this random possession, in fact, belong? In the trash can, I suspected Gregory would say. I pushed the button above the hilt, but the light inside the plastic blade didn't turn on. Dead battery, I supposed.

Disappointed, I set the thing on top of the pile of books and papers that populated the surface of my coffee table. Hands on hips, I stood a moment, looking around. The first step would be to open the blinds so I could see better. The windows in the sitting area weren't large, the view was indifferent, and the sun tended to reflect harshly off the concrete outside. Having the blinds open caused a bad glare on my computer screen. So I never drew them. Still, light was light.

The problem with this plan was the blinds were so cheap and battered it was difficult to get them up and down. Plus, every time I raised them it seemed there were more gaps and cracks than ever when I lowered them again.

I turned to look at my desk. My gaming rig sat there, the orange light of my monitor in sleep mode watching the scene like the eye of Sauron. I again became aware of the mix of sweat, dust, and sunscreen on my face. It was sticky and uncomfortable.

Heading for my bathroom, I switched my computer on as I passed my desk. I washed my face and arms in the sink and returned to the dim apartment. My monitor now bathed the room in a soft white glow. I bent over, clicked the HotTS icon on my desktop, and waited as the game booted up. I'd turn it on, I decided, and set my avatar up by the entry portal to keep an eye out for Hawkeyez777 as I cleaned.

But my legs were tired. So I sat down in my desk chair. As my character was summoned into existence in the familiar landscape of the fake world, I looked at my XP progress on the week's challenge and my position in the Elite Squad. I realized with a little twinge of anxiety that I was behind. Or, if not behind, definitely not ahead.

I preferred to be ahead.

I'd just go run a few quick quests, I decided. After that, I would clean.

It took me three more days to catch up with Hawkeyez777. It turned out he found me.

I did not clean my apartment that day after my lesson. Instead, I gamed for hours, took a shower, ordered Chinese food and fell asleep in my chair with my laptop on my stomach. HotTS could run on my laptop, though not well. I wouldn't risk taking on any quests on such an underpowered machine, but for poking around safe places and watching the entry portal, it was sufficient.

Not that it did me any good. Hawkeyez777 was inexplicably absent.

When I ran into him at last, it was on Wednesday. I was on the very hillside where he'd saved my skin a couple weeks before. I was there because I had a new saddle for Buttercup and it gave her a neat new repel capability. I was considering trying to take on the forest alone again.

I was sitting there astride my horse among the dancing dust motes when I saw a flicker of movement to my left. It was the great, dark-pelted wolf, loping over the crest of the hill. A second later, Hawkeyez777 himself appeared, his shadowy armor seeming to swallow the light.

Feeling self-conscious, I turned to face him. He ran up to me, stopped, and said, "It can't be beaten alone, you know. They do that on purpose to force loners to group up." The voice masking software he used muddied the inflection in his words, making his tone robotic.

I flicked on my mic. "I know."

We stood there. In my apartment, the AC kicked on. Outside in the parking lot, a car alarm blared to life. As I wondered if my mic would pick up the sound, I told myself this was the moment. It would be so easy, so natural to say, "Would you help me?"

Instead, I said, "I guess you beat it ages ago?"

Hawkeyez777's wolf sat down on its haunches and scratched at an ear. All the animals had behaviors like this—programmed movements they would enact after they'd been holding still for a while. Buttercup's were all fairly stupid. When I was riding her, she would paw, shake her head, swish her tail, and snuffle at the ground. When I wasn't riding her she would do all those things, plus graze and even lie down if I was immobile for an excessively long period of time.

Still, the wolf's evident lack of interest in the conversation made me nervous. Insanely, I began to manufacture excuses to leave. I could log out without saying anything, of course, and blame it on a power outage or a computer crash. Or I could say, "I have to go." But that would be stupid since I'd been trying to track this guy down all week.

He said, "Yeah, I have a handful of friends I quest with from time to time."

He was so casual as he said it, so nonchalant. How did people do it? This making of friends? I, of course, had had friends over the course of my life. But those friendships had always formed organically in situations where I was forced into the proximity of other people on a regular basis. Such as in class in elementary and high school, or at camp. Even in college, I'd had friends. But when whatever it was that had made us part of each other's lives ended, these people always faded away for one reason or another.

In theory, the place I should make friends now was at work. But the wearying combination of Humanilism's supportive, hip environment and the soul-crushing nature of the actual work made it hard to cultivate friendships in that place. My primary goal every day was to tick off the required Interactions as quickly as possible and get the hell out of there.

So yeah. Friends. They were not a thing I had in my life right now.

Hawkeyez777 paused, expecting me to respond to what he was all but offering. When I said nothing, he added, "We've done the spiders a few times. If you want help, just send me a quest invite."

Perhaps I am unusually susceptible to the power of suggestion, but when I spoke with Hawkeyez777 or any other character in *Heroes of the Totem Spirit,* I tended to assume their avatar more or less lined up with who controlled them in real life. Of course, this made no sense. There was no rule that said you had to pick a gender or body type that matched your own. Being significantly overweight or underweight were not options. Everyone had some variation of a strapping warrior body, except the undead classes, obviously.

As I felt a rush of warmth at being not only accepted but sought out by this formidable warrior and his hulking wolf totem, I realized with a strange clench of trepidation that he could be anyone. Hawkeyez777 could be a scrawny 16-year-old boy or a sexual predator in his 50s. I had no way of knowing.

An abrupt wave of fatigue washed over me. This was another reason I had no friends. As soon as I made fractional progress with anyone, I began to doubt the entire basis of what connected us.

Flustered, I replied in a rush. "Thank you so much. I will definitely take you up on that. I have to go now, though."

Then, without waiting for a reply, I logged out of the game.

"Good morning, Jordan! Your first assignment today is: Ad Review."

I squinted at the screen, my eyes raw with lack of sleep. I had come in later than usual today, which meant I was stuck in the middle of one of the long, communal desks. On either side of me, a co-worker tapped and clicked away, focused on earning Merit points. The only silver lining on the horizon was the fact that it was Friday.

I stared at the 'Proceed' button as I popped open a can of DragonFire. The thought of clicking the button, of opening the sluice gate and watching the ads pile into my queue, seemed intolerable. And yet, not clicking the button was also intolerable. It would mean I would sit here in a kind of Humanilism purgatory, not racking up Interaction points, not earning any Merit, not getting any closer to being able to go home. It was both the carrot and the stick of the flexible employment model of the place. Since technically no employee of my ilk was ever required to be at work, if you came in and did not get your work done, were you never technically allowed to go home either? What would happen to a person who came in and didn't ever click proceed? How long before someone would come over, peel me out of my chair, and suggest there was no need for me to come back again tomorrow?

At the edges of my peripheral vision, I could see the screens of the co-workers on either side of me. One of them was doing BlockWeaver support. I recognized the chat layout and color scheme. The other was in an interface I didn't recognize. According to the brag sheet Humanilism posted on our employee board every week, we provided Humans to over 60 companies. Which meant there were people here I worked alongside whose jobs were nothing like my own.

I heard a step behind me. I sat up straighter, afraid the abnormally long time I had been sitting here staring at the 'Proceed' button had already been noted. I reached for my trackpad in a spasm as someone said, "Oh good, you haven't started. Jordan, do you have a minute?"

I recognized the voice. It made a little chill run through my body. I took my hand away from the laptop and shifted around on my understated chair made of elegant molded wood designed to be ergonomically correct and visually pleasing all at once.

Luke Rastenhaus stood behind me, wearing his trademark navy blue t-shirt, brown jeans, and leather work boots. He was a slim, stylish man who was too old to be a hipster, yet whose style leaned in that direction nevertheless. He was our office's "Director of Human Capital." Which meant he was my boss.

I felt a spasm of fear and embarrassment. I never looked precisely chipper in the morning, but today had to be even worse than usual. After logging out of HotTS following my conversation with Hawkeyez777, I'd been unable to sleep for hours upon hours. It had seemed I'd drifted off mere minutes before being awoken by the jangling of my alarm.

I didn't respond to Luke in any way other than to stare at him, but it seemed my answer was a foregone conclusion. He made a little inviting gesture towards his office and began to walk away.

I'm too tired for this. My thoughts were leaden and sluggish as I followed him, knowing that every person at the long tables who did not seem to be watching was, in fact, aware of our every move.

Ostensibly, Luke checked in with all his employee's on a regular basis. It was not at all uncommon to see him emerge from his secluded lair, escort an employee within, only for them to walk out again 20 minutes later, both parties laughing until they parted ways with a warm handshake.

But it was usually the high Merit folk Luke came out and collected in such a manner. People like me—those of us concerned with getting through Interactions and getting the hell out of this place ASAP rather than racking up points to cash in for rewards and perks—were rarely on his radar.

Luke's office stood at the top of a long, curved staircase with a balcony at the top. There were two chairs and a glass coffee table on the balcony. He often sat in one of them, watching the tableau of workers down below. Sometimes, when he called an employee to a meeting, they only went as far as the chairs.

Not today. Today, Luke proceeded all the way up the broad staircase, across the balcony, paused to set his fingers on the handle of a door at the top until a little light on the side flashed green, then led the way into his circular, airy office.

"Espresso?" he offered as I followed him inside, gesturing towards a gleaming brushed metal machine that crouched on a table along one wall. "Or tea? Regular coffee, perhaps?"

I shook my head, wishing I'd thought to grab my can of DragonFire. Luke gave me a smile tinged lightly with disappointment, then gestured for me to sit. I did.

There was a laptop open on the desk, oriented so I could not see the screen. As Luke settled in, he glanced at it, clicked something, and turned to face me. "Jordan," he said. "How are we doing this morning?"

It was an inane, unanswerable question. I had to either pretend he hadn't said "we" and answer in the singular or attempt to infer how he was doing based on the evidence available to me. I wasn't in the mood to do either. I said, "Look, I actually had a rough night. If we could get to the point, that would be awesome. I'm already running late."

This was not on script. I was not supposed to speak to my boss this way. I was not supposed to suggest that my work here might be un-fun or burdensome, or in any way imply his interruption of my day was anything but welcome.

Luke's eyes widened. He paused for a beat. When he replied, his tone was unchanged. "You know, running late isn't possible with our flex structure for employees. Your accomplishments are not contingent on timeline-based performance metrics."

I stared at him, floored by the ridiculousness of this explanation. For one thing, I had been working here for nearly two years. Surely, he did not think I still had not grasped the basics of our scheduling system? For another, while what he said was true in theory, it was also true that it was impossible to stay in good standing as an employee without coming to work on some kind of regular schedule. I was in good standing. I wasn't a Merit chaser, but my Interaction scores were consistently high. I put in the minimum amount of time in the office, but it still amounted to a full-time job.

I was unable to keep a hint of acid out of my voice when I replied. "I'm aware of how the flex structure works, yes."

My boss leaned back in his chair, folding his hands on his stomach as if he had a beer belly rather than flat, hard abs. He regarded me with a perplexed look, as if he was used to looking at exotic, tropical birds with riotous plumage but found himself faced inexplicably with a common sparrow. He said, his tone a little colder, "Are you unhappy with your work here at Humanilism?"

The question took me aback. Was I unhappy with my work? I had no idea. Happiness wasn't a concept I understood in connection with day-to-day life. As far as I was concerned, happiness came in snatches, in stolen slivers between the dragging monotony of the grind and the bombshells of disaster that fell on a regular basis.

I'd had less such disasters in recent years. And now, I realized, this moment could turn into one. While I did not like my job, I did enjoy being able to afford my rent, having health insurance, money for food, etc..

I sat up a little straighter, rallying my scant supply of energy. "Unhappy with my job? No, of course not. I'm not a morning person. I have trouble sleeping sometimes."

This answer seemed to make up for my previous rudeness. Luke relaxed, leaning even further back in his chair and looking pleased. "That's actually the reason I asked you in today." As he spoke, he pulled open a desk drawer. "Our employee health algorithm identified you as a great candidate for our new BodPod pilot program. I'm hoping you'll agree to participate."

My confusion was now total. BodPod? Pilot program? What could this have to do with me not being a morning person?

I said nothing, but Luke didn't seem to notice. He reached into the desk drawer and pulled out a small plastic box with what appeared to be a pink plastic bracelet mounted inside. He set it on the desk, glanced at me, and his smooth composure cracked for an instant. He quickly reached back into the drawer and drew out another box, this one containing a black bracelet. Finally he set out a third option, this one blue.

Satisfied with his save, Luke leaned back in his chair once more. "We're looking for ways to reward employees for making healthy lifestyle choices outside of work."

I stared at the three boxes, trying to remember the last time I'd made a healthy lifestyle choice and drawing a blank.

Luke rattled on. "If you agree to participate, we'll give you a BodPod activity tracker. You'll wear it all the time, and it will collect information on your daily step count, your sleep duration and quality, and your heart rate. It will also identify and log your workouts. Our system will aggregate this data with your work performance. You'll get Merit points for each day you hit your step goal or complete an exercise milestone. You can even enter all your meals if you want, to get a breakdown of how well you're meeting your nutritional needs."

I felt briefly indignant. Wasn't this a violation of my privacy? What right did Humanilism have to monitor my sleep and exercise habits?

Anger shot through me. I imagined standing up, walking out of this office, and straight out the front doors.

But then what? My anger faded as quickly as it had erupted. Luke was still talking, rattling on about incentives and improved health and community building. I understood that while this was being offered to me as a choice, it would be a very poor decision to refuse.

Feeling a little sick, I reached forward and picked up the box containing the black bracelet.

Chapter 4

The rubbery black band seemed stark and obvious against the pale skin of my wrist. I spent the rest of the day feeling subtly conspicuous at work—like Spock never quite aligning with his human crew. I resolutely ignored the BodPod as much as possible over the course of the day. I even managed to achieve a state of hyperfocus upon leaving Luke Rastenhaus' office, flying through my recommended Interactions in record time.

It was 5:51 when I arrived home. I walked into my apartment and plopped my bag onto the kitchen counter. The movement caused the digital face of the BodPod to light up, showing me the time. The little light also drew my attention to what I was doing. I paused, remembering my resolution to be a tidier person. I retrieved my bag and hung it next to my jacket. Then, with a feeling of mild trepidation, I opened my bag and drew out the BodPod box.

Luke had walked me through the set-up that morning, showing me how to use my employee email to create a BodPod account and then grant Humanilism access to my data. We then synced the device to my phone, and he sent me on my way. Now, I dug the little pamphlet out of the box and flipped through it, skimming the enthusiastic headlines and diagrams for information on how the device functioned. Mainly I was wondering how easy it would be to trick. Perhaps unsurprisingly, the slim instruction manual did not come with ways to dupe your employer into thinking you were healthier than you actually were.

I pushed the button on the side of the device. The clock appeared. I pushed it again and the numbers changed from 5:52 to 2,312. This was my step count, and it made me blink with consternation. According to what I'd just read, BodPod recommended users shoot for 10,000 steps a day. Humanilism had adopted this recommendation as the benchmark for their employees in the pilot program. To earn any points for wearing this thing, I would need to hit that goal. Every day. Which meant I had a formidable 7,688 steps to go.

The screen went dark as I stared at it. I consoled myself with the reality that I'd not been wearing the BodPod for the entire day today and thus the stats were definitely inaccurate. Still, though. It was going on 6:00. I was nowhere near even halfway to my goal.

I heard a faint chime. Annoyed, I pulled my phone out of my pocket to see a BodPod notification on my lock screen. "Getting fit is better together! Connect your friends, or join a local BodPod community."

I dismissed the notification. I had no friends and I certainly wasn't going to pit my meager stats against those of strangers. I carried my phone over to my desk and set it down next to my keyboard as I switched on my gaming rig and clicked the HotTS icon on my desktop.

As I settled into my chair, however, I heard the chime again. I glared at my phone and saw another BodPod notification. "Tony75 has sent you a friend request and a personal message: 'Hey Jordan. I guess Luke strapped one of these things to you also. Friend me?'"

A new feeling—something midway between consternation and fear—erupted in my sternum. I picked up my phone, moving cautiously, and tapped the notification. It took me to a BodPod profile page.

I knew Tony, of course. He was one of my co-workers and had been assigned as my Acclimator when I'd been hired. This meant he'd shown me the ropes around the Humanilism office, helped me understand the Merit system, and trained me on Interaction protocol. He was a short, pale man with thinning hair and a soft, round belly that hung over his belt and caused his button-down shirts to gap slightly where he tucked them in. He was socially inept but sweet.

And he'd sent me a BodPod friend request.

On my monitor, the *Heroes of the Totem Spirit* environment materialized out of gray mist. My avatar appeared, well-muscled, elegant, and clad in gleaming armor. I shifted my gaze back to my phone and the photo on Tony's profile. Like mine, his account appeared to have been preloaded with his Humanilism employee photo. He was wearing a wan smile under his over-sized glasses.

I felt trapped. Social niceties weren't exactly my area of expertise but even I could see there was no way I could decline Tony's invite without hurting his feelings.

With a heavy heart, I tapped the 'Accept Request' button. Then I silenced my phone, set it face down on the desk next to me, and mounted Buttercup. I rushed away from the portal, afraid I'd run into HawkEyez777 and he would ask me why I hadn't taken him and his pals up on their offer to help me with the spider forest.

I made for a quest zone I knew well. It was populated with overgrown rats that had some kind of disease that made them unusually ferocious. I was about to walk past the large boulders that marked the quest boundary when the BodPod on my wrist vibrated, scaring me so badly I nearly jumped out of my chair.

I stared down at my wrist and saw a message scrolling across the screen. "High five from Tony!"

Muttering to myself, I turned back to my screen. I was going to have to figure out how to turn these notifications off.

"Okay," Erin said, raising her voice so it would carry over the sand. "That's pretty good, but you're asking for the trot in a way that's saying, 'Hey Sally. When you feel like doing this, would you please maybe pick up the trot?' That's not serving either of you well. I want you to pick a footfall – a particular beat. Ask her to trot and make sure she's trotting *the next stride*."

Erin emphasized the last three words. I nodded as I turned Sally at the top of the arena. Sweat was rolling down my back and my jeans were damp.

I'd woken that morning to a strange sensation. It had taken me a moment to parse the feeling. Finally, I'd realized it was my BodPod. I'd set up an alarm the night before, telling the bracelet to soundlessly wake me in time to get to my lesson at the Tipped Z. It was an oddly soothing way to wake up. No noise, just the gentle pulsing of the bracelet against my skin.

Checking my stats before leaving the house, I learned I'd slept for five hours and fifteen minutes, with seventeen restless periods. The sleep goal BodPod and Humanilism had set for me was eight hours.

So far, no lifestyle Merit for me.

I'd been surprised to discover it was raining when I left my apartment – a light drizzle that left dusty smears on my windshield when I tried the wipers. It was the sort of soft rain that usually signals the end of true summer, and had all but ceased by the time I reached the ranch. It had left behind, however, an appalling heaviness on the air. Humidity was the worst.

As I set Sally up again, trying to hold all of Erin's new ideas about how to use my seat and legs and not my hands in my head at once, I tried to focus on the pattern of Sally's hoof beats. Earlier, Erin had said, "Cue the trot just before the inside hind foot hits the ground, so she can push off on the proper diagonal." I'd stared at her, certain for an instant she must be joking. How on earth could a person tell when one particular foot was about to hit the ground?

But I had seen in Erin's face she wasn't joking, so off I'd gone to attempt the impossible.

"Rise into a posting trot, and she should rise with you. If you are decisive in your expectation, she will feel it and stay with your rhythm." I muttered the words to myself, repeating what Erin had said earlier. Riding this horse, I was discovering, seemed more metaphysical than mechanical. I adjusted myself, picked a footfall, and tried to decide I was going to start posting and Sally was going to magically accommodate my post by beginning to trot.

I chose my moment, tried to post, and succeeded only in flailing awkwardly into a standing position in the stirrups. Sally halted entirely, further unbalancing me. Sweat ran into my eyes. I cast a plaintive look in Erin's direction.

"Okay," she said. Her tone was a little flat and frustrated. "Come on into the middle. Let's take a break."

Feeling chastened, I reached for the rein, remembering at the last minute not to pull Sally's head in Erin's direction. I softened my seat and turned the horse off the rail with my leg. We walked across the sandy arena and came to a stop next to Erin on her horse.

There was an unreadable expression on Erin's face as I approached. It filled me with an uneasy emotion. For a moment, I was convinced I'd done something truly terrible to Sally. I glanced down at the horse, looking for blood or other signs of distress I had somehow missed.

Erin was running her hand up and down her mare's neck in long, smooth strokes. We sat in silence for a moment. The sun was not yet out. A thin scrim of clouds hung over the landscape, shrouding the mountains. I waited, my heart pinging with consternation.

At last, Erin spoke. "There's something I need to tell you, Jordan. It's actually something I should have told you from the start."

My heart leaped into my throat. The consternation shifted to fear. I steeled myself for bad news. Was Erin dying of cancer? Was the Tipped Z about to be sold and bulldozed for sub-divisions? I couldn't imagine what she might be about to say that could match her bleak tone.

Resting my hands on the saddle horn, I gave a small nod.

Erin sighed. "I'm not a 5th generation rancher. I've only been riding for a few years. You're my very first student."

I blinked, the fear fading into confusion. I cast my mind back, trying to remember the ad that had caught my attention when I'd cleared it for approval. "But the ad said..." I stopped, trailing off when I saw the look on Erin's face. She looked deeply pained, as if I'd sidled up and slipped a dagger between her ribs.

I stopped. Silence fell. A damp breeze shifted my hair. Erin went on. "Me teaching the lessons wasn't the original plan. The whole thing was Grant's scheme. He only told the rest of us the same morning the ad went live. It caused a..." she trailed off again. She was speaking slowly, as if choosing her every word with exaggerated care. She began again. "Grant is still adjusting to his life here."

I sat on Sally's back, utterly at a loss. I had no idea what to say, no idea what to do with this strange confession. Questions swarmed in my brain. Inanely, the only thing I could think to say was, "So Grant's a 5th generation rancher?"

Erin's answering smile was tinged with sadness. "They all are. Grant. Clint. Nora. Even Wyatt, more or less. Everyone but me."

Clint? Wyatt? I had no idea who she was talking about. But before I could say anything more, Erin seemed to rally. She sat up straighter in her saddle, adjusting her reins. "Anyway, I'm telling you this because I want you to understand. I'm not an experienced instructor. When we get stuck, it's more likely my fault than yours."

I blinked, thinking back on my difficulties with the trot exercise. I still didn't understand the whole bit about the Tipped Z and the ad and Grant and his position, but I understood what Erin was saying. I felt a sudden surge of fondness for her. I smiled. "Not *all* your fault, I'm sure."

Cautiously, Erin smiled back. "As long as we don't blame the horse," she said, "we'll be fine."

I waited until we were back at the hitching post and Erin was occupied tying up her latigo on the other side of her horse. Then, I positioned myself so Sally's body was between Erin and me, and my back was to her. Surreptitiously, I checked my BodPod.

Riding with Erin took a good deal of attention, but once or twice over the course of my lesson that morning I had thought gleefully of how I must be racking up steps. Last night, I'd decided no one could really expect me to meet any goals on the very first day, so had gone to bed with my final count at 2,529. On Saturday morning, I'd taken it off to charge it and then forgotten to put it back on. Today, I'd promised myself, I'd do better.

And I was doing better. How could I not be? I'd ridden a horse for an hour, plus walked to and from the arena. As I pressed the little button on my BodPod to switch the display to my step count, I anticipated great things. Had I hit 20,000 steps? Maybe 30,000?

The number, when I saw it, landed like a mace in my stomach. 5,514. That was all.

Outraged, I looked up, my indignation great on my own behalf. My unit must be defective, I decided. I would complain about it to Luke Rastenhaus on Monday.

As I raised my eyes to the uncaring landscape, I realized I'd made a strategic error. By positioning myself to be out of Erin's line of sight, I'd opened myself up to observation from the other side. The barn side. The yard that had been empty only a second before was now suddenly, improbably, full.

First, I saw Grant. He stood in the bay doors that opened into the large section of the barn where hay was stored. His body was oriented to look off towards the mountains, but his head was turned in my direction, his bright brown eyes fixed squarely on me.

Next, I saw the riders. There were two of them, men on horseback, approaching from the direction Grant was oriented. Their horses were moving at a businesslike trot, their strides long and loose, their coats dark with sweat.

Behind me, I heard Erin say, "Oh good. Clint and Wyatt are back."

I stood as if frozen, my arm positioned to read my step count even though the BodPod's little screen had gone dark. I was arrested by the sight of the riders. I didn't notice Grant was moving until he'd sidled up to me. His voice was close and low when he spoke. "What's your count, then?" Before I could answer, or even process his question, he reached out with his blunt thumbnail and pressed the button on the side of my BodPod. Twice. That number appeared again. 5,514.

The riders were close enough now I could hear the thump of hooves and jingle of spurs. Grant spoke again. I couldn't decide if I was weird about my bubble or if he had come much closer than was normal for someone who essentially did not know me. "Not bad for 10:30."

I felt like I could feel his voice thrum in my sternum, his proximity bringing heightened awareness to the skin all down my side. I felt as if he'd dropped a freeze potion; I could not move.

Grant, not seeming to notice my discomfiture, tilted his own wrist, bringing it up so I could see the BodPod he wore there, black like mine. He pressed his own button twice. The screen flashed on. 5,124. "You've got me beat, anyway."

I said nothing. I was overwhelmed. The two riders had reached us. They stopped near the hitching post and dismounted. Erin approached one of them, the taller, thinner of the two. He had startling blue eyes and dark hair. She inclined her head so he could stoop a little and give her a soft, familiar kiss. Then she turned to me. "Jordan, this is my husband Clint. And this is my brother-in-law, Wyatt. Clint, Wyatt, this is Jordan."

Both men tipped their hats at me. If the gesture hadn't been so natural and easy and friendly, their synchronization would have struck me as comical. I gritted my teeth against the desire to mention Faith, which was easier than usual thanks to Grant's distracting presence right next to me. I nodded back. These were the final two 5th generation ranchers, then.

Clint and Wyatt led their horses by to take up positions further down the hitching post. Next to me, Grant shifted. He pulled a battered little Android phone with a cracked screen out of his jeans pocket. "What's your username? I'll friend you. No one else I know has one."

If I hadn't been so overstimulated, I might have thought to lie. But I could feel Grant next to me and Sally behind me, starting to wonder why I hadn't yet removed her saddle or hackamore. The sun was hot on my face. My nostrils were full of the scent of dust and horse sweat and Grant's strange blend of gasoline and desert. I told him the truth.

"My first and last name with an underscore. Jordan_ Falkenrath." Then I had to spell it for him, and watch helplessly as he punched it into the BodPod app friend search function, tapped, and pulled up my profile.

In my pocket, my phone chimed.

Grant was watching me. I had no choice.

The notification was familiar. "GrantCircleT has sent you a friend request."

Numb with disbelief, I accepted.

I found Gregory in the large, airy room at the back of his condo. He'd made it into his studio upon purchasing the place. I'd guessed he would be there this time of day, so walked up the long back hall to peep around the door. He was perched on a wooden stool drawn up against the back wall, staring at a massive canvas on an easel set at the opposite side of the large room. He wore a paint-smudged wife-beater, cargo shorts, and a pensive expression.

Other than the stool, the canvas, and the palette sitting on a slender white side table, the studio was utterly empty. The walls were plain white sheetrock. The flooring was over-sized white tile with white grout. The windows were covered in sheer white fabric screens that let in the light but blocked the view. There were skylights and track lights: brilliance and brightness everywhere.

This was how my brother preferred to work – in a space blasted free of any shred of shadow.

Standing in the hall, I hesitated. I'd come straight here from the Tipped Z, unable to stomach the idea of returning to my drab apartment after what had happened with Grant. So I'd come to Gregory's instead.

Now, seeing him at work, I wondered if I should slip out as quietly as I'd slipped in. My brother's art was something I'd never quite understood. I found it awesome in the classic sense of the word: inspiring great admiration, apprehension, and fear. It was his art, I understood, that allowed Gregory to transcend the terror and pain and confusion of our childhood. He took all that damage and threw it onto canvases. The resulting paintings pulsed with life and dark energy, freeing him of some of the burden he carried. The darker side of me resented his talent a little. It seemed to offer him an escape hatch, a means to move on.

The best I ever managed to do was forget for a short while.

The condo was silent. Gregory, regarding his painting, was as still as a Rodin. He wasn't wearing his persona now. His hair was soft and ruffled, as if he hadn't bothered to comb it after showering. Deciding I was unwilling to interrupt, I turned to go.

"Jor? Is that you?"

While Gregory himself insisted everyone call him by his full name in all instances, he occasionally shortened mine. I turned back around, moving to stand in the doorway to the studio. He was staring at the painting, but I said nothing. He knew it was me. I was the only person with a key to his condo. Neither of us left our doors unlocked. Ever.

Gregory was different when he was working. He became quiet, serious, reflective. His art brought out a side of him I sometimes feared no one but me would ever see.

Standing there, I became aware of the sunscreen/dust combo on my face. I should have at least gone home and showered before coming over here. "I didn't mean to interrupt," I said.

But Gregory was standing, easing himself off the stool. "I was just finishing. Let me wash up." He stood and stretched, the movement causing his shirt to ride up, revealing a few inches of flat, firm stomach and the terrible, jagged edge of his monstrous scar.

Feeling a chill, I looked away. The room was too sterile for me by far. Gregory straightened his shirt, picked up his pallete and headed for the white door in the corner that led to a smaller adjacent room that contained a utility sink and shelves of paint, canvas, stretcher bars, and brushes. I said, "I'll wait out here."

Ten minutes later, Gregory joined me in the sitting area. He came padding barefoot down the hallway, his hair still rumpled. But he'd changed into jeans and a tight cream-colored shirt, already resuming his characteristic air of breezy security. As soon as he entered, he fixed me with his brilliant, mega-watt smile. "This is a pleasant surprise," he said as he strolled past. "Everything okay?"

In spite of his casual tone, I recognized the weight in the question. It was code for, "Has she found you?"

As my brother walked to the kitchen and rattled around in the fridge, drawing out a tall, elegant glass pitcher full of some kind of pale, greenish liquid, I hurried to reassure him. "Everything's fine." This was code for, "No, she hasn't."

We said nothing more for a moment, but I could see his relief in the way his shoulders straightened. He filled two tall glasses with ice, poured the pale liquid over the cubes, and returned to the sitting area.

Had I not caught a glimpse of his scar minutes before, I might have rejected the glass. As it was, I was too filled with guilt and gratitude to do anything more than wrinkle my nose as he handed the beverage over. He noted my expression anyway. "Just try it." He sounded exasperated. "One of my clients makes it for me. It's an ingenious blend of seaweed, honeydew, chamomile, and various other magical elements. It's great for stress relief and replenishment."

I didn't have any DragonFire with me anyway, and I was thirsty after my long morning out in the sun. As Gregory settled onto the settee, I took a sip. It could have been sweeter, but other than that it wasn't too terrible. I swallowed and tried to gather my thoughts.

I'd come over full to bursting, feeling the need to tell someone about the BodPod and Grant, Erin's strange confession, and how hard it was to get 10,000 steps.

Now, though, the urge to talk had drained out of me. I felt the way I often did. I had things to say, but seemed bereft of any ability to gather the proper words.

Gregory was used to this shortcoming of mine. His eyes did a quick assessment of my person, taking in my dusty jeans and boots and coming at last to settle on the BodPod. "I gather you've been riding?" He sounded pleased. "And is that thing on your wrist an accessory of some kind? Something that might qualify as *adornment*?"

His tone had the desired effect. Gregory had long ago learned the best way to get me talking was to annoy me. "It's an activity tracker, not a charm bracelet." I snapped. "It's for work."

Gregory waited, sipping his drink and watching me with the expression of someone prepared to hold out.

I sighed. "It's super depressing, actually. I'm supposed to get 10,000 steps a day, which I swear is literally impossible unless you're a professional athlete or something. Also, these two guys wanted to be my BodPod friends, which means every time I look at my own stats, it ranks my step count against theirs."

Gregory, of course, zeroed in the juiciest piece of this confession. "Two guys?" He leaned forward. "Do tell."

I thought of Grant and Tony. A stranger pairing could hardly exist. "One of them is Tony, my Acclimator from work. He's..." I paused, fishing for the right word. "He's just Tony."

Gregory nodded, his expression becoming avid. "And the other?"

I remembered Grant in a sudden rush, his low voice so close to my ear, the press of his thumb as he checked my step count. He hadn't actually touched me, and yet a rush of warmth and confusion swept over my body as I remembered. "Grant," I said. His name felt smooth and heavy on my tongue. "He's a ranch hand. Or something. He's around sometimes when I have my lessons."

Gregory looked more titillated than ever. "Is he cute? Do you like, like him? Is he one of those silent and handsome types?"

I considered throwing the magical beverage at my brother but checked myself. Instead, I considered the three cowboys I'd seen that day. "No," I said, pressing my palms against the cool sides of my glass. "Erin's married to the tall, silent one." Clint really had looked like a cowboy out of a cheesy Western, down to the intense expression and the belt buckle. He and Wyatt were both good-looking, to be sure, but neither one intrigued me.

I thought again of the way Grant had walked right up to me and suggested we be friends on the BodPod platform. "Grant is friendly," I said. "Although why he's showing any interest in me, I have no idea."

Gregory sat back in his chair, looking exasperated. "Possibly because he has two eyes and a brain."

"Whatever," I said, standing up. "I'm going to go wash my face."

I tapped the 'Conclude Chat' button at the bottom of my BlockWeaver support window, then leaned back in my chair, stretching. I could feel the muscles in my legs unkink. They weren't sore today. They just felt a little used. This was progress.

My screen shifted to the screen with my score for the Interaction I'd just finished in a column beside my progress for the day while in the corner, the countdown for my next Interaction began. I hit the 'Pause' button, followed by 'Take a break.' I needed a fresh DragonFire and a trip to the lady's.

I stood, picking up my empty can and glancing around the Humanilism office. It was midday on Monday. The long tables were full of Humans trying to rack up Interactions and Merit points. I could see Tony, his bald spot gleaming at the next table over. I scowled at his back. He'd hit the 10k step goal both Saturday and Sunday and was already at 5k for today. As I tossed my can into a recycle bin, I surreptitiously checked my steps. 1,821. Either I was an unusually pathetic specimen of humanity or Tony was wearing superhero spandex and a fat suit beneath his drab office chinos.

Grant, too, was crushing me on the BodPod charts. But whereas Tony was clearly clawing his way towards his 10k and stopping once he hit that mark, Grant wasn't even paying attention. He regularly racked up 15,000 steps a day. On Sunday, he'd topped 20k. At least in Grant's case, though, it made sense. He worked at a ranch, after all. Lots of his steps probably came from riding. It was harder for those of us who were chained to desks for the work week.

Not that even my weekend performance had been stellar. Sunday was my best count so far, and I'd topped out at 7k. After spending part of the afternoon with Gregory, I'd gone home, showered, and logged into HotTS. But the thing on my wrist had been so distracting, the thought of Grant checking his own dashboard and seeing that I wasn't moving, hadn't moved, in hours, was so embarrassing, I at last got up and hauled myself outside. Sweating in the twilight, I'd walked around my apartment complex's perimeter.

Still, I hadn't achieved 10k. I hadn't hit my XP goal for the day in HotTS, either. I was clinging to the bottom of the Elite Squad roster by the skin of my teeth.

After I washed my hands and left the restroom, I returned to the beverage area to find Tony there, stooping to fish a bottle of Coke Zero out of the fridge. He straightened when he saw me, and beamed. "Oh, hey Jordan. How's it going?" He spoke brightly, affecting mild surprise.

For my part, I was not fooled. I understood what was happening here. He'd seen me get up and had orchestrated this little encounter. Tony wanted to gloat.

"Nice work on your steps on Sunday," he added unselfconsciously. "Did you get out for a hike or something?"

The question struck me as invasive. Tony and I weren't good enough friends to ask one another how we passed our leisure hours. Were we?

Nevertheless, I answered. "Horse riding."

"Ah." Tony, blinked behind his glasses, then unscrewed the top on his Coke Zero. "I've been getting my steps on the treadmill," he admitted. "Every morning until I get 4k, every evening until I get 10k. I've got it set up in front of the TV. It's a bit brutal, but it works." He gave me a quick, uncertain smile.

I gaped for a moment, floored. Tony had a treadmill? Wasn't that cheating? Shouldn't you have to go outside to earn steps?

But then, I reflected, most of my steps on Sunday had been taken by a horse's legs rather than mine. If one of us had grounds to accuse the other of cheating, it wasn't me.

I sidled around Tony, edging for the fridge where I'd stashed my day's supply of DragonFire. Tony watched. I realized he was expecting a response of some kind. "Ingenious," I managed to mumble as I grabbed a can and popped the top. "I've been wondering how you were doing it."

Tony beamed at that, his round cheeks flushing a little. "Oh, I realized I was going to have to be systematic about it, or it wasn't going to happen."

"Right." I took a sip of DragonFire and glanced over my shoulder. "Well," I said, trying to sound aggrieved, "Gotta get back to my Interactions."

Tony raised his Coke Zero can to me in a one-sided toast. "Sounds good. I'll see you on the BodPod dashboard."

Chapter 5

I dispatched the oversized rat, moving forward to collect the small spray of coins and glancing around to discover I was alone in the landscape of twisted, infected fungi. No more rats, or foes of any kind.

I'd cleared the quest. Again.

Turning, I moved Buttercup back the way we'd come. As I crossed back between the two stones, the words 'Progress Saved' flashed across my screen.

I glanced at my XP bar. I was behind. Then I checked the step count on my wrist and let out a groan of despair. It was just past 8:00 pm on Monday, and I had less than 3,000 steps.

I sat up straighter in my chair for a moment, then hunched forward, staring dismally at the mini-map in the corner of my screen. Where on earth was I going to earn my XP for the day? And how was I going to endure Tony's smug aura at work if I continued to let him thrash me like this?

And then, there was Grant. Gorgeous, 5th generation rancher Grant, who'd gone out of his way to speak to me several times and then added me as a BodPod friend. Was there a spark between us? I wasn't sure. But I did know that, if there was, my lame stats were not going to do anything to fan it to flame. They might even snuff it out entirely.

I sat staring for one more moment at the mini-map, then resolutely logged out of HotTS. I stood up, filled with a sense of determination. I was going to go for a walk. Again. And this time I was going to do more than wander around in my apartment complex.

I was halfway to the door when I realized I should take my phone. I went back, scooped it off my desk, and shoved it into the back pocket of my jeans, where it protruded but seemed secure enough. Then, I made my exit. But once outside, I found myself stuck again. I needed to either take my keys with me, I realized, or leave my apartment unlocked. Neither option seemed desirable.

I stood for a moment in the muzzy darkness of my little entryway, stymied. As I weighed my options, my wrist vibrated, nearly causing me to expire of cardiac arrest on the spot. I raised my wrist to stare at my BodPod and the words scrolling across the screen. "High five from Tony!"

I drew in a lungful of dank, warm air. "Screw you, Tony," I muttered. Then I stepped back indoors, grabbed my keys, and made my exit.

Traffic hummed all around in the warm, Tucson night. My keys were an uncomfortable bulge in my pocket as I walked gingerly to the edge of my apartment complex and stood gazing down the sidewalk in some bewilderment. Cars flowed by on the road and the sidewalk radiated the day's heat back into the sky. I hesitated, uncertain which way to turn. I chose right for no reason whatsoever. A truck rattled by, belching exhaust fumes into my face. I held my breath for a moment, walking faster. How could this possibly be healthy? I was going to develop lung cancer by the time I got home.

But thoughts of Tony's calculated treadmill routine and Grant wondering if I was the most sedentary creature on the face of the earth spurred me on. I walked. I walked until I reached an intersection, then turned onto the street that looked quieter. I did this a few times. At one point, a low-slung car blasting bass cruised by, slowing slightly. I wondered if I should be carrying mace as well as my keys and phone. But the car didn't stop, and neither did I.

It was 9:45 by the time I got home. My t-shirt was damp with sweat, my Vans had raised blisters on my heels, and I'd gotten lost in some weird neighborhood. But my BodPod screen said 10,254. It had vibrated shortly after I'd sorted out my location using the maps app on my phone and navigated my way back to the edge of my apartment complex, startling me but making me smile when I looked to see the screen erupting in a pattern of exploding lights around the flashing number 10,000.

I'd achieved my step goal for the day.

I let myself into my apartment, locking the door behind me, hung my keys on their hook, kicked off my Vans, and headed for the bathroom. After a quick shower, I discovered I was starving and also exhausted. I rummaged in the fridge, gave up, ate a DragonFuel bar, and at last collapsed into bed. It was only 10:30, and I was going to fail to earn enough XP to max out my HotTS gains. In the morning, I'd be off the Elite Squad.

As I lay in the dark, feeling my heels smart and sting when my blisters came into contact with the sheets, I found I didn't care.

I woke with the muzzy, disoriented feeling of someone who has made poor choices but cannot yet remember what the practical fallout might be. For a moment, I lay in the quiet of my apartment, trying to gather myself. I shifted. The muscles in my legs protested. I shifted again and felt my chafed heels.

At last, I remembered. The walk. I'd left my apartment last night and walked around in potentially sketchy neighborhoods for an hour and a half.

I rolled over, groaning, and fumbled for my phone. I squinted as the screen lit up, fearing I must have somehow slept through my alarm. But the screen said 7:02. I had thirteen minutes before I usually rolled out of bed, took a five-minute shower, pulled on my clothes, grabbed my bag and my case of DragonFire, and left for work. It was a fifteen-minute drive from my place to Humanilism, and it took me less than half an hour from the moment my alarm went off to get into my car.

Mystified, I sat up and ran my fingers through my hair, smoothing it away from my face and trying to remember the last time I'd woken up before my alarm. After a moment, I gave up, stood, stretched, and went to my computer. Turning it on, I pulled up my BodPod dashboard. As the screen loaded, a pop-up window appeared. "Congratulations! You crushed your 8-hour sleep goal. Click to see your stats."

I clicked and was astonished to discover I'd slept for eight hours and twelve minutes, with five restless periods and zero times waking.

For me—a confirmed insomniac—this was unprecedented.

As I stood staring at the chart of my night's rest, my stomach rumbled. I thought, improbably, of eggs. When we'd moved into our first apartment together, Gregory and I had had an omelet phase. Every weekend we'd traded off making them, trying out different fillings and toppings.

I hadn't cooked an omelet in years, and there definitely were not any eggs in my refrigerator. But I did have those extra fifteen minutes. Besides, as Luke Rastenhaus had so assiduously reminded me last week, with Humanilism's flex schedule, it was impossible to be late.

Wincing at my throbbing blisters, I stepped into my Vans, grabbed my keys from their hook, and headed for Bessie. I was back a scant 20 minutes later bearing eggs, cheese, red pepper, onions, and sliced ham. As I rooted around for a knife and cutting board, I began to feel annoyed by the dim overhead lights. I walked to the blinds covering my windows but stopped short of pulling them. They were such a pain to get lowered again, and the glare really did make gaming impossible.

So I returned to my breakfast, determined to make do. I had to move my map off the stove to turn on the burners, so I draped it over the mound of random belongings on my coffee table. My only pan was warped and heated irregularly. But I'd gotten by with worse before this. The end result of my efforts was hardly a culinary masterpiece, but it was edible.

By the time I dumped my dishes into the sink and hurried to the door, it was 8:15. But I felt buoyant as I crossed the parking lot for the second time that morning, as if I'd won some sort of adulting award and prizes would be forthcoming. I climbed into Bessie, cranked the engine to life, and began my commute. I would only be half an hour behind my usual starting time, and I'd not only had a real breakfast, I'd gone shopping.

The good feeling lasted approximately ten minutes, at which point I realized I'd forgotten my case of DragonFire. "Shit," I said, glancing around the crowded street in a panic, searching for a grocery store. But I knew I was out of luck. The blend of neighborhoods and businesses where I lived had ceded to industrial complexes. I could stop at a gas station, but buying individual cans instead of a case costs a small fortune. I could turn around and go home, but every minute I delayed decreased my chances of getting a good station at Humanilism for the day.

I stopped at a red light, gazing at the Chevron station one block ahead with indecision. When the light turned green, I drove on by and went straight to work.

Gregory had the windows open, and a fitful late summer breeze snaked through his condo. He stood at one end of the granite-topped island in his kitchen, chopping meat. I stood at the other, chopping vegetables and sipping at intervals from my can of DragonFire. Having gone without it all day, it tasted like the nectar of the gods.

I'd made it to work that morning, claimed a passable station, and settled in. But by 10:30 I'd had a raging headache. I'd purchased a Mountain Dew from one of the vendors in the cantina, but by then it had been too late. The stabbing sun falling through the windows, the constant chatter of my co-workers, and the ceaseless, stressful mundanity of my job had never seemed like such a toxic combination. By the time I logged my last Interaction of the day, I was having fantasies of storming up to Luke Rastenhaus' office, flinging my BodPod in his face, and telling him he could keep his Merit from now on. Because I was quitting.

But I knew better than to talk to anyone when I had a headache. Several times over the course of the day, I'd seen Tony try to catch my eye, no doubt wanting to discuss my incredible achievement of 10,000 steps the day before. But I avoided him and slipped out with the stealth of a very uncomfortable cat the moment I could log off.

Now, sipping my DragonFire, I could feel the headache receding. Part of it was the caffeine, no doubt. The other part was the Ibuprofen Gregory had all but shoved down my throat after I'd spent the first half hour at his house wincing every time he spoke. Now, a feeling of marginal contentment began to creep over me as I listened to my brother rattle on about the logistics of packing and shipping a show to a small gallery on the east coast.

As I scooped up the peppers I'd slivered and dropped them into a bowl, my BodPod came to life. I couldn't help but glimpse at the screen. 7:44. With a vague feeling of dread, I pushed the button on the side. It switched to my step count. 4,121.

Defeat settled in the pit of my stomach like a cold, glass ball. It was endless, I realized. Hitting 10k yesterday had gained me nothing. I'd woken up not one step closer to hitting my goal again today. My trip to the grocery store had given me a small boost, but it wasn't enough.

Gregory, noticing my distraction, shifted the topic to accommodate my wandering attention. "So how are the BodPod wars? Are you crushing your chubby mentor, at least?"

I was not crushing Tony. I had yet to out-step him, even once. I filled Gregory in, telling him about my late night walk. As I spoke, he finished with the meat, washed his hands, and grabbed my phone from where it sat on the counter. Before I could even manage a protest, he'd opened my BodPod app and was poking around my stats. "Hey," I said. "Invasion of privacy."

He raised his eyes to me for a moment, winked, and returned to the app.

I felt embarrassed heat rise up to prickle my cheeks. It's one thing to know you're sedentary and pathetic. It's another to have the evidence charted and organized for all to see. Resolutely, I looked away.

"It doesn't even matter, though. It's, like, endless," I said, resuming my tale of the night before. "I got all those steps in, but then today I'm back at zero. You don't earn anything. Nothing accumulates."

Realizing how whiny I sounded, I shut my mouth. Gregory set the phone back down on the granite. "Wait," he looked up with wide, outraged eyes. "Let me get this straight. You have to be at least a teeny bit active *every day*, and the only payoff is you will improve your health and wellness?"

I lunged across the counter, grabbed my phone, and shoved it into my pocket. "Oh shut up. You physical types just don't understand."

For a moment, I thought Gregory was going to run with the sarcasm. He watched me for a moment, though, and then turned away. He pulled open the cabinet that contained his elaborate, rotating spice rack. He began to season the meat. I caught the sharp scent cayenne pepper. My stomach turned over with a rumble. He said, "Your steps were quite good on Sunday. That was when you went to ride horses, right?" He set down the cayenne pepper and began dusting paprika over the slivers of beef he would soon transform into fajitas.

"Right." I glanced at my brother's profile, suspicious of this turn in the conversation. It was impossible, looking at him, not to draw certain unflattering comparisons between the two of us. He had our mother's looks: the light hair, refined features, and perfect complexion. I looked nothing like either of them, with my dark hair, eyes that couldn't be called anything more flattering than hazel, a nose and mouth that were all too clunky to suit. All my life, I'd wanted to look like they did—to fit in even that much.

Gregory always argued I was hung up on superficial markers of beauty. He'd even postulated several times that I was the best looking member of our family, or would be if I bothered to stand up straight and look people in the eye once in a while. The idea was so patently ridiculous I had to conclude our mother's abuse had made him incapable of seeing any of us objectively. Grimacing, I dropped my eyes back to the veggies.

"What if you rode more often?" Gregory's tone had a forced casual note I immediately distrusted. "Maybe you could lease a horse or something. That's what you did before, right? When it was off-season at the camp? You could ride that horse Butternut whenever you wanted in exchange for doing chores?"

His words made a still pool of loss form inside me, broken by the ripple of resentment that disrupted all my memories of those days. My temper flared. "Buttercup," I corrected him. "And the Tipped Z isn't a kid's ranch camp. I doubt they'd let me ride their super fabulous horses without supervision."

Shrugging, Gregory traded paprika for chili powder, then pepper. He looked up at me with a quick smile. "Maybe you should just walk to work, then."

By Friday, I was exhausted. And in spite of my best efforts, my stats across the board were dismal.

On my way home from Gregory's, I'd stopped at Walmart and purchased a little handheld can of mace equipped with a panic button I could push if someone tried to murder me while I was out racking up steps at night. I also purchased a lame little fanny pack. Then I'd gone on another late night walk, my phone and keys stored in the pack, the mace clutched in my hand.

I walked again on Wednesday and Thursday, but both nights I was too tired to make it all the way to 10k. Plus, I felt the need to accumulate at least some HotTS XP. This was difficult because I found it inexplicably impossible to stay up super late after my walks. Which made no sense. Wasn't exercise supposed to energize you?

Day after day, as I put effort into goals I fell short of meeting, I kept thinking of Gregory's comment. *Maybe you should just walk to work.*

It was a ridiculous idea, of course. It took me 15 minutes to *drive* to work, and for much of the year the heat was crushing. Beyond that, I'd be walking through a deeply unpleasant stretch of town—all gridlock and strip malls and industrial complexes—not meant to be traversed on foot.

Nevertheless, I mapped it. According to Google, Humanilism was 8.1 miles from my apartment, and the walk would take me two hours and thirty-seven minutes, assuming I took the most direct route.

Always before, I'd been pleased—smug, even—about my commute. Many of my co-workers complained about the endless hours they spent driving in from the foothills or Sahuarita or even just the other side of town. My fifteen minutes had felt like nothing—a brief warm-up. But to walk it? Surely, such a thing wasn't even possible.

I was sitting at my desk looking at Google Maps when my phone rang. It was sitting on my desk next to my left hand, and it began to vibrate as it rang, dancing around on the cheap resin surface. I jumped, swore, and snatched the phone to silence it. I stared down at the screen. It was a local number I did not recognize.

I felt a tide of panic wash over me. I set the phone down again and shoved my hands under my legs as if I was afraid they would defy my will and answer the call without my consent. It had been quite a while since my mother had last violated the restraining order that made it illegal for her to contact Gregory or me. But I knew it was only a matter of time. Several of her old numbers were saved in my phone and blocked so they never rang or got sent to voicemail. But she could have gotten a new number for the express purpose of calling me. It wouldn't be the first time.

I stared at the phone. Silent and still now, the screen continued to display the unknown number for what seemed an eternity. At last, the screen changed as the call was sent to voicemail. I sat there, my heart racing, my hands growing clammy against my jeans. One minute passed, then another. The screen went dark entirely.

I waited.

At last, my phone gave a chime and lit up again. Two notifications appeared on my lock screen. "Missed call," and "New voicemail."

I didn't move. The AC kicked on. I shivered. The air around me already felt too cold. The message was a good sign, I told myself. My mother, as a rule, did not leave messages until she'd already failed to get me to answer her calls quite a few times. At least, that's what had happened the last time she'd gone off the rails and decided to get in touch with me at any cost.

Still, I sat there staring at the lit screen until it went dark again. As the AC continued to pump cool air across my chilled skin, I tried to give myself a pep talk. "You're being ridiculous. Just listen to the message. If it's her, you can delete it without listening."

But it wasn't entirely true. No matter how fast I was, I'd have to hear her voice say at least a few words. And I knew what they'd be because I'd heard them a billion times. *Faith, honey. I'm so sorry.*

I blinked hard as the old anger roused. I seemed to hear my old reply, the one I'd said equally as often. *If you were really sorry, you would change.*

As it always had, the anger gave me strength. I shifted in my chair, snatching up the phone and tapping the voicemail notification. As my phone went through the tedious process of dialing into my mailbox, I stood up and began to pace. The robotic female voice cheerily informed me I had one new message and zero saved messages. Then added, "To listen to your messages, press one."

I felt a brief surge of hatred for the voicemail interface. This gave me the wherewithal to press one. There was a pause. A female voice sounded in my ear.

"Hi, Jordan. This is Erin at the Tipped Z, your riding instructor. I was calling because something has come up and I'm not going to be able to give you a lesson on Sunday. I'm sorry to give you such late notice. If you want to reschedule for Saturday or maybe even Monday, we could work something out. Give me a call if that's something you'd like to discuss. Otherwise, sorry again and I'll see you a week from Sunday."

As the recording ended and the robotic voice chimed in again to instruct me that I could save, delete, or archive the message, I let out a long, quivery breath.

Erin. It had been Erin. I deleted the message, then created an entry in my address book so I would recognize her number if she ever called again. "You should have answered," I chided myself as I hit the save button and set my phone back down. Had I done so, I would have taken her up on her offer to reschedule the lesson. As it was, I doubted I'd be able to bring myself to call her back.

It was nice sleeping in on Saturday morning. No silent, vibrating alarm buzzed me out of sleep. I woke up at 10:30 to lie there for a while, relishing the fact that I didn't have to drive to work. I didn't have to do anything at all.

I rolled over in bed, stretching. The muscles in my legs ached a little, even though I hadn't gone out walking the night before. After Erin's phone call, I'd felt jittery and unnerved. So I'd logged into HotTS. I'd galloped Buttercup around the familiar landscape for a while, gathering what XP I could. I had fallen off the bottom of the Elite Squad charts days ago and there was no way to claw my way back for the week, but I told myself it didn't matter. The week's prize was a two-handed greatsword, which didn't fit with my fighting style, anyway. Sure, I could have sold it in the marketplace, or traded it for something more useful, but it wasn't worth losing sleep over.

What I needed to do, I knew, was clear the spider forest. Doing that would not only make *Heroes of the Totem Spirit* fun and interesting again, it would make the Elite Squad XP goals so much easier to achieve. I'd have access to more formidable foes and the corresponding XP rewards for killing them.

My stomach grumbled. Although I was still regularly falling short of my step goal, I was finding my appetite increased. Gregory often expressed confusion on how I even functioned on my habitual diet of DragonFuel bars, DragonFire energy drinks, pizza, and the occasional eegee's sandwich. He was convinced the only thing that kept me going was the one night a week he cooked for me.

It wasn't that I couldn't cook. It was just that ever since I'd gotten my own place at the beginning of my senior year in college, there hadn't seemed any point.

Lying in bed, I began to imagine the omelet I was going to make. My stomach rumbled with increased enthusiasm. I sat up, blinking, and stared at the disaster of my apartment. Although I had stowed the paper towels that had occupied the bulk of the kitchen counter, otherwise it was in no way improved since I'd resolved to tidy up. But no matter. I decided I would make my breakfast. Then I'd clean.

I used the bathroom, shrugged into some jeans and a shirt, and padded my way into the kitchen. I felt a strange swell of pleasure as I opened my refrigerator and saw the eggs and cheese and ham waiting. I was out of peppers, but I found I didn't care. Later, I'd go shopping again and get some more, along with mushrooms. Gregory did not like mushrooms in his omelets, but I did.

I cracked the eggs into a bowl and whipped them into runny yellow slime. Then I set my warped pan on my uneven stove-top and turned the knob to start the burner. I poured the eggs into the pan, sprinkled pepper over the top, and turned my attention to dicing cheese and ham.

A few minutes later, I returned to the pan. With my plastic spatula, I attempted to lift the edge of the omelet to get some idea of how it was cooking. But the beaten egg remained as it had been before—gooey and viscous and cold.

Frowning, I glanced at the light on the top panel of the stove next to the words 'Hot Cooktop.' It was unlit.

I blinked, double-checking the burner to confirm it was, indeed, turned to on. But there was no heat. I tried a different burner, then the third, then the fourth.

The stove remained lifeless and unresponsive. I tried the oven light. That didn't work either.

"Shit." I stared at my pan of uncooked egg and the tidy cubes of ham and cheese I'd prepared. "Shit, shit. Shiiit." I felt intolerably disappointed, like the girl who'd been invited to prom by the most popular boy in the class only to discover the whole thing was a cruel hoax.

I stood there for a while, completely at a loss. What would make a stove stop working? The kitchen light was on, so it was not a general electrical outage. I looked up at the microwave installed above the oven, and pressed the button that said, 'Add 30 Seconds.' The appliance beeped and whirred happily to life. I pressed the cancel button.

I returned my attention to the cold stovetop. Did ovens have a reset switch? I ran my hands along the back of the control panel but felt nothing.

Out of ideas, I flopped back to lean against the cupboards, crossing my arms across my grumbling belly. "Shit," I said again, feeling real despair now as my final hopes fled. "This is bullshit." I would have to contact the apartment manager. And someone would have to come into my embarrassing pigsty of an apartment to fix the stove.

I stalked out of the kitchen and retrieved my phone from my bedside table. I sat down on my bed and sent Gregory a text. "I think my oven is broken."

I glanced at the clock. It was almost 11:00. Unlike me, Gregory was a morning person. He'd doubtless been up for hours. However, he didn't always have his phone on him. So I was pleasantly surprised when he texted back immediately. "Oven???"

I could practically see his expression of astonishment at the idea of me cooking. This served to further fuel my feeling of annoyance. "I'm trying to make an omelet."

There was a pause. I wandered back into the kitchen, where I tried all the burners again, one after the other. It seemed like they would have to work if I kept trying. After all, ovens didn't just break. Did they?

But the knobs turned and the burners remained cold and my eggs stayed runny in their pan.

At last, my phone chimed again. "Does your microwave work?"

I stared at the message in stupefaction. I stabbed out, "Yes."

As I waited for a reply, I considered the question. I began to wonder. Could one cook eggs in a microwave? I pulled up Google.

By the time Gregory replied, I'd already found a recipe. It turns out one can, indeed, make an omelet without an oven.

Energized, I returned to the kitchen and began to root around in my cupboards. I doubted I had the 9" glass pie pan the internet recommended, but I was sure I could find something close enough.

As I withdrew a stack of baking ware from a cupboard to look behind it, Gregory texted again. "So use that. But seriously. Don't you think it's time you moved somewhere a little less ghetto?"

Chapter 6

By Tuesday, I felt I'd mastered the art of the microwave omelet. The method even had some advantages. In the back of one of my cupboards, I'd found a plain glass plate with enough depth for my purposes. Which meant I could whip the eggs, pour them atop the melted butter on the plate, and pop them into the microwave. While the eggs cooked, I could clean the bowl and tidy up the kitchen. Midway through, I would add extras and fold the eggs over. Then, when the omelet was done, I could eat straight off the same plate I'd used to cook, leaving fewer dishes to deal with. Perfect. There was no need to complain about the broken oven, after all.

At least, this was the way I saw it. As I explained this to my brother, however, he listened with a look of pronounced skepticism. When I stopped speaking, he rubbed lightly at his temples. "You still need to tell them the oven is broken, Jordan. Otherwise, they might take the cost of the repair out of your security deposit when you move out."

I scowled, shifting in my chair. It was a lovely late summer afternoon. We were sitting out on his small balcony. He'd poured my DragonFire into a glass against my protests. Now I watched bubbles rise in their marching rows as we talked. I couldn't prevent myself from arguing. "Why would it make any difference if I tell them it's broken now or later?"

He cast a weary glance at me. He held his glass of white wine in one paint-stained hand, his bare, slender feet propped up on the railing. "Because there's probably a clause in your lease about reporting any maintenance concerns in a specified amount of time."

I felt a small surge of triumph. "I don't have a lease." I took a lazy sip from my glass. Ahead, I had a view of the mountains shouldering up beyond the scrubby vegetation of the desert. A flock of small birds wheeled out of a tree, their bodies dark specks against the bright sky.

Gregory was beginning to sound uncharacteristically annoyed. "What do you mean you don't have a lease? I was there. I co-signed it for you."

It always made me feel like I'd won some small prize when I managed to annoy Gregory. He annoyed me all the time, but he was a much harder mark. I smirked. "It ran out ages ago and they never made me re-sign. I never mentioned it. Neither did they. I pay my rent and no one has kicked me out. So I guess it's all good."

The annoyance smoothed out of Gregory's face to be replaced by something a good deal less welcome. Interest. He set his glass down on a side table, stood up, and left the balcony.

He was back a moment later with a slim, chrome sided laptop. He settled back onto his lounger. "In that case," he said, "we can make a list while we finish our beverages. Then, we're going apartment hunting. I don't like this idea of you walking around in those neighborhoods alone at night. And anyway, you're not a student anymore. You're a young professional. You can afford something a little nicer."

I settled deeper into my chair, not looking at his laptop. "Young professional?" I repeated with a snort. "Is that what I am? I thought I was a working stiff."

Gregory gave me a severe look. "Should we be job hunting instead?"

I sighed. This was my brother. Always trying to improve my life. I shook my head, running out of energy for sarcasm. "The job's fine," I said. I paused then, remembering his comment from the week before. I admitted, in a timid voice, "I've actually been thinking it would be nice if I could, you know, walk to work."

I could see Gregory contain his shock, stifling it with diplomacy. Historically, I hated walking. I'd been the sort of college student who preferred to stand in the sun for twenty minutes waiting for the shuttle when I could have hoofed it from one part of campus to another in less time.

But my perpetual status in last place on my BodPod friends list was eating at me. When it came to stats, I had my pride. Clearly, I had to do something.

Gregory's reply was deceptively mild. "That would be great. You'd save on gas, too. And wear and tear on your vehicle."

I thought of Bessie. She was already about as worn and torn as a vehicle could get, but I didn't reject his optimism by pointing this out. Instead, I leaned forward to look at the map of Tucson he'd pulled up on his screen. "There's this neighborhood, and this one," I said pointing. "Both back up to the bike path that goes behind Humanilism. It'd be a nice walk. First a few blocks of quiet streets, then along the path."

Gregory was nodding with enthusiasm, zooming in and opening multiple new tabs on his browser to type in streets names and pull up apartment listings. I took another sip of my beverage. It tingled across my tongue as I felt a small, answering thrill of excitement down my spine. I hadn't mentioned this to Gregory, but those two neighborhoods were also much closer to the Tipped Z. Not walking distance, but close enough the drive would be quick and easy.

As always when I thought of the Tipped Z, I thought of Grant. It seemed an age now since he sidled up to me and checked my step count, but I could remember the rush of feeling that had come over my body at his proximity, his blunt thumbnail pressing the button on my BodPod.

Gregory was staring down at his screen, brow lightly creased as he perused my options. "Do you think you want another studio, or maybe something with a..." He looked up, then trailed off, staring at me.

"What?" I snapped, returning his surprised expression with a glare.

His eyes narrowed. "Are you blushing?"

My cheeks, which had grown a little warm at the memory of Grant, heated further. "No," I snapped as blood surged through my body. I jutted my chin at his computer. "Did you find something?"

Gregory regarded me for one more long moment, then shook his head with a little sigh. "You're totally blushing," he said. "But I'm going to let you win this one." As I scowled, feeling the burn in my cheeks, he turned the computer around. "This place looks pretty good, don't you think?"

○

I stared at the message I'd typed in the quest invitation box, re-reading it for the millionth time. It was as bland and casual as I could make it. Yet I had been sitting here for half an hour, tweaking it compulsively instead of hitting send. "To: Hawkeyez777. From: PonyPrincess090. Hey, if you're still up for helping me take on the spider forest, here's the invite. Feel free to share and suggest a time. Any evening except Tuesday works for me."

As I sat staring at the words, my avatar stood below them on the screen. In the background I could see the entry portal, other players moving into the world. It was raining in the HotTS environment – a thin gray mist sifting down and causing fog to gather in the low-lying areas of the landscape.

It was not raining in Tucson. It was Wednesday. I was recently home from work. The mild temps of the last few days had fled. It was one of those hot, flat, days that popped up when the worst of the summer was supposed to be over and seemed to be trying to bake the vital fluids out of anything that moved between the earth and sky.

I adjusted my BodPod on my wrist. It had a tendency to hang up on the lip of my desk when I was gaming. I changed "Hey" to "Hi" and back again. Then I sighed and stood up, pacing into the kitchen where my printed map once again draped across the dysfunctional stove. As I stalked to the fridge for a can of DragonFire, I replayed my conversation with Hawkeyez777 in my head once again. There could be no mistaking his offer to help me clear the spider forest. There also was no shame in accepting that help, since the game designers had made this quest impossible to beat without assistance.

So why couldn't I send the quest invite? I stooped before the fridge, wrapped my hand around a cool can, and straightened. Gregory had once asked me how much money I spent on DragonFire. I'd asked him how much he spent on wine. That had shut down that conversation.

I wandered over to one of my windows as I popped the top, positioning myself to look through one of the crooked gaps in the blinds. Outside, I had a view of a blank, stucco wall with the heat-warped parking lot beyond. It wasn't a nice view, I conceded. Not nearly as nice a view as any of the apartments Gregory and I had toured yesterday.

I walked back to the computer. In my absence, my avatar had sat down, and my name above her head had turned gray—an indication to other players I was away from my computer. I read the message again. Then again. "Just send it," I said out loud. It did no good. I turned away from the screen and my eyes fell on the mound of clothing on my armchair. I'd put some laundry away, I decided. *Then* I'd send the message.

I had grabbed a handful of empty hangers from the jumble of mismatched options in the closet when my phone chimed. I walked to where it sat on my desk, knowing what it would be. Gregory's text was one word. "So?"

I sighed and returned to my laundry, picking up shirts one at a time to spear onto hangers. We'd looked at three apartment complexes yesterday. One, neither of us had liked. But the other two were both nice. The one we both preferred had a one bedroom apartment with a small deck and an office nook available right now. All I had to do was write a check sign a lease, and it would be mine.

The advantages of moving were almost too many to list. I could walk to work. I could have biked to the Tipped Z if I'd owned a bike. The complex had a pool and a great view of the mountains. Bessie would have covered parking. The office nook was dim and windowless, so I could have both a view out other windows and a glare-free computer screen. The oven worked. There was even room for a table if I wanted somewhere to eat other than a tiny, cramped island with stools.

The rent was a good deal higher than what I was paying now, but there was no doubt I could afford it. After returning to Gregory's after the three visits, he'd badgered me into letting him look at my finances. He'd seemed shocked at the state of my bank and retirement accounts.

The first thing he'd done was convince me to increase the amount of my salary going into retirement up to its maximum, since I, "Clearly didn't need the cash right now anyway." Then he'd moved the bulk of my cash from my checking account into my previously neglected savings account, and set up an automatic transfer so most of my paycheck would go straight into savings. Then he'd looked at what would remain of my cash flow and said, "You can definitely afford this. Assuming you don't pick up any expensive new habits, that is."

I thought briefly of the Tipped Z. A horse would qualify as an expensive new habit, I suspected. But I said nothing about this to Gregory. As he logged out of my accounts and padded into the kitchen to serve up the enchiladas he'd baked for dinner, he'd said, "So which one do you think you'll go for?"

I'd told him I'd have to think about it. He'd frowned at me. "Don't think too long. The one that's open now isn't going to stay that way."

I hooked the hangers onto their bar, wincing at the unpleasant scrape of metal on metal. I'd hang up my clothes more regularly, I thought, if not for how annoying the whole process was.

I walked back to my phone and unlocked it. I stared at Gregory's text for a while, considering. There was no good reason not to move and plenty of good reasons to move. Just like there was no good reason to not send my quest invite to Hawkeyez777.

Abruptly, I thought of my mother, and the thing she'd said over and over when we were kids. "I'm my own worst enemy." She always said it with a sort of wistful regret, as if she truly believed she couldn't do any better.

If I had one goal in life, it was to be as little like my mother as possible. And yet, at times, I failed miserably at this.

In a sudden spasm of decisiveness, I picked up my phone and walked over to where I'd left the rental materials each place had given me. I sifted through for the one with the empty apartment. I didn't allow myself to think. I dialed the number. When the phone was answered, I told the person on the other end that I wanted the rent.

Less than five minutes later, it was official. I could drive over this afternoon and sign the lease.

Feeling oddly giddy as I ended the call, I decided to roll with the momentum. I walked over to my computer and looked at the message on the screen. I stooped down and tapped, 'Send.'

○

It felt like an age had passed since I'd last been to the Tipped Z. I experienced a faint, irrational thrill of homecoming as I parked Bessie in front of the barn on Sunday morning and walked into the dim expanse of the hay room. The place seemed deserted. Not even the dogs came out to stare at me in their stiff way.

I crossed my arms against the morning chill that lingered in the shadows and made my way towards the open bay doors. As I approached, I heard voices on the other side. They were pitched low, reaching my ears as a murmur rather than distinct words.

I sidled up to the wall. Due to my angle, I couldn't see the hitching post. But I heard a horse stamp at a fly, its hoof making a solid thud against the earth.

I listened. Probably, this was not a good idea. No conversation around here was any of my business. If anyone noticed me eavesdropping it would be embarrassing at best. Still, the thought of stepping out of the barn and interrupting whoever was speaking seemed equally intolerable.

So I drifted up to the wall and stood there.

One of the voices belonged to a man. It seemed to be the one doing more of the talking. Was it Grant? My skin prickled at the thought. I strained to catch the words.

"...can't understand that," Erin was saying. She sounded tired, her tone listless.

The other voice replied with urgency and purpose. "I think it was less about the idea itself and more about how we began. He needs something to rebuild his confidence. I don't see why it couldn't be this."

There was a long pause punctuated be another stamp of a horse hoof. When Erin spoke again, she sounded exhausted. "Look, Wyatt. I understand what you're saying, but I'm not sure what can be done. Hank feels his position is reasonable. Clint is fine with giving Grant whatever time he needs, but I think he actually agrees with his father on some level."

Wyatt let out an annoyed huff of breath. "And what do *you* think?"

Standing in the dimness of the barn, I began to feel uncomfortable. This was not a conversation I had any right to overhear. But what could I do about it now? Step out and reveal myself? Go back to my car and pretend to come in again in a few minutes?

When she answered, Erin's tone had gained a crisp quality. "I think my student will be here any minute, and I need to get ready."

I twitched in my spot, feeling guilty. I was afraid Wyatt was going to come striding through the doorway and discover me. In a sudden spasm of movement, I stepped out of the barn.

To my right, Sally and Esperanza stood at the hitching post. Sally wore a saddle, while Esperanza's bare back gleamed in the early sun. Wyatt was a few steps in front of me, wearing a hat and chinks. As Erin said, "Oh, hi there. Wyatt, you remember Jordan?" I thought I detected the mildest note of triumph in her tone.

Wyatt turned to look at me, his face smoothing into an easy smile. He was a solid but slim man, with light hair, blue eyes, and a face that was not at all unattractive. He and Nora were a good couple—aesthetically speaking, at least. Their child would probably be good at sports and popular at school. He offered me his hand. "We met, but only briefly." His palm was rough with calluses, his grip strong.

I was too busy resisting the urge to explain to him that my given name was Faith to make any reply. He released my hand and said, "Erin says you're doing well with Sally."

I swallowed and found my voice. "She's amazing," I blurted out. Then I realized the comment wasn't very specific. "Sally, I mean. Erin too. I mean, riding here is great."

I was now so flustered by my own lame statements I was beginning to blush. Wyatt's smile had gone a little fixed. He pushed his hat back and rubbed his forehead. "The Tipped Z is a special place." Then he glanced at Erin. "I'll grab your saddle, shall I?"

Erin looked up from tightening Sally's girth. "Thank you," she said. If I hadn't overheard their disagreement, I would never have noticed any tension between them.

As Wyatt walked away, I sidled over to Sally. The mare raised her head and wuffed at my shirt. "I'm sorry about last week," Erin said.

It took me a moment to figure out what she meant. Then I remembered the canceled lesson. Before I could form an answer, Wyatt was back. He came striding out of the barn, carrying a pad in one hand, a saddle in the other. In a fluid series of movements, he flipped the pad into place and followed it up with the saddle. He made it look effortless—as if the bulky tack weighed nothing at all. I found myself wondering if Grant could saddle a horse so smoothly.

"Oh, it was fine," I hurried to reassure Erin. "Turns out my oven broke anyway."

Erin looked up with a faint smile, trying to parse the logic of my statement. I cursed my social ineptitude and tried to clarify. "I mean, it was good I had time to get that taken care of." It was a lie, of course. The oven was still broken and would stay that way until I moved out.

But Erin nodded, seeming to accept this explanation. Wyatt straightened from doing up Esperanza's girth. He gave Erin a quick smile, tipped his hat at me, and disappeared once more into the barn.

Erin jutted her chin at the hackamore hanging on a hook as she picked up her two-rein. "All right," she said. "Put that on Sally and we're good to go."

"Collection comes from the energy in your body and engagement in the horse. It's not about the reins like most people think. Now pick her up and try again. Your hands are providing structure only. There shouldn't be any weight on that hackamore."

I was sweating buckets. My focus had narrowed down to all the points at which my body came into contact with Sally's body. If I'd thought the horse lively before, now she felt like a coiled spring. And not in the way of a horse about to spook or have a meltdown. She was 100% with me, ready to apply her speed and strength when I asked. At least, as long as I asked in a way she understood.

I collected Sally again, shortening my reins and asking her to walk forward with my seat. "Good," Erin said. "Now leg-yield over to the fence, and cue the canter."

I did as she asked, feeling as if I was actively building new brain cells to deal with the complexity of the maneuver. As Sally shifted to a leg yield and neared the fence, I heard Erin say, "Remember to ask on the correct footfall."

I knew a moment of despair. I would have stared at Erin with incredulity except I was too busy attempting this impossible task. *Leg yield over to the fence*, I reminded myself. *Then cue the canter.* It sounded so simple. The idea was to send Sally straight from the lateral movement onto the correct lead.

I felt the soft energy in Sally's body—her expectation we would accomplish great things. I was focused as hard on riding this horse as I'd ever concentrated on anything in my life.

We reached the fence, I cued the canter. Sally didn't miss a beat. She hopped straight into a smooth right lead, and we proceeded down the fence.

I found myself laughing as I gave Sally her head and we swung for the top of arena. I lifted my eyes to the landscape. Before me, the scruffy pastures of the Tipped Z rolled towards the mountains. I noticed a cloud of dust and a herd of cattle moving along the top of the ridge. As we rounded the top and began to head back down the fence, I turned in my saddle to keep my eye on the cattle. I could just make out two men on horseback riding in their wake. I felt a little thrill. Wyatt, I knew, wasn't one of them. Did that mean Grant was out there, moving cattle across the desert?

I returned my attention to my horse. We cantered back down to where Erin sat on Esperanza. She was smiling as I eased Sally to a stop next to her. I was grinning ear to ear. She said, "You've spent a lot of time on horseback, haven't you?"

The question took me aback. I suppose I had spent a lot of time on horseback. At first, it was just summers. But by the time I was 10 I'd worked out my pseudo lease deal, which meant I could ride any day I could make it out to the ranch camp.

I'd first discovered the ranch camp because of our neighbor, Maria. She was an assistant director at the camp, and she went out four evenings a week to do whatever assistant directors do. After I expressed interest, she started taking me with her whenever I asked to go. I would put out hay for the small herd of horses that lived at the camp year-round, spread manure in their pasture, then spend a blissful hour on some horse or other's back. The first few years, I didn't favor any horse in particular. I also didn't bother with a saddle since it meant more time tacking and less time riding.

In retrospect, of course, I could see Maria had felt sorry for me. I thought of her as old at the time, but she couldn't have been more than 30 when she first started saying hello to me and Gregory when we walked past her house on our way home from school, asking us kind questions about our lives at first but eventually progressing to offering quiet generosities, like letting us shower at her house and bring laundry over when our water got shut off, and bringing us "leftovers" I now suspect she cooked just for us.

Despite all that kindness, Maria betrayed me in the end. She failed to keep a promise.

A few years into our friendship, a few of the camp horses were sold without warning. I had attached myself to Buttercup by then, identifying her on the day she arrived as something special. When those horses went without warning, I had a breakdown in Maria's car, babbling about how I would have nothing to live for if Buttercup went that way.

Maria, always steady and solemn, looked over at me and made a promise. She promised she would protect Buttercup, that the horse I thought of as mine but wasn't would always be at the camp, would always be there for me to ride. Further, she said, someday, when I grew up and could afford it, she'd make sure I could buy Buttercup so she was really mine at last.

In retrospect, I can see it wasn't a promise Maria ever should have made. She was most likely trying to add a sliver of stability to my chronically unstable life. But it had been a mistake. The camp was not hers. Buttercup was not within her power to promise.

Still, I'd believed her. I'd been comforted. Later, realizing the one adult in my life I'd believed I could trust had lied to me had been almost as bad as the loss of the horse I'd adored.

In the years since the camp closed, my anger at Maria had faded. I'd finally come to accept the terrible circumstances of our parting did not negate all the good she'd done for me. Still, the memories carried with them the ache of old loss.

To Erin, I said, "Yeah. I rode an average of five days a week from when I was 10 until I turned 18. Daily, in the summer. After that, my first couple years in college, I rode less, but still consistently. Then..." I paused, my voice sticking in my throat. "When I was 20, I stopped."

"How old are you now?" Erin's voice was gentle, her eyes soft, as if she could sense my inner turmoil.

"24," I said. "Just."

She nodded, letting out a soft sigh as if making up her mind to broach some subject she'd been avoiding. "So, riding once a week probably doesn't feel like much to you."

I blinked. It was true. It seemed a small eternity elapsed between each time I came to the Tipped Z. I gave a timid nod of assent.

Erin reached down and smoothed Esperanza's mane, something I was beginning to realize she did when she was nervous. "I don't want you to feel like I'm pressuring you," she said, as I felt my curiosity begin to mount, "but Nora suggested I offer you a lease. For a monthly fee, you could come ride Sally whenever you wanted. I'd still give you a weekly lesson, to keep teaching you the finer aspects of how we ride. But you're clearly a person who can get on a horse without supervision." She stopped and looked at me.

I felt a small surge of joy, followed by a moment of mild panic. What had Gregory said after we went apartment hunting? *You can definitely afford this. Assuming you don't pick up any expensive new habits, that is.*

I sat wondering if it would be gauche to ask how much this would cost before accepting or declining. On the horizon, I was disappointed to see the horses and riders moving away now, having changed their angle.

Anticipating my concern, Erin pushed ahead. "Nora suggested a fee of $350 a month. That would be for full use of Sally, her tack, and one lesson a week."

I blinked, taken slightly aback. The number seemed exceptionally reasonable considering what I was already paying for a weekly lesson. If I rode even two extra times a month, my cost per ride would go down. Still, I suspected I should probably do something adultish, like consult my brother, or at least sleep on it.

Instead, I found myself grinning like a kid in a candy store as I said, "That sounds awesome."

Chapter 7

I sat staring at the jumble of items on my coffee table, stupefied by their very existence. Behind me, the lights on my computer were like a silent siren song, dancing in my peripheral vision, tempting me to not worry about packing. There would be time for that later. For now, I should play.

It wasn't true. I did not have much time. The wheels of my decision, once set in motion, had gained momentum with surprising speed. It was Sunday, the 1st of October. This morning, after my lesson, I'd signed a lease document that granted me permission to go to the Tipped Z and ride Sally whenever I wanted. On the way home, I'd picked up the keys to my new apartment. It had seemed appropriate, somehow, that these two things happened on the same day.

I had not yet, however, told my current landlord I was leaving. Gregory was not happy with this decision, saying it was a waste of money. But I was happier knowing I had the month to move, clean, and inform management that no more rent from me would be forthcoming.

I didn't really have that much stuff. Gregory was going to come by tomorrow. He had a Mercedes G-Class he'd modified for maximum interior space, which he used for hauling his art around. He was going to help me with the furniture. He'd suggested this would be easier if smaller items had already been boxed, at least to the extent that my larger belongings could be moved without first excavating for them under the detritus of a working stiff's life.

So I was trying to put things in boxes. The problem was, much of what I owned seemed to belong in a dumpster instead. Where, for instance, had I acquired five sets of water-warped Las Vegas themed playing cards? Why did I own a pair of red rubber boots that were clearly much too large for my feet? Where had this cane with a duck's head and a cheap sword inside come from?

The objects made me think wistfully of college. For a few years, I'd been out on my own, free both of my mother's tyranny and Gregory's steadying influence. I'd found there were other people like me on campus – people who played HotTS and drank copious amounts of DragonFire. People who still played *Dungeons and Dragons* old-school style, with a Dungeon Master and dice and paper character sheets. Such escapades we'd had, roving as a group late at night, binge gaming for hours, or crashing the Halloween parties of by much cooler people in our nerdy costumes. Still reeling from my loss of the ranch camp and Buttercup, I'd thrown myself into that world for a time.

None of those people remained in my life. Oh sure, we were friends on Facebook. But whatever force had united us when we lived in the dorms and went to classes each day had lost its ability to bind us together. Many had moved away. Some were still in town, but my systematic failure to respond to their invitations to hang out had led to a steady draining off of the lifeblood of friendship's vitality.

Still, I had these *things*. As incomprehensible as each random item seemed, each was a glimpse into the past, an uncomfortable reminder that my life, for a short time, had once been full.

Sighing, I set a red rubber ducky with devil's horns on top of a leather belt pouch with dice inside. My computer sang to me. Its song was especially seductive due to my changed status on HotTS. Thanks to that quest invite, I'd beaten the spider forest at last, which meant I had access to three new portals and the lands beyond.

It had been easy, it turned out. That afternoon after claiming my apartment, I'd sent Hawkeyez777 my message. He'd responded within minutes. By the evening he had assembled a squad of six players, all ready to help me take down the nasty arachnoid queen. Between the fact that I myself was far stronger than most who took on the spider forest and every member of Hawkeyez777's squad had cleared it long before, we had the forest defeated in what seemed no time at all. The squad guarded my flanks and prevented the spider minions from using their surprise strike. We cut through the forest with ease. When we reached the queen, Hawkeyez777 and his warrior buddies fanned out to guard my flanks while a player named Solo8Sol—who had several good ranged attack abilities and a kickass stoat for a totem partner—stood by to prop me up if I took some hits.

I didn't need the help by then, however. The queen fell before my Double Slash Charge attack and Buttercup reared over her body in triumph.

The spider forest was no big deal, it turned out, when you had friends.

Since then, it seemed every time I entered HotTS there was at least one quest invite waiting for me. I participated whenever I could, feeling obliged to help those who had helped me. In this way, I'd already cleared a formidable quest region in one of the three new worlds that I could never have managed alone at my current level.

The problem was work and the move and now even my agreement to lease Sally. For the first time in ages, I had little time for the game. And for the first time in ages, I was actually excited to play.

I stood, stretched, and checked my BodPod. I had 7,545 steps. After my lesson, Erin had shown me around the tack room to familiarize me with Sally's gear and where to find everything I would need to ride alone. Then she'd had me lead Sally back to the pasture where she lived with Esperanza and a handful of other horses. I could easily hit 10k if I went for a walk.

I would do that, I decided. I'd do that after packing up a couple of boxes. But first I'd energize myself with a DragonFire and a quick quest or two.

I stood, grabbed a can from the fridge, and sat down at my computer.

With a weary spin of the steering wheel, I navigated Bessie into the Humanilism parking lot. I parked, killed the engine, and sat for half a moment in the front seat. My eyes felt sandy, my body leaden. And it was only Monday.

Sighing, I grabbed my case of DragonFire and my bag, and exited the vehicle. As I did so, I noted where the bike path at the back of the building connected to a sidewalk that led straight to the front door. This would be how I would be arriving at work every day, very soon, I promised myself. Just as soon as I settled in at my new place.

Gregory had been more than a little annoyed with me when he'd arrived with his SUV on Sunday to find the only way I had prepared for moving was by creating mounds of belongings and shoving them into corners to get them out of the way. I'd seen him clench his jaw, and say nothing. Together we'd carried out my dilapidated armchair and kitchen stools. These had been the first items to arrive at my new apartment.

The next trip was the bed. "If you had boxed anything," Gregory had informed me testily as we wedged the frame into the back of his SUV, "we could have filled the extra space with smaller items."

I'd nodded sadly, as if unable to comprehend why the Jordan of last night had so failed in her resolve to prepare for this day's work. But I was secretly not at all remorseful. I'd stayed up until 3:00 am, running with Hawkeyez777's squad in a frenzy of questing. My XP gains had me well positioned to be back on the Elite Squad by the end of the week.

After the bed came the coffee and bedside tables. Next, the dresser. When we returned to my old apartment having moved those things, the place had already begun to acquire an empty and alien feel. I turned to Gregory, giving him a grateful nod, and said, "Thanks. I guess that's everything I need help with."

He speared me with his level gaze, his tone unamused. He was looking unusually rumpled in cargo shorts and a ragged t-shirt. "What about the desk and chair?"

I glanced at my gaming rig, which sat in solitary splendor atop the cheap IKEA surface. Before it stood my desk chair, which happened to be the sole piece of quality furniture I owned. I felt a flutter of sudden nerves. "Oh, we don't need to take those yet."

I wasn't looking at Gregory, but I could feel his stare. His tone was low and steady—as if he was explaining something simple yet elusive to a particularly dense child. "You're moving, Jordan. We've taken your bed, so we're taking the damn computer. If we don't, you'll wind up sleeping on the floor next to your lightsaber."

I considered denying this, but my brother knew me too well for that to fly. He took a step forward and began to roll my desk chair towards the door. "I'm taking this," he informed me. "If that computer isn't all unplugged and ready to go when I get back, I'll take it apart myself."

Appalled by the very thought, I'd powered down my machine on the spot. And so my desk and computer had gone to the new place, where I'd arranged them in the delightful, windowless office nook. Gregory had driven me back to my old place and left me standing in the wreckage that was my life without furniture.

I'd shoved a few piles of clothes into garbage bags, heaved them into Bessie, and made the drive from old place to new place one more time that day. I hadn't unpacked anything there. But I had set up my gaming rig, set up my wi-fi, and then fired up *Heroes of the Totem Spirit* to make sure everything was in working order.

I'd discovered upon materializing at the entry portal that the Hawkeyez777 squad was about to depart for a run at an endless foe tunnel. Hurriedly, I accepted my invitation to join them and ran off to swell their ranks.

At 2:00 am, I'd finally taken my leave of the other questors. Yawning, I stood up to find myself disoriented as I glanced around the office nook. My bedroom door gaped behind me. I wandered in that direction, ready to collapse. Only when I flicked on the light did I realize I hadn't thought to bring either sheets or pillows.

Now, the next morning, I stepped out of Bessie and headed for the front doors of the Humanilism building feeling monstrously and extravagantly tired. I was also fairly hungry. On my late night pilgrimage through the deserted Tucson streets to collect sheets, pillows, and clothes to wear to work, I hadn't thought to bring my omelet fixings, or even a box of cereal. So I was running on little more than a few scant hours of sleep and a good deal of caffeine.

Shuffling to my locker and fetching my laptop, I squinted at the available workstations. When I'd imagined arriving at work after spending my first night at my new place, I'd seen myself stride in with vigor, flushed with the exultation of having hit my step goal before 8:00 am. Instead, I teetered towards the end of one of the long tables and slouched, zombie-like, into a chair.

It was going to be a long, long day.

As I logged into the Humanilism interface, the chirpy morning greeting popped up on my screen. Except instead of giving me my first assignment, it said, "Good morning, Jordan. It's time for your annual review. Please click 'proceed' to continue."

It was all I could do not to groan audibly and sag out of my chair. I clicked 'Proceed' and took a sip of DragonFire to fortify myself. I expected the usual litany of performance questions. Instead, the screen resolved into a message I'd never seen before. "You're participating in our BodPod pilot program. Thank you for being a Humanilism Pioneer! On a scale of 1-5, how much would you say your BodPod has changed your daily habits?"

I stared at the words on the screen, feeling helpless and exhausted. Then, abruptly, I closed the lid on my laptop, stood, and returned it to the locker on the wall.

I would take a personal day, I decided. I had more than enough Merit to cover one. I would take a personal day, and I'd use the time to rest, bring enough over from my old place to make my life functional, and get my new place feeling like home. Maybe, if I was a total rock star and accomplished enough this morning, I'd head out to the Tipped Z and ride Sally in the afternoon.

Gregory straightened, shut the oven door in one crisp stroke, and turned to face me across the island of my new kitchen. "Okay," he said, reaching for his waiting glass of wine, "we've got twenty minutes for those to finish up. Let's choose one final task for the day. Then, we can relax."

From my perch on my stool, I glanced around the apartment without much enthusiasm. There was so much that needed doing. Completing any one task struck me as utterly futile. Still, I knew better than to argue with him.

It was Tuesday evening. The previous afternoon, Gregory had called to suggest we have our weekly dinner at my place to, "Season the kitchen." I'd rallied myself to a vague and ultimately useless resistance, trying a number of arguments that moved my brother not at all. When, in desperation, I'd confessed I hadn't brought over any of my kitchen items, Gregory had been merciless in his reply. "You'd better get going then. It's almost 5:00."

I'd been sitting in my desk chair in my office nook when he said this and had experienced a moment of pure shock at his comment. I'd been between quests when he called, and so hastily logged out of HotTS. "I'll bring the groceries," he said. "You have the place ready. Got it?"

I'd agreed mostly out of stupefaction. I'd gotten off the phone, stood, unkinked my leg muscles, and blinked around like an owl rooted out of its tree in broad daylight. That morning, I'd justified fleeing from work by promising myself I'd spend many productive hours putting my life back together, and then going out to ride Sally.

Instead, I'd spent the whole day gaming.

Now, watching Gregory pad into my mostly empty living room and grimace at my battered old chair, I wondered what would become of me if my brother ever tired of forcing me to maintain some semblance of a functional adult lifestyle. After his call, I had rallied at least to the extent of returning to my old apartment and packing up two boxes of kitchen implements, then unpacking them in my new place. It had taken forever since everything breakable needed to be swaddled in protective paper.

I'd kept at it, however, until 9:00 pm. At which point I thought my new kitchen had enough in it to render cooking and eating a simple meal possible. I'd gone to bed early, slept well, and driven to work in the morning so I'd have plenty of time to get home and prepare as much as possible for his arrival that afternoon.

While he'd cooked, Gregory had gamely made do when he found himself missing implements or spices while relentlessly prodding me to unpack and tidy away the random assortment of belongings I'd so far brought over from my old apartment.

As I considered my internal question, I decided there were two possible ways I might react if Gregory ever gave up on me. One was to descend into total dysfunction and lose even the semblance of maturity and independence I now maintained. The other would be to pull my act together, since my poor choices would never have the satisfying result of causing my brother to swoop in and fix things.

One nice thing about the new apartment was it was much larger than the old one. This meant there were plenty of closets and nooks in which to stow my stray belongings. It also left an empty feel once everything was stashed out of sight. "You should keep an eye on Craigslist for furniture," Gregory said, turning away from my chair to take in the view of the mountains. "This would be a nice room if there was somewhere to sit."

Behind me, the oven clicked. I sipped my DragonFire and followed Gregory's gaze. The mountains were there, shouldering up into the sky. Somewhere at the base of them lay the Tipped Z, and Sally, who I had not yet gone out to ride alone in spite of the signature I'd scrawled onto the lease agreement. I hadn't told Gregory about that decision. I decided I would not. For a while, at least.

Gregory lifted his eyes to the large, blank wall to the left of the windows. "And you need something big and eye-catching for this spot."

I had a few of Gregory's smaller paintings. They were still in my old apartment. But he was right. The wall he was staring at was very big and very blank. Anything I had would be dwarfed in that space. I leaned back against the bare wall. "If only I knew an artist or something."

Gregory gave me a dark look and settled himself to perch on my armchair with a look of distaste. "How about a bargain? I'll give you something for that wall when you get some halfway decent furniture."

I turned away from him to look out the window. "Or we could go back to having dinners at your place," I responded with poor grace. "Then my blank walls and cheap accouterments wouldn't have to offend you so." I stared out the window at the maze of manicured gravel and low shrubs that populated the empty space between my building and the next. I was watching a roadrunner skulking in the shade of a mesquite when a movement near the parking area caught my eye.

A man was walking along one of the paths that led through the complex. Something about the sight of him arrested me. He had a way of walking that struck me as unusual—as if he was placing his feet with particular care.

He was wearing a leather jacket and had a motorcycle helmet tucked under one arm. As I watched, some sound made him glance back over his shoulder towards the mountains.

When I got a clear look at his face, I let out an involuntary gasp.

It was Grant.

Gregory was saying something, but his words were mere noise in my ears. I felt suspended in perfect disbelief.

The path Grant was following curved and began to approach my door. My heart, which had been sluggish all day, suddenly began to imitate a frantic teenager with a brand new drum set. Grant must have seen my new address on the lease, and now he was coming here because....

Because why? Why would Grant be here? The question towered in my mind, unanswerable.

But he was coming. His deliberate steps were bringing him steadily, steadily, towards my door.

"Hello? Earth to Jordan? Who is that guy?"

Gregory sounded annoyed, and I suppose I couldn't blame him. He'd come up to stand next to me by the window and was staring at Grant with asperity. My brother did not approve of motorcycles.

I couldn't answer. I felt frozen in place, stunned to silence.

Grant came closer. As I watched, he reached a fork in the path. One branch turned slightly right and led to my front door. The other continued left and led past my apartment.

Grant reached the fork and glanced up, for all the world as if he could see me watching him through my window. I darted to the side like a minnow evading the groping paw of a cat. Grant, however, walked without hesitation onto the left branch. There was no hint in his face or his body that he was aware I, or anything else for that matter, could see him.

Peeping around the window frame, I watched as he made his way to a different building and pulled a ring of keys out of his pocket. He unlocked the door, stepped inside, and disappeared.

I felt as if oxygen had been returned to the atmosphere after a brief, inexplicable absence. I became aware of my brother staring at me. I stepped away from the window as if nothing interesting had ever been seen through a glass pane in the entire history of humanity. I said, "I was thinking my last task before dinner would be to hang the shower curtain." I began to move in as nonchalant a manner as I could manage towards the bathroom.

"Jor..." Gregory's voice was dangerous as he drifted after me. "Who was that?"

There was an unspoken pact between me and my brother. We did not lie to each other. I might withhold some things, hedge my way around divulging certain facts, but I could not fail to answer such a direct question, and he knew it.

Still, I made him wait. I went into the bathroom and stood on the bare tile floor. He trailed after me and stopped in the doorway. "His name is Grant," I said. "I've seen him around at the Tipped Z. I think he's like a ranch hand. Or something. I'm not exactly sure."

I thought of the strange vibe I picked up between him and Erin, his status as both a very distant relative and a 5th generation rancher. In truth, I understood very little about his role at the Tipped Z. I had thought he lived there. Now, I realized with a dipping sensation of incredulity, it appeared he was my neighbor.

"This is the BodPod guy? You didn't mention he was a total hottie." Gregory was watching me closely, trying to goad me into revealing more than I wanted to.

I glanced around the bathroom. It was larger than my old one, and a lot less dingy. The fixtures were clean and gleaming, the tile large and modern. Nothing was dripping, sagging, or corroded. "Really," I said, beginning to feel desperate, "it's not a big deal. I was surprised to see him. That's all. I thought he lived out at the ranch."

I picked up the plastic bag I'd shoved my shower curtain into. It came out in a creaking wad, its rubbery texture having been forced into a space too tight for it. As I made an effort to straighten it out, one of the plastic connectors meant to affix it to the rod fell, broken, onto the floor.

Gregory and I both stared silently at the piece of cracked plastic for a moment. Off in the kitchen, the oven beeped. Gregory said, "The Tipped Z is near here, then?"

I felt as if I'd been caught orchestrating an elaborate and unkind deception. I stooped and picked up the broken ring, tossing it into the unlined trash can. It landed with a sharp rattle. "Yeah," I said casually. "Just a few miles up in the foothills."

Gregory stood for a beat, watching me with a speculative air. I could feel the confession bubbling up in me, the rising desire to tell him not only was the Tipped Z nearby, there was a horse there that was mine to ride, at least until I stopped leasing her.

But the oven beeped again, this time with greater insistence. My brother turned away, leaving me holding onto both my wadded shower curtain and my secret.

I followed the decaying trail through the humpy swampland, steering Buttercup with care. I had nearly gotten lost in this place the first time I'd entered. The trail had a way of petering out into boggy pools or wrapping back on itself. But it lay between the entry portal and several super fun, repeatable quests. I was growing more adept at making my way through.

The sun was setting at my back as I moved, causing the cattails and rushes to throw long shadows in front of me. All around, frogs sang, insects buzzed, and the wind rattled the tall grasses. Not for the first time, I marveled at the detailed, immersive nature of the *Heroes of the Totem Spirit* environment.

At last, the trail before me widened and grew more distinct. Soon I was moving along a broad avenue that led to the bustling town square around the portal that led from here to the world where I'd spent so much time stymied by the spider forest. Merchants waited with various goods: weapons, spells, potions, and food. I wasn't in the market for anything specific, but I dismounted anyway and slowed down to see if anything caught my eye as I drifted past.

As I neared the last of the stalls, a familiar figure at the edge of my vision made me turn. It was the hulking wolf stalking alongside the warrior in black and red armor, the name Hawkeyez777 floating above his head. He seemed to be heading in my direction.

I shifted in my desk chair, glancing down at my BodPod to see the time. It was Friday night, and I'd promised myself I would go to bed at a decent hour. If I was being honest, I was growing a little tired of the constant group quests Hawkeyez777's pals were endlessly inviting me to join. I had declined to participate in the last several. Now, I felt oddly guilty as I turned to face my virtual friend.

The warrior and the wolf walked across the marketplace to park themselves in front of my avatar. As I flipped on my mic, Hawkeyez777 said, "Hey, what's up?" His voice was its typical deep, distorted tone, as much robotic as human.

"Not much," I said, feeling awkward. "I was about to log out for the night."

The problem with interacting with someone's avatar in HotTS is the utter lack of facial expressions and body language. I had no way of knowing, as I said this, whether Hawkeyez777 found my statement interesting, boring, surprising, confusing, or none of the above. His wolf sat down, its unblinking gaze directed at Buttercup.

I expected him to tell me he was off to quest with his buddies, and suggest I come along. Instead, he was silent for long enough I began to wonder if the human operator of Hawkeyez777 had left his computer. I was beginning to consider logging myself out when he finally spoke again. "I was wondering if you'd like to join me for a drink." He paused, then added, "Not now, if you need to go. But some time."

I stared at him in wonder. There was, I knew, an entire layer of HotTS I had never explored. While most of the worlds one could access with an avatar had to do with facing and fighting monsters, there were also places you could enter which gave you access to a completely different set of interactions. These areas were called social zones. Like quest zones, they came with their own special rules and could be entered and exited at will.

When you were in a social zone, players could not engage in duels or violence of any kind. You also had access to a whole myriad of new interactions with regards to other people's avatars. You could, for instance, sit with someone and enjoy a meal or a drink. There were options for playing board games and various other non-violent competitions.

There were also, if you had them enabled, provisions for flirting and romance. Though I had no experience with this myself, I had heard some people had extended relationships in HotTS. Your avatar could marry another avatar, purchase property in one of the residential areas, and even have children. These children were not real people, of course, but you could level them up and train them to do various things for you, much like you could with an animal companion.

I had gone into a social zone once or twice when I'd first begun playing, but found the experience awkward. Now, I stared at my screen in stupefaction. I was fairly certain Hawkeyez777 had just asked me out on a date.

Quickly, I clicked the name floating above his head. This led to his in-game profile, which was sparse. It indicated his gender (male) and age range (25-35), as well as region (Southwestern United States). I'd seen all this before, and none of it was necessarily true. *Heroes of the Totem Spirit* did not even pretend to try to encourage players to be honest with the facts they fed into the system. Hawkeyez777 could be a guy around my age who lived in Phoenix or Prescott. He could also be a 12-year-old girl who lived in South Africa. I had no way of knowing.

Realizing I had been too long in answering, I closed his profile. The bulky warrior stood waiting, his wolf by his side. Behind him, other avatars ran about, their companion animals always nearby.

I couldn't say no, I realized. After his help bringing me through the spider forest, I owed him at least this much.

So I forced myself to say, "Yeah. That sounds great. Maybe tomorrow?"

The wolf stood up as Hawkeyez777 turned to go. "I'll send you a social invite," he said. Then, before I could say anything more, he'd run off past the vendor stalls, towards the swamplands.

Chapter 8

"So," Erin said brightly, looking up from tightening Esperanza's girth, "did you ride during the week? How did it go?"

I felt a twist of something midway between guilt and embarrassment. I drifted up to stand next to Sally, setting a hand on the mare's warm neck. "I didn't, actually."

There was a beat of silence. I could sense Erin's surprise in the way she went still. Feeling I'd disappointed her, I hurried on. "I ended up moving into a new apartment. It was unexpected. So between that and work I just…"

I trailed off. Erin unpaused in her tacking, moving towards Esperanza's head. "Moving is such a hassle," she said with genuine sympathy. "Particularly when it's unplanned."

I realized with a sense of mild surprise Erin could not possibly have lived at the Tipped Z her entire life. She was Clint's wife, which meant she must have grown up somewhere else, met him somehow, fallen in love with him, and married him. From what I'd seen of Clint, he was the reserved type. I wondered how that story had unfolded.

Lamely, I said, "Yeah. It's the worst."

Erin slipped Esperanza's bosalita into place, then picked up her heavy bit. She nodded towards Sally's hackamore. "You can put that on her if you'd like."

I did as she suggested, but my mind was adrift. I now found myself wondering about Nora and Wyatt as well. Nora was Clint's sister, but Wyatt had been the one having that awkward conversation I'd overheard before my lesson a couple weeks before. I found myself suddenly curious about his connection to the Tipped Z. Was it just that he was Nora's husband? Or was it something deeper than that?

I looped the reins around Sally's horn and looked off over the rolling landscape that fell away behind the barn. I felt a little spark of surprise when I noticed three riders on horseback approaching at a fast trot. Erin saw them too. She paused in the act of beginning to lead Esperanza away from the hitching post. "That's odd," she said. "I didn't expect to see them back for hours."

The riders were little more than specks moving before a plume of dust, but I squinted anyway, trying to figure out which one was Grant. We waited. Erin's stiff, attentive posture made my stomach begin to coil with nerves. Time seemed to suspend itself in the odd glare between the flat blue sky and the sandy ground.

At last, the three riders paused. One of them opened a gate, let the others through, and closed it again. Then they grew rapidly, changing from distant, silent apparitions into full-sized men approaching on sweat-slicked horses whose hooves thumped the ground in a rolling thunder.

There was a movement to my left. I turned to see an older woman emerge from the barn, wearing pale leather chinks and carrying a saddle and a pad. There was another movement to my right. I saw Grant approaching at a jog, leading three horses on ropes. The horses were trotting to keep up with him.

I began to feel a little overwhelmed as the three riders, the small woman, and Grant and his horses all converged on the hitching post. Erin's face showed her confusion was just as total as mine.

The woman reached us first. She tossed the saddle over the hitching post railing with a practiced fluidity that belied her frail appearance. She was a short, fine-boned woman with wispy gray hair and flinty eyes. "Is something wrong?" Erin said.

"Clint sent me a text," she said. "Someone cut the fence at the bottom of Bobcat Canyon. We've got cattle straying all the way up into the pools. They left the dogs on the gap so no more cross over, but it's going to be a long day collecting strays."

Erin let out a low curse as the three riders reached us at last. The instant their horses stopped, two of them dismounted. I recognized Clint and Wyatt as they strode for the barn, leaving their horses standing. The third man remained on his horse. He was, I noted with surprise, wearing a sling across his torso so his left arm was strapped to his chest. But he was tall and lean and sat his horse with every bit of the confidence you might expect from someone who has ridden every day of his life. This must be Clint and Nora's father.

As I tried to take all this in, Grant was suddenly behind me, running a quick curry over the horses he'd led up and tied. The short woman moved to join him. The two of them worked like well-oiled machines. Self-consciously, I led Sally to the edge of things, trying to get out of the way.

Over the course of the next few minutes, Clint and Wyatt's sweaty horses were stripped of their tack, and their saddles were moved to two of the animals Grant had brought up. The woman tossed her own saddle onto the third horse's back.

Erin had moved to help with the tack transfer. By the time Clint and Wyatt had returned carrying a few bulky saddlebags, their fresh horses were ready. They tied their bags in place and moved to mount again.

No one had spoken during this activity, but now the man with the sling looked at my riding instructor. "Erin, we need you. And tie a rope to your saddle, for heaven's sake." Then he turned his sharp gaze on me.

I don't have a great deal of experience with older men, but this one struck me as particularly formidable as he took me in. I felt peeled raw—as if his eyes could see past my exterior and guess all my darkest secrets.

It was a nonsensical notion, but nevertheless I felt my arms prickle with gooseflesh. Erin, her cheeks flushed, hurried off to the barn and returned a moment later with a coiled rope. The man looked away from me, and back at his daughter-in-law. "Is that one worth taking?"

Erin answered quietly in the form of a question directed at me. "Jordan, would you like to ride with us and see if you can help? With a situation like this, cattle scattered over an irregular landscape, every rider makes a difference."

I blinked, suddenly short of breath. Wyatt and Clint were mounted again. As I hesitated, the older lady swung into her saddle. Erin was tying up her rope, putting her foot into her stirrup.

I turned towards Sally as if the mare could make this decision in my stead.

That's when I saw Grant. He was standing with the two sweat-slicked horses Wyatt and Clint had unsaddled. His expression was so intense, so conflicted, it made me startle. As my silence extended, he spoke up. "I can bring the dirt bike and follow after. If I..."

But the man with the sling cut him off. His tone was not harsh, but I saw Grant flinch. "Those machines are no good up in that country. Unless you want to get on a horse, you can stay here."

I saw blood rise into Grant's face. A heavy silence fell. A horse stamped. Erin arranged her reins. "Jordan," she said. "No pressure. If you don't want to come, you can ride Sally here in the arena. Just turn her out when you're done."

I found my voice at last. It came choking out of me, dry and dusty as the warm breeze. "No," I blurted in a rush of sudden decisiveness. "I want to help."

I hung up Sally's hackamore and double-checked I'd arranged the saddle properly in its place. Then I stood a moment in the stillness of the Tipped Z tack room. I could hear the quiet sounds of the evening coming on. Cicadas sang in the distance and doves let out their low cries.

I drew in a long, slow breath and let it out again. Certain everything was in order, I turned to head back towards the door. I could feel that rubbery sensation in my legs that foretold massively sore muscles tomorrow. The sensation made me smile. It had been quite a day—exhausting but wonderful.

I exited the tack room, stepping out into a dim hall lined with stalls. The sun was setting and the light was low, but I could make out a single horse watching me over an open half door, its large eyes dark in its pale face.

I turned, took a few more steps, and hesitated in the hay room. To my left stood the small door to the parking area where Bessie had waited all day in the baking sun. To my right stood the large bay doors which opened onto the hitching post with the pastures beyond.

When I'd left to hang up my tack, Erin, Wyatt, and Clint had just been departing to lead the six horses to their respective pastures. Clint's mother and father, Nell and Hank, had already left the barn, heading back towards the ranch house with its long, low porch, all but one of the dogs trailing after. The last dog had followed Clint, keeping to his heels like a shadow.

After all day surrounded by horses, dogs, cattle, and people, I was abruptly and starkly alone in this place.

The question was, what to do now? There was no reason to linger. And yet, it felt incomplete. I didn't feel ready to get in Bessie, to drive off without saying goodbye to anybody. Yet waiting around to tell Erin I was going to leave seemed even stranger.

I wandered back out to the hitching post, glancing around for some chore to occupy myself with. But these people were thorough, meticulous, and practiced in their ways. By the time I'd been off Sally's back and picking up her halter, everyone else seemingly had their horses untacked, rubbed down, and ready to turn out.

In the distance, the sun was a riot of lurid orange and reds on the horizon. The clouds were flat shelves of liquid gold in the sky. I gazed off towards the pastures and could make out three figures walking back in my direction.

I heard a step behind me and turned. I had thought myself spent for the day. I was so tired I felt ready to collapse. And yet I also felt energized and content.

At least, I felt that way until I turned and saw Grant stepping out of the hay room. Surprise, consternation, and hot adrenaline swept through me at the mere sight of him. All the questions I hadn't had time to think about for most of the day swarmed back into mind.

Why hadn't he ridden out with the rest of us? If I—someone with no experience with cattle whatsoever—had been able to make myself useful in this situation a 5th generation rancher would have been able to do much more. I'd seen feats of riding and roping today that had taken my breath away. Clint's horse facing down a calf that wanted to flee up the canyon instead of down while keeping its footing on the flaky, rock-strewn terrain. Wyatt's loop landing deftly over the shoulders of a struggling cow that had gotten tangled in the cut wire, his horse backing up to pull the rope taut so the creature couldn't struggle while they cut it loose and doctored its wounds. Even white-haired Nell, riding flat out to turn a small group of cattle that had pushed through a clump of trees and begun to thunder off down the fence on the wrong side. She'd had to go around the brush, but had opened her horse up to make up the lost time. For a moment, she and her mount had been nothing but a gleaming streak as they raced across the desert sand at just the right angle, stopping the strays and herding them back in the proper direction.

I myself had not done anything so remarkable. But I had flushed calves out of bushes, sat Sally in gaps the cattle would otherwise have tried to go through, and once pushed a small group that was thinking of trying to move through the cut fence back onto the Tipped Z's land.

It had been a long day. And tiring. But also very satisfying. There had been a problem to solve. We'd worked until it was done.

Now, looking at Grant as he stood in the fading sunlight, I tried to read his face. He was a good-looking man, but there was something sharp about his eyes that pricked me as he swept the hitching post and surrounding area. I did not think he'd come in search of me, so I supplied the information I suspected he wanted. "They've gone to turn the horses back out."

He was silent for a moment. In the brush beside the barn, a cricket chirped twice. Grant said, "Nora sent me out to find you all. We've got the grill going at Clint's place. Everyone can come down when things are wrapped up here. You, specifically, are instructed to stay and eat with us."

The way he phrased it made it clear the invitation did not come from him, but still his words made my body tingle all over.

The three approaching figures were closer now. I could hear the thump of their boots, a man's quiet laugh joined a second later by Erin's. Grant turned away from them and looked at me, "Unless you have somewhere else you have to be, that is."

I blinked. For the first time all day, thoughts of my normal life pushed into my mind. It was Sunday evening, I realized. I looked at my BodPod and saw the time. A swell of consternation washed over me. I was supposed to meet Hawkeyez777 in a small, out of the way social zone tavern in eighteen minutes.

"Shit," I said, turning to stare back in the direction of the greater Tucson area as if I could somehow peel away the miles between here and my apartment and observe the computer I was not sitting at right now.

Grant's look had grown more interested. He said nothing, but I could feel the curiosity in his gaze. I began to explain. "I have a ... I had a ... I ...." I stopped.

"Date?" Grant suggested. There was humor in his tone. Had my body not already been singing with adrenaline, I'm sure I would have felt a wave of consternation. As it was, I was glad the fading light would conceal the heat in my cheeks.

"No," I said in quick retort. Then felt compelled to add, "Not really. At least, not like a date date." I stopped, exhausted by my inability to communicate with others of my own kind.

Grant watched me for another heartbeat. I thought he would say more, but Erin, Wyatt, and Clint stepped up to us. I felt I knew all of them so much better now. Wyatt walked with a mild but persistent limp. Clint and his father shared the same aloof, distant body-language, but whenever either man looked at or spoke to his wife, he grew softer in some indefinable way. Now, Wyatt and Erin were both smiling, and even Clint's mouth was turned up in a slight grin. They drew up next to us and stopped. Seeing me, Erin spoke. "Oh good, Jordan. I was afraid you'd have left. After all that riding today, you must be starving. You'll stay for dinner, I hope?"

Grant said to me, "There's plenty for everyone," then added to the group at large, "And Nora's going to skin me alive if I don't hurry and round you guys up."

The statement held all the trappings of familiar ease, but there was something in Grant's tone that kept it from sounding entirely natural. Still, if anyone else noticed, no one reacted.

I looked at my BodPod again. Fifteen minutes until I was supposed to meet Hawkeyez777. I felt terrible at the thought of standing him up, but also I desperately did not want to leave the ranch right now. Today, for the first time since my years at the camp, I had caught a glimpse of what it might be like to belong somewhere.

Clint turned and began to walk into the dimming evening. The group moved with him. The dog left his heels and began to trot purposefully ahead. I drifted along like a small fish caught in the undertow of a much larger vessel.

Clint did not re-enter the barn. Rather he set his feet onto a dusty path that led along the fence-line. I had been expecting to approach the long, low ranch house that sat across from the barn. We did not. The path continued past that, dipping and wrapping around a sudden, lumpy drop in the landscape.

As we descended, another house came into view. This one was smaller than the ranch house and of a more modern style. It had large windows at the front, and light blazed within. There was a front patio surrounded by a low wall. Inside the wall, I could see Nora standing next to a gleaming grill wielding a spatula while the two children I'd seen that first day played on a brightly colored rubberized mat that had been laid across the flagstones of the patio.

This was where Clint and Erin lived.

We walked single file down the path, and my conscience pricked me with every step. Canceling a meeting was one thing, but simply not showing up was terrible. Vainly, I scrambled through options. Clint and Erin might have a computer. I could access my HotTS account easily enough, but I didn't think there was any way to send another player a message without actually logging into the game.

Or was there? I honestly had no idea. In spite of all my time playing, I had never really interacted with someone within the game before beyond randomly running into them. Now that I thought about it, I remembered seeing ads for an app that allowed avatars to communicate while not actively manifest in the gaming environment.

I paused. My phone was back in Bessie, where I'd left it all day. I didn't have a secure pocket for carrying the thing on horseback. Erin noticed my hesitation. She turned to look at me with an inquisitive air. I was about to tell her I needed to go back and grab my phone when Nora turned and shouted, "Jordan! How do you like your burgers? Bloody? Burnt to a crisp? Cheese? No cheese?"

Clint opened a metal gate in the wall. One by one, the others filed into the yard. Again, I felt towed along. I drifted in and managed my most lucid statement of the day. "Just medium. No cheese. Thank you."

Satisfied, Nora began flipping the burgers that were already arranged on the grill. The scent of the cooking meat and the char of the smoke swept into my nostrils. I felt suddenly weak with hunger.

Erin had gone to the mat to stoop down next to the little girl, who had begun to attempt to crawl in her direction. Clint had lifted his son into his arms and Wyatt had wrapped Nora in a hug from behind. I felt awkward and alone.

But I wasn't alone. Grant, too, was on the edge of things, standing beyond the light the large windows threw across the scene. As Nora said something that made Wyatt laugh, he turned to me. "You'll want to wash up, I guess."

He turned as if to move off, but I managed to blurt out after him, "Actually..."

He turned around. I trailed off, feeling awkward. Although I'd seen Grant several times before now, it felt strange to be in such close proximity to him in the near dark. He gave me a look, waiting for me to go on.

"I need to get my phone," I said. "It's in my car."

He seemed to take this as a request for an escort. He turned away from the door and moved smoothly back towards the gate, tossing a quick response back at Nora when she asked to know where we were going. Soon we had proceeded around the ridge, leaving the light and sound of the small gathering on the patio behind. Next to me, Grant said, "Bet your step count's pretty great right now."

I'd hardly thought of my BodPod all day. As he spoke, I felt suddenly curious. I pushed the button on the side to reveal the number 25,194.

He tipped his screen towards mine so I could see his. 15,244.

I gaped at the little screens in astonishment. Grant grinned at my evident shock. His teeth were even and straight, but I noticed a scar below one side of his nose that made his smile kink slightly. My awareness of his lean, solid body was making me giddy. I found myself asking the question that had flitted in and out of my mind all day. "Why didn't you come?"

I knew as soon as the words were out that they were a mistake. The desert was busy around us, with crickets chirping and a few birds calling to the fading sun. Grant's smile faded. Something seemed to go out of him. Instantly, I wanted to take it back, to hit the 'undo' button and un-ask the question.

The gathering dark seemed to press in on us. It had seemed such a short walk down. Now I strained ahead for a glance at the barn. I began to think Grant might not answer the question, might not even acknowledge I'd spoken. But at last, he replied. "I was in a wreck."

As he spoke, Grant ran his right hand over his left forearm. In the low light, I saw the long, thin scars. There were two of them, one on each arm. They weren't identical, but they each ran up from the inside of his wrist nearly to his elbow. "Since then," he went on, "I don't ride."

He said this casually, but I could sense the well of dammed emotion beneath the words. I struggled for an answer, but none came.

He picked up the pace a little, his boots crunching in the sandy soil. When he spoke again, his tone had changed. "Anyway, I'm glad you went. I'm sure Sally enjoyed the work." His voice regained energy as he spoke. Abruptly, we came out behind the barn as the little path cleared the ridge. "Parking lot's just there," he said and led me towards where Bessie sat in the warm glow of the solar lamps set up around the parking area.

"Wait a minute. Now you're roping cattle?"

The incredulous question came from Tony. He stood by the counter in the beverage station, holding not a Coke Zero, but a glass of water.

It was Monday morning, and I was back at work. As I stood, waiting for Tony to move so I could get into the fridge and my stash of DragonFire within, I could feel the muscles that ran up and down the insides of my legs. They were very, very sore. And it wasn't just my legs. My shoulders were sore. My abs were sore. Even the arches of my feet were sore. I had never realized horseback riding could be such a full-body workout.

The sore muscles were distracting. They'd been cramping my style all morning. I'd taken a break from my Interactions after a particularly annoying exchange with a person who claimed the BlockWeaver interface was deleting photos from his computer when he deleted them from his website. He wanted to know how to change his settings so this would stop happening. When I patiently explained there was no such setting because what he was describing was impossible, the guy flew into a seething rage and started slinging profanities at me in all caps. I had tried to calm him down to no avail and finally sent him on to a supervisor. This was not an ideal solution. We could only send so many Interactions to supervisors a month for free. After that, doing so cost Merit points.

It wasn't until after I finished the Interaction and hit pause for a break that it occurred to me the guy had probably been trolling me. That thought had soured my mood even before I stood up and felt the elaborate tracery of screaming muscles throughout my body.

So I wasn't exactly thrilled about this interrogation from Tony about how I'd netted so many steps on Sunday. He'd couched his question in congratulatory terms, but I'd caught the undercurrent of accusation. Tony thought I was cheating.

"Not roping," I said, trying to keep the irritation out of my voice as I wondered how rude it would be to simply shove Tony out of the way to get to the fridge. I needed DragonFire like a vampire needs lifeblood.

As I considered my predicament, I noted Tony's body between me and the fridge was not the obstacle it had once been. Oddly, his pleated khakis hung a little limp on his soft frame. There was even an extra dimple on the left side where the belt cinched them in for a tighter fit. "Excuse me," I said. "I need to get into the fridge.

Tony, perhaps seeing the insane glint in my eye, stepped out of my way. I stooped, opened the door, and felt a mild sense of relief as my palm touched the cool side of a DragonFire can. I straightened, popped the top, and took a sip. My mood equalized at the familiar flavor. I decided I could be magnanimous with Tony. "We were gathering. Like, herding the cattle together with horses and making them go somewhere."

Tony adjusted his glasses. I waited for some sign of interest, perhaps an inkling of awe that I could get on a horse and use it to move cattle. But his attention appeared to have shifted. He was staring at my can of DragonFire. "That stuff's bad for you, you know." His tone was conversational with a hint of self-righteousness mixed in. "I came across an article this weekend. It was all about artificial sweeteners, and how the body doesn't know what to do with them, so they build up in your system. They can have adverse effects on your satiation levels, and also your gut biome. I've given up all soft drinks." He held up his glass of water with an air of mild superiority. "This looks like water, but it's actually an advanced formula of vital minerals and electrolytes, plus it's got a little caffeine. It gives you the boost without the crash or the toxins."

I wasn't really listening. All plausible arguments against DragonFire and the things that were in it had already been exhaustively laid at my feet by Gregory. If my brother couldn't get me to stop drinking the stuff, why would I listen to a mere colleague? "Yeah well," I said mildly, "we humans have a 100% mortality rate, so what can you do?"

Tony blinked, apparently too stunned by the blatant lack of logic in my response to muster any kind of answer. He adjusted his BodPod on his wrist. I noticed a faint tan line forming around its band. Was Tony perhaps going outside to get some of his steps, then?

I would have asked, but then he would have answered and the conversation would thus continue. That didn't strike me as an ideal outcome. So instead I gave him a small, ridiculous wave, and returned to my workstation, clutching my can of delicious toxins.

As I settled gingerly back into my chair, I thought again of that day out at the Tipped Z. It had been on my mind almost constantly since I finally drove home that night, having spent the evening with a family that was not mine but didn't seem in the least thrown off by my presence. Nursing a tall glass of water, I'd listened to Wyatt tell Nora about the day, smiled at the antics of the children, and surreptitiously kept an eye on Grant at all times. Now that he'd told me about his wreck, I found myself attaching meaning to certain details I'd noticed long ago. His careful way of walking, I perceived, was an effort not to limp.

Since then, I had spent a good deal of time trying to imagine an accident that would have left him not only physically battered but unwilling to get on a horse, ever again. And if he was so dead set against riding horses, why was he working at a ranch?

Still feeling too fried to take on more Interactions, I pulled my phone out of my pocket and checked my BodPod stats. In spite of my steps haul on Sunday, Grant was leading in the 7-day average chart. Tony was in second. But I wasn't as far behind him as I normally was.

Not wanting to dwell on my last place status, I tapped Grant's photo. His BodPod profile appeared, which was sparse. His photo showed him leaning against a truck. He wore a t-shirt and jeans, work boots, and a half smile. I tried to pick out the scars on his arms, but either this photo had been taken before his accident or the resolution wasn't high enough.

In the lower left-hand corner of my laptop screen, my break timer shifted from green to yellow, signifying my time away was getting long and would soon begin to cost me Merit points. Sighing, I shoved my phone back into my pocket and hit the 'Next Interaction' button.

With a strange shiver of excitement, I turned off the neighborhood street and onto the Tipped Z's long, narrow driveway. The breeze from Bessie's open window stirred my hair. The sun was a muted presence in a hazy sky. The air was so mild as to be almost cool. It was, in short, the perfect fall afternoon. And I was on my way to ride Sally alone for the first time.

As I steered my battered Ford around a curve, passed the entrance sign, and eased my way up to the barn, my entire body felt charged with adrenaline. I told myself this was due to the thrill of having a horse I could show up and ride without anyone's particular permission.

But that was a lie. It was a lie I was allowing myself to believe in order to keep from having to admit the real source of my newfound motivation for making use of my lease.

I had become mildly obsessed with Grant.

It had been building each day since he'd told me why he hadn't ridden out to help with the straying cattle. On Sunday, night, he had crossed my mind on and off. On Monday, I had pulled up his BodPod profile at least a dozen times to stare at his photo as if it could tell me all his secrets. On Tuesday, Gregory had gotten annoyed with my utter failure to hold up my end of the conversation and forced me into a MarioKart match while dinner cooked.

Now it was Wednesday, and I'd woken with the conviction I would go to the Tipped Z after work. I would ride Sally. And who knows? Maybe I'd run into Erin. Or Nora. Or Wyatt or Clint.

Or Grant.

No dogs came to greet me as I parked in front of the barn and stepped out of my battered vehicle. I took this to mean Clint and his father were both out on horseback. The dogs, I had learned by now, mostly belonged to Hank. The three ubiquitous barn dogs, Chet, Fuzzface, and Peach, dwelled in the barn when not accompanying him on ranch business. Then there was Clint's dog, Dots, who was always either at his heels or down at the house attending the next generation of Tipped Z ranchers with a patient but mildly aggrieved expression.

Finally, there was Lop, who appeared to belong to Nora, but sometimes shadowed Wyatt.

Grant did not have a dog. Which meant the quiet barnyard told me precisely nothing about whether or not I might expect to see him.

The hay room felt vast and empty as I entered. I stood a moment inside, listening for signs of life. I heard nothing except the cheep and flutter of sparrow nesting in the rafters. I proceeded into the tack room in search of a halter.

At the ranch camp where I had learned to ride, the tack room had been organized around the horses. Each horse had his own hook, where his halter, bridle, and saddle all hung. Grooming tools for each horse waited in a caddy below. Students and counselors alike had been instructed to never, ever use so much as a hoof pick on a horse other than the one whose name was written on it in permanent marker.

Even at the time, I had suspected this had to do more with keeping things organized than the actual needs of the horses. Still, I wasn't quite used to how differently the Tipped Z tack room was laid out. Here, things belonged to people, not horses. And nothing was labeled.

During the tour of the tack room Erin had given me after I'd signed my lease, I'd asked Erin which was Sally's halter. She'd given me a mild, mystified look and answered in her tactful way. "Well, you'll be using Nora's gear." She'd gestured to a row of hanging rope halters, "but you can pretty much use any of these." She'd handed me a faded blue halter with a long white lead rope tied on.

Now, I fumbled along the wall in the dim hall in search of a light. I found a switch and flipped it. The room became abruptly visible. I stepped to the end of the short hall and stared around. So much tack. There were walls upon walls of bridles, with headgear ranging from simple headstalls with snaffle bits to the elaborate spades decked out in silver. It was strangely intimidating to stand in the presence of so much equipment.

I turned to the halters and searched among them for the faded blue one. I found a darker blue one and one midway between blue and green, but nothing in the shade I was sure I could remember. Although Erin had explicitly told me I could use any halter, this failure to find a familiar one threw me off balance. I felt suddenly like an imposter.

What if most of the halters on this rack were okay, but one or two were not?

As I stood agonizing over the halter situation, another thought crept into my mind. Erin had said any halter and any grooming caddy would do, but she had pointed out a specific hackamore for me to use on Sally, and a specific saddle for me to ride in. The adrenaline in my veins turning a little sour, I spun to stare at the wall of hackamores. They were more varied than the halters, with bosals woven of many different colors and textures, many different widths and sizes. The ropes were varied too, with no two seeming the same combination of color and pattern.

My heart skipped a beat as I scanned frantically for one that looked right. Sally's hackamore had been half rawhide, half reddish leather. I remembered that. And the rope had been a pattern of solid rows interspersed with little dots. Hadn't it? Or had it been more like little dots interspersed with solid rows?

Feeling genuinely panicky, I took a step backward, experiencing an urge to give up before I got too far into this. It wasn't too late to go get in Bessie and leave, pretend I'd never come. During my next lesson, I would pay better attention to Sally's tack.

Just when I was about to turn around, two things happened. First, my eyes snagged on a familiar mecate pattern down at the far end of the row. Staring, I stepped forward. As I tried to decide whether I was certain it was the right one, I noticed a piece of ribbon tied to the reins. Tied to the ribbon was a little scrap of paper on which was written, "Jordan."

Relief flooded me like molten mithril. Bless Erin's kind heart.

Then, the second thing happened. As I turned to look at the saddles and saw another piece of the same ribbon tied around the horn of one I recognized, I heard the thud of boots outside in the stall barn.

I spun towards the door and tried not to look guilty. It was Erin, I told myself. Or Clint. More likely Clint. And that was fine. I wasn't doing anything wrong. I had paid to be allowed to come here. I'd signed a contract.

The footsteps came closer, and then stopped. The cadence of the steps had struck me as manly, but I did not hear the light patter of dog paws on concrete or the panting breath of a canine.

My heart, already putting out a good deal more effort than usual, seemed to flip and twist in my chest. A single man, no dog.

Grant. It must be Grant out there.

I stared at the faded paint on the jutting corner wall that obscured my view of the short hall and doorway. I heard another step and then, sure enough, Grant stepped into view. He saw me, and surprise froze him in place for the space of two heartbeats. Then he smiled and let out a quick breath. "Oh, Jordan. Good. Erin said you might be out this week."

I breathed in the smell of leather and horse, acutely aware of how good Grant looked in his worn jeans and dusty work shirt. He had a pair of gloves tucked into his belt and his sweaty hair was pushed back from his forehead.

I wondered if he remembered my name was really Faith but managed to push the question into the dim corners of my mind before it could hijack my thought process. I said, "Yeah. It's my first time out to ride Sally on my own. I'm just making sure I remember what tack to use. There's so much stuff in here."

I felt a brief surge of pride as I finished speaking, and an uptick in my confidence level. I had managed to deliver a perfectly lucid account of myself.

Grant moved further into the room. I caught the scent of dust and salt and creosote—as if he carried the desert with him. He answered my observation with surprising energy. "That's what I've been saying," he said, making a quick gesture with his hand to encompass the racks and racks of saddles and bridles and various other types of equipment.

"Anyone could walk in here. I've been trying to convince Hank he needs to put a lock on this door, but no one listens to me. It's like they all believe that just because something hasn't happened yet, it never will."

His last sentence carried a slight twist of bitterness. I sensed he was thinking about more than just tack. He must have seen the open door and the light, I realized. He'd come in here thinking he would find a thief—or a bunch of empty hooks.

I looked around the room again. Suddenly I saw the room in a new light. How much was all of this worth? The silver bits? The luminous saddles? The woven ropes and gleaming conchos? I felt a sudden surge of anxiety.

I spoke without thinking. "Maybe you could install a hidden camera or something. Then, at least if things went missing, you could check the footage and see who took it."

Grant blinked and looked at me, his expression shifting away from frustration and into amusement. "That sounds both economical and easy." His tone was sarcastic but playful.

I laughed. "It's probably not as difficult as you think." I turned away from the saddles and sidled up to the halters. I selected a rusty orange one I was certain I had never seen before, picking it up with a bravado I didn't feel. "They sell these home security kits now. There's nothing to them."

Grant's sharp eyes tracked my hands as I forced myself not to exert a nervous death-grip on the rope. "You do some kind of tech support. Right? For work I mean?"

At first, the question threw me off-balance. I was certain I hadn't mentioned my job to anyone at the ranch. Had Grant Googled me? The thought sent a strange thrill shooting from the sternum to the base of my spine. But then I realized the truth. My BodPod account was connected to Humanilism, and my profile included both my job title and description by default.

I felt abruptly embarrassed. There was nothing truly lame about my job, but it didn't take any real skill or expertise. "It's just customer service and quality control," I admitted. "It's not like a real IT job, where you have to know things about computers."

Grant's expression was curious now. He was standing between me and the doorway. As I began to feel self-conscious about how long we'd been in the tack room together, I reasoned I could hardly shove him out of the way in an effort to leave.

"But you do know things about computers." It was less a question than an observation.

I shrugged, feeling the thrill of being in his presence begin to fade. "Some things." I could hear how my own tone had gone suddenly flat. The worst part of being even marginally competent with any sort of tech was that you then became the defacto support team for friends and family. This had been the story of my undergraduate life. There was nothing more annoying than trying to work out why a friend's girlfriend's ancient laptop refused to connect to the internet, or why your roommate's wireless printer suddenly demanded a password when its owner was certain no password had ever been set for it. If Grant took this opportunity to tell me about an issue he was having with his router, I was going to be very, very disappointed.

Instead, he had seemed to withdraw inside himself a little. He was staring at the rows of saddles. The sharpness in his eyes had grown sharper still. "At least you have marketable skills. Relevant skills. Skills that will help you make a living in today's world."

He turned his head. His work shirt was long-sleeved, concealing his forearms. But the scar above his lip was clearly visible.

I remembered what Erin had said. Grant was a 5th generation rancher. And then he himself had told me he'd had a wreck and didn't ride anymore. And now, another piece of the puzzle clicked into place.

Grant was here because he felt he had nowhere else to go.

I had so many questions. What had happened? How long ago? Did Grant not ride because he physically could not? Or was it just that he didn't want to?

Silence stretched in the small room. Grant's eyes flicked from the saddles to me. Something dark stirred there now, beneath the sharpness. I felt a different kind of shiver. "Sorry," he said, and his tone had changed. "I'm keeping you from your ride."

Chapter 9

My apartment, I thought with pleasure as I placed my dust-covered riding clothes neatly in the hamper that resided in my utility area next to my washer and dryer, was looking less and less like the abandoned dorm room of a cluster of freshman frat boys and more and more like a space inhabited by a responsible adult. I still hadn't brought over entirely everything from my old place, but what was left was unimportant. Winter clothing and worn out shoes, stacks of books, spare sheets, several old PCs I'd found wedged and forgotten in the back of my closet, and various miscellany still waited to make the pilgrimage. I had a few more days before the end of the month. A few more trips, and I'd be done.

Meanwhile, Gregory had given me the magnanimous gift of enough matching white plastic hangers for my entire wardrobe. My clothing was hung and organized in my capacious new closet. What art I owned hung tastefully on the smooth white walls. The kitchen was fully functional. The irredeemable wadded up plastic shower curtain had been replaced with a new fabric one, with elegant metal hooks to hold it to the pole that rolled easily on little ball bearings.

This was all thanks to Gregory, of course. Not me. Still, I couldn't deny I was deriving a sense of pleasure from my tidy surroundings I would never have felt a few years ago. Maybe I was finally maturing.

Putting my dirty clothes straight into the hamper instead of leaving them thrown over the back of an armchair was, regardless, a clear act of adulting. As I left the utility area and padded into the kitchen to grab a can of DragonFire from the fridge, I couldn't help but think that if Grant ever figured out I lived here and happened to drop by, he would not be completely repulsed by the state in which I chose to live.

The only problem was the living room. Gregory had loaned me a round dining table and four chairs he'd had stashed away in storage, so my eating area was occupied. However, my battered coffee table alone occupied a spacious expanse of conspicuously empty real estate, my armchair having been stowed in the corner of my bedroom at my brother's insistence. The large wall Gregory refused to provide artwork for until I acquired proper furniture was stark and empty. The bare tile floor seemed huge and cold before the large window that looked out upon the mountains.

I sighed. Furniture. That was what I needed. New living room furniture. And then my manipulative brother would give me a large and gorgeous painting for my bare wall.

I had made a few desultory efforts to turn up hidden gems on Craigslist but had gotten overwhelmed by the stream of terrible floral print sofas and sagging computer desks. I didn't know much about furniture, but I knew my brother. In his world, flowers were not to be used for decoration unless they were literally alive.

I realized I was staring out the window, tracking the few people moving across the apartment complex grounds and the sidewalk lit by solar lights. When I saw a lone male appear near the parking area, I felt a surge of anticipation. But then he came closer and I saw it was not Grant—didn't even really resemble him in any way.

I was doing it again. Resolutely, I turned away from the window. I needed something else to occupy myself, to prevent me from standing here mooning. The logical thing would be gaming, but I'd felt uneasy in HotTS lately. Ever since I'd missed meeting HawkEyez777 in the social zone, I had stopped receiving quest invites from his friends. Now I lived in fear of running into one of them, perhaps being challenged to a duel for his honor.

In the bathroom in Clint and Erin's house that night, I had managed to download the HotTS app and send off a hasty message explaining I was stuck offline and would not be able to make it to a computer in time to meet him. He had never replied. I couldn't decide if I preferred to believe he'd never seen the message and so was mad at me, or he was taking it badly.

The thought of rounding a corner in a virtual town and finding myself face-to-face with the armored warrior and his hulking wolf was enough of a deterrent that my glorious office nook had seen hardly any use in days. Since I hadn't made it back onto the Elite Squad, falling off was not an issue. And it was easy not to miss my virtual Buttercup when I had the very real Sally to think about.

I'd had a wonderful first ride with her. At first, my experience had been marred by my preoccupation with wondering if Grant was still nearby somewhere, close enough to see me. This had persisted through tacking, grooming, and leading my leased mare to the arena. But as soon as I'd climbed aboard, I'd forgotten all about Grant. I'd lost myself in wonder at the horse's smooth gaits, her energetic softness, and at the fact she was mine to ride whenever I wanted.

We'd both arrived at the end of the ride hot and sweaty, but happy. At least, I'd ended the ride happy and I projected that emotion onto the horse. As soon as I'd dismounted, I thought about Grant again. But he'd not appeared as I untacked Sally, returned her to her pasture, and carefully restored her things to their places in the tack room, even going so far as to tie the ribbons back in place.

I'd driven home through the gathering dusk, my mind feeling fresh and still and clear. I'd stopped at Taco Bell for a couple soft shells on my way through town. Now, here I was. It wasn't time for bed, but my day felt strangely complete.

I pulled out my phone, intending to check my steps and saw a BodPod notification on my screen. "Grant has sent you a message: 'Nice riding today.'"

That was all it said, but it was enough to send a surge of adrenaline pounding through my veins.

I checked my BodPod for the time, then my step count. As I brushed my hair back from my sweaty forehead, I felt a small surge of triumph. Ahead of me, the bike path I'd been walking along adjoined the narrower sidewalk that edged the Humanilism parking lot and approached the large front doors.

I had done it. I'd finally walked to work.

Admittedly, it had taken slightly longer and earned me slightly fewer steps than I'd expected, but that didn't keep me from feeling undisputedly pleased with myself as I stepped out of the warm morning into the pristinely cool interior of the building. Shifting my bag on my shoulder, I waved my ID at the desultory watch girl and entered the open floor plan office where I would spend my day.

Although I made a point to arrive earlier than most of my colleagues, I still felt a little dip of disappointment as the door swung closed behind me. The large room looked as it always did in the morning. The long rows of desks were sparsely populated. One bleary-eyed night worker was packing up his things. A different morning employee was fishing her laptop out of her locker.

I didn't see Tony anywhere. No one stood up to applaud my grand achievement. No one seemed to even notice my arrival at all.

I turned from my survey of the room to approach my locker. As I entered my combination and opened the door, I had to reach in at a slightly different angle than usual to accommodate the stash of DragonFire I had been accumulating over the last week or two. Normally, I brought a case in with me a few times a week. But carrying a case of DragonFire on my back while I walked to work seemed both impractical and uncomfortable. I'd been squirreling away stray cans in my locker until I could devise a better system.

I set up my laptop at an open station and returned to my locker to ferry cans to the nearest mini-fridge. It was awkward, holding the individual drinks, and it took me a few trips before I was satisfied I'd have enough to get me through my required Interactions. This was a guess, though, as I refused to keep track of how many caffeine-impregnated energy beverages I consumed on a daily basis.

I had left a few cans in a fridge from the day before bearing oversized, gaudy labels Humanilism provided for this purpose with my name scrawled on. I popped one open and was on my way back to my station when I looked up to see Luke Rastenhaus waiting next to my chair. He stood in place, regarding the looming brick wall and its enormous logo with an abstracted half smile on his face.

He turned as I approached. The wattage of his smile ticked up a notch or two. "Good morning, Jordan. I was hoping to have a chat with you upstairs before you got started."

The high of walking to work was beginning to wear off. I became suddenly aware of the sweat-dampened waistband of my jeans, my flushed face, my flyaway hair. I hadn't even had a chance to look in a mirror. The section in the Humanilism employee manual on personal dress and grooming was decidedly relaxed, but I do think there was something in there about being clean and tidy. I wasn't sure I was either of those things just now.

I followed my boss up the grand curvature of the staircase, across the little landing, and into his spacious, airy office. Still clutching my DragonFire, I settled into the chair pulled up to face the large desk as Luke took his seat on the other side. He took a quick look at the screen of his slender laptop and began. "So, I wanted to check in with you. It's been four weeks today. How are you feeling about your BodPod? It looks like you've been wearing it consistently, and your step average has been on a steady rise."

As Luke spoke, I noticed his wrist. A bright orange BodPod rested against his smoothly tanned skin. He saw me looking and raised his arm a little as if this would allow me a more complete view. "BodPod is excited about our program. We got some new colors in—shades that haven't even been released to the public. Are you happy with black? We've got purple now, and teal, and red. Plus orange, as you see." He bent down as if intending to open his desk drawer.

I spoke quickly. "Black is fine. Really. Black is perfect."

He straightened with a little shrug and a grin, then folded his hands on the desktop in front of him. "The pilot program you were good enough to participate in has been very successful. We're about to open the BodPod program as an option for the entire company. We were thinking of rolling out a few other lifestyle incentive programs as well."

I took a sip of my DragonFire. It fizzled pleasantly against my tongue. I thought of Tony's baggy chinos, of my own walk to work this morning. Those did seem like good results, taken together.

Luke continued. "We thought we'd offer our early BodPod participants first crack at these, too. One of the programs we're going to try out is offering Merit incentives for lifestyle changes. So, if you have a habit you're trying to break, or a behavior you're trying to establish, you can declare this on our interface and then input your progress. It takes 21 days to form a new habit. We've built that in as the goal."

I nodded vaguely, shifting in my chair and feeling a little chilled as the sweat in my clothing began to dry. I wondered if it would be practical to store some jeans at work but do my walking in something a little more breathable. Then I could change when I arrived. Though I'd never used it, Humanilism employees had access to a whole gym, complete with showers, washers and dryers, and large lockers where clothing could be stored between uses.

Luke adjusted his BodPod on his wrist and the face lit, showing the time. I was later getting started on my Interactions than I'd intended. I hadn't been planning on it earlier, but now I found myself wondering if I could make it out to the Tipped Z again after work today.

Luke was still talking about habits. My attention snapped back to the conversation abruptly when he said, "So, what do you think? You've been such a great ambassador for the BodPod program, is there a habit you'd like to try to change?"

I froze in the act of raising my can of DragonFire to my lips for another sip. I seemed to hear Gregory's voice. *Every time you drink one of these, it takes a few minutes off your life.*

Tony had recently given up his Coke Zero and switched to whatever all natural electrolyte booster he'd been touting the other day. I had plenty of bad habits, but DragonFire was doubtless my most public vice.

Luke was not looking directly at the can in my hand, but I could feel his awareness of it. When I didn't answer, he smoothly pushed ahead. "It has to be something trackable, of course. Common choices are things like ordering too much take-out, getting to bed at a certain time, decreasing screen use at night, drinking habits." He paused. My can of DragonFire could not have been more conspicuous if it had been glowing. "You know. Things along those lines."

"Yeah," I said casually, crossing and uncrossing my legs. I began to feel a small spark of defiance. I had walked to work this morning, for crying out loud. What more did they want from me? "I'll think about it, but off the top of my head I can't come up with anything about my life I want to change."

"So," Erin said, squinting into the early sun as she looked across from her perch on Esperanza to my position on Sally, "tell me about your week. Grant says you were out three times. That's great."

I felt surges of several competing emotions at her words. First, I was undeniably proud that I had, in fact, ridden Sally Wednesday, Thursday, and Friday. This had been made possible by the fact that between riding her and walking to and from work daily, I was consistently crushing the Humanilism step goal. This was earning me extra Merit points. I usually hoarded Merit points to a somewhat illogical degree. I'd decided to be extravagant this week and use them to buy myself some shorter days.

The other feeling was a strange blend of pleasure that Grant had noticed me and hurt he hadn't approached since my first visit.

I gave Sally a little pat on the neck. "She's such a ball to ride," I said. "I think I'm a little obsessed with her."

This was not untrue. Sally was truly a joy to be around. As I got to know the mare better, I only became more impressed with her work ethic, her easygoing nature, and her athleticism.

But the truth was, Grant was the one I was obsessed with.

Erin was smiling. "Nora will be so glad to hear you're enjoying her. This prohibition on riding is driving her up the wall. She and Wyatt said all along they'd probably have two or three kids. But with this first pregnancy being so rough, I'm honestly not so sure. With my two, I was able to ride until the third trimester."

I scanned the landscape, wondering from what vantage Grant had seen me without being seen himself. I spoke without thinking. "At least it works out pretty well. She might not be riding, but she can watch your kids, and that allows you more time to be useful and do ranch stuff, I'm sure."

There was a strange pause. I looked over to see Erin had flushed red under her light skin. Unlike the others, she didn't tend to wear a hat. Her eyes were squinted nearly shut against the bright day.

I sensed I had strayed onto a fraught subject. As the silence lengthened, I cast about desperately for anything else to say. It lit on the question I had been stewing over for days. Once again, my inner censor failed. "Grant said he was in a bad wreck and that's why he doesn't ride anymore. What happened? Do you know?"

It was such a random comment, so insensitive, invasive, and clearly none of my business, it seemed to do the trick. Erin snapped out of whatever emotional spiral she'd been descending. "He told you that?" She sounded surprised.

I nodded, remembering that look on his face, the way he'd said the words. *Since then, I don't ride.*

Erin shook her head, her eyes falling to contemplate the sand of the arena. "It was terrible. A really, really horrible situation," she said. "He broke his pelvis—shattered it, more like—not to mention his wrist and his forearm and his ribs and his ankle. He even cracked a few vertebra. Basically, his entire left side was crushed. As I understand, it was six months before he could walk again."

I tried to imagine the Grant I knew confined to a bed or a chair for half a year. It did not compute.

I couldn't help it. I was fascinated. "How long ago was this?"

Erin gave a little shrug. "Two years ago now, or about that. He lived up in Wyoming then. I didn't know him at the time."

The sun was growing warm on my back, but the breeze was cool. "So it's not that he can't ride, right? I mean, he gets around town on a motorcycle."

Erin looked at me, the barest hint of a smile on her lips. "You seem to have noticed an awful lot about him."

It wasn't a rebuke. Nevertheless, her playful tone made me flinch. "He lives at my new apartment complex," I blurted by way of explanation. "I didn't know that when I moved in. But then I saw him coming home one day."

I was blushing. I could only hope I was backlit enough by the rising sun that Erin wouldn't see.

Erin's smile faded again. "I don't mean to tease you. The truth is, he could use a friend."

I wanted more. It seemed the answers she'd given led only to more questions. What did she mean by "horrible situation?" Weren't all accidents, by definition, pretty bad? And why move from Wyoming to Arizona to work at a ranch when you refused to ride a horse?

Still, even my social ineptitude had its limits. Erin gathered up her reins. I couldn't bring myself to ask any more questions, but she threw out one more enticing tidbit. "He was exceptionally handy once. He's been winning ranch roping competitions since he was a kid."

Then, in response to some invisible cue I couldn't see, her horse began to walk. Erin shifted into a more businesslike tone. "Let's warm these ladies up. While we walk, you can tell me what you and Sally have been doing on your own."

I slammed Bessie's door shut with my hip and looked past the set of plastic drawers in my arms at the heap of boxes and bags on the curb. I felt a sense satisfaction. It was Wednesday evening, and I was free at last. This was it. My old apartment was no longer home to a single one of my worldly possessions. I had turned in my keys. I was officially moved out.

Then my eyes strayed to the expanse of sidewalk leading into the complex. I felt a dimming of my enthusiasm. Moved out, perhaps, but not yet entirely moved *in*.

I stared at the heap of stuff. Much of what had been leftover was random or awkward. The lightsaber jutted out the top of one box, balanced appropriately atop a stack of old *Star Wars* paperbacks. My map of the *Heroes of the Totem Spirit* world I'd been trapped in for so long was rolled up and rubber banded shut next to it. Around that box lay other boxes and bags. There was no way I'd be able to move it all into my apartment in one trip, or even two.

Stooping with the drawer unit still in my arms, I managed to loop a finger through the red loops of first one garbage bag, then another. I straightened. I'd forgotten what, precisely, was in these bags, but they were heavy. As I took a step forward they swayed ponderously, bouncing unseen sharp corners against my calves and shins. I muttered a curse, repositioned the drawers in my arms, and shambled on like a member of the walking dead with lingering klepto tendencies. The worst thing about my new apartment, I reflected, was its excessive distance from the parking lot.

I had reached the spot where the concrete sidewalk forked when I heard the tread of feet behind me. Hastily, I stepped onto the branch that led to my door, thinking whoever was behind me would walk on by. Instead, the footsteps stopped. As I lumbered onward, a familiar voice spoke into the gathering dusk.

"You know," Grant said, his voice amused, "you'd get more steps if you carried one thing at a time."

I stopped, feeling a mixture of embarrassment and pique. I strained to look over my shoulder. Grant stood on the path behind me, his leather jacket unzipped, his motorcycle helmet hanging in one hand.

"That's true," I said dubiously. I had heard of this. People who carried one grocery bag in from their car at a time, or parked in the spaces furthest away from the door. I was not sure I wanted to attain that level of BodPod devotion. "I guess I value efficiency over statistics."

Grant laughed. "I think, at the rate you're going, you're not saving any time either."

For a moment, I felt annoyed. Who was this guy to judge my stuff-carrying technique? After all, from what I knew of him, his every choice in life was hardly guided by rational reflection.

But then, still smiling, Grant stepped forward and relieved me of the two dangling bags. "I do the same thing," he confessed. And the sting of his laughter faded into a blush of warmth that shot out from where his fingers bumped mine. As I released the bags, he said, "Lead on."

Unable to think of a valid reason to refuse his help and disinclined to do so anyway, I did lead on. Moving with a good deal more alacrity with my lightened load, I traversed the final stretch of sidewalk and reached my front door. I paused then to fumble in my pocket for the keys. The door unlocked, I hesitated.

As a general rule, I did not have people over. Part of this was strategic. The fewer people who knew where I lived, the less chance my mother would dupe some well-meaning acquaintance into revealing my location to her. But that was not a rational reason to forbid Grant from crossing my threshold. He already knew where I lived, after all.

The other part had to do with the sheer degree of effort it usually required to make my place even somewhat presentable to other humans. Even with my things tidied away, my old place had never been able to shake off a squalid air. And being an under-furnished studio, there had never been anything for anyone to sit on except my one diseased-looking armchair, and my inevitably unmade bed.

None of those reasons were problems here. The apartment was tidy right now. It boasted blinds that opened and closed, floors that weren't peeling or bubbling, and a kitchen with bright, shiny countertops. My rumpled bed was privately stowed in my bedroom.

The only problem was my bare living room. But that was excusable. I had, after all, only recently moved in.

So, shoving my reservations aside, I stepped through the door and flipped on a light. Unlike the flickery fluorescent fixtures at my old place, these came on softly and stayed on. I walked through my short but pristine entryway, turned left, and deposited my drawers in the empty living room. Feeling gloriously disingenuous in the way of a tidy person with impeccable taste, I said, "Sorry. It's a work in progress."

As Grant set the bags next to my drawers, he glanced around with a non-committal air. That's when I realized he possibly lived in the exact same floorplan and was unlikely to be impressed by the base features of my apartment.

I added lamely, "I'm still shopping for furniture."

The reality of having Grant in my apartment was slowly beginning to feel both impossible and overwhelming. I could smell the leather of his jacket. The door, still open, let in a breeze that carried the cool of the coming night. We were well into October now. The heat faded quickly when the sun went down.

Grant took a step back towards the door. He set his motorcycle helmet on one of the stools pushed up under the overhang of the island's counter. "Do you want a hand with the rest? It's getting dark." And he seemed to take my answer as a foregone conclusion because he was moving towards the door before I could even reply.

○

Laughing and carrying my lightsaber, I hurried along the sidewalk. It was full dark now, but the solar lights that lined the paths had come on. I could see well enough. I tried the switch on the lightsaber's hilt with inane hope, but the thing was as dead as ever.

Behind me, I heard Grant's rapid footsteps. This was the last load, and we had made it into a game. The rules Grant had declared were simple. We could carry only one item at a time, no matter how small, and whoever got the most trips won. If we took the same number of trips, the person back across the threshold first would carry the day.

Also, no running.

Grant had casually fabricated these rules out of thin air on our first trip back to the parking lot. Where he'd found the inspiration, I had no idea. Playfulness seemed to come naturally to him. I'd been a little nonplussed when he'd finished explaining and then speed walked away from me, but my competitive instincts had kicked in before he gained too much of an edge.

We'd have finished the trip before, and Grant would have won, but then the lightsaber had toppled out of the box as I heaved it off the ground. I'd stooped to retrieve it, but Grant, already part way up the sidewalk, had heard the clatter. He'd glanced back. "Nope. Only one thing."

So, with an impish grin, I'd tilted the box a little further and allowed the HotTS map to roll out as well. "There's something left for each of us, then. Unless you want to forfeit," I'd called as I scuttled after him.

What should have been Grant's final load was a stack of hand-thrown bowls carefully packed in a cardboard box. Gregory had made the bowls when he'd taken a ceramics course the year before. This was after he'd finally gotten around to getting his GED and was flirting with the thought of enrolling at the university to work towards a BFA. In the end, his motivation fizzled out after the one semester. The bowls were lovely, but I'd always been too afraid of breaking them to do anything but hide them in the back of a cupboard.

To Grant's credit, instead of thumping his load roughly down in the entryway like I did, he'd carried the box to the kitchen and set it on the counter. As I darted back out the door, I was officially in the lead.

Now, the game was almost done. As I speed-walked to the fork in the path and scurried towards my front door, clutching my lightsaber, I risked a glance over my shoulder. Grant was there. The rolled-up map was a long, pale shape in his hand. He was moving with shocking speed considering he wasn't running. With a startled squeak, I redoubled my efforts at walking, resisting the impulse to jog. Jogging even a single step was grounds for a return to the parking lot.

I was just a few steps from my threshold when I heard a papery rustle and felt a light swat on my shoulder. I turned with an outraged gasp, bringing the lightsaber into an enguard position and blocking the sidewalk. "Hey," I said. "You can't attack the leader. And don't ruin my map, either."

But I was grinning. It was ridiculous, but I couldn't remember the last time I'd felt so light-hearted. The truth was, I should have thrown that map away ages ago. I had stopped needing it the moment I cleared the spider forest.

Grant's grin was impish. "The rules don't prohibit the use of violence to achieve victory." His eyes were on the door behind me. I could see him calculating the odds of being able to rush around my blockade.

I waggled my lightsaber at him and took a long, slow step backward, followed by another. He advanced as I retreated, feinting at me with the rolled map. But it didn't matter. Three more steps, two more, and I would win.

Then, all in a rush, Grant darted forward. I brought the lightsaber down across his shoulders, but it was blunt and light and made of plastic and I wasn't, obviously, trying to do any damage. He ignored the ineffectual blow as he got inside my guard, wrapped his arms around my torso, and scooped me off my feet.

I was so startled, all I managed to do was release a strange gasp. As I dangled in his arms like a mynock attached to a power cable, he swung me around so he was closer to the door than I was and took a few laughing, stumbling steps backward. He was surprisingly strong, particularly for someone who had been unable to walk in the recent past.

Before I knew it, we were inside the apartment, and he had won. I might have been outraged by his supremely unfair tactics, but as he set my feet on the tile of the entryway and kicked my front door shut with his foot, he did something that made me forget about our game and its rules and who had won.

Grant lowered his mouth to mine and kissed me.

Chapter 10

I woke with the distinct feeling I should remember something. Usually, when this happened to me, the sensation was one of dread. What terrible thing had I temporarily forgotten? What crappy reality would I have to face as soon as my brain finished booting up for the day?

This time, it was different. I woke with a sort of warm glow in the pit of my stomach. It was such a strange sensation, I simply lay in my sheets for a time. As I did so, it all came back in a rush.

Grant. The unloading game. The kiss. Everything that came after.

A thrill shot through my body. I wondered if it all could have been a dream. It seemed impossible that Grant, with his gorgeous face and sculpted body, would want me, of all people. He was a hot-house flower that thrived in full sun. I was some sort of delicate cave-dwelling fungus that collapsed when exposed to fresh air.

At least, I had been. As I sat up in bed and looked around my tidy room, I realized I had been undergoing a slow process of change. I looked down at my arms. I had tan lines from all my time spent on Sally in a t-shirt. There was the hint of visible muscle tone in my legs. Maybe I was more adaptable than I thought.

I stood up, stretched, and smiled. Turning to my bedside table, I checked my phone more out of habit than expectation. It was a few minutes before my alarm was set to go off. As I picked it up and glanced at the lock screen, I saw I had a new BodPod message. It was from Grant. It said, "Good night. ☺" He'd sent it at 10:15 pm.

My smiled widened. I felt my heart begin to beat a little faster. I was, I realized, behaving like a teenager. Except I'd never kissed any boys when I'd been an actual teenager. And in college, I'd had a bad habit of sleeping with any guy who hung around long enough and showed interest. Some of these relationships hadn't been bad, per se. But they hadn't been good, either.

I'd certainly never felt what I was feeling now, which was the enraptured glow of a reciprocated crush.

I tapped the message, intending to reply, but then felt suddenly paralyzed by the enormity of this moment. Grant had helped me carry a bunch of stuff into my apartment. Then he'd kissed me, and we'd enjoyed a steamy make-out session. I, not being a person who was good at setting or enforcing boundaries, would most likely have let it go farther. But Grant had backed off before things escalated, checking himself with visible effort.

As we'd disentangled our bodies, I had defrayed the awkwardness of the moment by offering to put a frozen pizza in the oven and giving him one of the beers Gregory had left in my fridge. When he'd asked with mild confusion if I was going to have a beer as well, I'd said only, "Oh I don't drink." He hadn't pushed the point, which was another mark in his favor.

We'd settled in, chatting about the ranch and the apartment complex and BodPod stats. It had been as easy to talk to him as it had been to kiss him. That was a novelty for me as well. In my experience, men who were good to kiss and men who were good to talk to were like Wookies and Trandoshans: unlikely to exist on the same planet unless there was a war on.

Which meant there was a lot riding on my reply. Now that Grant was no longer here, in my apartment, his very presence making it impossible for me to deny what was happening, I had trouble believing his interest was real. As I padded into my kitchen to start my breakfast, I tried to consider the situation from all possible angles. Could he have ulterior motives? A secret agenda? But as I cracked eggs into a bowl and began to beat them, I couldn't think what anyone had to gain by including me in their life.

I was waiting for my omelet to finish cooking when inspiration struck. I picked up my phone and typed out, "Good morning."

I paused, wondering if I should include any emoji. I decided against it. I hit send.

Okay, so no one was going to nominate me for the witty banter award. But I felt satisfied as I returned my attention to my breakfast. I had replied. I had not said anything that might make me seem over-eager or clingy. The ball was now back in his court. Mission accomplished.

The microwave beeped. I pulled my omelet plate free and carried it to the island overhang. Settling onto one of the stools, my eyes fell on the box of Gregory's bowls that still sat where Grant had left it. The rest of the boxes and bags lay in a heap in the living room. I'd tidy it all away this afternoon, I decided, and then make a serious effort at finding some furniture.

If Grant ever came over again, I wanted to make sure my environment would make me seem like a normal, functional human adult.

Rubbing my eyes, I closed my browser and sagged for a moment in my desk chair. I felt stiff and fatigued, even though the clock told me it was only 9:15 pm. When I closed my eyes, my head seemed to swim with competing images of over-stuffed chairs and designer sofas. I felt I had looked at thousands of potential pieces of furniture. None of them seemed quite right.

Sighing, I wondered how people did this. I'd never chosen furniture. Always before, it had come to me in the manner of stray cats. I'd bought my bed from the girl who was moving out of the first apartment I moved into. The dilapidated armchair had been left on the curb by someone else. My desk had been a gift from Gregory. Even my desk chair hadn't been a choice, precisely. It was just the chair everyone who spent a lot of time at a desk seemed to buy. I'd found it used on eBay and put in a bid. A few days later, it had shown up on my doorstep in a large box.

Now, though, the variables to weigh when choosing living-room furniture seemed overwhelming. What color? What style? Did I want to get just a couch or a few matching pieces? Was leather too pretentious? Was cloth more comfortable anyway? I felt paralyzed by the possibilities.

This, I understood, was decision fatigue.

More out of habit than real desire to play, I found myself clicking on the HotTS icon on my desktop. I hadn't logged in for days. It was even a little surreal, clicking past the animated logos and the intro video, hearing the familiar welcome music pour out of my speakers. As the image of my avatar and Buttercup loaded, I half expected the virtual horse to toss me a reproachful look.

She didn't, of course. She hadn't missed me because she was not a real horse. And then I glanced at the Elite Squad stats. The top five players of the week were there, followed by the minimum score required to qualify. My score and rank were listed below. I was nowhere near the low point cut off.

For a moment, I felt a flutter of panic. I had worked so hard to stay on the Elite Squad for so long. All that hard work was eroding away from me, day by day. I moved my mouse, intending to click on the entry portal that would send me into the game.

Then, my phone lit up. I'd placed it on the desk next to my keyboard. My heart skipped a beat when I saw the BodPod icon next to Grant's message. "You've been on my mind since I opened my eyes this morning."

A shiver shot up my arms. I realized with a strange clarity that while there were gamers who were also functional people, I, personally, did not seem to possess the force of will to play within reasonable parameters. I could have the Elite Squad, or I could have a real life.

As I stared at my phone, heart pounding, another message from Grant appeared. "Can I see you again soon? Want to grab apps this weekend?"

It took me a moment to parse that Grant was referring to food, not software. And then I understood. This was called a date. Grant had just asked me out on a date.

In a moment of foresight, I understood what would happen if I clicked the entry portal. I would stay up way, way too late chasing down questing points. I would wake up exhausted, and either be late to work or extra slow to finish my Interactions. I'd be late getting home, and I wouldn't have time to finish sorting and unpacking my remaining belongings. I'd be tired and grumpy on the date. If Grant happened to end up in my apartment again, the first thing he would see was the ungainly heap of boxes and bags.

If I didn't click the entry portal, I could put a few more things away and get to bed at a decent hour. I would wake up feeling refreshed, walk to work in plenty of time, fly through my Interactions, and be bright and spry for the date. I'd have time to deal with the last of my belongings before dinner. The front room would be nothing more offensive than empty if we ended up back here.

As I stared at my computer screen, the Elite Squad leaderboard numbers refreshed. Hawkeyez777 had just moved into 5th place.

Feeling a strange twinge of an uncomfortable emotion I could not define, I logged out of the game, shut down my computer, and accepted Grant's invitation to dinner.

Craigslist, I am certain, was left out of Dante's *Inferno* as one of the circles of hell only because it had yet to be invented at the time of the book's writing. As I stared blearily at yet another couch set, I took a long sip of DragonFire and tried to decide if all the hours of staring at furniture had caused critical damage to my brain's aesthetic center, or if I had found a winning option at last.

The items I was staring at seemed too good to be true. Occupying some medium position between the floppy floral monstrosities of my college days and the settee in Gregory's living room, the look was one of smooth, gray fabric with even and elegant lines. The set on offer included a lightly used couch and two padded chairs, with a coffee table that matched the wooden legs of all three. I chewed on my lip, flipping repeatedly through the photos and staring at the price. It was high, but I was beginning to realize it was probably reasonable.

It was Thursday night and I was in my office nook. Grant had responded to my response with a suggestion we meet in the parking lot and walk down to a lovely little Cantina a short distance away from our apartment complex later this weekend. It sounded like a nice plan and had the added benefit of incorporating steps. I had accepted. But ever since, I had been unable to shake the vision of having a wonderful date, inviting Grant into my apartment afterward, and being faced once more with the empty living room and my pathetic furniture. Perhaps it was too late to do anything about it, but maybe it wasn't.

So I'd returned home from work and thrown myself into shopping with renewed vigor. I had passed this ad over several times in the past due to the price tag. But now as I accepted certain realities about the costs of joining the adult accouterments club, I realized it was actually a steal. Flipping over to my email, I sent Gregory a link to the ad with the single word, "Thoughts?" Then I stood up and wandered into my kitchen, where I was unable to deny a little spark of a pleasant feeling it took me a moment to identify. As I looked at Gregory's bowls, now unpacked and displayed on a shelf along the kitchen wall, I realized it was pride. I was feeling a little bit proud of my apartment with its spacious rooms and large window with a view of the mountains beyond. I tried to imagine the furniture I'd been eyeballing in place of my battered coffee table. I thought it would all come together rather nicely.

Gregory was slow in replying, which was not unusual. He did not keep any devices in the room with him when he was working. Still, I was distracted by his silence at first—a feeling that trended towards annoyance as I rifled through my fridge and unearthed the remains of the frozen pizza I'd cooked for Grant. As I ate, I checked my phone more or less continuously. When a message popped up, it took me a moment to parse that it was not Gregory my brother, but Grant my budding romantic interest. It said, "Looking forward to Sunday. 6:00 still good?"

I felt a surge of something sweet and sharp as a flood of memories of Grant washed through my mind. The scent of sand and creosote and leather, the stubble of his jaw against my cheek, the warm touch of his hands on my back, my neck, my shoulders.

Feeling breathless, I tapped out a reply at once, then stood there, chewing on my cold pizza and wondering if I should wait at least a little while to respond. To distract myself, I pulled my new broom and dustpan from the nook where my washer and dryer lived and did a quick sweep of the apartment. Then I returned to the kitchen and checked my phone again.

Gregory had emailed at last. "Buy it," the message said. "Buy it now." Feeling giddy, I sent my reply to Grant, then hurried back to my computer and punched the phone number from the ad into my phone.

I woke on Sunday with a sense of untapped potential. It was going to be the perfect day. Busy, but perfect. I had a plan. Step one involved going out to the Tipped Z for my lesson with Erin. Step two included giving myself and my apartment a thorough cleaning. Step three consisted of accepting delivery of my new furniture at 4:00. Step four was meeting Grant for our date. Step five ... well. Step five was still to be determined.

It said something about how my life had shifted in the recent past that I set out on this day with a sense of optimism. This was foolish, of course. Jordan of a few weeks ago would never have tackled so much in one day, much less assumed everything on the list would go according to plan. But I was caught in some giddy spiral of healthy living, blooming romance, and interior design inspiration. I didn't even stop to consider everything that might go wrong.

It started with Bessie. I woke easily to the vibrations of my BodPod, rolled out of bed, washed my face, and slipped into my riding jeans and boots. Grabbing a can of DragonFire from the fridge, I walked straight out into the fine, cool morning, looking up at the mountains with their shoulders bathed in the warm light of the sunrise. As I walked, I reveled in a feeling of promise and expectation that lasted until I reached my battered vehicle, climbed behind the driver's seat, and turned the key in the ignition. This act was greeted by a dull click rather than the sound of the engine turning over. Stymied, I tried again. And again. Two more clicks.

And that was when I remembered. This was not a movie or a story in which the plot must work towards a meaningful resolution. This was my life. And my life, I had long suspected, was cursed. Any time I started to get it together and things began to feel right and good, it meant not that I had finally cracked the code to functional living. No. It meant doom was waiting just around the corner.

The unraveling always starts with something small like this—a dead car—that interrupts my plans for the day. It progresses from there, a tiny pebble starting an avalanche that releases a deluge of disaster. Once the roaring mess of scree has all settled again, everything I thought I had accomplished is flattened and paved over by the new features of an alien landscape.

Staring through my windshield at the innocuous parking lot, I felt my heart begin to pound. *Stop it,* I told myself. *A dead car is a dead car, not some harbinger of doom.* I tried the key one last time and again heard that dull, lifeless click.

In my pocket, my phone began to ring. I stepped back out of the car, fished it out, and saw a number I did not recognize. It was a 520 number, which meant local. My mouth went dry. I felt abruptly light-headed.

I let the call go straight to voicemail. I waited for a minute, then another, standing next to the beached Bessie, waiting for the message notification to pop up. It never did.

And that's when I knew she'd found me again. My mother, whatever else might be said of her, had always had an exquisite sense of timing.

All the vigor and optimism drained out of me. I slammed Bessie's door, not bothering to lock it, and trudged back to my apartment. Once inside, I texted Erin. "Sorry," I said. "Car trouble. I won't be able to make it out for my lesson." I sent the message and stared dully at my phone. What did you even do when your car wouldn't start? I knew how to troubleshoot a computer or a phone, but not a vehicle. Most likely, I needed to call a towing company so they could take it to a mechanic so they could figure out what was wrong.

In my hand, my phone locked itself. There on the screen was the missed call notification. I felt the old anxiety writhe in my belly, felt the familiar dread of the cycle I knew was about to begin anew.

I sipped my DragonFire, enjoying the taste of the frothy, sugary beverage, and turned to look at my computer. It sat, neglected, in my lovely new office nook, the screen gorgeously free of glare.

I walked over, woke it up, and clicked the HotTS icon. I'd game for a little while. Just until I felt a little less anxious. Then I'd call for a tow truck, and see about salvaging the day.

I walked to work on Monday. This wasn't due to a resurgence in motivation or optimism, but necessity. Bessie was still broken. I had done nothing to pursue repairs.

Sunday had not gone at all as planned. My new furniture did arrive as scheduled, delivered by two burly young men supervised by a middle-aged woman with steel gray hair who watched them maneuver the pieces into my living room only after accepting and counting the large pile of cash I had procured from the bank after work on Friday. She fastidiously reminded me of a ding on the leg of the couch, which had also been detailed in one of the Craigslist photos. I shrugged, said it was fine, and declined when she offered to have her sons remove the plastic and arrange the pieces. The three of them left, the sons striding out, unbothered, the mother glancing back with a look of concern as I closed the door behind them.

The new furniture sat in my front room, swathed in protective plastic. I had barely given it a second look before turning back to my office nook, grabbing another DragonFire on the way.

At the time the furniture arrived, I was still in my riding jeans. There was no need to prepare for the date with Grant because I'd canceled that too, citing the same car trouble I'd used on Erin. He'd texted back offering help. I had not replied. I was many hours into a HotTS binge by that point. While it would be a long time before I was anywhere near regaining entry to the Elite Squad, I was on the leaderboard for the daily points race by the time 6:00 pm rolled around. If I pushed myself, I'd thought I might be able to get onto the top 20 list before the cut-off at midnight, and thus earn myself a points boost.

It had been something to shoot for, anyway.

My phone had spent the day on the desk next to me, facedown and set to silent. Still, I checked it with compulsive regularity, noting as the calls from the unknown number piled up. They were coming at irregular intervals, but I knew the pattern. Soon, the frequency would increase, eventually starting to come on the hour, every hour, until I either blocked the number or gave in and answered.

If I answered, I would have to talk to her. If I blocked her, she would get another phone. Or, worse, she would show up in my real life somewhere. There was no way to stop her, no recourse I could take until she'd actually crossed the line and either approached me or made contact. Even then, it was tricky. There was the restraining order, but I had learned over the years it was a pale thing, useless in the face of my mother's determined phases.

I should warn Gregory. I should block the number. I should ignore her, not let her get to me. I shouldn't let her derail my life this way. Again.

I did none of those things. I plunged into HotTS, feeling my anxiety spike every time my phone lit up and vibrated with an incoming call. I could hear the voice of one counselor after another, the people Gregory had sent me to talk to, thinking it would help. *She only has power over you if you give it to her.* Simple words, spoken, always, by people who had never met my mother.

At midnight, I'd gotten my boost, then played another couple of hours to make a good start on the next day's stats. In the morning, I'd dragged myself out of bed at the insistent vibrating of the silent alarm on my BodPod and stumbled into the kitchen. After staring at the eggs in the cool light of the fridge for a few minutes, I'd decided an omelet was too much work. I'd loaded up my shoulder bag with a few DragonFire cans and begun the slow walk to work. My phone, in my pocket, vibrated twice before I made it to the Humanilism building. I was late, so I ended up in a station crammed between two other Humans, neither of whom I particularly liked. As I logged in and waited for my assignment, my phone lit up again. When I did not react, the young man with a well-groomed beard and skinny jeans on my left quietly pointed. "Your phone is ringing." His tone was soft and apologetic.

"I know." My reply came out sounding exceptionally ungracious, but I was past caring. He gave me a long, affronted look, shrugged, and returned to his own Interactions.

Work dragged by in a fuzz. I ran out of DragonFire and was exhausted by the time I finally completed my Interactions for the day. I took an Uber home. When I walked into my apartment, the sight of the still wrapped furniture in my living room didn't even make me pause. I went straight to my computer.

My avatar and Buttercup had just phased into existence before the entry portal when my phone lit again, this time with a text instead of a call. It was Grant. His message was short but sweet. "Hey you. Any chance we can reschedule?"

I stared at the words on the screen for a while, noting with detachment the way they blurred as my eyes began to prickle with tears. I liked Grant. I liked him a lot. But there was no point replying. He was nice and talented and so very attractive. I was nothing. I had always been nothing. If Grant got to know me, he would see that, and call it off. Better not to disappoint him.

Still, I couldn't bring myself to text him back with a no. Instead, I texted Gregory. I told him I wasn't feeling well and we should skip our

Tuesday dinner. It wasn't a lie, I reassured myself as I hit send. I felt less well than I had in a long while.

I sat in the employee auditorium at Humanilism Enterprises, slumped in a chair at the end of a row as far back in the audience as I could be without being conspicuous. On the stage before us, Luke Rastenhaus stood beneath a large screen on which the details of the new BodPod incentives program were displayed. The program was mature now, and being offered to everyone. Along with the features I had enjoyed, a new suite of perks had been assembled for those who met step count and sleep goals. But the thing Luke Rastenhaus was most excited about, the thing he'd spent the last half hour building up to presenting, was something he called the Peer Challenge Program.

"Accountability," he now said, standing in his slim jeans on the black stage against the black screen. "That's the difference between a goal and a dream. With accountability, changes become real. They become transformative. Studies show you are 57% more likely to achieve a goal if you tell another person about it. So here at Humanilism, we are giving you both the means and the platform not only to declare personal goals but for your fellow Humans to step up and participate in group goals. Individuals can even give trusted friends Challenger status. A Challenger can set a custom goal, tailored just for you. You can then track your progress towards meeting that goal. You can also make your goal public."

He paused, beaming. I slumped lower, painfully aware of the BodPod on my wrist and its pathetic step count. It was Tuesday morning. Bessie still wasn't repaired. I'd taken an Uber to work, making the driver take me first to the grocery store so I could replenish my alarmingly depleted DragonFire stores.

I'd arrived at work two hours later than usual, due to sleeping in after another late-night gaming binge. I'd entered to find the workroom almost entirely empty, with only a small group of my fellow Humans migrating towards the door in the back. I stood on the threshold, mystified, until one of them, a young woman named Sonia who was always smiling, turned and called to me. "Mandatory presentation in the auditorium."

Belatedly, I recalled seeing a message about this a few days prior. Hustling to stash my case of cans, I'd rooted one out of the package and scurried into the auditorium as the lights dimmed and Luke Rastenhaus stepped onto the stage.

Now, I wasn't really listening. I was distracted by the fact that it was almost 11:00, which meant my phone would vibrate in my pocket and I would once more not answer the call. I sat in silent anticipation as Luke Rastenhaus continued. "To help you see how this could work, I'm going to give you an example. One of the most successful participants in the pilot program has agreed to help me with this today. I'm sure even if you don't know him personally, you were amazed at the before and after photos we published in the employee newsletter last week. Let me introduce Tony Firth."

I straightened incrementally, dumbfounded as Tony strode onto the stage. He had deflated even further since I'd first noticed his weight loss, and gotten some new pants to accentuate the changes. In a white button-down shirt tucked into a plain pair of chinos, he stepped into the spotlight looking not in the least bit pudgy. Tony, I was astonished to realize, was lean and tan and healthy-looking.

On the screen behind him, a photo appeared. It had been taken at the beginning of the year, the mandatory snapshot we all had to sit for every season. Larger than life, the old Tony loomed for a moment as Luke Rastenhaus chatted on about how the BodPod pilot program had helped Tony see his own unhealthy habits, and change them.

"And Tony isn't our only success story," Luke went on. "Far from it. We've seen astonishing progress almost across the board. So now, Tony and another one of our BodPod veterans are going to take it to the next level."

It was now 11:03. I peeked at my phone, but it still hadn't registered an incoming call. This struck me as ominous. My mother was as persistent as she was predictable. When she decided to force her way back into my life, she always managed. Somehow.

Up on the stage, Luke handed the mic to Tony. Tony said, "Thank you, Luke. Now I'd like Jordan to come on up and join me. Jordan, my fellow BodPod success story, I've got a Challenge for you."

The audience shifted, heads rotating and clothing rustling as all my co-workers began looking around in the darkness. I sat, frozen with horror until Sonia leaned back from the row in front of me and gave a little tap on the knee. "Jordan," she said. "That's you."

Jordan. I thought. *My name is not Jordan. Jordan is the construct, the fake, my effort to reimagine myself. Faith is who I really am. Faith, my mother's daughter. The failure. The child she tried so hard to love. Despite my lack of beauty, despite all the obvious flaws in my character, despite how unlovable I truly am, she tried. It wasn't her fault. I made it impossible.*

I stood in a spasm. "Stop it," I hissed to myself in the barest of whispers. It was not the truth. I knew that. It was the narrative my mother had nurtured at the core of my psyche, planted at the moment of my birth and painstakingly nurtured through all the years of my childhood.

"A round of applause for Jordan," Luke boomed, having acquired a second mic from somewhere. The audience started clapping.

I made my slow, bewildered way to the stage.

Chapter 11

Buttercup plunged through the final row of rushes. I directed her into a rumpled field dotted with rocks and small stands of dry brush. I poured on all possible speed for a moment, urging my horse to her fastest. We charged up to what I hoped was a strategic position beside a boulder, and wheeled around.

The three banshees hung in the air behind me, no more than shadows. Seeing them there, their smoky bodies pulsating in the dim light, I experienced both relief and trepidation. Relief that only three had followed me out of the swamp. Trepidation because I wasn't sure if I could take them all on. I gave Buttercup a mental pat on the neck. "If we survive this, old girl, I promise you I'll upgrade your breast collar."

The first banshee swept closer. These were more subtle fighters than the spiders I had once faced in a similar situation. The monsters at this higher level were a good deal more intelligent, which added depth and strategy to the game but also made plunging headlong into new quest zones a good deal more dangerous. I'd headed into this swamp thinking I'd poke around a little, only to stumble on these nightmarish creatures. I glanced at my health bar, which had fallen rapidly into the red zone during my first entanglement with one of them. Now it was creeping back up towards full, but there wouldn't be time to heal entirely before they were upon me.

Deciding to go on the offensive, I moved around the outside of the group and charged for the straggler. It was incorporeal, so could only be damaged by magical weapons. Fortunately, this included Buttercup's shoes. She reared and struck, and the creature fell back, stunned. I was able to sling a fireball potion into its smoky depths. It went up in flames.

"One down, two to go," I said, groping with my free hand for the can of DragonFire that should have been sitting right beside my keyboard.

Except, it wasn't there.

For the hundredth time that night, I remembered what had panned out on stage in the Humanilism auditorium, remembered how my before and after sleep logs and step-count stats had flashed up on the screen, fortunately having not been updated for several days. The picture they painted was indeed remarkable. The numbers plainly showed how I had transformed from a sedentary insomniac into a person who regularly walked 10,000 steps a day and slept for eight to nine hours a night.

That, Luke Rastenhaus had declared, was a success no less dramatic as Tony shedding 30 pounds in a matter of weeks. And so, me and Tony—the shining stars of the Humanilism BodPod program—were going to move together towards the next step.

There, on stage, with every one of our co-workers watching, Tony had challenged me to give up DragonFire. "It won't be easy," he'd declared into the microphone, showing a surprising flair for the drama of the spotlight. "But if you can give up that drink for just 21 days, I suspect you won't even want it anymore."

Staring at the banshee on my computer screen, I returned my hand to the keyboard. My persistent headache, which I had temporarily at least kind of forgotten about, roared back with full force. "Screw you, Tony," I muttered to the screen. "If I lose Buttercup to these creatures, it's your fault."

The two remaining banshees were circling, their tattered and transparent bodies eerie on the shifting air. Then, out of nowhere, one of them lobbed a glowing green ball of magic. I dodged, but the second one was ready for that. Its projectile spell hit me square in the chest.

My screen began to glow green around the edges. A message flashed up over my stats. "You have been entangled and are taking 5 damage per second." Far worse than that though, was the fact I could not move, at all, until the spell wore off.

Retreat or maneuvering no longer possible, I watched as the two monsters moved in, one on either side. As I tried to decide whether to stand and fight or simply force-quit out of the game, I glanced longingly at the edges of my screen, remembering when the warrior in red armor and his wolf had come to my aide. But I hadn't seen Hawkeyez777 in weeks—not since I'd blown off his invitation to hang out in the social zone.

I took a quick stock of my inventory. No miraculous spell sat forgotten in some unused corner of my storage pouch. I had a few healing potions, but one wouldn't be enough to help, and I wouldn't survive long enough to use multiples. "Shit," I said into the quiet of my computer nook. "Shit, shit. Shiiit."

The first banshee struck, sliding its bewitched weapon toward my immobilized form. I struck back, but my hit did little damage. My screen flashed red. "Shit," I said again as the second hit me from the other side. Feeling sick with regret, I understood I was not going to survive.

Suddenly, the banshees fell back. I had a moment to feel astonished as a wolf appeared, bounding up from behind a boulder and hurling itself at one of the two apparitions, glowing with some kind of spell that gave it the ability to attack non-corporeal creatures. The hulking warrior, Hawkeyez777, was hot on its heels. Even as relief flowed through me, it carried a healthy dose of suspicion-tinged confusion. This was twice now he'd been there, impossibly, to save my skin. Why?

The two banshees screamed, enraged, and fell on these new foes. But they'd used up all their tricks on me. Also, Hawkeyez777 had clearly spent the time I had not played very much building up his avatar and companion animal alike. He was several levels above me now.

It was over in a moment. As the green tint faded from my screen, the familiar, comforting message popped up in its place. 'Progress Saved.'

The warrior turned, a new lock on his helmet flowing in the same breeze that had stirred the ragged banshee bodies. I flicked on my mic, but he spoke first. "You don't look like a damsel in distress. And yet, I keep finding you in these predicaments."

The social zone was a strange place. Like the quest zones, it was delineated by an invisible boundary. Once you crossed inside, the rules of engagement changed. In this case, all weapons became inaccessible, both on human-controlled avatars and on totem partners. The entire fighting interface, in fact, went away. It was replaced by an entirely different set of interactions, with new behaviors for introducing yourself, playing games, and transitioning into a romantic interaction.

It was this last option that preoccupied my mind as I moved next to the burly warrior down the street. His wolf padded at his side. He'd removed his helm when we entered the social zone. I could see his face for the first time. It was a stern, handsome face, more grizzled than I'd expected, with a large scar running from eyebrow to jaw on the left side. An avatar couldn't get scars. No matter how badly injured, we all healed without leaving the slightest mark. Which meant he'd chosen that scar and placed it on his own face, intentionally.

That was interesting, as was the fact he'd twice now appeared out of nowhere to save me from my own stupidity. He'd told me as we'd returned to the central town in this portal that the banshee zone was like the spider forest: impossible to clear without friends. But he had not offered to go back and take it on with me.

As we walked, I tried to determine whether the silence between us was friendly or frosty. This was difficult, as body language was pretty much generic, even in social zones. I still didn't know how Hawkeyez777 felt about my last minute cancellation, didn't know why he'd invited me into a social zone in the first place, and certainly didn't know who he really was. All I knew was he'd been gaming a lot during my absence.

The hulking warrior turned and led me into a low-slung tavern with a painted sign out front. It wasn't crowded, but there were other avatars present, sitting in small groups or pairs around the large, dim room. As she always did in these moments, Buttercup disappeared. Overlarge totem partners that couldn't fit inside buildings simply stored themselves in their owner's inventory until they could once more exist in the real world.

The warrior's wolf, however, was not too large to exist in the tavern. It continued to pad next to him as Hawkeyez777 selected a table and sat. I did the same, beginning to feel nervous. My avatar, too, had reverted to less warlike attire. My long hair was swept back in a set of intricate braids, my pointed, elfin ears revealing me as not quite human.

The man across from me was human. Or, at least, he was wearing a human skin. There were creatures in *Heroes of the Totem Spirit* that could shape-shift, though I thought if this was a talent Hawkeyez777 possessed I'd have seen evidence of it in battle by now.

"Can I buy you a drink?" Hawkeyez777 asked.

It was a strange question. Seeing as how we weren't really in a tavern, we could not drink. And the mention of beverages made my head pulse with pain. Resisting the urge to curse Tony again, I decided to go with the flow. "Sounds great."

Signaling the proprietor, Hawkeyez777 completed some sort of interaction, the details of which I wasn't privy too. He then offered me a tankard, which I had the option to accept, decline, or purchase. I chose 'Accept' and a set of bars I'd never seen before appeared on the lower right-hand side of my screen. The area was labeled with Hawkeyez777's name, and there were two bars. One appeared to be a record of how much time we'd spent questing together. This was about half full. The other, labeled 'Social,' was empty except for one tiny sliver of green. I stared at the two bars with mild consternation. What happened when they became full, I wondered?

"So," Hawkeyez777 said, wrapping his two large hands around the tankard of foamy brew and looking across the table at me with his large, gray eyes. He was a handsome man, but that was not surprising. Everyone in HotTS was handsome or beautiful. Except for the undead, of course, and people who went out of their way to build ugly avatars. "I haven't seen you around much lately."

His voice was modified by the filter, but his intonation sounded more curious than accusatory. Still, I felt myself flush. I was glad my avatar wouldn't give away my nerves so easily. I found myself spilling out the truth in far more detail than was necessary. "I'm so sorry about standing you up that day," I blurted. "I was at this ranch, where I have a horse. A real horse, I mean. And it's not my horse, exactly. I just lease her. But anyway, I was going to ride but then it turned out some cattle had gotten out because a fence had been cut. The ranchers asked me to go with them and help gather them up. I went and it took the entire day. I was still out there when I should have been meeting you here."

When I finally ran out of breath, Hawkeyez777 absorbed my long explanation without apparent interest. I bit back more words, feeling a surge of annoyance. I was not the most socially adept individual on the planet, but this utter lack of facial expression and physical cues was extremely off-putting.

After a beat of silence, Hawkeyez777 said, "No worries. It's cool."

Across the room, a woman with runes painted all up and down her arms and face made an extravagant gift of a potion to another woman, this one with the coloring of a dark elf. The dark elf accepted. Hearts bloomed in the air above the two of them.

I turned my attention back to my companion. Scrambling for a way to continue the conversation, I said, "You've been busy these last few weeks."

Hawkeyez777 shrugged. I stared in confusion. How had he done that? He must know about some menu I had yet to find. I didn't know how to make my avatar do anything but walk or fight.

In real life, I shifted in my chair. On my desk, my phone remained ominously silent. It was almost worse than the constant ringing. I knew better than to think my mother had given up. She had merely changed tactics. And until I knew what her new one was, I felt distinctly at a disadvantage.

"So why a horse?" Hawkeyez777 asked. It struck me as an inane question. Before I could contain myself, I shot back, "Why a wolf?"

Hawkeyez777 smiled. I blinked, astonished. Facial expressions in HotTS? He definitely had access to a menu I hadn't found. I stared around at the edges of my screen, cursing the UI designers who liked to hide critical functions inside tiny little collapsible bubbles. "I like dogs," he said. "So I thought a wolf would be even better."

There. In the upper left-hand corner, where I could usually access combat spells, I saw a tiny little button with a smiley face icon. I clicked it and an entire menu appeared, slithering down the left side of my screen in a waterfall of complex potential. "Holy shit," I murmured, noting that actions were colored according to some algorithm, recommended or not, depending on your social progress with the person you were speaking to.

"What's that?" Hawkeyez777 said.

"I just ..." I trailed off, reading quickly, then clicked 'Sip drink.' My avatar picked up the tankard and took a small swig. An indicator bar appeared beneath the tankard, showing me how much there was left to drink. "Sorry," I said, deciding to be truthful. "I have to admit I've never gone into a social zone before. I mean, not really. I came in once alone but I never talked to anyone. I just now found the interactions menu."

Hawkeyez777 laughed. That is, his voice laughed. His avatar's expression remained fixed. "I'm not that good at this either," he admitted. "Did you know there's an entirely different set of leaderboards for people who are devoted to the social zones instead of fighting?"

I had not known this, though I could hardly pretend to be surprised. In the background, the rune-covered woman and her dark elf partner were now making out, locked in a passionate embrace as other patrons skirted around them. "Weird," I said. But even as I said this I couldn't help but think it probably wasn't any weirder than spending all your time trying to kill imaginary monsters.

By Thursday morning, I was certain my headache was a sign that my death was imminent. I tried to imagine what the ravaged inside of my skull must look like by now. Deprived of caffeine, all the important pathways and circuits had shriveled shut. Whole regions of my brain were falling into dry and dusty ruin. The only thing that got me out of bed was the unappealing alternative of lying there all day, staring at the ceiling, waiting for the end to come.

I took an Uber to work again, skipping breakfast and stumbling past the girl at her podium with an impatient wave of my ID. I had no DragonFire cans to stash, so I merely fumbled with my locker until I freed my work machine and stomped with it over to a free station at the end of a long table. I was aware of the stares of my co-workers as I blearily logged in to gaze with murderous intensity at the spinning icon, waiting for my first assignment. After the presentation during which Tony had ambushed me with his challenge and I had accepted it out of pure shock, several people had informed me that my progress was inspirational, that I gave them hope, that they couldn't wait to see how giving up DragonFire would launch me into even better health. Now, I was painfully aware of how I must look. My eyes were red and there was something wrong with my vision. It seemed the edges of my eyes were dancing with strange lights and odd, fuzzy patches. There was nothing to be done about it, I decided, but ignore the stares and pretend I felt perfectly normal.

On the screen in front of me, the narrow, chirpy Humani Sans font greeted me by name. When I clicked the button that said 'Next,' a new screen appeared. This one prompted me to enter my progress on my "Give up DragonFire" goal. I entered a zero in the box for cans of DragonFire consumed in the last 24 hours which, at the very least, did give me a small feeling of satisfaction. While my step count and sleep logs were only visible to my BodPod friends, my challenge progress could be seen by every employee at Humanilism.

My daily entry completed, I continued to my work assignment. Once again, I faced the spinner. I waited. My phone suddenly dinged. I looked down to see the message from BodPod. "Sophia221 has sent you a friend request."

"You've got to be kidding me," I muttered under my breath. I looked up. On the other side of the open office, Sophia was looking straight at me and smiling. Resisting the urge to groan with despair, I accepted the request. Then I silenced my phone, setting it face down on the table next to me.

My first assignment was ad review. I worked for about an hour, narrowing my focus down to the words on the screen. Most ads, I approved. A few I adjusted for grammar problems and sent back to their makers. A few others I flagged for a superior to look at. As I hit my stride, I forgot about my headache and Tony's obnoxious challenge. I forgot about all the missed calls on my phone, the swaddled furniture in my living room, the strange drink with Hawkeyez777 and our stilted conversation, which had yielded no new information about him other than that he'd never ridden a horse, had never initiated a romantic relationship with anyone in the *Heroes of the Totem Spirit* environment, and was curious about the impact of MMPORGs on social development. That last bit had slipped out when I'd said something about our social indicator bar filling up as the night progressed. He'd tossed it out casually, sounding very academic, then backpedaled when I pressed him, spouting inane comments like, "It's weird no one knows anyone for real," and, "Like I could pass you on the street and we'd never know."

It had been a strange way to spend a couple of hours, but not bad. When I'd finally said I had to go, there had been this strange, jerky moment of hesitation before Hawkeyez777 had asked if I'd like to meet again for drinks in a few days. I'd accepted, more out of confusion than any real desire to spend more time with him in that context.

I'd gone to bed at a reasonable hour but spent quite a while lying in the dark, my head full of thoughts of the warrior and his wolf, the missed calls on my phone, Grant's unanswered texts, my canceled lessons, my canceled dinner with Gregory. My brother, so far, didn't seem suspicious. But if I pulled out on two dinners in a row, he'd come looking for me. He knew the signals, knew what it looked like when I started to fall apart. Again.

So it was a nice break, in a way, to simplify my existence down to reading ads, looking for errors, ferreting out the trolls. I'd almost achieved a state of relaxation, or something close, when a little box popped up in the corner of my screen. This was the intraoffice communication system. It could be used by management to send messages to workers. This one was apparently from 'Front Desk,' but that was all the information I could get before clicking it. I could not click on it until I approved or denied my current ad.

Being careful not to rush, I read the ad a few times: an inane bit of copy advertising life-coaching that was just cheesy enough I worried it was a secret message for something far more nefarious. At last, however, I had to conclude I had no grounds to flag it. I clicked 'Approve.' Then I clicked 'Pause,' to take a break, and opened the message from the desk. It was brief. "Visitor for you in the public lounge."

My tenuous feeling of contentment vanished. My heart began to hammer and my headache surged back full bore. I stood in a jerk, then crouched down to type, "Be right out." I clicked the 'Take a Break' button on my ads interface, which would remove me from the active queue. Then I turned, heart pounding, and headed for the door.

The public lounge was the place security stuck unauthorized visitors. No one who was not an employee or invited guest was allowed into the office, so anyone who turned up unexpectedly was funneled here. It was a large, tastefully decorated room with a handful of nooks separated by folding paper screens, so employees who might be having unexpected or sensitive conversations could do so with a modicum of privacy.

Currently, the lounge was empty except for one figure. I recognized her with a frisson of mixed emotions, too muddled and complicated to parse into any kind of order. She stood there, examining a painting on the wall, her graceful, willowy figure as elegant as ever, wearing stylish jeans with expensive boots, and a flowy, white top. Ungraciously, I thought, *She must have a new man in her life.*

My mother turned. Her hair, as light and fine as Gregory's, caught the muted light. It had always struck me as both illogical and incredibly unfair that someone so deceitful, so cruel, so violent, could also be beautiful.

"Faith, darling," she said the moment I stepped into the room, the smooth planes of her face breaking into a radiant smile. "It's so good to see you." She stepped forward as if to offer an embrace.

I shriveled inside, feeling the familiar tug and pull on my emotions. It was so difficult, so impossible, not to be drawn in. *Think of Gregory,* I reminded myself. *Think of his scar.*

Memories rose up behind my eyes—the broken bottle, the blood, the iron tang in my mouth, the gagging flavor of fear.

I stepped back, crossing my arms. "Candace." I used her name instead of any version of "mom," which she hated. "I did not invite you to come here. It's a violation of the restraining order for you contact me or approach me. I've been keeping a record of your calls. Now I have the corroboration of the staff here. I will be reporting this."

Something flickered in my mother's eyes, a tiny flaw, a crack, in her smooth exterior. Here in public, she would never show her true colors, never seem anything but loving and reasonable and beautiful. Which meant anyone watching the two of us talk would conclude I was the jerk.

My mother sighed, her slender shoulders sagging beneath the flowing white top. "I should have known better than to hope we might be able to move forward and leave the past behind." Her tone was full of gentle regret. I felt the tug again, remembering other things from our childhood.

She could be a blast, our mother. There were the days we had turned the entire kitchen into an art experiment, painting the floor by sliding around on sponges, our bare feet and legs becoming covered in splatters and smears of color. There were the crazy games she would invent out of thin air, Gregory and me rushing to fulfill her bizarre rules, laughing so hard we could hardly breathe.

No. I pulled myself up short, refusing to remember. Because for every one of those good times, there were a dozen others. Nights Gregory scrounged in the cupboards, cooking the bottoms of several abandoned bags of rice after picking the little brown beetles out, or refusing to eat his half of a frozen burrito and then soothing me when I cried myself to sleep listening to the growling of his empty stomach. Days going to school in clothing that no longer fit. Evenings locked in the bathroom, a chair dragged in from the kitchen braced beneath the door while our mother shrieked and raged on the other side.

"If you don't leave now," I said, "I'm going to call security."

She sighed again, her mouth going hard around the edges. Reaching into a spangled clutch she wore on a thin strap around one shoulder, she pulled out an envelope. Her tone was both hurt and aggrieved. "I thought you might like to know. I've heard from your father."

She extended the envelope. When I failed to move to accept it, she set it down on a small table nearby. Then she turned, white shirt fluttering like a halo of light, and strode out the door.

I stared at the envelope. It was a bland, innocuous thing, white with nothing on its front at all except the word "Faith" written in my mother's flowing script. Even after all this time, she knew me well. If there was one thing that could entice me to let my mother back into my life, it was this.

Still, I wasn't stupid. I'd been tricked by my mother enough times—duped, manipulated, played. I did not open the envelope at work that day. I shoved it into my bag and did my best to return my focus to where it belonged. When I was done with my Interactions for the day, I went home, fished the envelope out of my bag, and stuck it in the top drawer of my desk. Then I logged into HotTS and played for hours.

Hawkeyez777 was logged in also. We'd achieved a new status as "friends" thanks to our time together in the social zone. This had granted us the ability to see whether or not the other was online. As I ventured into a portal—one of the three I'd gained access to after defeating the spider forest but still hadn't explored very much—I sometimes looked at the glowing green dot next to his name. Who was Hawkeyez777? He'd seemed like any normal guy during our conversation. Except when he hadn't. There had been these moments, popping up here and there between safely bland topics, when he shifted somehow, becoming suddenly more mature, using a more fluid, educated style of speaking. It was disconcerting when it happened, and it never lasted long, but it made me feel, for the first time, the strangeness of this thing we did. It was like a masked ball times 1000%. One thing I hadn't detected at all, however, was the slightest hint of flirtiness. This left me feeling a strange blend of relief alongside a vague and irrational sense of rejection.

After my avatar materialized in front of the entry portal, I went to my profile. I checked it over for sensitive information, but there was very little. I'd entered the minimum required to create an account. Although *Heroes of the Totem Spirit* made you use your real name corroborated by some form of ID, this was automatically set to private status, so no one but you could see it. Then there was your public profile, which didn't have to match your private data in the slightest. As I skimmed through the meager facts the game knew about me, I reassured myself that it wasn't anywhere near enough for anyone in the game to know who I was IRL.

Still, I felt oddly self-conscious as I moved into the game world, running into a little canyon full of bouncing fluffballs that looked harmless until they opened red maws and tried to bite off your legs. Buttercup and I mowed through them without trouble, all the while aware of the fact that Hawkeyez777 knew I was online, even if he didn't know where I was.

On my desk, my phone beeped. It was a text, which I ignored until I'd cleared the combat zone and received the 'Progress Saved' message. Then I looked at the message. It was her, of course, not even bothering to pretend now that she wasn't breaking rules. "I'll need an answer by tomorrow." Unsurprised, I set the phone back down. Patience had never been one of my mother's virtues.

I moved on, finding a nest of bandits whose leader challenged me to a duel, then cheated by calling in reinforcements when it looked like he would lose. I annihilated all my foes with my double slash charge attack. That victory netted me a healing potion, which was always welcome. I continued on, feeling rather pleased with myself. But the longer I played, the more the weight of the envelope seemed to increase in my mind, like a brick of some strange metal that gets heavier the longer it's left in the dark. At last, I exited a combat zone and rolled my chair back, sitting for a moment to stare at the front of my desk.

My father. He was a man I had never met and who, according to my mother, did not know or care about my existence. He'd known Gregory, briefly, but hadn't cared about him either. The way she told the story, he and my mom had never married but they'd been involved for a few years. Then he'd realized being a father was too much work. She hadn't heard from him since he walked out on us, and had no means of tracking him down.

We had no way of knowing whether or not her story was true. Given her propensity to lie on other topics, even as kids, we'd thought it unlikely. And so, one favorite way Gregory and I had used to pass the time was to make up stories—alternative explanations for our father's conspicuous absence in our lives. Some of them involved his heroic death, others memory loss caused by a tragic accident. But even us—kids with no shortage of ingenuity—found it difficult to craft a story in which he was alive and well and not a total jerk.

The brick in my mind grew heavier. I reached out at last and yanked open the drawer. On top of the rolling pencils, jumbled rubber bands and sticky pad notebooks, it was there. I picked it up, slammed the drawer, and ripped the envelope open, surprised to see my hands were trembling, surprised my heart was pounding, that I was seeing red. *How dare he?* I thought. *After all these years of silence.*

Inside, there was a newspaper clipping. On top of that, a note, this also written in my mother's hand. "He's come back to Tucson," it said. That was all.

My rage dialing back a notch, I peeled the note off the clipping. The headline read: *Renowned Behavioral Psychologist Says Other Worlds Inform New Social Trends.*

Sitting back in my chair, I skimmed the article but gleaned little more than the name Professor Jason Hawkins. On the back was another sticky note, also written by my mother. "Let me know if you want to meet him."

I made myself slow down and read the whole thing closely. When I was done, I sat back in my chair, stunned. Then I reached up and hastily logged out of HotTS.

I jerked in my chair, startling at the sound of a loud rapping on my front door. Wide-eyed in the dim light, I glanced towards the exit of my office nook as if I could somehow divine who stood outside by peering through walls. This was the third time in as many days I'd heard a knock. To the previous two, I hadn't responded. This one, though. This one sounded insistent.

I returned my attention to my screen, but the rapping came again. On my desk, my phone gave a buzz. I'd put it on silent to escape the constant ringing, my mother growing angry as her noose failed to close around my neck. It was her now outside, I was sure, having somehow discovered my home address as well as my place of work.

More banging, and a raised voice. That piqued my interest. My mother only yelled when she was drunk, and she was careful never to drink in public. Throwing a fit in full view of anyone who might be passing by in the apartment complex was not characteristic. I disengaged from the gnome creatures I'd been fighting and retreated from the combat zone I'd been trying to clear.

By the time I'd dispatched the enemies who followed me out of the quest zone, the banging had stopped. My phone, however, was all but dancing across my desk as it vibrated from one incoming text after another. I stared at it for a moment, then snatched it off the desk. My lock screen was cluttered with messages I had been ignoring, both from my mother and from Gregory. The former, I had not responded to since she'd given me the envelope. The second, I was keeping at arm's length by the skin of my teeth, and only because he'd spent the weekend in Phoenix for a show opening. He'd told me in no uncertain terms we *would* have our usual dinner tomorrow, even if I had to eat propped up in bed. He was still under the impression I was ill.

But the most recent texts were neither from my mother nor my brother. They were from an unknown number with a local area code. For a moment, I thought my mom had gotten a new burner cell, something she did any time I blocked her number. Then I read the first message. "Jordan, it's Nora from the Tipped Z."

The second, sent a few second later, said, "Open up." The third, "Look, I know you're in there. We need to talk."

Bewildered, I stumbled out of my nook and into the kitchen. It was a mess. A few dirty dishes lay scattered across the counter next to a pizza box with a few slices inside. This sat beside the discarded case of DragonFire I'd left behind when I'd gutted it in order to stow its contents in the refrigerator. My BodPod lay beside it, where I'd dropped it after unstrapping it from my wrist.

That had been Friday, after the contents of the clipping had led me to stunned understanding. Completely overwhelmed and deeply rattled, I'd decided Luke Rastenhaus and his Peer Challenges could eat my shorts. I'd taken an Uber to the grocery store and purchased three cases of DragonFire. I had no intention of ever giving it up again.

Now it was Monday, mid-morning. I was not at work because I had not bothered to go in yet. I had done nothing but game and drink over-caffeinated beverages all weekend, once more canceling my lesson with Erin. I'd also figured out how to set my gaming mode to private so even my so-called friends in the game couldn't see I was online unless they physically ran into me.

Still, I'd played these last days with a jittery feeling, sticking to obscure, out-of-the-way, unimportant quest zones and backwater portals, nevertheless fearing I'd run into Hawkeyez777 at any moment. What would I do if that happened? Logout, I decided. But what if I was in a combat zone? That was harder. Avoiding him wasn't worth the loss of Buttercup, was it?

I became vaguely aware of the disaster of my apartment as I shuffled towards the door. It dawned on me that I, too, was a mess. I hadn't really slept or eaten in days. I'd been drinking DragonFire non-stop since I'd crawled out of bed this morning. I was in a full-on state of total dysfunction.

I could have simply failed to answer the door. There was something formidable about Nora's personality, but she was not a human battering ram. Short of breaking a window and climbing in, she couldn't force access to me.

But she was here. Nora, a person I had spoken to only a handful of times but whose horse had taught me many things. Nora, Erin's sister-in-law, Grant's muddled cousin of a sort. Why was she trying to root me out? Curiosity was enough to make me reach the door, turn the deadbolt, and crack it open.

Nora was there, sitting on my stoop. She was facing away from me, holding a phone in a brightly colored case. She was texting someone, but she looked over her shoulder when she heard the latch. "Oh good," she said, heaving herself to her feet. In the two months since I'd first met her, her belly had transformed from a cute bump to a significant protrusion. She rose, sighed, and stepped towards the door. "Can I come in?"

It was a warm day, despite being November, with a clear blue sky and full sun. I am not a socially gifted individual, but even I can see that refusing to let a pregnant woman in out of the sun is a non-starter. I moved aside, wincing as Nora stepped through the door and stood for a moment, disoriented by the total gloom. "Wow," she said as I closed the door behind her. "Have you really been sick, or is this something else?"

It was a perceptive question. I'd used the excuse of being under the weather to cancel my second lesson with Erin but had sensed skepticism in her reply. At the time, I'd wondered if I was being paranoid. Now, Nora's presence in my apartment suggested I'd failed to fool them.

"Can I offer you a glass of water?"

As I deflected the question, I moved into the kitchen. Nora waddled around the living room furniture—still made lumpy and translucent by its wrappings—and rotated the blinds. Light poured in, blinding in its pure brilliance. She shoved the blinds to the side and moved on to the next window.

"Do you have any tea?" she said. "Decaf."

I stared at her. She was a tall woman, normally lean but made larger by the pregnancy. I tried to imagine barging into a near stranger's apartment and asking for tea. It didn't compute.

Still, I found myself opening the cupboard Gregory kept stocked in the hopes I would occasionally consume liquid that wasn't DragonFire. As more light flooded in, I read a few labels. "Rooibos Red," I said. "I think that's decaf? Or here's peppermint, green tea, and something called Mango Tango."

Nora left the living room and proceeded to the kitchen, continuing on her quest to illuminate every corner of my pathetic existence. "Mango Tango," she laughed. "Let's try that."

I had to rummage around for a while before I could find the kettle. By the time I had the water on, Nora had seated herself on one of my stools and was watching me with her too-perceptive gaze. I put the pizza in the fridge, broke down the DragonFire box, cleared away the other random items on the counter, and set out two of Gregory's hand-thrown mugs. As the water in the kettle began to pop and hiss, Nora skewered me with her level blue stare. "Okay, then, Jordan. Why don't you tell me what's really going on?"

My name isn't Jordan, I thought. *It's Faith.*

Chapter 12

In spite of myself, I told Nora about my mother. I started without much conviction, skirting the truth, sticking to evasions and platitudes. But as the water came to a boil and I poured it over the tea bags, Nora listened to everything I said and honed in like a scent hound on the things I glossed over, the details I left out. Somehow, before I knew it, I'd given her a more complete picture of my childhood than I'd ever shared with anyone but Gregory.

She'd started out seeming brittle, maybe even annoyed. But as she rooted one fact after another out of my reluctant mouth, something in her changed and softened. By the time I told her about the night my mother had nearly killed her own son with a broken bottle, the night he'd refused to let me call 911 because he'd been afraid we'd be placed in foster care and separated, the night I'd sat with him, both of us soaked in his blood, sobbing as together we tried to patch the terrible hole in his side, I thought I even saw her eyes go slick with tears.

"And that was the easy stuff," I went on. My momentum up, I could not seem to stop talking. "When she was angry and violent, it was easy because you could defend yourself. It was the other times it was hard— when she was loving but then said things, terrible little jibes and barbs she'd slip in around your armor. She always knows how to strike where it hurts. Worse, she takes care to seem not just normal, but loving and beautiful to everyone else. So even if you try to confide in someone, they think you're exaggerating or confused."

I thought of the note, her graceful handwriting. Before I could stop myself or think through possible ramifications, I said, "And now she's trying to convince me some professor at the U of A is my long-lost father. But the joke's on her, this time. If she's telling the truth, I already know him. Or, at least, I kind of know him."

I fell silent, thinking again of what I'd learned in the article, the section in which the interviewer had asked about the professor's methods. His answer: "I game myself, of course. Quite a lot, though with different objectives than most players." When asked what game he was currently studying, he said, "It's an MMPORG called *Heroes of the Totem Spirit*. The developers have been really cool about my research, actually. They've given me a deeper level of access than is afforded to other players so I can collect more data. It's all anonymized, of course, but it's been really useful, nonetheless."

Nora was holding her teacup between two hands. We were on the second cup by now. She'd started to shift uncomfortably on her stool from time to time. She looked around the apartment, seeming to take in the contrast between the hand-thrown mugs and the dirty dishes, the swaddled furniture and the nice tile floors. She noted the BodPod on the counter. Her eyes returned, at last, to me. "So," she said, "to sum up, you have a mother who is emotionally and physically abusive, who has recently reappeared in your life despite a restraining order and is trying to blackmail you back into a relationship with her by offering up this professor as the father-figure you've longed for your entire life. Your resistance mechanism is to hide from her, which unfortunately means shutting down emotionally and withdrawing from everything and everyone else in your life as well."

I blinked, stunned. I wanted to argue with her. That was far too simplistic an explanation. She didn't know what it was like, trying to talk to my mother. The way she always made you feel wrong, even if you won an argument. The way she always made you feel brutish, even if she was the one behaving badly. She couldn't possibly imagine growing up with the persistent hope that a benevolent father would swoop in and fix everything, only for him to never appear.

Sitting up straighter on her stool, Nora pressed both hands to her lower back. She glanced pointedly at the jumbled living room. "Are those furniture items coming or going?"

I was still stunned, still at a loss for words, still half offended by her tidy summation of my life's problems. Nora glanced at me, stood up, and fished a utility knife out of her leather purse. As she approached the furniture, she gave me an inquisitive look. I nodded and she knelt with a groan to begin slicing tape.

Seeing a pregnant woman working on a task I'd been neglecting for days was enough to snap me out of my strange stupor. I found my tongue at last. "No, no. This is ridiculous. You sit down. I'll unwrap them." I walked up to her, hand extended for the knife.

She stood with alacrity, making me wonder if the groan had been theatrical in nature. But she snapped the blade shut and picked up her cell phone instead. "Actually," she said, "I have a better idea."

Five minutes later, Grant was there. Nora answered his knock because I had hastily dashed into the bathroom to brush my hair and teeth and stare into the mirror in futile desperation. I looked terrible. Pale skin. Rings under my eyes. Too wan. Too thin. But there was nothing to be done about any of that now.

By the time I emerged he was there, looking as handsome and perfect as ever. At least, that was what I thought at first glance. But as he greeted Nora and accepted the utility knife, his gaze flitted to me. Was it just me, or did his eyes have a bruised look to them? There had always been that sharpness to his expression, but now there was something else there, too. Something worse. He looked a little dull, a little haunted.

He greeted me with a casual, "Hey Jordan." As I stood there, flooded with memories of his mouth on mine, his hands on my shoulders, the leather and oil scent of him surrounding me, he crouched and deftly cut away the protective wrapping on my new furniture. I watched him work. His forearms were well-muscled and tan, his movements swift and certain. I thought of what Erin had told me about his accident. *It was six months before he could walk again.*

I felt a sudden flush of embarrassment. I still didn't know what had happened to him—not exactly. But whatever it was must have been terrible. Yet here he was, back on his feet, fighting, refusing to give in. I'd never been the one my mother hurt, not really. Her target had always been Gregory. When she went after me, it had always been to get to him, to hurt him, to mobilize him into rallying to my defense. And yet I was the one who broke, who failed, who had to be propped back onto my feet time and time again.

The silence would have been awkward if not for the squeak and pop of the plastic Grant removed from the furniture in great swathes. The moment he had the first chair unwrapped, Nora collapsed down into it with her tea, sighing and propping her feet up on my old coffee table, which was shoved in next to the new one and would need to be disposed of somehow. I hovered back by the counter, trying to decide how this had happened, how I'd transitioned from sitting alone in my office nook to having my home invaded by two 5th generation ranchers. Belatedly, I said to Grant, "Do you want some tea?"

"Sure he does," Nora said before he could answer. In the absence of any protest from Grant, I turned around to put the kettle on once more.

I stood awkwardly on the sidewalk in front of my apartment complex in my riding jeans and boots, feeling conspicuous despite the fact that plenty of people in Tucson wore boots as a rule rather than the exception. Squinting into the afternoon sun, I felt like an albino bear rudely extracted from hibernation and forced to face the light. It was Tuesday afternoon. I'd gotten home from work a short while before. As soon as I'd arrived, I'd texted Nora, as promised, and she'd texted back. "On my way." I was going to the Tipped Z to ride Sally because Nora had insisted she had nothing better to do than come and get me anyway.

My living room, I'd been forced to admit, looked quite nice with the new furniture. Grant had finished unpacking it the previous afternoon, arranging the pieces to Nora's satisfaction and even going so far as to haul all the wrappings to the dumpster. I'd shoved the old coffee table into the corner in the kitchen area, where it was at least out of the way. Then Grant had returned, downed his cold tea in three huge swigs, and bolted for the door. Nora, standing in the living room surveying her handiwork, had said, "You're going to need something big and bold for this space," gesturing at the large, blank wall, mimicking Gregory almost perfectly.

Watching the door close behind Grant, I'd said, "I do. I mean, I will. I mean, my brother's promised me something."

Nora had nodded, seeming satisfied, then turned to set her empty mug on the counter. Once again, she'd skewered me with that blue-eyed gaze. "What time do you get off work tomorrow?"

I'd fumbled through an explanation about Humanilism's Interactions system. She'd frowned, taking it in, and then said, "So, text me when you're home and I'll head over. You're riding Sally tomorrow, broken vehicle or no."

I'd found it impossible to argue. She'd gone, then, giving my hand a squeeze as she headed for the door. Her parting words were delivered in a soft, sympathetic voice. "Forcing you into seclusion every time she reappears is how she continues to control you, you know." I'd closed the door behind her, then walked into the living room and collapsed onto my new couch.

Now, I waited on the curb, scanning traffic for the telltale rusty pickup. Instead, a sleek white SUV ghosted up in front of me, Nora waving from the driver's seat. "Don't worry," she said as I opened the door, "its Erin's car. The Power Wagon lives on, but she refuses to let me take it on public roadways with her children inside."

As I settled into my seat, I glanced into the back. Two child seats were strapped in place, one containing the tiny cowboy, the other his infant sister. I expected him to say "ma'am" or something equally adorably stereotypical, but he was absorbed in the contemplation of a set of rattling wooden rings.

I buckled in. Nora pulled out into traffic. "It's a puzzle," she said conversationally. "My great-grandfather whittled it out of the tree they had to cut down to build the ranch house. Or so the story goes. Every member of my family seems to find it compelling at that age."

Outside, traffic drifted by, sun winking off windshields, the mountains rearing on the horizon. We headed against the flow. Soon were bouncing along a dirt road I didn't recognize. "Wait," I said in confusion. "I thought we were going to Tipped Z."

"Nope," Nora said, tilting her head towards me with a smile. "We're going to where I live. The Rocking J."

She explained then, about Wyatt's connection to the Tipped Z. The Tipped Z, she told me, had been built by a rancher who'd come down from Wyoming with a good friend, looking for affordable land. That friend had founded the Rocking J right next door. The two men had lived and worked side by side, building their ranches, raising families. For generations, the partnership held strong. But then, at last, Wyatt's father had grown up and decided he wasn't interested in ranching. He sold the land—against the young Wyatt's protests—to developers. All that was left of the Rocking J now was a single house on a few acres, where Nora and Wyatt lived.

It was a sad story, but Nora told it without apparent rancor. As we whipped around a bend in the narrow road, going a bit faster than felt entirely safe, a little house came into view. It was nestled against the back of a long, high ridge, utterly secluded from the surrounding housing developments. We pulled up outside a carport next to a pipe corral containing two horses. The house lay directly ahead. To the left stood a gate, a defined trail leading away into the empty land on the other side of a wire fence. "That's the Tipped Z," Nora said. "The back of it, anyway. So Wyatt just saddles up and rides to work every morning." She grinned, opening the back door and working on the buckles that held the baby in place. "You can let him out if you want," she said, gesturing to the mini cowboy.

Feeling awkward and self-conscious, I opened the back door. Little Garth looked up at me with serious blue eyes, still clutching the wooden rings in one small hand. I pressed the obvious buckle. To my relief, the elaborate harness came apart easily. I was able to extract his short limbs and scoop him out of the seat.

He was heavier than I'd expected, but patient as I caught his boot on the lip of the seat, reoriented him to free it and, at last, set him on the ground. As soon as he was upright, he set out towards the house with such speed and purpose, I started after him in dismay. But a quick glance at Nora showed me she was smiling, and I saw it was a dog the boy was going for, who had emerged from beneath the porch to lick the child's face, wiggling all over. "Lop is supposed to be a working dog," Nora confessed to me as she balanced the infant girl on her hip. "But he's turning into more a nursemaid these last few months."

I looked around the scrubby desert landscape. The house was modest and simple with a weathered look to the adobe that made me think it had been here a long time. But the roof was new, the yard was tidy, the horse pens clean. The massive, rusty Dodge parked out front lent the scene a sense of picturesque tranquility. I felt a pang of envy. And also confusion. Why had Nora brought me here?

As Lop flopped into the dust of the driveway and Garth plunked down next to him with a squeal of delight, Nora approached the pipe corral. The two horses stood in the shade, tails swishing at the lazy flies. "The little one is Shiner," Nora said. "He's a stud prospect Clint and Wyatt are considering as a sire for one of the ranch lines, but he's just two and they only breed proven bridle horses, so he's got a while to grow into himself. For now he's over here, keeping Balin company."

I looked more closely at the two horses. One was indeed shorter and leaner than the other, his chest narrow, his eyes curious and youthful. That one took a step in our direction, ears forward.

I looked at the other horse. "Balin?" I said. "Like the dwarf?"

It seemed an odd name for the creature in question. He was a tall, rangy animal, with leaner lines and a flatter head than I'd seen in most of the Tipped Z Quarter Horses. He was a blue roan, his coat a deep black scattered over with a layer of silvery white hairs.

"That's Grant's horse," Nora said. "He brought him down from Wyoming when he came to work here with us. His family lost their ranch. It was called the Circle T, and they'd been struggling to keep it afloat the last many years. The day before Grant's accident, he and his mother had finally decided to sell. So he can't ever go home now, not really. All he has left of the place he grew up is that horse."

We stood a moment, listening to the giggling child as the dust rose softly on the slight breeze. The sun was bright in my eyes. I felt my heart inexplicably begin to beat a little faster. "I thought Grant didn't ride anymore."

Nora adjusted the child on her hip, bouncing her in a little rhythm. "He doesn't," she said. "But he tries. Every morning, he's here at sunrise. He does groundwork, saddles up, does everything short of climb into the saddle. Balin is a bridle horse, just like his brother, Dwalin, was. They were full brothers, Grant's pride and joy."

I felt a strange, mounting sense of dread. Behind us, the dog stood up, shook, and sneezed. I said, "And where is Dwalin?"

Nora turned and looked at me. "Dead," she said. "Killed in the accident that nearly killed Grant as well."

Dead. The word had such finality. It hung in the air between us, seeming to mute the call of quail and mourning doves. Lop stood up and walked off, heading towards the gate and the path beyond. Garth got up also, dusted off his jeans, and walked over to solemnly reach up and take Nora's hand as if understanding the gravity of what we were discussing. I stared at the blue roan, thinking of Grant's careful way of walking, the bruised look in his eyes sometimes.

Nora wasn't looking at me. Her eyes were raised to the horizon, the little humped hill that separated the quaint, secluded house from the shiny new subdivision on the other side. "We all have our demons," she said at last. "We all carry the weight of loss. Grant may not look it, but he's fragile right now. I ask only one thing of you, Jordan. Be straight with him. Either go for it, or don't, but don't dance back and forth with him. Don't leave him hanging if you're not going to give him a chance."

I flushed, feeling the sting of the reprimand. I thought of our silly game unloading the car, the plastic lightsaber, the heady kiss. I could think of only one way to excuse my behavior. "I didn't mean to," I said. "It's just ... he deserves someone better than me. Someone sturdier. Someone more whole."

Behind us, there was the clang of a gate latch, followed by the squeal of hinges. I turned to see Erin on Esperanza, riding through the gate as she ponied Sally behind.

"There's your ride," Nora said. "But I think it's up to Grant to decide what he does or doesn't deserve. Don't you?"

With that, she turned, walking across the driveway to greet her sister-in-law. Erin swung down from the horse to gather her children in a quick hug, handing the two get-down ropes to Nora. I hung back, turning again to look at Balin. The horse stood with one hip cocked, dozing. Nora's words seemed to scroll on repeat in my mind. *Two bridle horses, one of them dead. Grant's pride and joy. He can't ever go home. He's fragile right now.*

Abruptly, I thought of Buttercup. The real Buttercup. The horse I had fallen in love with at the camp. I could still remember the day I received the terrible news that the camp was folding. It hadn't come from Maria. She had been inexplicably absent from the camp the last few weeks. I hadn't been out in nearly a week myself as I'd been busy with school and recovering from a cold.

I saw the story on the home page of the Tucson paper I cruised by most mornings in those days. It was a tiny snippet shoved in between more important stories. I could remember the slow donning horror in my sternum as I clicked the link and learned how the land and buildings had been sold to a developer. The stock was to be auctioned off. The article had a date and time.

At first, I tried to convince myself it would be okay. Maria had told me I'd never lose Buttercup, after all. How often had I replayed that scene in my mind—reassured myself with the words she'd spoken? She'd *promised* Buttercup would be mine eventually, one way or another. And I'd believed her. Because up until that point, the camp had been the one solid thing in my life, the one constant other than Gregory.

I called Maria only to find her number disconnected. When I called the camp, no one answered at all. When I tried to go to the ranch, I found the gates closed and locked.

I was in college by then. It was a long time since Maria had been my neighbor. I actually hadn't seen her around the camp for quite a while, I realized as panic began to set in. Our relationship had changed in the last few years. We were still friendly, but I had placed distance between us. It was embarrassing, now that I was older, to remember all Maria had seen of my dysfunctional childhood.

I tried going to her old house only to find it empty. Standing on her dark stoop, I realized she was gone. Maria would not stand and fight for me. Buttercup would be sold, along with all the other horses. The horse I had believed was mine would be taken from me, along with the camp and everything that place had allowed me to become.

I'd gone to that auction, clinging to a terrible shred of hope. At first I focused on the crowd, searching for Maria's quick smile, her enthusiastic wave, ready to hear her explanation of how we were going to buy Buttercup now, here, together, and take her somewhere safe.

But Maria wasn't there. I watched horse after familiar horse as they were sent into the little pen, herded around, the known facts about them read off on the loudspeaker. Most of them didn't go for much. I learned afterward that any sold for less than $500 most likely went to a kill buyer. Buttercup, being on the young side, with good conformation, and a palomino to boot, was less in danger of that fate. She sold for $1500. It was a sum that, in retrospect, was not that much for a nice horse. At the time, though, it was an amount as impossible for me to imagine having at my disposal as a private jet.

We all carry the weight of loss. What a strange way to put it. I looked at Nora, who stood with Sally, running a gentle hand along the mare's neck. When she saw me looking, she headed in my direction and handed me the horsehair get-down. I accepted the rope, more out of reflex than conviction. "I still have a long way to go before my due date," she said, giving her belly a fond pat. "Because of one little hiccup in the beginning, the doctor says no riding until after the delivery. Period. So I expect you to keep this girl in shape for me."

Then she was moving off, collecting the baby from Erin and shooing Garth towards the house. Erin glanced towards me, smiled, and swung into the saddle. I slid the get-down through my belt and mounted as well, remembering my confusion that first day when I'd been presented with Duke and the first hackamore I'd ever seen. I was used to it now, all the ways in which riding at the Tipped Z was different from riding at camp.

Erin walked Esperanza in my direction. "Good to see you, Jordan. We've missed you around here." Her eyes were warm, her words entirely sincere. I wondered at them. Missed me? These people? How was that possible? They were all so competent, so self-sufficient. What use could they possibly have for someone like me?

I looked past her at the low hills, the mountains shouldering up beyond. "I missed this place too."

It was true. The truth of the statement crystalized for me as I spoke. I reached down and set my hand on Sally's warm neck. Then, before I even knew I planned to say anything at all, I added, "Is Grant a Tolkien fan?"

Erin, who'd turned Esperanza for the gate, gave me a quizzical look. "Tolkien?" she repeated. "The writer?"

I blushed, feeling foolish but nodding in the affirmative. We reached the gate, which Erin had left open. We rode through and she stopped, waiting for me to clear it, then deftly stepped her horse over and swung it closed again.

Erin laughed. "I have no idea," she said. "We've never really talked about books."

She didn't know. But I did. It was obvious he was a Tolkien fan. Why else would he name his horses after a set of dwarves? As we rode off into the empty scrub desert, I found myself wondering how many 5th generation ranchers had read *The Hobbit*.

"Is he scared to ride, then?" This question popped out as the previous one had, completely without my consent. "Grant, I mean?"

Erin moved Esperanza into a trot. I cued Sally as well. Together we moved along at an easy pace, the wind sighing in our hair and the dust rising behind. "Not scared, no," she said. "At least, I don't think that's the main problem."

I struggled with that, trying to think what else could be wrong. Physical pain? Flexibility? He seemed fit enough, even if his gait was a little strange.

I waited. After we'd been trotting for a time, Erin glanced over at me, her expression troubled. "I don't know that he'll thank me for telling you this, but you might understand him better if you know. What happened to Grant, his accident, was an act of violence. His family, like ours, has always ranched. They kept cattle, and believe it or not, cattle thieves are still a thing. There's been a resurgence of the problem lately, particularly in small communities with a lot of out-of-the-way pastureland. The thieves just drive up with a truck and trailer, load up a few cattle, and haul them off. A fully grown beef cow is worth $2000 - $2500. A few of those go missing, and most ranches are going to feel it in a major way."

I listened, mesmerized, trying to imagine sneaking onto someone's land and loading up stolen cattle.

Erin was rising and falling with Esperanza's trot, smooth as can be. "Anyway," she went on, "one morning, Grant was out checking fence. He saw a couple guys finishing loading some of his family's cattle in a stock trailer. He was on Dwalin. He came trotting up the road, in the middle of the road, to confront them. They hopped into the cab and pulled out, coming towards him. He kept riding straight at them, determined to force them to stop."

I felt my stomach begin to sour, a sick feeling spreading through my limbs as I imagined Grant astride a beautiful bridle horse, refusing to back down.

Erin's voice was subdued as she finished. "Well," she said, "they didn't."

"Perfect," Gregory said, stepping into my living room to gaze at my new furniture with a strange blend of fondness and incredulity. "These are by Unit, you know. Nice design and solid quality." He stooped as he spoke, running his hand over the gray fabric of my couch. "It's too bad about that ding in the leg, though."

I sat on one of my stools by the counter, watching my brother, wishing there was some way I could spare him from the information that buzzed in my mind like a swarm of angry hornets. Nora's intervention and the trip to the Tipped Z had been a nice break, a temporary reprieve. But now, Gregory was here, in the flesh, not yet knowing what I knew. I had to tell him, but I didn't want to.

Gregory was holding a glass of white wine, looking slim and sophisticated in light slacks and a gray t-shirt. He took after our mother. The resemblance was undeniable. I did not. I had often wondered if this meant I looked like our father.

Gregory settled onto the couch and set his glass on the coffee table. "What are you doing over there? Even attractive furniture is meant to be sat on, Jor." His tone was playful, his eyes alight. I felt dread roll over inside me like a monster surfacing from the black depths of the ocean. As soon as I opened my mouth, as soon as I told him, that light would go out. She'd have ensnared him again, too.

I thought of Nora's words. *Forcing you into seclusion every time she reappears is how she continues to control you.*

But Nora had never met my mother. She hadn't been there through the manic ups and downs of our childhood, didn't know what it was like to be raised by a master of manipulation.

Gregory knew. And even now, he had begun to suspect. I could see it in the tightening of his jaw, the new tension beginning to build in his shoulders. He sat, his posture perfect, as usual, but growing a little more rigid by the moment. "Jor," he said again. "I know you haven't been sick."

I closed my eyes for a moment and stood up from my stool. If I had been a better person, I would have been able to keep this from him, shoulder her reappearance all on my own and spare him from her latest gambit. But I had never been the strong one. I walked into the kitchen, opened a drawer, and pulled out the newspaper clipping. He waited as I approached, accepting the small piece of thin paper when I offered it to him. I watched him read, his eyes darting back and forth, seeking out information that would connect the story to me, to us.

He glanced up when he was finished, a forced smile on his lips. "Are you trying to convince me gaming is a worthwhile practice because someone in academia has decided it's worth studying?"

I walked back to the island and picked up my can of DragonFire. Facing away from him, glaring at the smooth faces of my kitchen cabinets, I dropped the bomb. "She claims he's our father."

Silence. The apartment was well insulated. There was none of the street noise and bustle of my old place. The windows were shut, the fridge didn't rattle. My PC was asleep, its fans still. It was way too quiet. I stood within that quiet for a few heartbeats, giving him time.

When I turned around, Gregory had set the clipping on the coffee table. As it often did when he was stressed, his left hand had strayed to his side, his fingers resting softly on the fabric of his shirt. Underneath, I knew, lay the ragged knot of scar tissue left by the messy wound the two of us had inexpertly patched. He'd been feverish for days after she cut him with the bottle. I'd been certain he would die. But every time I left his side he woke up enough to say to me, "Don't do it. Don't call anyone. I'm going to get better. After that, we're going to leave."

He'd been as good as his word, too. He had, indeed, healed. And as soon as he was up, at age 16, Gregory had dropped out of school, gotten a job, and gotten us our own apartment. Our mother, deep in a binge at that point, hadn't bothered to track us down for months. When she finally found us, she was back on her feet, on the other side of her swing, and in love with her latest gullible benefactor. She'd left us alone for long enough for Gregory to become a legal adult.

But then, she'd fallen apart again. That was when she came back, asking for money, for food, for a place to stay. When Gregory refused to let her move in with us, she set out on her campaign of sabotage.

At first, it was little things. A broken window and a few things missing, small valuables disappearing. We moved and that helped for a while. But then she found us again, and again the problems began. Missing mail. Stolen credit cards. The landlord and neighbors falling for her act every time, letting her in when we weren't there.

We moved again, selecting for barred windows and a secure door. That's when she set our apartment on fire. After Gregory turned her away from our door one day without allowing her to so much as come in, she came back at night, when we were asleep, and punched a smoldering cigarette through a window screen.

And that's why we have a restraining order against our mother.

Gregory shifted on the couch. He didn't look at me. His eyes were distant, perhaps seeing his own version of our shared trauma. "You don't believe her," he said at last. It wasn't a question.

My mother was an accomplished liar. It was how she duped men into supporting her financially sometimes mere days after meeting them. "I don't know if I believe her or not," I admitted. "The thing that's weird, though, is I know him. In the game, I mean. That game he talks about studying, it's the one I play. His handle, it says in the article, is Hawkeyez777. He's a friend of mine."

Gregory looked over at last. There was a building intensity in his eyes. "How many people play this game?" he asked.

I walked to the window. Outside, the sun was throwing warm golden rays across the decorative gravel. "Millions," I said.

Gregory frowned. "So the chances that you met this person by accident, that you just happened to bump into each other, they're..."

"Low," I finished for him. I turned around and leaned against the wall. "Particularly if you factor in the small but relevant detail that he's my *only* friend in the game."

Normally, this would have earned a sarcastic remark of some kind, but Gregory was focused on the puzzle I'd placed before him. "How did you meet him?"

I shrugged, thinking back, trying to remember. "I don't know," I confessed. "I just kept bumping into him. Often when I was in trouble." I remembered the time I tried to defeat the spider forest alone and nearly got myself killed, how his wolf had come bounding over the hills, straight for me. Almost as if he'd known I was there, known I'd needed help.

"You think he knew who you were?" Gregory said.

I gave a small nod. There was no other explanation.

Gregory sat back against the couch cushions, staring up at the ceiling fan. "So either he really is our father," he said, tone solemn, "or he's some poor sot our mother is stringing along for some reason of her own. He's skeptical. Not skeptical enough to dismiss her, but enough to get to know you on his own terms rather than going through her."

I walked over and collapsed onto one of the chairs. Despite looking somewhat stiff, it was surprisingly comfortable. "Yeah," I said. "That's what I think too. Do you want to meet him?"

It took Gregory almost an hour to build his avatar. On the one hand, I could sympathize. I had spent far more than a single hour honing my own appearance. Still, it was difficult to be patient. As he scrolled through the different races, hairstyles, clothing options, and totem partners on my desktop computer, I fired up my laptop and logged into the game. Once in, I moved a short distance from the entry portal and sent Hawkeyez777 a message. I could see by the green dot next to his name that he was online. "Hey," I said, "there's someone I'd like to introduce you to. He's new, so it'll have to be on Char." Char was the first portal all new players got access to. Most experienced players avoided it because it was so crowded with noobs. "Is there a social zone there where you'd like to meet up?"

I sent the message before I could second-guess myself, before I could wonder at the tone I'd taken with him, before I could convince myself I was doing the wrong thing.

"What's your totem partner?" Gregory asked from my office nook. I was in my bedroom, sitting on my sagging old chair in the corner it now occupied next to my closet.

"Horse," I said shortly. Gregory made a small noise halfway between disgust and amusement. "Can I get a flamingo?" he asked. "I've heard those beaks can take a finger off in one lop. They'd be formidable in battle. Particularly with some armor. I bet if..."

"Gregory, come on." I shifted in my chair, trying to ignore the mounting tension in my shoulders. I suspected my brother was taking his sweet time to torment me. Our temperaments, always so different, were often in conflict on points like this one and so many others.

Gregory loved drama, the slow reveal, the gradual increase of anticipation. I liked to get things over with.

"Fine fine fine," he said, waving a hand at the screen as if giving it permission to hang up his coat. "I'll do the fox. Even though that seems generic."

"Good," I said, moving back towards the portal. "What's your handle?"

"GregorThePiebaldPainter," he said just as I saw a tall, slender druid step out of the portal and into the street. A tiny red fox followed him, pouncing on the toe of his boot when he stopped to look around. "Woh," Gregory said, gazing in my direction. "Is that you? Your horse looks like she could eat me for breakfast."

A message from Hawkeyez777 flashed up in the corner of my screen. "Brick and Bones," it said. "Meet you there in 5."

"Follow me," I said to Gregory. Then I stood up to close the bedroom door. "Turn on the mic," I said, pointing. "If we can hear each other in real life as well as in the game, it's going to be crazy confusing."

Gregory watched dubiously from my chair as I shut my bedroom door. I retreated to the far side of the bed, where I turned on my Bluetooth headphones and paired them with my laptop. By the time Gregory and I had found the Brick and Bones, settled into chairs, and declared each other friends, seven minutes had passed. Which meant Hawkeyez777 was late. Not an auspicious start to my supposedly long-lost father's brand new roll in my life.

Each minute dragged by, agonizing in its length. While Gregory fiddled with his controls and watched the interactions in the social zone around us with a mix of wonder and amusement, I stared fixedly at the door, waiting.

"It says I can flirt with you," Gregory said. "His voice came through, scrambled by the default filter so it sounded alien. "My own sister. That's just wrong."

In my bedroom, I sat up straighter and felt my heart begin to pound. The tavern door swung open, revealing the silhouette of the hulking warrior with the shaggy wolf by his side.

"That's him," I said, terse and low. "The guy with the wolf."

There was a pause as Gregory figured out how to scan the room. Then he let out a low whistle. "His wolf looks even meaner than your horse. And the dude. He might not have fangs, but I wouldn't want to bump into him in a dark alley."

Hawkeyez777 approached, passing two nearly identical blonde human women, a shadowy man with a crow on each shoulder, and a table of elves that could have stepped straight out of Rivendell. He reached us, sat down, and did something so that the three of us were suddenly in a group chat interface together, friend bars and all. "Hi Faith," Hawkeyez777 said. "Good to see you."

I froze, going as still and silent as if a rabid dog had just appeared and begun to growl. *Faith.* He'd called me by name. By my real name.

That was impossible.

Impossible, unless he had some kind of deeper access to my life than he'd let on.

I could not see Gregory IRL. He was in the other room. I had no way to share any kind of incredulous look with him. I felt the fluttery edge of panic seize me. If not for my brother's presence, I might have crashed the game right there just to escape.

Whether or not Gregory understood the enormity of the moment, he recovered without missing a beat. "She prefers Jordan," he said. "And I'm her brother, Gregory. I don't really play computer games, but she thought we should meet."

Gregory's avatar extended a hand. Gregory was apparently having no trouble finding his way around the interaction menus. There was a single beat of silence as Hawkeyez777's avatar sat in utter stillness. What was the man doing? Did he realize he'd made a mistake, using my name? Had he figured out I was on to him? Or was he actually on to me, somehow?

The hulking warrior accepted Gregory's handshake and I managed to collect my scattered wits. There are doubtless any number of graceful, logical approaches to take when confronting an online entity who may or may not be the father you've never met. In that moment, however, I could think of none of them. I said, "Do you know someone named Candace Falkenrath?"

Gregory sighed loudly enough to make it through the noise filter on the mic. Hawkeyez777 was very still for a time—so still I found myself wondering if his human operator had fled the scene. Any moment now, the hulking warrior might begin to fade, disintegrating out of his seat as my so-called-father fled the game.

At last, he spoke. "She told you." It wasn't a question. The words sounded both tired and sad despite the gravelly overtones the voice filter put in. "She promised she wouldn't, that she'd give me some time."

He trailed off. I wondered what he was doing in real life. Standing up and pacing around his room? Slumped in his chair? Rubbing his hands through his hair. I'd Googled the name from the article, of course, so I now had a mental picture of what the man who controlled the hulking warrior looked like. Or, at least, as clear a picture as one can get by staring deep into the eyes of snapshots on the internet. He had dark hair with a loose wave, quite similar to mine. His skin was lightly tanned, overlaid by a hint of stubble. He was thin, tall—all of my mother's men were tall—and wore round, professorial glasses.

Now, staring at the warrior in red and black armor, I tried to meld the image of the academic I'd seen in the photos with this formidable avatar. It was difficult and disorienting. I felt a sudden flash of anger. It was also unfair. All this time, I'd thought Hawkeyez777 was my friend.

We all waited. In the background, an undead ghoul walked in, looked around the room, and went back out. Hawkeyez777 addressed Gregory. "Your given name is Christian?"

Gregory didn't answer, which was confirmation enough. The warrior's face was impassive, but even around the voice filter, I could hear the nerves in his voice. "I'm sorry. This isn't how I wanted it to happen. I have so much to tell you both, so much to explain. Do you think we could meet in person? In real life, I mean?"

Chapter 13

I stared down at the text I had composed, reading the few words over and over. Around me, my apartment was quiet. Gregory had gone home. I'd shut down both computers. We would meet the man who may or may not be our father tomorrow evening. For now, there was nothing to do but wait.

Nothing, that is, except make a decision. Despite the distracting revelation of Hawkeyez777's identity, I had not forgotten Nora's words to me, hadn't forgotten the sickening events Erin had told me about, hadn't been able to forget the image of Grant sitting on a horse, standing his ground as a massive truck pulling a trailer full of stolen cattle ran him down. It was a terrible story, so much worse than anything I had imagined. But it still didn't totally explain why he hadn't yet gotten back on a horse.

I had to make things right with Grant. I was in the process of ghosting him, and he deserved better. I also thought he deserved better than me, in general. But the thought of breaking things off with him entirely, closing that door forever, filled me with a kind of squirming regret that made me ache with a feeling of loss.

It was 2:00 am. We hadn't stayed in the tavern long. We'd worked out when and where to meet in person, and then we'd all logged out of the game. Gregory had stayed at my place for a subdued meal and gone home early. I hadn't logged back into the computer. I'd spent the intervening hours cleaning my apartment, then fallen to organizing the contents of my kitchen cabinets. This was not a characteristic late-night activity for me, but the thought of lying down to sleep was as impossible as the thought of logging into HotTS and either seeing or not seeing the green dot next to Hawkeyez777's name.

In bed at last, I couldn't sleep. So I was composing this most likely ill-advised text to Grant. "Sorry for ghosting," it said. "I hit a rough patch. Family drama. Is offer to help with broken car still good?"

It was a self-serving message. I legitimately didn't have a clue what to do about Bessie, but also it seemed easier to ask for a favor than to reschedule a date. Still, I had not actually sent the message, only written, deleted, tweaked, rewritten and reread it compulsively for the last half hour.

Sighing, I dropped my phone into the sheets next to me and rubbed my temples. My hands smelled like dust and the lemony cleaner Gregory had given me because it was, in his words, both all-natural and effective. Earlier, when Hawkeyez777 had asked to meet, Gregory had stepped in, handling the whole thing, setting up a rendezvous in a place that was public but not noisy, then chatting smoothly for a few minutes before suggesting we should save the important conversations for offline. Why was it, I wondered, that Gregory had come out of our childhood sure and capable, strong and certain, while I was entirely the opposite?

It was far from the first time I'd wondered this. Usually, I concluded he was simply made of sterner stuff. Even when we'd been kids, Gregory would shout back when our mother was drunk and I would cower in the corner. This had set up the dynamic she'd eventually honed and used against us. When her barbs and bad behavior began to fail to get a rise out of Gregory, she'd shifted to directing them at me, forcing him to intervene to protect me, and therefore entangle himself again.

For my part, I had never defended myself. Had Gregory not been there, I'd have slunk away from her, hidden, evaded, sidestepped, refused to engage in conflict. That was my MO even now. It was one of the reasons I had no friends. Relationships, in my experience, always led to tension sooner or later.

Such as this thing with Grant. I picked up my phone again, woke it up, stared at the message on the screen. Who did I want to be? The person who hides in the corner and lets other people do the living? Or the person who steps into the light and does something?

In a sudden spasm of determination, I hit, 'Send.' I regretted this act an instant later, staring at my screen in fatigue-laced consternation. "No no no," I mumbled. Why didn't messenger apps have an undo button? I read the message one more time, groaned, and dropped my phone into my sheets again. It was official. I was an idiot.

Ten seconds later, my phone beeped. I sat up in bed, fumbling through the sheets until my fingers found the familiar shape. I looked down at the screen. *It's her,* I told myself. *Or Gregory. Or some notification from the phone about app updates.*

But it wasn't. It was Grant. The message was characteristically short but sweet. "Offer stands. Meet at curb in 5 mins?"

I looked at the clock. It was 2:11 am. Apparently, Grant wasn't any better at sleeping than I was. Laughing, I texted back. "Sounds good."

He was standing next to Bessie when I walked out into the quiet of the night. It was November now, and the breeze had an edge to it. Grant, his face illuminated by the fading solar lights set along the sidewalks, smiled as I approached, but there was something a little cautious in his body language. My silence had damaged the easy rapport that had existed between us.

This reality made me want to draw back into myself, retreat like I always did. But I fought the urge. *No,* I told myself. *You can make it right. You can fix it. You just have to try.*

I stepped up to him and said, "It's unlocked." Then I handed him my keys.

He took them from my hand, our fingers brushing. Electricity shot through me in a surprising burst as I heard the creak of his leather jacket, smelled his familiar blend of desert scents. He opened the door, leaned into the car, put the keys in the ignition, and turned. Nothing happened. Not even a click now. "Battery's dead," he said. "My guess is the alternator. Have you ever had to replace it before?"

I knew what a battery was. Phones had batteries, as did many common household appliances. I did not, however, know what an alternator was. Cars had never been of interest to me. "No," I said. "At least, not that I recall."

He drew the keys back out of the ignition and held them up. "Can I keep these? I'll run by AutoZone tomorrow and see about getting a new one. If it's a simple swap, I should be able to manage it myself."

I folded my arms, regarding him with bemusement. "Don't you have work to do?" I said, "The ranch?"

He shrugged. "It won't take me all that long. I bet I can fit it in tomorrow. How about it? I'll repair your car, but only if we can reschedule that dinner."

"Oh, so it's going to be blackmail then?"

Grant took a step forward, grinning. For a moment I thought he was going to reach for me, kiss me soundly in this moonlit parking lot. But he checked himself. "Only a fool works for free," he said.

"Fine." I rubbed my arms, wishing I'd put on a jacket before stepping outside. "Tomorrow, I'm hanging out with my brother. How about Thursday?"

"Friday would be better," he countered.

"Then Friday it is."

I walked into the Humanilism workroom as the Uber that had brought me to work glided away from the curb. I strode to my locker, noted the crowded state of the long tables, and felt my heart sink a little lower in my chest. I was late. Very late. It was almost 11:00 am. I had to get all my Interactions done in time to get home and get changed so Gregory could pick me up to go meet our maybe father. It was going to be a long day.

I took a moment to transfer the case of DragonFire from my backpack to a mini fridge, ignoring the surprised glances several of my co-workers cast at the cans. Since deciding to ignore Tony's Peer Challenge, I had embarked on a silent, passive mutiny. Despite the fact that I had returned to drinking DragonFire like most people drink water, I still blithely put in a zero every time our interface asked me how many cans I had consumed the day before. It was evident to anyone who saw me over the course of the day that I was lying. And I didn't care. If Luke Rastenhaus had wanted a better response to the challenge, he should have asked if I was willing to participate first. I also had yet to put my BodPod back on. It was still on my kitchen counter, out of batteries.

I booted up my work laptop, passed the challenge screen by inputting a zero, and sat watching the spinner as the system acknowledged my presence and began to calculate where the greatest need for me might be. As I stared at the swirling dots, I was unable to keep my mind from straying towards Grant. What had he been doing awake at 2:00 am? Why wasn't he working at the ranch today? Where had he learned how to replace an alternator?

The icon had just been replaced with the large message, "Hi, Jordan. Please check in with your supervisor," when I heard a step behind me. I swiveled in my seat as Luke Rastenhaus' familiar voice sounded cheerily above the chatter of keyboards that filled the large space. "Good morning, Jordan. I hope your day is starting off well. Might I have a word?"

I felt a dip in my stomach. Turning, I plastered a smile on my face and got to my feet, closing my laptop on the strange message. I focused for a moment on extracting myself from the long table without jostling the oversized Human on my left whose shoulder and elbow had clearly strayed into my territory. *Shit,* I thought. *This is it.* I glanced guiltily at the open can of DragonFire sitting next to my laptop. I should have known better than to carry out my rebellion so publicly. Had Luke noticed the beverage? I tried to position myself between him and the can, hoping he'd turn away.

Then, in a flash, I thought of Grant, thought of him sitting on a horse in the middle of a dirt road while a truck hauling cattle roared towards him. I felt an unfamiliar surge of an emotion I'd rarely felt before—some blend of certainty and resolve. I turned, picked up my can, and followed Luke up the staircase towards his airy office. If he was going to fire me for failing some stupid public challenge I'd been coerced into against my will, so be it.

We reached the top of the stairs. Luke opened the door to his office by resting his fingers on the handle until something clicked and a light flashed green. He gestured for me to go through.

Inside the office, sunlight filtered through the large windows, muted by expensive screens. Silence fell as the dull hum of indistinct noise cut off with the closing of the heavy door. Luke walked to his desk, sat down, and gestured to the opposite chair. I sat too, and fixed him with what I hoped was a steely glare.

Luke looked at my beverage, then at my bare wrist. He sighed. "I realize we put you on the spot the other day. I'd like to apologize. It was unfair to present you with a challenge like that, on stage, before the entire company, without first assessing your willingness to participate. I can see I got over-excited about our prior success. When Tony came to me with the idea ... well ... I said yes before thinking it through."

I barked a short laugh, remembering the terrible dread I'd felt in the pit of my stomach as I'd walked down the aisle in the dim auditorium to the stage. The black painted wood of the stage had felt hollow beneath my feet as I walked over to Tony and stood there, hating myself for even going that far. Then I'd accepted his challenge like a training parrot while he put words in my mouth, talking about my DragonFire habit, the cost—both financial and to my health—of drinking a processed beverage in such quantities. I'd been too flustered to do anything but nod and respond to the cues as they came while Luke Rastenhaus beamed and had his tech guy plug the challenge into the new interface right then and there.

Now, in his office, Luke sat back, ran both hands through his normally well-groomed hair, and closed his eyes in a long blink. "We've actually had a string of complaints about the Peer Challenge Program," he said. "A number of them on your behalf, but others as well. People feel pressured to accept friends. Then people go around challenging other people to give up this or that or participate in some new activity. It's a total mess. So, I wanted to tell you personally, we're shutting the whole thing down. Not the BodPod program as a whole," he rushed to reassure me as surprise registered on my face. "Just this one aspect."

I took a sip of my DragonFire, pretending Luke was a truck and I was a cowboy and I wasn't going to give an inch, no sir. "So I'm off the hook," I said.

Luke laughed, some tension seeming to go out of him. "I wouldn't like it if some random co-worker asked me to quit my coffee habit," he confessed, "even though I almost certainly drink too much espresso." He shrugged. "Besides, without my coffee, I'd cease to function and this entire department might collapse, so I don't see how that would be much help to anyone."

I leaned forward, preparing to leave the chair and return to my drudgework. "Anyway," Luke pressed on, staying me with a small gesture of his hand, "that's only one part of why I asked you up here today. In watching your data a little more closely these last weeks while you were in the BodPod program, I've noticed some patterns I wanted to discuss with you."

A cold rock formed in my stomach, heavy and solid. *Cowboy*, I told myself. *Face of iron*. It was only then that I belatedly remembered how Grant's stand-off with the truck had ended. With him getting run over.

"I've noticed you come in early as a general rule and work quickly through your Interactions. You rarely spend your Merit points even though they pile up fast due to your consistently high feedback ratings, and you have a bit of a habit of using CSS hacks to solve design problems for our BlockWeaver clients."

My mouth went dry. Though the first two comments could possibly be construed as positive, my last habit was sort of unofficially frowned on. Flustered, I hurried to explain. "It's just that sometimes the things they want are so simple. A few lines of code and they're happy, versus twenty minutes of explaining why I can't do it and a frustrated customer in the end."

Luke held up a hand. "How well do you know CSS, Jordan? And do you have any experience with HTML? I ask because we just opened a position in one of our internal teams. I thought you might be perfect for the job. I'm not convinced your current position as a Human is allowing us to make use of your full potential."

I stood in my bedroom, staring at myself in the mirror. Wearing my usual jeans and black t-shirt, I looked pretty much like I always did. But I felt jittery, unsure, and anxious. It was the way I always felt when I knew I was about to see a parent.

Of course, in this case, it was not my mother. It was my supposed father, who I had never met before. At least, not IRL. And while his abandonment of his two children was not exactly auspicious grounds for the start of a relationship, it was true he himself had never directly done anything hurtful or manipulative or abusive towards us, other than failing to be a part of our lives.

Sighing, I turned away from the mirror. I doubted he'd be impressed, but I was what I was. He could take me or leave me. I wasn't going to try to come off as something other than myself for our first meeting. If we continued to get to know each other, he'd find out the truth, anyway.

It was Wednesday afternoon, an hour before Gregory was due to pick me up. I'd gotten home from work early because my Interactions requirement had been waived for the day by Luke Rastenhaus. After mentioning the job opening, he'd taken me through a door downstairs that had a security pad my ID could not open and into an internal part of the building I'd never visited before.

As we'd walked, he'd explained. "As you know," he said, leading me down a wide, cool, hallway, "most of our Humans here don't work for Humanilism, or at least, not directly. We rent out their attention and expertise to our own clients."

I nodded, resisting the urge to mention I'd worked here for years and understood this basic concept. We reached a fork in the hall, turned left, and he continued. "But we do have a number of internal teams," he went on. "These people do work for us, directly, and they have jobs here at the company. I'm an example of this, obviously, and our other teams include marketing, brand positioning, outreach, research, payroll and accounting, and, of course, web development. We have our own website. It's our primary portal for receiving new client inquiries. We also have an entire interface for our current clients where they can access records and statistics on how many Humans they are currently using, details on their Interactions with the end user, and so on."

We entered a sunny foyer with an entrance from the outside, also barred with a security swipe. Before us stood a plain, solid, double-door. Luke stopped walking. "Right now we're going through an entire UI overhaul of both sides of our website – the client side and the public side. Our goal is to be more agile with updating both features and design in the future, breaking advances into smaller pieces so we can iterate more rapidly in response to feedback and changing technology. The current team is full of senior members. We want to inject some fresh blood."

He began to move again, pushing through the door to reveal a spacious, sun-filled office. There were elements I recognized. The wooden lockers along one wall. The workstations scattered around. But there were differences as well. There only appeared to be about 12 people present. Each worked in a quiet nook, often surrounded by plants or partially obscured by a portable screen. In the middle of the room was a single long table with workstations like the ones I was used to, but this was currently unoccupied. "It would be a promotion, of course," Luke said, lowering his voice. "And you'd need to go through a starter training course, then pass a proficiency test, then continue in a training capacity for six months to a year. But if you're interested, we can do it immediately as an internal hire before we formally even open the position."

I felt stunned. "But I'm not a developer," I said. "I mean, I know a little CSS and HTML, but that's all. My degree is in Communications. I only took a few Computer Science courses. Like, for fun."

Luke smiled, unconcerned. "We've found it leads to a better team dynamic if we hire for work-ethic and personality rather than technical skill. Programming can be taught. Don't worry. They'll start you on what you can handle, and train you up as you go."

In the back of the room, a man stood up. He was African American, with steely gray hair and deep smile-wrinkles around his eyes. He approached us, beaming. "You must be Jordan. My name's Jamie. I'm a Senior Developer on the internal team and Team Leader. I'm told you might be joining our ranks."

I shook Jamie's hand and it finally crystallized. This was real. My days as a Human were over.

The rest of the day passed in a blur of meeting the rest of the team and learning about the job. The new position, Junior Developer in Training, seemed too good to be true. The daily pattern would feel a good deal like my old position, with a few key changes. For one thing, there was the raise. Even Junior Developers in Training, it turned out, earned more than Humans, but a more substantial raise would come when I passed a few proficiency tests and became a plain old Junior Developer.

But almost better than that, there was the workroom. So quiet, so spacious, so full of nooks and crannies, one of which I would select to be my own so I would work in the same physical place every day with no one's elbow spilling into my comfort zone, ever. The hours were a little less flexible as there was a daily team meeting and more coordination between members of small teams. But still, there were many hours of flex time I could push around as I saw fit.

In short, it felt like an incredibly lucky break.

It had also been such an unexpected turn of events, it had kept me from dwelling overmuch on what was to happen that evening.

Now, in my apartment, I grabbed a can of DragonFire from the fridge and walked into my living room. The wall above the sofa was still blank, but otherwise the room felt far too sophisticated to belong to me. The view was nice, the furniture was nice. It felt good to sit and watch the light change on the mountains while I absorbed the events of the day.

Outside, the solar lights along the walkways began to glow as evening fell. The moment felt surreal. The nice furniture. The new job. The maybe father.

In my pocket, my phone gave a chime. I fished it out and saw a message from Grant. "New battery and alternator did the trick. She's good to go."

I smiled. Emboldened by that odd sense of certainty I'd begun to feel that morning, I texted back. "If you've run out of charitable acts for the day, I've got an hour before my brother shows and a lonely beer in my fridge."

The restaurant Gregory had selected was a low slung stucco structure, utterly unassuming on the outside in plain white paint with an understated sign hanging above a door made out of rough planks of dark wood. We stepped into a low entry space, where a hostess took our names and led us through another door. And from there, the place transformed. The room we walked into was broad and golden, lit by warm round lamps. Tables were separated by partial walls overflowing with leafy plants as low music piped in over the sound system.

It wasn't crowded, but those present were like Gregory—well-groomed and well off. "How do you even know about these places?" I asked in a theatrical whisper. Looking to the side, he winked. He wore gray slacks that looked like they were woven out of real silver, a white shirt without a collar, and a jacket of the same stuff as the pants. When he'd arrived to pick me up, he'd taken one look at my typical ensemble of jeans, black t-shirt, and gray canvas jacket, and frowned. But then I'd introduced Grant. That had shut him up.

Still, I felt conspicuous as we made our way around diners who looked like they'd been selected and arranged to appear in the background on a movie set. It was a winding route to our table. When the hostess stopped with a gesture for us to seat ourselves, the table she indicated was not unoccupied. This was a surprise. We'd arrived almost ten minutes early.

The man at the table had apparently watched our approach. He stood now, looking nervous but determined. This, I thought to myself in a kind of stunned bemusement, was Hawkeyez777, only without armor or wolf. For a moment, I foolishly searched his features for resemblance to his avatar.

What I saw instead completely floored me. I saw myself.

Putting on a smile, the man offered Gregory his hand. Gregory took it. "Jason Hawkins," the man said. He had a nice voice, smooth and even. Nothing at all like the gravely the rumble the filter in *Heroes of the Totem Spirit* gave him.

Jason released my brother's hand and turned to me. "Jordan," he said. His eyes were hazel, the exact same shade as mine. The shape of them behind his round glasses was also familiar, as was the bridge of his nose and a million other tiny details in the way his face was put together. He was taller than me, but he had the same complexion that suggested it would tan if he would go outside a little more.

I shook his hand. It was soft and warm. As I turned to take my seat, I noticed the stunned look on Gregory's face. He'd been staring at us, eyes flicking from Jason to me and back again. I gave him a quick glare and he snapped out of it. I walked around him to pull back the chair on his other side.

We all sat. I tried to tamp down the feeling of excitement that had begun to rise within me as I'd noted the physical resemblance between Professor Jason Hawkins and myself. It came through far more strongly in person than it had in the photo I'd seen. Also, it didn't necessarily mean anything. My mother was an observant woman. It was possible this man really was my father. It was also possible she'd seen him, noted his resemblance to me, and somehow orchestrated this entire meeting as a means to dupe us. For now, I needed to remain distant, remain skeptical, remain aloof.

After we were all settled, our server came over, introduced himself, and left us with a basket of steaming, fluffy white bread. We all stared at it, enveloped in a bubble of silence amid the quiet murmur all around. Across the table, Jason adjusted his glasses. Next to me, Gregory's hand strayed to his side, resting on the place where his scar lay concealed beneath his shirt for only a moment before he realized what he was doing and pulled it away.

For my part, I wished I'd brought a can of DragonFire.

Behind Jason, a couple rose, donned their coats, and walked towards the exit. Oddly, this felt only marginally different from sitting in the HotTS social zone staring at each other's avatars. Except now I didn't have the comforting knowledge that I could escape at any time by simply logging out of the game.

"I know you're wondering why I haven't been a part of your life," Jason began at last, launching into what sounded like a practiced speech. "And I don't have a good answer for you. I knew, by the end, that

Candace had a tendency to..." he trailed off, eyes going a little distant before continuing, "...embroider or entirely obfuscate the truth. I was there at first, you know. Through Gregory's birth and the first year and a half of his life. I was there. But then she told me Gregory wasn't my son. She said she'd been sleeping with other men throughout our time together. There was no way I could be the father. She was very cruel and unapologetic. She told me as a way to end things, explaining she and Gregory's real father wanted to make a go of it. I was out of luck." He broke off, removed his glasses, rubbed his eyes, and put them back on. "I had reason to believe her, see. We'd been very careful. Before Gregory was born, we never once had..."

Jason broke off suddenly, looking up as if he'd just remembered who he was talking to. A deep flush appeared on his neck. He swallowed. "That is," he said, "these things happen, of course, but given the precautions we'd taken, I had been very surprised when she first told me we should expect a child."

He stopped. Gregory took pity on him. "So when she told you I wasn't yours..."

Jason nodded, fiddling with his fork. "I was so hurt, so devastated to think she'd been so systematically and cruelly unfaithful, I left. I applied to graduate schools, and ended up in Oregon working on my Ph.D. I put it behind me. Not my son, I thought. None of my business. He'll have his real father to get him through life. I didn't know at the time, Jordan, that she was pregnant with you. I didn't even know you existed until about six months ago. I'd been back in Tucson for many years by then. I came back after I finished my dissertation, to teach at the university. But I never ran into Candace or thought to look for her."

I felt a dull anger begin to burn in the depths of my stomach—the rage I always felt when I realized our mother had gotten away with a lie. All our lives, she'd told us an entirely different story. Our father had abandoned us, she'd say whenever we asked. She had lawyers looking for him. He owed thousands in child support. He'd left us all in the lurch. We'd be better off if he never came slinking back because he was a no-good nobody.

"But why?" I burst out, unable to contain the question. "Why do that? Why send you packing? It's all a blatant lie. There was never a man around she told us was our father. She always said you'd run off, abandoned us without warning. Why would she say that if it wasn't true?"

Gregory leaned back in his chair, looking not in the least surprised. "Control," he said. "If we had a father who loved, us, that would mean we'd have somewhere else to go, someone to support and protect us. The first step an abuser takes it to isolate her victim. You know that, Jordan."

I did know that. But it didn't make it any easier to look across the table at this man with eyes the same color as mine and wonder what my life would have been like if he'd somehow discovered the truth decades ago.

"It was a glitch, actually," Jason said, setting his fork down and picking up his glass of wine. He and Gregory had consumed the better part of a bottle and were seeming a good deal more relaxed. I had reluctantly ordered a Mountain Dew, which sat in all its fluorescent glory next to my plate of pan-seared quail looking as out of place surrounded by all this finery as I felt.

It had been over an hour since we'd sat down. Gregory and Jason had clearly hit it off. That's not to say I didn't like the man. He seemed very nice. I was just having trouble letting go of the fear that this wasn't real, that Mom was about to waltz in to reveal how she'd outplayed us all, that his simple story was untrue. We'd left the topic for a while, talking instead about Gregory's prodigiously successful career as an artist, mine as a Human who rode ranch horses, and Jason's as a professor who played video games to study human behavior. That had brought us around to the topic of how he'd discovered me.

"Like I said in the article you mentioned," he said, leaning back in his chair with the mildly professorial air he seemed to adopt out of habit while speaking, "the devs at *Heroes of the Totem Spirit* have been awesome. They granted me access to their data on a level no public user has ever been allowed. This access was supposed to be totally anonymous, but there was a little loophole I stumbled upon by accident. When I looked up users with the same zip code as me, I could see their full account. This included things like real first and last names and the image of the photo ID they'd provided to verify their account."

I grimaced, thinking of the driver's license photo that would forever be my biological father's first impression of his child. I look like a psychopathic ax-murderer in that shot. An ax-murderer named Faith.

Jason looked at me. Some of the nervousness from earlier came back into his voice as he continued. "I was searching for local players because I thought I might be able to start a MeetUp and find a few people willing to help with some of my research goals. Looking at the list, I saw your last name. Falkenrath. I thought, 'How many Falkenrath's could possibly live in the Tucson area?' So I snooped. It wasn't ethical. I was looking at data I shouldn't have been able to access, even with my agreement with the devs. Still, I couldn't help myself. I saw your age and realized you'd been born only six months after I moved away. I thought you must be Gregory's sister, the child of your mother and the man she'd cheated on me with. I Googled you and came upon a few photos of higher quality than the driver's license. And that was when I knew she'd lied."

He stopped as a quick, shaky smiled flashed onto his face, then vanished. "From my perspective, at least, I think you look a good deal like me."

I blinked hard and took a sip of Mountain Dew. Gregory murmured his quiet agreement as I stared at the tablecloth, trying to pretend my eyes hadn't begun to burn. Jason continued, letting out a long, shaking sigh. "So, I began to investigate. I had my lawyer help me look into it. He found I am listed as the father on two birth certificates."

He stopped talking. Around us, the restaurant had grown busier as more tables filled, the occupants laughing and chatting. Most people, I thought bitterly, were out for a nice evening, enjoying time with their friends or family with easy familiarity, not risking life and limb picking their way across a relationship tableau littered with the explosive mines my mother had planted decades in the past.

"It's not your fault," Gregory said, sitting up straighter and pushing the base of his wine glass on the table in a short, tight circle so the liquid inside swirled. "She told you the most hurtful lie she could concoct. No normal person would have received the news she gave you and thought, 'Maybe this isn't true. Maybe what's really going on here is she's pregnant with my second child and she wants to get rid of me so she can raise the two of them in the kind of isolation that enables abusers to maintain total control over their victims.' You only knew her for a few years. We all know she can seem perfectly normal and even loving when it suits her."

Jason's face had grown pale at Gregory's words. I cringed. One of the things we'd been taught to do in therapy was not shy away from the facts, not hesitate to define our childhood in accurate terms. Gregory and I were used to calling a spade a spade, but Jason clearly wasn't. I could see pain in his eyes, colored by a hint of doubt. The memories he had of our mother, I was sure, did not jive with the childhood Gregory had just described.

"She nearly killed him with a bottle once," I said. The quail had been tasty, but my appetite now deserted me. I shoved the half-eaten meal to the side and leaned forward, fixing Jason with the eyes I'd evidently inherited from him. "She stabbed him in the side with a broken bottle because he tried to take her keys away when she was falling-down drunk and ready to drive off to get more booze. She stabbed him, and then she left. He wouldn't let me call 911 because he was afraid social services would take us away from our mother, and separate us."

"Jordan," Gregory said, reaching over to put a hand on my wrist.

I shook it off. "No," I snapped. "If we don't tell him the whole truth, he's always going to have doubts, which means he'll be vulnerable." I turned back to Jason. "So yes, she nearly killed her own son—your son. But Gregory got better and we moved out even though we were both still minors. After that she'd show up at intervals, break or con her way into our place, and steal from us. Finally, she set our apartment on fire while we were inside, asleep. That was terrifying, but a good thing in the long run because it led to a court case that resulted in Gregory taking on legal guardianship of me. So now we have a restraining order against our own mother, which she violates whenever it suits her. Just like she did a few days ago when she popped up at my place of employment to give me that article."

I trailed off, uncertain now about the point I was trying to make. The spark of anger had drained out of me. Jason was staring at me in horror. I sat for a moment, feeling my heart pound. I dropped my gaze back to the Mountain Dew.

"I tracked her down," Jason said after a moment. "All that time I was getting to know you in HotTS, I had a PI working for me. It took a few months, but the investigator, Jillian Diehl, found your mother. I confronted her and demanded the truth. She tried to lie again. She said she'd put me down on your birth certificate because her other partner went to prison. But I don't believe her. I've hired a lawyer, and I am hoping the two of you will agree to a simple DNA test. Not because I need evidence, but because then I'll have the legal connection to you, no matter what your mother says. Now that I know you exist, I do not intend to abandon you again."

I thought of our interactions in HotTS, the way I had bumped into Hawkeyez777, seemingly at random, over and over again. "All along," I said, "you were running into me on purpose."

Jason looked embarrassed. "One of the things I can do is track players I've selected and see a few extra stats—their life bar, for one, and the zone they're in. The stats flash if someone is rapidly losing life. One of the things I'm studying is how players react when their peers are in distress."

He trailed off, seeming to have to force his mind back to the matter at hand. "Of course," he continued, "since I'm not supposed to know who anyone is, this shouldn't have been as powerful a tool as it turned out to be. I told the devs about the loophole in my access, of course. They closed it, but I already knew who you were. So yes. I tracked you. I orchestrated our meetings, trying to get to know you, trying to come to terms with the thought that you might be my daughter. But you're a tough nut to crack. Saving you from the spiders that day was kind of my lucky break."

I smiled without meaning to, remembering the way the hulking warrior had come bounding over the hill to assault the monsters tailing me. Then I remembered our brief conversation at the end of that meeting. "Pony girl?" I said.

He looked sheepish. "My greatest challenge when it comes to in-game interactions is using language that doesn't alienate other players. I've learned to adopt certain speech patterns to fit in."

I laughed. Jason's face lit briefly with a smile in response. "Anyway," he went on, "I thought things were progressing nicely between us after that, but my lawyer kept cautioning me to wait until we had real evidence that Candace wasn't lying. When you failed to meet me in the social zone that day, I got scared. I was afraid I'd pushed too hard, or given myself away somehow. Then you were hardly around for a while. I realized I would never forgive myself if I lost track of you and I missed my chance. I had decided the next time we spoke, I would tell you what I knew. But then you took the matter out of my hands."

A brief silence fell. Across the table, Gregory was watching us intently. He said, "I, for one, will happily take a DNA test."

I glanced quickly at my brother. He was sincere. I looked back at Jason. *Father.* The word echoed in my mind, wonderful and strange. *This is my dad.* "Me too," I said. Jason raised his glass in a silent toast, his eyes slick with unshed tears.

Chapter 14

Grant "picked me up" at 6:30 on Friday, on the dot. His knock sounded on my apartment's door right as I was strapping on my BodPod. I'd finally rescued it from the kitchen counter when I'd gotten home from work a few hours before and plugged it into its charger. It was now restored to life, the green heart rate monitoring lights flashing in their blinking rhythm.

Turning, I crossed my apartment and opened the door. It was mild out despite being November. A few hours before, Grant had confirmed via text that I was still up for walking to dinner. Now he stood on my stoop, smiling, his face lit by the last rays of the sunset.

We walked mostly in silence, but it was the companionable kind. Grant, I thought, seemed a little less cautious about his gait than when I'd first met him. We walked easily and steadily together, our BodPods racking up the steps as we went.

As we stepped into the little gastropub Grant had selected for our first date, I looked around with mild wonder. I tried to remember the last time I'd gone out twice in one week. It must have happened at some point when I was in college.

The evening Gregory and I spent with our father had ended pleasantly. He'd insisted on picking up the tab, then walked us out to the parking lot. As Gregory and I drove off, we shared a stunned silence. When Gregory asked, at last, "Do you think it's legit?" I wasn't surprised. We'd both been tricked enough times to be skeptical of any story that connected to our mother, even tangentially.

But I couldn't see how Jason could possibly be lying. He'd given Gregory a manila folder in which we found copies of both our birth certificates, along with a printout of Jason's and a scan of his driver's license. We'd also set up a time the following day for the three of us to meet in his lawyer's office, where we had collected the DNA samples with a legal witness present. As we'd parted ways after that meeting, Jason had said, "I've paid for expedited results. We should know within a few days." It was getting harder and harder to think this could be a scam of some kind.

To Gregory, I'd said, "I'm going to let science be the judge of his story," and we'd driven the rest of the way home in thoughtful silence.

Now, settling into a seat across from Grant, I tried to focus on the present. Either Jason was my father, or he wasn't. If he was, my life would change a little. If he wasn't, we'd go on as before, having fallen for my mother's most ambitious lie yet. Either way, Grant was here right now. He was looking at me with those keen, dark eyes. "You seem preoccupied," he said.

I was saved from responding to this probe by our server coming by to take a drink order. Grant ordered a beer of some kind. I asked for a water. As the server walked off, Grant waited a beat, as if giving me a chance to respond to his previous observation. When I didn't, he said, "You don't drink, ever?"

The question annoyed me. Not because of Grant, specifically, but because of the long, long list of people who had previously poked and prodded at me on this subject, from my brother all the way down to random strangers at parties who had introduced themselves by way of pressuring me to consume alcohol. Most people, it seemed, thought themselves original and entertaining as they repeated questions and arguments in favor of getting drunk all the time that I'd heard a million times before.

My mood darkened a notch. Before I could reply, Grant grimaced. "I'm sorry," he said. "I'm sure you get that all the time. I was just curious."

He looked remorseful. I softened. "My mother was an alcoholic," I said. He blinked, looking surprised. Without totally deciding to, I went all in. "An abusive alcoholic who once stabbed my brother with a broken vodka bottle. You could say I don't have a positive association with drinking."

In spite of myself, my tone had grown a little acidic as I relayed the story. It wasn't something I'd ever talked about outside of therapy, and now here I was, telling the second person in as many days about the most traumatic night of my life.

Grant sat back, looking stunned. "Fair enough," he said as the server returned, set down Grant's beer and my water, and asked if we were ready to order. Grant told her we needed more time. Then he looked at me and said, tentatively, "Associations can be changed though, you know. With time and effort."

Now I really was annoyed, both at Grant and every person I'd ever had this conversation with in the past. I sat up straighter and shot back. "You don't ride horses, ever?"

Grant looked as if I'd slapped him. There was a long awkward silence as he set his beer down and said, "You're right. I don't. At least, not lately."

Around us, the gastropub was full of lively chatter and the snappy beat of some indie hit song. I unwrapped my straw and began to poke at the ice in my glass.

We sat in frosty silence. I was certain I'd just ruined everything. He was annoyed, and so was I. We'd never recover our equilibrium now. He'd worn a leather jacket on the walk down, which he'd removed. He looked good in his finely made gray t-shirt, but the scars on his arms were there, as was the one next to his mouth. I thought again of the terrible scene Erin had painted for me.

Grant cleared his throat. "I'd like to ride again," he said, seeming to be deliberately containing his more intense emotions, keeping them out of his voice. But his shoulders were tense, his posture rigid. "It's just..." he trailed off. I could see his jaw working as he clenched and unclenched his teeth.

I sat, transfixed and silent as my mind scrambled, searching for some way to change the subject, to let him off the hook. Why had he brought up drinking? Why had I brought up riding? These were not things to be talking about on our first real date. I flailed about for some other subject—any other subject. But my brain was frozen, my tongue still.

Grant began again, his voice low and strained. "I was raised to see horses as partners. When you train an animal to set aside all his natural instincts, when you systematically work to teach him to follow you as a leader, to trust you more deeply than his own natural programming, when you get him to the point that he will do anything you ask simply because you ask it of him—when you do that, you become responsible for his safety."

I knew what he was talking about. Erin had spoken this way, too, of the bridle horse tradition the Tipped Z adhered to when training their horses. It was all about building up trust and precision through long-term partnership.

"So if you ask a horse to stand and face something he should clearly be afraid of, it's on you to keep him safe. If you ask him to stand in a road because you're sure the truck will stop, he will be sure the truck will stop, also. He will do as you ask. He will stand in its way."

He stopped. His eyes had gone dark. He was sitting in a rigid posture of pain. "So let's say you ask him to do that, and then the truck doesn't stop, and the horse dies a brutal, traumatic death because he trusted you..."

He broke off again, a kind of shudder going through him. "How can you ever risk making that kind of mistake again? Better to not have that kind of power."

As he said this last sentence, he raised his eyes to mine. In them, I saw all the pain of his accident. Not the physical pain, but the pain of his mistake. He believed he'd betrayed his horse, and his horse had died as a result.

That was why he didn't ride. Not because he was afraid. Not because he didn't want to.

Grant thought he didn't *deserve* to ride.

It was possibly the saddest thing I'd ever heard.

I swung onto Sally's back and settled into my saddle, looking over at Erin for instructions. She'd been in the arena before I arrived today, but she wasn't riding Esperanza. She was on a different horse, one with a coloring I'd never seen before. He was, quite literally, silver and gold. Not gray. Not yellow. His coat was short and burnished. He gleamed in the sun like a precious metal. As I looked at him with curiosity, Erin gave his neck a quick pat. "This is Snoopy. He belongs to the TruGlide corporation."

She spoke this name as if it should mean something to me. I searched my memory for some prior mention but came up with nothing. Seeing my blank look, Erin went on. "They make shoes for competitive reiners. Snoopy lives half in a stall, half in the pipe corral attached to the barn. Nora has an arrangement with his owners. She keeps him in shape so that he can show up to events and photo shoots, always looking his best. He's got a degenerative hock condition, so he can only handle light work. Still, he does need regular exercise. Nora can't ride right now, so he's fallen to me."

I took all this in, but once again my brain failed to manufacture a suitable response until a little too much time had passed.

The truth was, I was having trouble focusing. This was due to a mix of fatigue and pure distraction. Since Grant had escorted me back home and given me a sweet but not exactly steamy kiss goodnight, I'd had trouble thinking about anything but him for more than a minute or two.

A short silence fell. Erin ran her fingers through the horse's silvery mane. "He's tough to keep sound," she said with a sigh, "though he's undergoing a stem cell treatment right now that seems to be helping. At least he's photogenic and popular enough with their audience that they keep him around."

I considered the horse. Although he was a Quarter Horse, he wasn't built anything like the other horses I'd seen on the ranch. He was bulky with muscle and stood on small, upright feet. He had a dished nose, a pronounced jaw, delicate ears, and a bored expression. The work Erin had done with him before I'd arrived had produced only a light sweat, but he stood with his head so low he looked exhausted.

"We're going to start today with a mirroring exercise," Erin said, moving her horse into a walk and indicating I should join her. "Try to make Sally walk the same speed as Snoopy, and do whatever I do."

She walked off. Immediately, I saw this would be challenging. Snoopy's walk was a good deal slower than Sally's. As I asked Sally to walk as well, Erin looked over at me. "So how was your week? Did you ride again after Monday?"

Sally fell in smoothly next to Erin and Snoopy as I felt myself flush with embarrassment. So far, the number of times I'd ridden Sally on my own was embarrassingly small. "I'll be better next month, I promise," I said. "It's been crazy with the changes at work and all this stuff with…" I trailed off, trying to think of a word to use to describe Jason. I wasn't ready to start referring to him as my father, not without the DNA test. "There's this guy," I resumed, then realized I'd made it sound like a romantic entanglement. I stopped again, wondering how people like Erin always managed to sound so smooth and collected when they spoke.

Erin turned to look at me, her expression having gone a little serious. Meanwhile, Sally was steadily creeping ahead. I tried to slow her with my seat. "Someone you're seeing?" She prompted. "And he's not Grant?"

"No," I groaned. We reached the top of the arena and my thoughts once more returned to my dinner with Grant. Despite the awkward start, we'd managed to turn the conversation away from examining the darkest places in our respective pasts and eventually settled in to have what I'd thought was a pleasant meal. I'd been all set to invite him in. The whole walk home, I'd imagined it, using our previous make-out session as a model for what might happen this time.

But before we even got to my door, Grant had pre-empted me. "I had a really nice time," he'd said, putting his hand in mine to give it a light squeeze as we left the main walkway and stepped onto the path that led to my door. "Thank you for a wonderful evening."

There was the undeniable suggestion of goodbye in his tone. Before I could think of a way to convince him to un-say it, we'd reached my door. He kissed me and walked off into the night.

I'd gone inside, thrown myself onto my lovely new gray couch, and proceeded to engage in a minute by minute review of the entire evening. Other than the very beginning, when we'd discussed the things we didn't do, it had felt so normal, so easy, so right. So why hadn't he given me the chance to invite him in?

Erin was watching me. Sally had slowed, but not enough. More flustered than ever, I tried to explain. "It's not that kind of guy. He's someone my mother knew. Gregory and I went to dinner with him. To meet him. Because ... well ..."

I stopped again, unable to think of a way to explain this without sounding like a person Erin might not want to continue to associate with. But she was curious now, watching me with keen eyes. I gave in, deciding only the truth was going to get me off the hook now. "According to our birth certificates, he's our father," I said. "But according to our mother, he's not."

Erin turned Snoopy in a half circle and set off in the other direction. I mirrored her, speeding Sally up since my horse had further to go. Erin glanced over at me, her expression perplexed. "Wouldn't your mother, um, know who she ..." It was her turn to trail off looking flustered.

I released a short laugh. "I've no doubt my mother knows. But what she knows and what she says are often two different things." There was a short, surprised pause before I added, "She's mentally ill."

Great, Jordan, I told myself. *Keep digging the hole deeper and deeper. Next thing you know they're going to stop encouraging Grant to date you and find a reason to cancel your lease.*

Then, more to forestall further questions than any desire to continue to discuss my personal life while on horseback, I said, "But I went out with Grant again last night. We had dinner. It was nice."

Erin turned Snoopy again. Again I mirrored her. She said nothing, so I continued to prattle on. "I think he might have changed his mind about me, though," I confessed, feeling the rock in my stomach that had nestled there when he'd walked away the night before and continued to gain density since.

Erin stopped Snoopy, backed him up, and stepped his front end around to face the other way. I did the same, hardly even noticing how smoothly and effortlessly Sally followed my practically unconscious signals. "Why do you say that?" Erin said.

I found myself blushing as we walked down the length of the arena, towards the mountains. "He seemed a little cool at the end of the night."

Erin pushed Snoopy into a trot. The horse had an impossibly slow jog I wasn't even sure Sally could match.

"Well," she said, "one thing I know about boy trouble is horses are the best cure. Collect Sally on the hackamore, now. Yes, she can trot this slow. Gather her up, keep her soft, and slow her cadence with your hips. Good, Jordan. That's good. You two are starting to be a good team."

And just like that, Grant was gone from my mind.

For a little while, at least.

The knock on my door was both unexpected and sudden. I jerked in my desk chair, snapping out of my bubble of pure concentration. I'd been working on trying to figure out where a persistent discrepancy in line height was coming from on the sample website I was building for my course. In Chrome and Microsoft Edge, it was the same. But in Firefox, it was totally different. It was a maddening problem. Not necessarily relevant to the site's performance, but something that needed to be worked out, nevertheless. It was Monday. I could think of not a single person who should be showing up here unannounced at this time.

At the sound of the knock, I surged out of my chair and spun towards my door, looking around blankly for my cell phone. It wasn't in its usual place next to my keyboard, which meant I'd left it lying around somewhere. *It's her,* I thought, my heart beginning to pound. My mother, tired of being ignored, had found me at last. And now I'd never be rid of her again.

Or, could it be Grant? He'd sent me a couple texts since our date but hadn't suggested we hang out. It was Monday afternoon, now. I was growing worried. What if he never asked me out again?

Shuffling across the tile in my stocking feet, I pressed my eye to the peephole. Then, sighing, I threw the deadbolt and opened the door. "Gregory?" I snapped. "What's wrong with you? You nearly gave me a heart attack."

He was standing on the stoop, his blonde hair rumpled, holding an open envelope in his hand. He said nothing, only thrust it into my hand. "I texted," he said. "And you haven't made me a key yet. So..."

He didn't chide me, didn't ask why an unexpected knock on the door should be such a big deal. Turning sideways, he stepped past me. As I looked at the envelope and drew out the folded single sheet of paper inside, he walked into my living room to stand in front of the large blank wall, his hands shoved into his back pockets and his gaze as intent as if there was already more to look at then some drywall texture.

I closed the door, locked it, and unfolded the piece of paper. It had a logo at the top above the address of some company with a name that sounded sciency. The first paragraph was a wordy disclaimer, but down below was a single sentence in a fixed-width font, as if the letter had been stuck into an antique typewriter for the final message to be added.

I read. "There is a 99% probability that subjects B and C are the immediate descendants of subject A."

I blinked, understanding pouring into me in a rush of warmth. I looked up at Gregory, who had turned from the wall and was now watching me with eyes that had grown intense with some emotion I could not name but felt the mirror of in my own heart. "It's real," I said. "He's really real. Jason is our father."

Gregory nodded. I closed my eyes. *You should hate her for this. This, and so many other things. She deserves to be hated by her own children.*

It was an uncharitable thought, one some of my therapists would have applauded and others would have chided. Hatred, one of them had told me once, was a burden. It took an enormous amount of energy to hate someone. Indifference, that therapist had explained, was a far worse punishment to dole out.

Others would have encouraged me to feel the hatred, explaining that emotions can only be moved through once they'd been felt.

I didn't know which was right, I only knew my life seemed to improve as my mother's presence in both my mind and my day-to-day life decreased. It was useless to wonder what our lives would have been like if our mother hadn't driven Jason off, if he hadn't believed her then, if he'd been present for us all along.

Gregory was watching me, his eyes calm and assessing. Despite the fact that he was the one our mother had physically scarred, we both knew I was the fragile one. I drew in a quick breath. "Well," I said. "That's good. I mean, that's cool."

Satisfied I wasn't going to have an immediate emotional break, Gregory turned back to the wall. "I invited him to join us for Tuesday dinner this week. I thought we could have it here."

I stared at him. "Here?" I looked around my apartment, alarmed. "Why here?" My apartment was nice enough, but Gregory's condo was both more spacious and more aesthetically pleasing.

He turned, moving back towards the door. "To celebrate," he said, unlocking the door to step outside. Annoyed, I trailed after him, stepping into a pair of flip-flops and then gasping as the cool evening air bit at my toes. "Celebrate what?" I called after him, wrapping my arms around my stomach as he strode out along the gravel path to his Mercedes, which was parked in one of the guest spots.

We reached the curb. I stopped, my annoyance curdling into a bad mood. Gregory could be incredibly obtuse when it suited him.

My brother reached his vehicle, opened the back, and pulled out a toolbox and a drill. He returned to me, thrusting the items into my reluctant hands. "I have my own drill," I protested. Of course, mine was some corded, generic off-brand special I'd picked up on the cheap. His looked like it had been designed by the same team of engineers that made the Mars Rover.

A few minutes later, he had pulled a thin but massive rectangular object from the back of the SUV. Even swaddled as it was in foam and a paint-stained sheet, I knew what it was.

My annoyance downgraded a notch. I stepped off the curb to close the rear doors, then followed as Gregory navigated his way back to my apartment. We made it through the door without incident. He set the piece down to prop it against the living room wall.

I closed and locked the door, my curiosity beginning to win out over other feelings. Gregory had, of course, given me loads of art over the years, starting with collages made of dried pasta and crayon and growing more sophisticated as he grew older. I had any number of small pieces that had ended up in my possession one way or another. But, as far as I could remember, this was the first time Gregory had made a painting just for me.

Leaving the painting wrapped, Gregory opened the toolbox, pulled out a tape measure, and once again approached the large, blank wall. I made a strangled noise. Walking to the swaddled canvas, I pulled the sheet aside and released the rubber bands that held strips of foam to each corner. Gregory liked to paint on deep canvases. This piece was already framed in something heavy and chunky.

Gregory made no comment as I continued in my unwrapping process. He worked rapidly to measure off the wall and search for studs. His silence communicated tacit approval. He'd always been shy about his work. Even now that he was an improbable sensation, his paintings in galleries all over the country and selling almost as fast as he could create them, he still had no ego whatsoever. He had trouble talking about what inspired him and drove him to paint. As much as he enjoyed painting for a living, he did not like the attention that came with his notoriety.

So now, he left me alone as I unwrapped the piece and removed the fat foam to access a thinner layer beneath. Under that was a layer of semi-opaque plastic, which I unfastened and let fall away. Then I stepped back to look at the piece my brother had made for me.

Gregory's work was difficult to describe. He tended towards the abstract now, but when we'd been younger he'd been obsessed with creating visual landscapes full of minor impossibilities. He could draw a perfectly accurate sketch of any scene in seconds, so instead of going for reality, he stretched it. Gravity was often in question in his work, as was perspective, proportion, and color. The results were somehow both beautiful and haunting.

This piece had no immediately identifiable subject matter. It appeared, at first glance, a pixelated tableau where a sea of muted color stretched endlessly towards a horizon that was lost in a kind of luminous fog. It was violent in places, serene in others. It was more or less monochromatic, using a palette of browns that teetered towards red in some places and often got bleached over by layers of nearly opaque white. It was framed in white as well, a massive frame at least five inches thick and cut at a steep angle so all planes pointed in.

I stared at it, feeling gooseflesh rise on my arms. While no one else on earth could have known what it was, I did not need him to explain. This was a rendering of something that was not normally visual at all. It was a painting of us—our relationship in all its layers and complexities, all its pain. But when I stepped back and let myself see the whole, I realized it was absolutely beautiful.

Gregory had been pretending not to notice I was unwrapping the painting, but as he marked the wall with the chewed off stub of a pencil, he could no longer maintain the charade. He looked in my direction. Suddenly I remembered him at age 10, standing with his hands and face smudged with charcoal as our mother screamed at him for making a mess and I stared at the papers spread out neatly across the kitchen table, wondering how she could fail to see how talented he was.

"It's perfect," I said before he could ask. "Absolutely perfect."

I dropped the last rag into the basket with the others and stood looking around my apartment, hands on hips. The place positively gleamed. Gone was the dusting of plaster left behind by Gregory's installation of the painting, which now hung above the gray couch in unapologetic splendor. He'd departed after seeing it safely mounted, leaving me with the ominous comment, "Now all you need is a rug to tie it all together." I'd experienced a moment of mild panic, staring at the gray furniture and the magnificent canvas in its heavy white frame and wondering how on earth I could ever find one that would compliment both. My brother, seeing my look of dismay, laughed. "I'll help if you want. Next week, maybe." And then he was gone, disappearing out the door before I could even find words of thanks, taking my poor old coffee table with him.

Now, it was 6:00 on Tuesday. Gregory was due to arrive at 6:30, Jason at 7:00. It would be the first time in our lives Gregory and I would spend time in the presence of someone who we knew without a doubt was our father.

I'd spent the last hour scouring every surface of my apartment, hiding away any evidence that I might ever be anything less than fastidiously tidy and was still terrified our new parent might look around and find this place lacking. Hot, tired, and needing to shower, I glared at the gleaming floor. I thought I understood why Gregory had fobbed the hosting off on me. If I was this anxious about how my new and fairly bland apartment would reflect on my character, I could only imagine the kind of anxiety he'd feel about showing our brand new father his condo.

I picked up the rag basket, placed it in the laundry closet, and closed the door. As I turned for the bathroom, I heard my phone chime. I detoured, walking to where it sat on the counter, glowing softly. The message was from Grant. "Nice step count today," it said.

I scowled at the phone and proceeded to the bathroom, where I stripped off my t-shirt and jeans and stepped into the shower. Grant and I had been exchanging texts daily since the date, but still there was this coolness between us. He had yet to ask me out again. Our exchanges were trending towards shallow.

My step count was high for the day because I'd walked to work and, once there, remembered Jamie had promised me a tour of the rest of Humanilism's inner sanctum, which was called the Canary Complex. He'd taken me all around the area behind the security door, introducing me to the various internal teams that kept the whole enterprise running. Then, after lunch and a few hours of training, I'd walked home. After that, I'd cleaned non-stop, which was good for step accumulation as well.

I stood under the warm stream of water, letting it course over my face and muffle my ears. What was Grant's deal? If he liked me, why was he holding me at arm's length? If he didn't, why was he continuing to text? It was a frustrating puzzle—one I didn't know how to piece together. All I knew was I still got an adrenaline rush every time I remembered that first kiss. He'd been so certain then, so solid. What had changed?

It was tempting to take a long, slow, shower, but soon enough I began to worry I'd been in there too long. I stepped out into the fogged up mist of my bathroom. Donning a fresh pair of jeans and black shirt identical to the ones I'd recently removed, I placed my discarded clothing in my hamper and walked into the kitchen. Standing there, I once more surveyed my new domain. It wasn't perfect. Gregory was right the living room conspicuously lacked a rug. The light fixtures were a little outdated. It might be nice if the walls were a light gray instead of white so they contrasted slightly with the molding.

I pulled myself up short, feeling disoriented. Since when had I ever cared about things like light fixtures and wall color? My brother's aesthetic values were infectious, evidently. To steady myself, I turned to the fridge and popped open a can of DragonFire.

On the counter, my phone chimed. Grant, again, this time sending an emoji of running shoes. Exasperated, I set the phone down.

I looked at the clock. It was almost 6:30. Gregory would be here any minute. I removed two wine glasses from the cupboard and set them on the counter, then stared at their winking rims and remembered the strained beginning of my conversation with Grant the night we went out to dinner. *Associations can be changed, you know.* I turned back around and closed the cupboard just as I heard the deadbolt on my door unlock. As Gregory let himself in with the new key I'd had cut for him, I walked around the counter to relieve him of two bottles of wine he held cradled in one arm while several bags of groceries dangled below. "I could have helped you unload," I chided him as I set the bottles down. He stepped out of his leather loafers, situated them neatly by the door, and walked over to place his bags on the counter. I stared at the tableau. "That's is a lot of food," I added.

Gregory was as stylish as ever in a white shirt and a pair of brown, lightly pinstriped slacks, but he looked uncharacteristically nervous as he reached into a drawer for a corkscrew and began to open one of the bottles. "Four people is a lot more than two."

I froze in the act of pulling groceries out of bags. "Four people," I repeated, feeling a sudden bloom of terror spread through my belly. "What four people?"

Gregory popped the cork out of the bottle and sniffed it, then rotated it free of the opener and set it aside. "Jason's wife, of course. I forwarded you his email. Didn't you see?"

Starting to feel panicky, I stared at my phone. No, I had seen no such email. But then, my day had been so busy. Had I cleared a notification by accident? I almost scurried to my computer to investigate this outrageous claim but realized it was irrelevant now.

Jason had a wife, and she was coming to dinner whether I was prepared or not.

I tried to corral my frantic emotions, tried to readjust my worldview to see this as a normal, sane, well-adjusted person might. Of course Jason had a wife. He was in his 50s. He was a functional human being. He'd had his relationship with our mother when he was quite young and gone on to be an entirely normal person, never knowing he'd fathered two children and left them behind. "I didn't realize he was married," I said lamely as Gregory poured salsa into a bowl and opened a bag of chips.

My brother gave me a withering look. "And you didn't notice his wedding ring?"

I felt my cheeks heat with a flush. No, I hadn't noticed his wedding ring. And, I realized, I'd put astonishing little thought into the reality of Jason as a person. I'd been so busy obsessing about what his absence had meant to me, it had never even crossed me that he'd been elsewhere all this time, living a life, meeting people, doing things.

A new thought struck me. I felt a sudden thrill of new terror. "Oh God, Gregory. Do they have ... kids?"

Gregory had finished unpacking the food. He collected his four black reusable shopping bags, folding them neatly down in small squares which he stowed in a leather pouch. He met my eyes, "Jordan," he said, his tone somewhat stern, "I have no idea. I imagine these are the sorts of things we will learn as we get to know him better. Now relax and help me set out these appetizers."

"And do you know what he did next?" Jason said, looking from me to Gregory and back again as his eyes twinkled behind his glasses. "He said, 'Because goose doesn't rhyme,' and walked away."

Gregory and I laughed. Jason's wife, Sonia, who had seemed demure at first but turned out to have a quick wit and a surprising way of tossing sharp observations into the conversation, laughed as well but in the indulgent way of a person who has heard the joke before. She was a striking woman, with dark hair shot through with gray, dark skin, and large, intelligent eyes. It turned out I knew her too. She was the priestess avatar Solo8Sol who would run with the quest group I'd been a part of for a while. In those runs she'd played a mainly supporting role, since she had awesome healing powers and the ability to cast buffs that enhanced the stats of everyone around her. She also had several highly effective ranged attacks, and the ability to teleport short distances. Her totem partner was a pure white stoat that also had healing abilities, along with a distortion shield that deflected incoming projectiles and drew mana out of foes to channel into his mistress. Her fighting style was all about baiting, evasion, and keeping her distance while firing projectiles to cripple and slow the enemy before bringing them down. She was fantastically useful to have at your back in close combat.

She was also my step-mother, which was weird. As Gregory stood, cleared our plates, and returned to the table with the nearly empty bottle of wine, I watched Sonia out of the corner of my eye, trying the term on for size. It felt a little clunky. As I sipped my DragonFire from the glass Gregory had poured it into when I wasn't looking, I found myself wondering what life would have been like if this person—quick, clever Sonia—had been my real mother.

It was a hopeless train of thought, of course. Gregory towered over her, pale and lean and very, very genetically dissimilar. She could never have produced a son physically like him. I was also taller than she was, though my coloring resembled my father's and so was not as far off from Sonia's.

My father. When I thought the still-new word, I turned my eyes to Jason where he leaned back in his chair, raising his glass so Gregory could pour.

The evening had turned out to be a good deal of fun. It had started a little tense, with Gregory opening the door and taking coats, all four of us crowding around my little island and attempting to make small talk.

Before long, however, Sonia was commenting on the new painting. Instead of asking arcane questions about subject matter and inspiration, she asked technical questions about the depth of the canvas, the paint application technique, and where Gregory had found such a unique frame. This kind of question about his art, my brother was always more than happy to answer. And while they'd been discussing the relative merits of various canvas stretching techniques, Jason turned to me and said, "I've been meaning to ask, where did you find that mithril coat for your horse? I've been looking for something similar for Gnarl, but I've never seen another artifact like that one."

Gnarl, of course, was Jason's wolf. I blinked, momentarily disoriented by the convergence of my game life in *Heroes of the Totem Spirit* and the reality of this tidy academic sipping wine in my apartment, who was both Hawkeyez777 and my biological father. I said, "I found it in this chest I came across in an endless tunnel. It opened up a dialogue that basically let me create a custom artifact via a series of prompts. I've gone back loads of times. I've never seen that chest again. It must have been an anomaly."

Jason, looking avid, gave a quick nod. "If you don't mind showing me where some time, I'd be interested on both a personal and academic level. The devs are known for hiding powerful opportunities around the easier levels, but even if you're looking they aren't easy to turn up. You must have gotten lucky."

And I also spent about a gazillion useless hours playing below my level thanks to the spider forest, I added sourly in the silence of my own mind. But I didn't say that. Instead, I looked over, startled, as Gregory laughed at some quip made by Sonia, who was smiling mildly while her eyes danced with a kind of wicked glee.

Jason followed my gaze. "She'd love something similar for Bajista too, of course, but it's not quite as important because he's not in close combat most of the time."

I nodded. Jason continued easily, asking me questions about Buttercup, when I'd first started playing, and why I'd been online less lately. I found myself telling him about the Tipped Z, Sally, and even the lost Buttercup of my youth. He listened attentively and asked clarifying questions at regular intervals—as if he was going to write a paper on it later. When Gregory and Sonia joined us and the conversation turned to broader topics, I found myself mildly disappointed. Who'd have thought my father would be so easy to talk to?

Now, dinner was over, the evening was winding down. I found myself feeling it would not be at all unpleasant to socialize with these people again. As we sat for a moment in comfortable silence, I realized this was what it was supposed to be like to have a family.

Twenty minutes later, when all wine glasses were empty and Sonia was loading the dishwasher and Gregory was trying to shoo her away from it, Jason collected his coat, put it on, and turned to me. "Thank you," he said quietly. There was a seriousness about the words that made me understand he was referring to more than the meal. "Thank you for being open to having a relationship with me. With us. Sonia and I met in graduate school, and we've both poured all our time and our hearts into our research. We never had children, and we don't regret that. But..." he trailed off, watching his wife politely concede the fight and allow my brother to herd her away from the stack of dishes. He sighed. "I suppose everything you decide to do is a choice to not do something else. But it's a nice surprise, meeting you two. I feel terrible I didn't know about you sooner, but I'm glad I do now."

Sonia joined us then, accepting her coat from her husband and slipping it around her slim shoulders. Gregory made a joke I was too dazed to catch, everyone laughed, and then they were gone. As the door closed behind them, I found myself standing in a kind of trance. My apartment felt quiet and empty.

I turned to Gregory. His cheeks were a little flushed, his eyes bright. "You know," he said, "Jason's lawyer managed to get copies of our birth certificates."

I blinked, feeling stunned as I realized what he meant. We'd talked about changing our names for years, but we had never followed through because our mother had ferociously blocked us whenever we tried to get our hands on the required legal documents. It hadn't felt worth fighting her over. "Right," I said, feeling a sudden spark of excitement.

My whole life, I'd carried Faith with me everywhere I went, an invisible weight and constant reminder of my broken relationship with my mother. What if I became Jordan at last, totally and for real?

"I was thinking," Gregory said, "Gregory Hawkins has a certain ring to it."

I was silent for a moment, stunned. It was a solid point. If we were going to change our first names, why not go all the way?

"Jordan Hawkins," I said, testing it out. "It's the name of a person who has a father."

Wordlessly, Gregory put an arm around my shoulders and gave me a quick, light squeeze. This was unusual for us. Physical affection was not a thing either of us found natural or easy. But I didn't push him away or make a face or crack a joke.

For a moment, I squeezed back.

I flipped the latch on the gate, pushed, and led Sally back into the large pasture where she lived with a number of the Tipped Z's other saddle horses. She waited patiently as I untied her halter, then turned and ambled off when I stepped away. As I walked back through the gate and fastened it behind me, she flopped down with a sigh to have a good roll in the sandy soil. I watched her, smiling, until she stood up, shook herself, and popped into an easy canter, moving to join the rest of the herd that was picking around the sparse desert a short distance away. I turned and began to walk back towards the barn.

It was Wednesday afternoon, late in the day. The sun was falling in the sky, staining the clouds in lurid hues as the shadows grew long. A chill was gathering on the air, but I was feeling too content to notice. I'd passed my initial proficiency exam at work earlier, which meant I was now officially a Junior Developer in Training. This basically meant I still had no idea what I was doing but was at least qualified to begin learning to do the real work of my new job.

It was fun, too. The new job. I liked my team. Jamie was both knowledgeable and affable, and some my new co-workers even seemed like the sort of people I might eventually become friends with. It was early days, still, but I found myself going to work every morning full of curiosity and optimism instead of dread.

Upon passing my exam and therefore officially earning my new job title, I'd decided I needed to celebrate with a ride on Sally.

I'd found the barn at the Tipped Z silent and empty, and gone about my ride in a bubble of pure solitude. Now, as I walked back to the hitching post, I saw a movement to the right of the barn. I squinted and made out a figure in the shadows, crouched down in some strange posture.

I stopped in mid-stride, arrested by the frisson of fear that leaped into existence in my sternum and banished my feeling of easy contentment. I stopped, staring, trying to make out more detail. When I couldn't, I scanned the horizon in the futile hope I would see Clint or Wyatt or Hank or Erin riding to my rescue.

I saw nothing, though, not even a stray cow. For all intents and purposes, I was alone.

I began to walk again, realizing I was entirely exposed and visible in my current position. Abruptly, I remembered the awkward conversation I'd had with Grant in the tack room. That felt like ages ago now. His concern about the unsecured room made a lot more sense in light of his experience with violent cattle thieves. Now, though, I wondered. Was this person here to steal things? Tack? Cattle? Horses? Why else would they be skulking that way, dwelling in the long shadow of the barn?

As my heart began to pound, I tried to decide what to do. My phone was in my car, where I always left it when I rode. To get to it, I'd either have to go through the barn or around it, and either would be difficult to accomplish without alerting this person to my presence. "It could be nothing," I told myself. "It could be the UPS guy, with a delivery. Maybe I didn't notice his truck pull up. Maybe he's waiting on the far side of the barn in the deep shadows because he's an albino and the sunlight hurts his skin."

I'd begun to walk again, but now my steps lagged, growing slower as the distance between me and the strange presence decreased. I squinted, seeing movement, and realized the person had begun to make a strange, quick, repetitive motion with his body, flinging one hand out in front of himself, then dropping into a kind of half squat, then doing it again. And there was something in that hand, something round and heavy-looking.

The movement stopped. The figure set the thing down, straightened, and set hands on hips. It walked a tight circle, stepping briefly into the sun. And I recognized him.

It was Grant, and he wasn't wearing a shirt.

I noticed a number of things all at once. First, there was his skin. It was tan and smooth, covered in a thin sheen of sweat that made the pronounced muscles in his chest and shoulders gleam in the fading light. Second, there were his scars. So many of them. The scars on his arms were thin and precise, the work of surgeons. The scars on his back were different – lumpy, chewed up patches of skin that were reminiscent of the brutal incident that had placed them there. I thought of Erin's quiet words about the accident, his own explanation. *The truck didn't stop.*

I shuddered, unable to comprehend what it would feel like to be impacted by a massive machine of metal and glass, backed by a trailer pulling several tons of cattle. The fact he'd survived at all seemed like some kind of miracle.

Grant walked back into the shadows, stooped, and began again with the repetitive movement. My fear having abandoned me to be replaced by voyeuristic curiosity, I continued to drift closer. Gradually, I figured it out. The thing in his hands was a weight—a kettlebell. I'd seen them in the Humanilism gym but never used one. He was doing some move that, judging by the sweat rolling down his back, was a good deal more difficult than it looked.

He finished his set, put the weight down, and turned. I froze in place, realizing I had drifted close enough that I was no longer en route to the barn doors. I was quite obviously doing nothing at all but staring at Grant in his shirtless state.

I saw him jump when he saw me, saw a number of expressions flicker across his face before his look settled into something neutral but slightly guarded. He took a step to the side and retrieved a towel hanging on a nail that had been pounded into the side of the barn. I could see now there was a little concrete pad on the side of the building. Several kettlebells of various sizes were scattered around this, along with a little table bearing a water bottle and a folded shirt.

Grant wiped the towel over his face. "Hey Jordan." He sounded unflustered. "I didn't realize you were here. What's up?"

I blinked. What was up? We'd texted every day since our dinner date, but the conversation had stayed superficial. I hadn't seen him around the ranch in ages only to suddenly stumble upon him mid-workout, looking sexy as hell and acting like I was his annoying little sister instead of someone he'd recently been making out with over a lightsaber.

I bristled, confusion making me irritable. He used the towel to wipe off his chest, then picked up the shirt. He pulled it on quickly. It covered the gnarly scars on his back, but not the thin, precise ones on his forearms or the one on his lip that put that small kink in his smile.

I thought back to our date, the awkward start, the sparring over our respective boundaries, his question, *You don't drink? Ever?* Could that be the problem?

I'd always told myself I didn't drink because I didn't want to be like my mother. And yet, Gregory drank without being like her. Jason drank and Sonia drank. Grant drank. Drinking didn't turn you into a monster by default.

I thought of our mother's latest play, her attempt to use Jason's existence to worm her way back into our lives. I thought about the way she'd lied to him, sending him packing when she learned about my existence. I thought about Gregory's answer to my question about why. *Control,* he'd said. For my mother, it was always about control.

Was that it for me, too? Did I refuse to drink because it gave me some leverage, a little sense of superiority and sobriety in the face of other people and their sloppy reveling? Or was it because I didn't trust myself?

I thought, too, of Grant's explanation—of being unable to ride a horse because he felt he didn't deserve its trust.

In a flash, I understood why we'd stalled out, why we'd been trading inane texts instead of moving forward.

Grant and I both had trust issues.

All around us, the light was fading. The vast desert was cooling, the light in the sky changing in hue, the mountains growing dim on the horizon. Grant was watching me, expecting me to ask about a piece of tack or a gate or a horse or some other bit of ranch trivia. Instead I said, "I'll drink a beer if you'll get on a horse again."

Chapter 15

The bottles clinked as Grant set them on the counter, five of them, followed by a tall can. Each had a label that said things that meant nothing to me. Some were plain and traditional looking. Others were elaborate, with intricate text and graphics woven together. One had a leering gargoyle in the corner.

"I thought we'd do a sampling," Grant said, opening my cupboard and gazing at my meager selection of glassware. "Hopefully we can find one that tastes good to you. We can start light, with a Kölsch. But the one in the can is a stout so if you trend dark, we've got you covered."

He was in a remarkably good mood. Despite his initial stunned silence after I'd issued my bizarre challenge, now that he'd had time to digest the idea, he seemed entirely on board. Of course, this was possibly due to the fact that I'd agreed to go first on the grounds that I'd been the one to set the stakes. In all fairness, he should have chosen the weapons. But since this wasn't actually a duel and we weren't trying to kill each other, the only other option was for him to choose the order of completion. He'd decided I would go first.

Now, staring at the beers, watching Grant's firm back as he reached into my cupboard and pulled out one of Gregory's whiskey tumblers and a large pint glass, I wondered if I had made a huge mistake. I'd literally never had a beer. I'd never consumed alcohol of any kind. Not even a sip. All my life, my refusal to become even the least bit intoxicated had stood as a kind of permanent critique of my mother and the weakness that had destroyed first our childhoods, then whatever relationship we might have been able to have with her as adults. Now, my heart began to pound. My palms felt sweaty. Was I really willing to give that up?

Several counselors had told me that although a person with alcoholism in the family is wise to be careful about drinking, not doing something simply to make a point to someone else isn't the healthiest means of making lifestyle choices. One had even gone so far as to suggest my refusal to drink was the final way in which my mother controlled me, still, despite the restraining order and all my attempts to break free. I hadn't gone back to that counselor. As my anxiety ramped up a few notches, I wondered if he'd been on to something. I'd always told myself I didn't drink because I didn't want to. But if my racing heart was any indication, I didn't drink because I was afraid.

Setting the glasses on the counter, Grant gave me a quick smile. "For the record, we will not be consuming six beers tonight. You will have a small sample of each, and choose one to finish. After that, you're cut off. The last thing we want you to do tonight is get drunk."

I frowned at the six beers, looking at Grant. "What will happen to rest? You can't recork a beer, can you?" Gregory had a fancy little wine pump he used to save bottles he didn't finish, but I'd never seen him use such a thing on a beer.

Gregory laughed, "I'll drink a couple," he said, shrugging. "We'll dump the rest.

I found myself frowning. "Waste them?" I said, unable to keep a note of accusation out of my voice. "That seems ... well ... like a waste."

Grant laughed, cracking one of the bottles and pouring its pale amber contents into the tumbler. It fizzled and frothed and the yeasty smell of beer filled my nostrils. "For someone who doesn't like beer, you're awfully concerned about its welfare."

I ignored this, watching Grant's hands as he stopped filling the tumbler and poured the rest of the beer into the pint glass. When the bottle was empty, he raised the glass. "Cheers."

I picked up the tumbler. We clinked rims. My heart was beating faster now, my palms gone a little slick. The glass was light, holding only a few sips of liquid. I raised it to my nose and sniffed.

Grant was watching me. It was Friday. Ever since he'd accepted the terms of our strange duel, we'd been texting back and forth with easy regularity. Now he was smiling, waiting for me to take a sip. I felt the warm fuzzy feeling of having reignited his interest fade as it was subsumed by anxious dread. Was I really going to do this?

I set the small glass back on the counter when I noticed my hand was shaking. I squeezed my eyes shut and seemed to see the old rental we'd grown up in, the narrow hallway that led from the backyard to the kitchen with the cracked tile you had to be careful not to step on, our mother sitting in her chair at the wobbly table, clutching a glass in one hand and a bottle in the other. The way she would lift her head and look at us when she hadn't made anything for dinner and we would come in to scrounge around for anything edible—the blankness in her eyes showing us she wasn't there, not really. Those were the good nights. When she was silent and still and left us alone.

I sank onto one of my stools and drew in a long breath. When I opened my eyes, Grant's eyes hadn't strayed. His expression had grown serious, taking on an edge of concern. He reached out and put a hand on mine. "Jordan," he said. "You don't have to do this if you don't want to."

My name isn't Jordan. It's Faith. The old dialogue started up in my head, making me wince. *My name is Faith, but it's not a name I've ever deserved. Ever earned. Faith is a disappointment. A failure. A waste.*

Out loud, I said, "My mother named me Faith, and my brother Christian. So if you wrote our names together, we were Christian Faith. In between her phases of binge drinking, she would always go evangelical. That's how we survived. She drank until the money ran out, then sobered up, got some menial job, went back to church, and found another man she could dupe into thinking he was saving her, that his support was a way to bring God back into the life of a prodigal woman and her two innocent children."

I stared down at the bubbles in the glass. They rose in tidy lines, marching towards the surface with a kind of urgent order I found oddly endearing. "She made us play along, play the part. I think I got baptized four times, always in a different church."

I stopped talking, refusing to go down the morose thought spiral that was thinking about my mother. I let go of the glass, rubbed my hand, and grasped it again. "But now that we've found Jason," I said, my voice gaining momentum, "we're changing our names. Me and my brother both. We submitted the initial paperwork yesterday."

Grant's hand was warm on mine, his touch comforting. He said nothing, did nothing, only waited for me to go on or drink the beer or say I didn't want to drink the beer. "So really," I said, "my name isn't Jordan. Not yet."

Grant's warm eyes were serious and steady. He was quiet for a moment. When he spoke, he did so slowly, choosing each word with precision and care like I'd first observed him choosing his steps. "A birth certificate is just a piece of paper."

I looked at the glass, feeling the fear roiling in my gut slowly coalesce into something else: something firm and solid and positioned at my very core. He was right, I realized. The legal name change *was* just a formality. I hadn't truly been Faith for a long, long time. Not since that day all those years ago at the ranch camp with Maria, when she stepped out the door of the office to call me in from my ride.

That day, for the first time, I'd ridden a horse named Buttercup—a new mare who was said to have a little bit of attitude. Horses that washed up at the ranch camp always had some story. Buttercup's was that she'd been bred and raised by a determined older woman who was friends with one of the camp directors. When the woman died unexpectedly, Buttercup came to the camp.

She wasn't ridden by the campers—not at first anyway. She was too "unpredictable." Maria warned me about riding her, but I wasn't to be deterred. So many of the camp horses were old and sour and disinclined to go. I saw Buttercup, who was young and fit and beautiful, as an opportunity.

My ride that first day had been unlike anything I'd ever experienced before. On Buttercup, going wasn't a problem. The problem was control. I'd realized within minutes of getting on her back, much to my surprise, that I didn't know anything about riding a horse that wasn't half-dead and used to hauling around clumsy children.

We had a lot of trouble that first day. But as I'd dismounted, Buttercup turned to sniff my shoulder. She gave a sigh and let me pet her face, clearly not holding a grudge.

As I pulled her saddle and bridle, I made a sudden but complete decision. Buttercup was new here, and all alone. I was going to be her champion. And in being that champion, I was going to learn to be the kind of rider she needed. I was going to have to change, but I thought I was up for the challenge.

Gregory had called himself Gregory for a long time by then, but I hadn't yet found the courage to instruct anyone but my brother to use my preferred name. I'd spent the whole afternoon in the sun and the dust, feeling strength build inside me as I realized for the first time that a horse cannot be forced into doing what you ask. It must want to go with you. I was determined to become a person Buttercup wanted to be with, and that person would not be the scared, cowering Faith my mother had created.

I walked up to Maria, looked at her, and said, "I prefer to go by Jordan, actually."

My voice had sounded quiet and firm. Maria smiled as if it was no big deal. She never called me Faith again.

All these years later, in my own apartment, staring at the glass in my hand, I finally completed the transition I began that day. "My name is Jordan," I said. "And I'll have a beer if I bloody well feel like it."

I raised the glass and took a sip.

The Kölsch, it turned out, was rather good. As was the Pilsner we tried next. I didn't like the Amber. The IPA had potential but seemed too intense for my first time. The nut brown ale seemed too sweet and heavy, and the stout was bitter and smooth and complicated.

We went down the row, tasting them all, and then I settled on the Kölsch. As I claimed the pint glass, Grant poured the IPA. I said, "You know an awful lot about beer." Now that I was a few sips into the Kölsch, I was finding it quite refreshing; it was somehow reminiscent of lemonade on a hot day but without the lemon or the sugar. Having pushed past the initial barrier, I was also feeling a distinct lifting in my mood—an easing of the anxiety that had dogged me all day. I was drinking a beer, and it wasn't half bad.

Grant shrugged. "My dad always gives me shit about it, wants to know why I can't just drink a Bud like everyone else and get on with my life. I just think it's interesting, I guess. Like everything in life, there's so much to learn if you're curious."

I took another sip of the Kölsch. Even the word was nice, crisp and foreign and yet not at all intimidating. I sipped again and felt a lifting sensation in my forehead, a kind of lightness that was not unpleasant as long as I didn't think about it too hard. *This must be a buzz,* I told myself. *You have a buzz.* The idea was entertaining, for some reason. I suppressed the sudden urge to giggle.

I forced myself to focus. Grant had just said something about his father. I was interested in fathers. I had one too. His name was Jason and he was surprisingly cool considering he'd accidentally abandoned us when we were kids. I said to Grant, "Does he live around here?"

Grant blinked. "My dad? Oh no. He and my mom are up in Wyoming. Always will be, I expect." He cast a critical look at my glass, which was already more than half empty. "You might want to slow down a little. Beers like that are easy drinking, but since you've got no alcohol tolerance whatsoever, I'd guess you're going to feel it soon."

I watched Grant as he spoke. He really was an extremely attractive person. I'd always thought that, but the fact seemed more obvious to me than ever before. I took another sip of beer, then realized what he'd said. I set the glass down and put my hands in my lap, like a child trying to resist a bowl of candies. He laughed. His glass, I noted, was still nearly full.

The lifting sensation grew more pronounced. I was aware that I was sitting alone with Grant in my apartment, doing nothing, really, and that this was something I might in normal circumstances feel somewhat awkward about. I felt very relaxed, however. *Very* relaxed. It was a nice feeling—as if years of accumulated layers of stress were unpeeling themselves and falling off of me in waves. *I understand,* I thought suddenly. *I understand why she does this.*

Grant was saying something, telling me some story about the first time he went to a bar and realized there was more than one kind of beer.

At the thought of my mother, however, my sense of relaxation burned away in a flash of terror. All of a sudden, the lifting sensation was not pleasant. It was scary. "How do you make it stop?" I asked, blurting out the words right in the middle of Grant's story, interrupting him in a way that was terribly rude.

He looked nonplussed, then concerned. He leaned forward, examining my eyes as if he thought they might have changed colors. "You feeling okay? How do you stop what?"

I put my hands on my head. It was a ridiculous thing to do, but I needed the reassurance that it was solidly there, firmly attached, not floating an inch or two above my shoulders. "The buzzing."

Grant relaxed a little, sitting back and taking a long sip. "You can't," he said. "You have to wait it out. That's why you want to be careful you don't drink too much tonight."

I felt the panic return. I stood up and felt the world wobble. Grant rose too, putting his hand on my arm to steady me. "Easy now," he said. His voice was low and smooth, relaxed and confident. "You're okay. You've had a little over half a pint of very light beer. That's not enough to do any harm. I promise."

He'd moved close to steady me. I looked up at him. The lighting in my new apartment was nice, warm and soft. Grant's expression was equal parts amused, concerned, and ... something else. "The only thing I can offer," he said, "is a distraction."

The look in his eyes made my heartbeat shift from anxious to interested. As he leaned down and kissed me, I tasted the IPA again, sharp and cool on his mouth. His hands found my hips. I felt myself come alive. I leaned against him as my focus seemed to narrow in. I drew in the smell of him, the texture, his shirt beneath my palms.

The kiss grew longer and more serious. His body was so firm, so solid and reassuring. Still, under the cotton of his shirt, I could feel the lumpy scars on his back, the ones I'd seen at the ranch. I remembered how he'd looked then, his muscles so hard and smooth in the late light. I threw myself into the kiss with even greater abandon.

Grant responded, pressing me up against the counter, his chest beginning to rise and fall at a faster rate. But then he stopped, pulling back to look at me, his expression serious. "Let's not get too carried away, okay? I won't risk pushing you somewhere you wouldn't go if you were sober."

I felt a little surge of annoyance at his words. What if I wanted to get carried away? I was a consenting adult. I had the right to make my own choices. I pulled away from him and took another sip of the beer. It still tasted good but seemed a little flatter. I eyed the other bottles, lined up in a tidy row, their labels all facing in my direction. I reached for the pilsner. Laughing, Grant grabbed my hand. "Oh no, you don't." He swept me into his arms and lowered his mouth to my neck. Thoughts of beer went entirely out of my head.

I woke the next morning in a state of muzzy confusion that pulled me out of sleep into horrified wakefulness in the matter of a few heartbeats. I opened my eyes, staring up at the ceiling fan above my bed, anxiety shooting through my veins like a cloud of poison. *Beer,* I thought. *Grant. The kissing. All that kissing.*

I tipped my head to the side, and there he was. Grant, wearing nothing but a pair of black boxer-briefs, his long, well-muscled body stretched out and half exposed, only wrapped in sheets from the waist down. As my terror lapsed into a mild headache, my memories began to return in greater detail.

After our initial steamy interlude, I'd wanted to drink another beer. Grant had tried to stop me, then relented, and portioned out a careful half of the pilsner, pro-actively pouring the rest down the drain. The others, he'd disposed of as well, except for the stout, which he drank himself. We'd kissed for a while longer. I'd made a joke about the lightsaber in our first romantic encounter, which led to a discussion of Star Wars that somehow led to me purchasing the entire extended set of movies on Amazon, setting my laptop on my coffee table, and navigating to the relevant scene in *The Phantom Menace* to prove my argument that Darth Maul did not use two lightsabers, but a single weapon with a blade on either end. We'd then left the movie on, cuddling up on the couch.

And then ... then I had tried to convince Grant to sleep with me. I could remember that, though my mouth had gone oddly numb and even at the time I could recall thinking it wasn't my mouth, saying the words. It was someone else's mouth, but it was okay because I agreed with what it was saying.

I remembered him kissing my forehead, smiling, and saying, "Okay. I will sleep with you."

And that's what he'd done. He made me brush my teeth and change into my sleeping t-shirt. I could see he intended to be literal about the sleeping thing. So as we'd gotten ready for bed, I'd had a plan—a strategy to jar him out of prude mode. But as we'd crawled beneath the sheets, a strange, heavy fatigue had seized me. I could remember nothing more. I must have fallen asleep the moment my head hit the pillow.

Now, the next morning, I sat up and stared down at Grant, feeling myself smile. He'd been right. The 1.5 beers had been more than enough. And now, clear-headed except for the tiny ache behind my right eye, I was glad, also, that he'd resisted my advances. It was a little embarrassing now, in retrospect, the way I'd thrown myself at him.

As if feeling my eyes on him, Grant rolled over and looked up. For the sliver of an instant, I felt afraid. Had he found my behavior last night ridiculous? Lame? Off-putting? But no. As soon as his eyes focused, his face broke into a sleepy smile. He reached up and touched the side of my face. "You're really cute when you drink," he said.

I felt myself smiling back. "And you're too damn honorable for your own good."

His smile faded. His eyes grew serious. They held mine as he searched my face as if looking for permission to speak. "I want to be with you, Jordan," he said. "But I don't ever want to have to wonder if our first time only happened because we'd been drinking."

I considered this. Lying among my sheets with the early sun filtering through the blinds, he looked no less attractive to me than he had the night before. "How long does it take 1.5 beers to wear off?" I asked.

He blinked. "Depends on the beers," he said, "and the person who drank them, how fast they drank them, how much they'd had to eat..."

I didn't let him finish. I flopped down on top of him, kissed him once, and glanced at the clock. "Not eight hours, no matter what. Right?"

His hands came up and settled on my shoulders. He kissed me once, slowly. "Right," he said.

I sat astride Buttercup on the top of a ridge, gazing through the bleak, gray atmosphere at the cluster of zombies down below. They stood in a ragged group, shambling around aimlessly, sometimes raising their grotesque faces to moan at the sky. To my left, Jason's massive wolf stood beside the warrior in black and red, Hawkeyez777. To my right, Bajista the stoat perched on Solo8Sol's shoulder, both his white coat and the lithe priestess' rippling gown oddly luminous in the dim light.

The zombies were guarding a chest. I could just make it out, partially sunk into the ground, only the slatted wood lid exposed. We were going to get that chest, by hook or by crook.

It was still Saturday morning. Grant had left only after we'd spent a good deal of time in bed getting to know each other in new and interesting ways. When getting up could be delayed no longer, we'd both showered and I'd made him an omelet. Finally, he'd said he had to go with evident reluctance. He kissed me goodbye and departed, at which point I'd spent roughly fifteen minutes wandering around my apartment smiling to myself, lost in a fog of blank happiness until Jason texted asking if I felt like joining him and Sonia for a quest.

Now, here we were. We stood together for a time, considering. The problem wasn't the zombies. They wouldn't have been a match even for Bajista alone. It was what we couldn't see that was the problem.

Word about this chest had been going around in HotTS the last few days. It was up a side canyon in a repeatable quest zone, one that threw a fair bit of heavy-hitting monster muscle at you before you even got to this point. We were all a little battered by now. At first glance, the zombies looked like a welcome change from the tougher foes we'd faced so far.

It was a trap, of course. The shuffling zombies were bait, set out to lure the unsuspecting. The real opponent was a djinn. And this one, if the rumors were true, was a real piece of work. The first thing it did when anyone attacked the zombies was trigger a massive area spell. This would teleport all but the three attackers nearest the chest—everyone in the entire quest zone—back to the beginning. Which meant the best odds you could get against the thing were three on one, with the three being battered and depleted already, and the one being entirely magical in nature, and also entirely ruthless. There was no waiting around the corner while someone else's gang wore the creature down and then dashing in for an easy victory. There was no way to face it on anything like equal footing.

Standing there, I wondered if I was crazy. Buttercup hadn't died in a long time, which meant she was as tricked out and leveled up as she'd ever been. Whatever was in that chest couldn't be worth risking her, could it?

But Jason hoped the chest was another like the one I'd found ages ago, one that would grant a type of artifact not otherwise available in the game. He was ready to risk anything if that was the case.

We'd been in this quest zone for an hour and a half already, clawing our way this deep into the winding string of canyons. It was raining now—a fine mist—so the air had a kind of murky quality that made the zombies even creepier. I'd never liked the undead. I couldn't fathom that some players chose them as their avatars.

"Well, here we are," Jason said, his voice distorted and robotic due to the voice filter. The mild academic who was my father and the hulking warrior who'd saved my life a few times were still completing the uneasy merging process in my head, overlapping most of the time but sometimes struggling free and refusing to let go of old associations. Right now I was having trouble not thinking of him as Hawkeyez777, my anonymous gaming buddy who could be anyone in the world.

Sonia answered. "No pressure, Jordan. If you're not up for the risk, just say so." Her voice was also distorted, but less so.

I gazed down at the zombies and the corner of the chest poking up through the damp ground. It was so clearly a trap, and yet it was irresistible. There could be anything in there. Or nothing. We'd never know if we didn't try to win it.

I sat up straighter in my desk chair, adjusting my mic. "I'm in. Let's do this." And without further ado, I leaped Buttercup into a gallop, careening down the ridge straight into the midst of the zombies.

Our plan was a simple one. There were very few creatures on this plane that could outrun Buttercup. I would do an initial charge, damaging as many zombies as possible and drawing the djinn out. Sonia would hang back, using her ranged weapons and healing spells as support. Jason would engage the djinn when it appeared. I'd circle back and guard Jason's back. When I finished the zombies, we'd take the djinn down together.

It was a good plan, considering how little we knew about the enemy. As I plunged towards the zombies, I even thought it might work.

Then, the moment I engaged the first zombie, the world flickered blue. It wasn't just blue light. The entire environment shifted so everything seemed suddenly to be made of blue crystal instead of earth and plant and stone. I was spared from the effect, but instantly I saw the problem. The blue was a conduit of some kind. My magic stores had started to drain, sapped by whatever shift the djinn had just initiated in the world. "Sorry if this gets you killed, old girl," I said to Buttercup. And then I knocked the head off the first zombie.

It was a long fight. The djinn was a teleporter, which I hated. It was also a sapper, stealing magic from its foes and throwing it back at them in the form of attacks. Fortunately, we had Bajista. The little stoat saved the day, siphoning what the djinn took back into Sonia so she could hurl it at Jason and me in the form of healing spells and various buffs. In the end, we brought the djinn down, but only barely. I was out of mana entirely and down to a sliver of life. Jason literally died, but Sonia used her last remaining mana to cast an ultra-rare resurrect spell she'd been hoarding for over a year before his death became permanent. If there had been one more foe, even a single zombie lying in wait, we'd have been toast.

But there wasn't one more foe. There was only the chest. As we stood in the light rain, the djinn's body fading out of existence and the world shifting so it wasn't blue anymore, I breathed a sigh of relief. It was just the three of us again, standing around the half-submerged chest. Jason was laughing, the sound made alien by his voice filter. Sonia said, "Well open it already, you idiot." I could hear the fondness in her tone even around the distortion.

My father, I thought, the word still new and surprising. *My father just kicked some serious djinn booty.* I was smiling as Hawkeyez777 stepped forward and knelt to open the chest. The lid sprang back and a bloom of white light burst forth, eradicating the dismal canyon scene and replacing it with a dialogue. "You have discovered a godshard. What form do you want it to take?" The options were as follows: weapon, armor, artifact, secondary totem partner.

I spoke into my mic, growing excited now. Although I could no longer see Hawkeyez777 or Solo8Sol, we were still in a questing group, so we could hear each other talk. "That's what it said last time! Godshard. I'd forgotten that part. Do we all three get to pick separately?"

Hawkeyez777 answered first. "Seems that way. I'm going with armor. For Gnarl of course."

Solo8Sol spoke next. "I think an artifact will suit me better."

I looked at Buttercup's stats, still showing in the upper corner of my screen. She was a wonderful totem partner. She gave me speed and strength and charging capabilities. But over the last few days, I'd grown somewhat infatuated with little Bajista. I'd never really considered all the ways in which a small, subtle creature like a stoat could be of use.

Grinning, I moved my mouse. "I'm going for a secondary totem," I said.

I stood up, my legs creaking, and watched as my computer shut down for the night. It was almost 11:00. After using our spectacular win to make our various new toys, Jason, Sonia, and I had had to test them out, of course. Jason had made Gnarl a reticulating suit of plate mail that covered the wolf entirely and regenerated when damaged. Sonia had made Bajista a collar to wear with a stone that created a force field around the stoat, so he was translucent and invulnerable whenever it was activated. With his mana draining capabilities, it was going to be a powerful upgrade for the little creature.

I was, admittedly, a teensy bit jealous of both artifacts. But it was okay. I had Cruger. He was a falcon. Agile and quick, he could ride on my shoulder and had a haunting cry that disoriented enemies. He wasn't actually at all powerful right now. In fact, he was basically a fledgling—tiny and clumsy and more of a liability than an asset. But that would change as time went on.

In any case, it had been a fun day. And spending it playing games had helped me not obsess over the night with Grant. As soon as I turned away from my computer, though, he leaped back into my mind in a rush. I couldn't get over how sweet he'd been. Going out of his way to find me a beer I liked, patient at my initial hesitation, and vigilant to make sure I didn't drink too much or do anything I'd regret.

In short, he'd been a total gentleman.

He'd texted once, from out at the ranch, and I'd replied. But now as I walked into my kitchen and scrounged a DragonFuel bar out of my cupboard, it almost seemed like it had all been too good to be true. Could anyone really be so nice, so attractive, so interesting, and into me, all at the same time? The prior evidence I'd gathered in my life would suggest not. There had to be a fatal flaw somewhere, something I hadn't seen.

Chewing on the bar, I wandered into the living room, where I stopped to stare up at Gregory's painting. It still gave me goosebumps, just looking at it. My brother was a marvel. I'd known that all my life, of course, but it amazed me how he'd somehow taken the pain of our childhood and made it beautiful, made it work for him, made it into a kind of visual challenge to the world as a whole. He would always be the first to say his success was incredibly lucky—that the art world was a crapshoot and he'd happened to catch the right person's eye at the right time. But I always pointed out that things that went viral did so for a reason. His work spoke to something universal. It resonated with everyone who had ever so much as stubbed a toe and gotten ridiculously mad about it.

And me. What had I done with that pain? I'd let it swamp me, drag me down, consume my verve and energy and optimism. Even if Grant was the real deal, how could I be worthy of someone so solid, so real, so kind?

In my hand, my phone chimed. I looked down. It was a text from Grant, a single emoji of the moon. I glanced out the window in the direction of his apartment. He wasn't asleep either, and he was thinking of me.

I found myself smiling, my dark thoughts fuzzed over in a haze of dopey endorphins as I remembered the way he'd kissed me that morning, long after my buzz had worn off.

I texted back the emoji of an empty bed. Then I waited. Three minutes later, there was a soft knock on my door.

He had me in his arms the moment I turned the knob, sweeping me into a kiss that all but knocked the wind out of me. He closed the door, flipped the deadbolt, and spoke into my hair. "I've been thinking about you all day," he breathed. "I keep telling myself to play it cool, to give you space. But then I tried to go to bed and all I could do was lie there and remember how serious you got when I said Darth Maul used two lightsabers and you were like, 'No. No, you're wrong. I will show you.'"

He laughed against my neck. I laughed too. As he stepped back a little to look into my face, I forced myself to look stern. "If you were smart you wouldn't keep bringing that up. And you call yourself a fan. Pssht."

"I know one thing for sure," he said. "I'm a fan of you."

And then he was kissing me again, and I stopped caring about lightsabers.

Later, we lay in the dark under the sheets, listening to the distant howl of a coyote. He had a hand on my hip. I was in a blissful state of total fatigue and total relaxation. We would sleep now, I thought in a kind of happy haze, and when I woke up tomorrow, he'd still be next to me. Again. It seemed too good to be true.

My mind had started to drift when Grant spoke, his voice low and serious, waking me all the way up again. "There's still the other half of the bargain." Something in his tone suggested he was hoping I actually was asleep, so I wouldn't have heard what he said.

I rolled over, looking at him across my pillow. In the moonlight, there was a kind of vulnerability to his face. He had one of his hands drawn up next to his chest. The pale scar on his forearm seemed to glow. "You don't have to do anything you don't want to do," I said, magnanimous in my drowsy contentment.

His expression didn't change. Under the sheets, his other hand gave my hip a little squeeze. "I do, though. I saw how hard it was for you to take that first sip of beer. You didn't want to do it, but you did anyway. And something in you changed when it did."

I considered trying to deny it but knew it wouldn't fly. I thought about beer and wine and alcoholism. I didn't think I would ever drink a lot, or even on a regular basis. But every now and then, when I was with friends, it might be nice not to be the only one drinking DragonFire.

I said, "I should have done that a long time ago. I'm free of something now. Some final weight I was carrying, leftover from the way we grew up."

Grant nodded. He drew in a long breath through his nostrils. "That's what I mean," he said. "That's what I want. I've done everything else. I did the impossible. The doctors said I'd be in a wheelchair for the rest of my life. I proved them wrong. It took years, but I can walk again. I can run. I can lift weights. I had to fight for every step at first, but my body is strong enough now. It has been for a long time."

I remembered the day I saw him with the kettlebells, the day I'd proposed this bargain. I set my hand on his warm skin, feeling the firm muscle beneath. I thought about what I knew of his accident—a truck, men stealing cattle, Grant on his horse in the road. I said, "You know, it wasn't you who failed that day. Your horse didn't die because you made a mistake. He died because those cattle thieves were monsters. He died because other men chose to put profit before basic human decency."

Outside, a coyote raised its voice in a lonesome, mournful howl. Grant's tone was low and distant. "I was so angry that day. Even before I saw that truck. I woke up knowing the fight was lost. I was going to lose everything I loved. I was heartbroken and sick with anxiety about what I would do after the ranch went. I saw those men, and I filled up with rage. In that moment, the only thing I could care about was stopping them. I thought I could. I thought I could preserve at least a few head of cattle just a little longer."

He sighed. In the quiet dark, I could all but feel the pain radiating off of him. I thought about the day I lost the camp. Grant had experienced that same anguish, only times a thousand.

"You got hurt fighting for something you loved," I said. I thought of Gregory, of all the times he'd put himself between our mother and the damage she might do. "You took a risk. You did it standing up for something worth protecting. There's no shame in that. Quite the opposite, really."

Shifting in bed, Grant propped himself up on an elbow. His warm brown eyes met mine. I saw something in them—a new look of determination.

"Will you come with me tomorrow, then? To the ranch?" he said. "I'm going to ride Balin."

We took my car. Like the day Nora had picked me up, we didn't go in through the neighborhoods and take the hard right turn, then approach the main barn. We went in the other side, skirting the subdivision so we approached what was left of the Rocking J—Nora and Wyatt's little homestead. I was surprised, when we pulled up, to see Sally in the pen with Balin, the young stud nowhere in evidence. "I texted Wyatt this morning," Grant said, looking a little sheepish. "And asked him to bring her over."

I could tell he was nervous. There had been a kind of coiled energy in him all morning, the re-emergence of that sense I had gotten from him early on, the sharp quality about him that made him seem a little dangerous. I realized now I'd misunderstood him, back then. I'd thought that brittle aura had something to do with the way he thought about other people. Now I saw it had always only been directed at himself.

As I parked my car and we stepped out and Grant led me to a little shed where Sally's tack waited alongside a few other saddles, bridles, hackamores, and pads, I thought back again to that first lesson—the day Grant had come in to ask Erin about some colts he was supposed to feed. "What was the deal between you and Erin when I first started coming around?"

I'd asked the question before I had time to wonder if this was a good time to broach the subject. I glanced at Grant, afraid he might be annoyed, but his eyes were only a little sad. "Oh, it was stupid. When I first came down, the idea was that I could help out around here since Nora's pregnancy got complicated so early. Hank kept giving me these jobs to do and I'd do them, but without riding horses. He got mad about it and said he wasn't going to give me any more work until I got back on a horse. I talked to Nora, and she suggested I teach some riding lessons. So that's when I put the ad out on the internet. But Hank found out and he was furious. He said a man that won't ride a horse has no business teaching other people to do it. Hank forbade me to use his horses to teach. He said Erin would have to take on anyone who inquired. He told me to take the ad down as soon as I could. Nora thought the whole thing was hilarious, but I was pretty frustrated at the time."

I thought of that ad, feeling a little shiver at how near a thing it had been. It was a staggering stroke of luck that it had come into my queue that day, that I'd ever seen it at all.

Grant continued. "Erin wasn't thrilled about the whole thing either. A few weeks before, she'd made a mistake roping that caused a wreck for Hank. It wasn't a big deal, but he had to wear a sling for a while. She was embarrassed and shaken up, and tried to argue she was the least qualified one to be teaching. Hank said she was also the least qualified one to be doing just about anything. He meant it kindly, I think. But he can be pretty gruff sometimes. She took it as a reprimand. So she agreed to teach the lessons, but then she thought I was making excuses to hang around to watch so I could be critical of her. I was angry, but not at her and not even really at Hank."

Grant paused. In the distance, a dog barked. Grant shook his head. "After that, Clint intervened between me and his father. He sees I have work, but it's all stuff that keeps me out of Hank's way. That's the way it's been now for months. Some days it feels more like charity than employment."

All the pieces of the puzzle slowly clicked into place as he talked. I saw the whole thing now, that strange tension between Grant and Erin, Nora's odd reaction when I first called asking about lessons, even Grant's irregular presence around the barn.

While Grant explained all this, we haltered Sally and Balin and led them to a hitching post made of three massive logs sanded smooth. No one appeared to be at home. It was quiet with the little ridge between us and the subdivision. The horses swished their tales and stamped their feet at flies. We moved easily through the familiar process of getting them ready to ride.

"Well," I said, "and here I thought Erin looked at you that way because you were some kind of rogue bandito, plaguing the women folk with your wily ways."

He laughed, but it was half-hearted. I could see his mind pulling away from me, beginning to dwell on the fast-approaching moment when he would need to put his foot in the stirrup and step up.

I thought about all the things that had been going through my head right before I sipped my beer, and I let the silence wash over us. I couldn't know what he was thinking, not exactly, but I understood he was preparing to face his own demons.

Grant went back into the little shed and came back carrying a saddle and pad. He flipped them onto Balin with the smoothness of many repetitions, let the cinch down, and began to snug up the latigo. He was done by the time I was back from the tack room, carrying just a pad. I returned for my saddle while he slipped on the pencil-thin bosalita and neck rope, then eased a spade into Balin's mouth.

I guided Sally's hackamore over her nose, looped the reins over the horn, and gave Grant a look. He was standing with his nostrils flared, breathing as hard as if he'd just run a mile. I could see the tension in his shoulders, the blankness in his eyes. I didn't know what he was seeing, but it surely wasn't this desert.

I didn't know how to help him, so I led Sally off. I returned to the area before the gate where Erin and I had mounted up. "We're going to ride over to the ranch, I presume?" I said it calmly—as if it was something we'd done a million times before.

Grant unstuck himself, led Balin up next to me, and said, "Yep. That's the plan."

I threaded my get-down through my belt and thought about the way Grant had lined up those beers for me, distracting me with options and information so I had less time to worry about the reason I'd never had a sip of alcohol in my entire life. I put my foot in the stirrup, swung into Sally's saddle. "I don't have much experience with gates. I could use the practice."

Not looking at Grant, I stepped Sally over to the gate and side-passed her up to the latch. She moved lightly off my leg. I reached down to flip it open, then stepped her back and to the side so I swung it open next to my leg. I thought we executed the maneuver very smoothly. I glanced at Grant to see if he'd noticed.

He hadn't. He'd been standing with one foot in the stirrup, his body rigid with tension. I turned. Our eyes met. "Cheers," I said, raising my free hand as if to make a toast. He grinned, a quick flash of a smile that was there and gone in a heartbeat.

And then, Grant swung into the saddle.

"Cheers," he said, adjusting his reins.

Balin sighed, rolled his cricket, and pricked his ears in my direction. Grant gave him some invisible signal. The horse moved forward, stepping out with energy but not with nerves.

Grant rode through the gate. I closed it behind him, stepping Sally to the side until it was shut.

When I turned around again, Grant was sitting there, a look of pure joy on his face. "We go that way, I think." He pointed at the sandy trail I'd followed once before, with Erin. I realized he'd have never come this way. He hadn't been on a horse his entire time at the ranch.

"I'm right behind you," I said.

Grant gave me another quick grin and moved Balin into a trot.

Exclusive Short Story

This is the end of Grant and Jordan's love story. Although they appear as characters in later books in the series, they're no longer in the spotlight.

There is a 30 page short story you might enjoy, though! It exists in the form of a story called *Thrown* which reveals a secret link between the first book in this series, *A Man Who Rides* and book two in this series, *A Man Who Starts*.

Thrown is available only to members of my mailing list!

If you want to check it out, please visit:
stefaniwilder.com/clintanderin

About the Author

Growing up in Tucson, Arizona, Stefani always hoped to marry a cowboy. She did not. (Instead she married a man who turned into a cowboy, but that's a story for another day.) She has always loved to write stories and ride horses, and now frequently writes stories about riding horses (and falling in love.)

Stefani Wilder is a pen name for Robin Stephen.

Please visit one of her websites for more details:

- stefaniwilder.com
- robinstephen.com

also from Brown Wing Press:

Vaquera's Haven

Tipped Z: Book #4

Stefani Wilder

Holly lost everything when her husband was thrown in prison. Divorced and broke, the only thing she has to fall back on is her cousin's offer to set her up in a little house at the edge of a ranch called the Tipped Z.

Holly has never spent time on a working ranch before. Though she grew up wealthy in California and once hoped to complete on horseback in the Olympics, by the time her cousin's wife invites her to go riding she hasn't been in a saddle in 20 years. She's not that interested in the idea of climbing onto a stock horse. But then she runs into her former trainer and secret love of her youth, Diego. She can't help but hope he'll be her second chance to live the life she feels she missed out on.

Meanwhile, there's a mansion going up on the ridge behind her tiny house. It's presence represents the loss of important grazing to the Tipped Z. Holly finds herself with an opportunity to help the owner with his own horses. She needs the money, and she finds she doesn't mind spending time with the super friendly and super rich Luke Rastenhaus despite the fact her cousin despises him.

Suddenly riding with Diego, Luke, and also at the ranch, Holly finds herself pulled in three very different directions. She realizes she's going to have to deal with some unresolved aspects of her past if she hopes to figure out which path forward will lead to happiness.